D0790549

"DON'T FIGHT ME, CHINA..."

His kiss was urgent and demanding, the kiss of a man who had waited too long to claim what he desired.

The sash of her scarlet robe fell to the floor, and he deliberately slid his hands inside, taking her by the hips and bringing her closer, her naked breasts brushing against his chest. As the robe rustled softly to the floor and his lean, dark hands molded her to him, she could feel the hard, alien heat of his desire. Though China gasped and shivered, she made no move to struggle free, for a languorous delight was filling her blood. She was no longer afraid, but was alive and willing and eager to learn what mysteries awaited her at his hands...

"MARSH COMBINES THE EXCITEMENT OF ROSEMARY ROGERS WITH THE DELICATE ROMANCE OF KATHLEEN WOODIWISS!"

Romantic Times

ELLEN TANNER MARSH

SILK AND SPLENDOUR

AVON
PUBLISHERS OF BARD, CAMELOT, DISCUS AND FLARE BOOKS

SILK AND SPLENDOUR is an original publication of Avon Books. This work has never before appeared in book form.

AVON BOOKS
A division of
The Hearst Corporation
1790 Broadway
New York, New York 10019

Copyright © 1986 by Ellen Tanner Marsh
Published by arrangement with the author
Library of Congress Catalog Card Number: 86-90764
ISBN: 0-380-89677-X

First Avon Printing: November 1986

AVON TRADEMARK REG. U.S. PAT. OFF. AND IN OTHER COUNTRIES, MARCA REGISTRADA, HECHO EN U.S.A.

Printed in the U.S.A.

K-R 10 9 8 7 6 5 4 3 2 1

To Jay Acton, who makes the best part possible

To Tom Huff, who knows how to make it fun

And to Grady and Zachary, who make it all worthwhile

Chapter One

Broadhurst, Kent
October, 1847

A crescent moon, half-hidden by black, racing clouds, shed its ghostly light upon the corniced rooftop of the stately manor house and turned its massive walls of Georgian stone to silver. An icy wind blew inland from the Channel, rattling the shutters of the tall, rectangular windows and bending the boughs of the ancient trees in the park. Candlelight glimmered behind the heavy brocade drapes, falling in bright patterns on the browned and brittle grass.

In the circular drive below, a queue of coaches creaked and swayed and inched its ponderous way toward the front door where the elegantly attired guests were escorted inside by footmen in black satin livery. The sound of animated voices swirled skyward in the teeth of the wind, and anyone chancing upon the festive scene would have been hard-pressed to believe that the master of the house, Esmund Louis Harcomb, the eighth Earl Linville, had been buried yesterday morning, and that this gay and garishly attired procession was in point of fact all that remained of his funeral cortege.

In a darkened bedroom on the upper story of the West Wing, a girl of some seventeen years stood with her face pressed to the icy glass, slim body unmoving as she watched the chattering guests hasten inside. A shriek of laughter from a matronly lady in shocking purple brocade floated to her on the cold night air, and she turned away with an exclamation of disgust, letting the drapes fall back into place and leaving her staring unhappily at the flames licking greedily in the hearth.

"Have they come then?" inquired a middle-aged woman sitting near the welcoming warmth, her thin hands moving methodically with an embroidery needle and floss.

"They have," the girl said bleakly. "And not a single one of them seems to remember that Great-uncle Esmund was buried only yesterday. Oh, Anna, why don't they just go home? Surely they don't intend to spend another night drinking and dancing."

Anna Sidney's prematurely graying head bent lower over the embroidery hoop. "I wish I knew, child."

Helpless anger burned in China Warrick's green eyes and her stiff petticoats rustled as she resumed her restless pacing. Dressed in mourning black, she seemed to fade into the gloomy shadows of the room, and only when she came to stand before the grate was the darkness dispelled by the reflected firelight dancing on her bright red curls.

"I wish we could get rid of them," she said darkly, "but how? Freddy says they're friends of Great-uncle Esmund's who've come to pay their respects. I don't remember any of them ever having been invited to Broadhurst when he was still alive. And furthermore"—China's voice shook—"there is nothing the least respectful about getting drunk and playing cards on the very night of his funeral!"

"Perhaps they'll be more thoughtful tonight," Anna said hopefully.

China's eyes flashed. "That I cannot believe! You should have seen them just now—how they were dressed and the way they were laughing and joking with one another!" Her small fist smacked into her open palm. "I vow I cannot sit by another night and let them do as they please. I cannot! God knows what they'll end up breaking or—or stealing!"

Anna pursed her lips, but there was nothing she could say in response to China's outburst. Just this morning two pieces of priceless Limoges china had been found smashed in the withdrawing-room fireplace, and one of the footmen had suffered a nasty gash on the head trying to subdue a visitor who had partaken of too much of the Earl's excellent brandy. Freddy Linville himself, China's cousin and affable host of the evening's festivities, hadn't lifted a finger to put an end to their rowdiness and Anna strongly suspected, given the young lord's own inherent wildness, that he had taken quite an active part in it himself.

"Perhaps they won't stay very long tonight," she repeated with an optimism she was far from feeling.

"You should know better than to believe that!" China said scornfully. "Once they start drinking they don't seem able to stop. I think I can understand Freddy wanting to celebrate the fact that he has come into his inheritance at last," she added slowly, "but Cassie—I find it hard to believe that Cassie would permit anyone to damage Greatuncle Esmund's antiques."

China had known, long before her great-uncle had died, that Freddy and Cassie Linville, her cousins and the Earl's only grandchildren, were thoroughly unscrupulous creatures who cared for nothing save the Linville fortune and the title that Freddy, as heir apparent, would one day claim for his own. That they were greedy, grasping, and coldly conniving had been plain to China from the first moment she had set foot in their stately ancestral home six long years ago.

Oh, they had been kind enough to her then, but China had been quick to learn that their friendly smiles and warm gestures could be all too readily replaced by menacing threats and the promise of physical abuse whenever the Earl went away. She had been too young in those days and too terribly afraid of their cruelty—Cassie's in particular—to dream of betraying them, yet perhaps she might have done so if Great-uncle Esmund hadn't been so frail and gentle-hearted and so firmly convinced that his grandchildren were the kind and devoted companions they pretended to be.

And because China had truly loved him and because she had looked on her years in England as an evil but necessary exile, she had accepted without question the appointment of Freddy and Cassie as jailers overseeing the term of her imprisonment. She hadn't questioned their cruelty, convinced in her lonely little heart that she must have done something very terrible to prompt her parents to banish her from Badajan, the sun-drenched, mountainous island of her birth, but she had quickly grown to fear and despise them and long for the day when she could go home.

Great-uncle Esmund, with his bristling whiskers and ready smile, had been the only comfort China had known, and she had adored him. Once it became clear to her that she was going to lose him, for his final illness had struck swiftly and left little doubt as to its outcome, she had steeled herself against the inevitable and tried to prepare for the changes that would invariably accompany the transfer of power from the Earl's capable and benevolent hands to the reckless command of twenty-two-year-old Freddy.

Yet none of her worst imaginings had prepared China for the ribald celebrations that had taken place on the eve of her great-uncle's funeral. Despite Freddy's insistence to the contrary, China didn't think a single one of the revelers had been a friend of the Earl's before his death, and as a great many of them had arrived long after the funeral was over and the mourners gone home, she could only assume they were acquaintances, and not entirely scrupulous ones, of Freddy himself.

Appalled by the behavior of the dissipated men and loudly painted women who had invaded the stately house, China had ventured downstairs late last night to beg them to leave. Hot color rose to her cheeks as she recalled her painful confrontation with the drunken Freddy, who had merely laughed and taken great pleasure in pawing her in front of his guests before sending her back to bed.

Horrified and humiliated, China had crept back to her room without awakening Anna, and though she had firmly resolved to speak to the older woman the following morning, she had not. Cassie had imperiously commanded her to turn over her cozy apartment to the additional guests expected to arrive that evening. Anna, too, had been ordered to take up quarters in the cold and sparsely furnished West Wing, a banishment that had brought tears of baffled pain and resentment to her eyes.

"His Lordship would never have permitted this," she had quavered, her blue-veined hands clasped to her bosom. "Whatever are we going to do?"

"Do?" China had repeated tiredly without pausing in her packing. "I suppose we'll have to do what Cassie says."

"But His Lordship—"

China had interrupted her with a terse shake of her head. "His Lordship is dead, Anna, and as my former governess you don't seem to rate the same importance as Cassie's guests—any more than I do. If she sees fit to usurp our rooms, then we have no choice but to give them up."

She had deliberately refrained from adding that it was clear to her that Anna's dismissal lacked only a formal announcement, for why else would Cassie have banished her to this remote wing of the house? It made her wonder uneasily, given the shocking humiliation she had suffered in the drawing room at Freddy's hands, if she was being utterly naïve in hoping for better treatment herself?

Now, as she listened to the doors slamming on the floors below and the murmur of the guests withdrawing to their rooms, China Warrick's soft mouth quivered and she turned to stare wretchedly into the fire. It was useless to hope that Freddy and Cassie could be persuaded to listen to reason, or expect that she herself would be welcome at Broadhurst much longer.

"Don't you be payin' 'em no mind, Miss China," a round-faced maid with a ruffled mob cap remarked with undaunted good cheer as she bustled into the room. "Sir Hedley didn't come tonight and I vow 'e were the worst of 'em yesterday. And Mr. Weston hid the keys to the wine cellar. Promised he'd limit the number of bottles he'll be bringin' up to 'em, he did."

"That was kind of him," China said softly, burning with shame because it was apparent to her that even the servants were aware of Freddy's vile and disrespectful behaviour and felt compelled to conspire like thieves against him.

"I've brought your supper, miss," the plump little woman continued in a tone of kindly understanding. Setting the tray near the fire, she lifted the lids of the chafing dishes and sniffed appreciatively. "There be cold roast beef left o'er from yestreen, and some chicken, though mayhap it's a bit dry."

"Thank you, Lyddie, but I'm not very hungry."

"Now, now, you'll be eating every bit," Lydia Broyles admonished in a tone that would have horrified any conventional-thinking Victorian chatelaine and seen her promptly dismissed for gross impertinence. But the acerbic Lydia had been at Broadhurst far too long not to speak her mind frankly, and she was familiar enough with the stubborn set of her young mistress's pointed chin to know how best to deal with it.

"You, too, Miss Anna," she added severely, thinking that both of them looked far too drawn for her liking. A hearty meal, Lydia firmly believed, would go a long way toward improving matters, though it would not, she admitted with a shake of her grizzled head, do much in the way of easing Miss China's burden or lessening her grief.

No, nothing could do that, and it was no small wonder, Lydia decided angrily, descending to the kitchen by way of the back stairs and hearing the raucous laughter that drifted to her from the library. Lord Freddy's cavortings were enough to send anyone to an early grave, not to mention the cruel way he and Cassie had started treating Miss China the moment the old Earl had drawn his final breath. Like a poor relation, that's what, and here she'd been living at Broadhurst for the last six years as the apple of His Lordship's eye!

"I'm afraid they've started in on His Lordship's best claret," wispy-haired John Weston said anxiously when the faithful cook waddled into the cavernous scullery to pour herself a cup of buttermilk fortified liberally with brandy. His expression was more than a little mournful as he thought of the cruel fate of the vintage bottles he had so lovingly tended during the Earl's lifetime, but when Lydia did not offer the hoped-for commiseration he added unhappily, "I had so hoped he'd be careful with it. It's very rare, you know."

Lydia's plump shoulders lifted in a shrug. "And just what did you expect, Mr. Weston? That Lord Freddy would display them bottles like paintings in some museum? Of course he'll drink 'em now His Lordship bain't here to stop 'im!"

"I had hoped," Weston resumed forlornly, "that Lord Freddy would display some moderation. At least in this particular instance."

Lydia responded to this with a derisive snort. "A lot you knows, Mr. Weston! Only way to protect it is to seal up the whole bloody lot in the family tomb!"

The elderly butler looked startled. "Lord Freddy and his friends?"

"Saints above, Mr. Weston, the claret! Though it wouldn't be a bad end for them vile creatures neither," Lydia added thoughtfully, tucking her blousy hair under the ruffled confines of her cap. "I'll tell you one thing," she went on darkly, "if it wasn't for Miss China I'd hand in my notice on the spot! Lord Linville'd never have stood for the way she's bein' treated. And I'll wager 'e never meant for Broadhurst to be turned into some—some common alehouse when he died! Drinking and gambling and letting those painted creatures what call themselves ladies have free run of the house!" She shuddered and took a sip of buttermilk, and after a moment mused unhappily, "Whatever be they up to, the two of 'em? They was never this awful when His Lordship were alive."

"Perhaps when Mr. Biggs arrives to oversee the disposition of the estate—" Weston began hopefully, but Lydia waved this aside with a work-reddened hand.

"Mr. Biggs indeed! I don't expect he'll do nothing but make Master Freddy the ninth Earl Linville, legal and proper. And once that boy has his hands on His Lordship's wealth, mind, it'll go bad for all of us."

John Weston's long face seemed to grow longer still. "I was rather hoping that His Lordship would leave Broadhurst to Miss China and not those scheming cousins of hers. As the Countess Linville she would never have permitted such scandalous behavior to occur."

Lydia Broyles compressed her fleshy lips and shook her head with sorrowful conviction. "His Lordship may've loved Miss China best, but he couldn't've made her his heir. Not when she bain't a true Linville. You'll be rememberin' her grandmother, Lady Delia, were only the Earl's adopted sister. Took 'er in when 'er parents died in that coaching accident, the old Linvilles did, them bein' such close friends and all. But that were before my time, and yours, too, Mr. Weston, but it still means Miss China's got no real Linville blood in 'er—more's the pity!"

Clucking sorrowfully, Lydia concluded with a dark and direly accurate verdict: "Even if she did 'ave fam'ly blood and Lord Linville did leave Broadhurst all to her, Lord Freddy and that snake-in-the-grass sister of his'd never stand for it."

"I imagine you're right." The elderly butler sighed, recalling aloud the number of times he had likened the two of them to circling vultures. Lyddie Broyles spoke the truth: Freddy and Cassiopeia Linville had schemed and quarreled and waited far too long to permit a mere seventeen-year-old girl to usurp their grandfather's fortune.

"Might've bin different if Miss China were a boy," Lydia pronounced sadly, the brandy loosening an already over-active tongue. "Or at the very least not the innocent child she be. On the other hand," she added pensively, "I suppose even an hardened harridan would have a real fight on 'er hands tryin' to take Broadhurst away from the likes of Freddy and Cassie. Rotten to the core the two of 'em be," she concluded with a sniff, "and mark my words. Master Biggs'll do no more than make their claim to Broadhurst legal and binding. You waits and see."

"If yer asts me," said one of the rail-thin scullery maids engaged in scrubbing the enormous oak table, "H'it bain't—"

"No one's askin' you," Lydia snapped, heaving her bulk around to scowl at her. "And I don't want you nor nobody else carryin' tales to the village and sayin' this or that about Miss China and them cousins of hers. Gorr! I just prays Lord Freddy'll loosen up 'is purse strings and send the poor mite back to that island of hers!"

The insistent jangling of the bells, summoning Weston

for yet another bottle of wine, silenced her tirade and seemed a mocking rejoinder to her passionate hopes. Pursing her lips, Lydia turned back to her buttermilk while Weston, his expression rigid, descended once again into the labyrinthine depths of the cellar.

In her bedroom far above, meanwhile, China had made a halfhearted attempt to eat her supper but found that she had no taste at all for Lydia's excellent fare. Wandering to the window, she laid her forehead to the cold glass and stood staring out into the moonlit garden. The coaches had been removed to the carriage house and the ghostly expanse of drive below was empty save for the leaves that scuttled and whirled to the coaxing of the wind. From the rose arbor came the haunting cry of a peacock, reminding her of the endless hours she had kept vigil at her great-uncle's bedside, praying he would recover while listening to the night birds calling one another across the fields, their mournful cries drowning out the sound of his shallow, raspy breathing.

China closed her eyes and sighed, and Anna, hearing it, laid her embroidery aside and turned to regard her young charge with anxious, loving eyes. Though she had taken great pains to conceal the fact from China, Anna was afraid, terribly afraid—of the future and what it might hold. Despite the tired slump of China's shoulders and the neglect her appearance had suffered since Lord Linville's final illness, she was still beautiful—far too beautiful for the likes of the rustic boors and fortune-seeking toffs who would doubtless begin beating down the doors now that the old Earl was no longer able to fend off their suits.

And there was also Freddy to consider. No, not Freddy—Lord Frederick Thurston Linville, the new Earl Linville. Anna shuddered with distaste and no small measure of foreboding, for she had been aware for some time now of the lecherous looks Freddy had been casting China's way ever since he had awakened to the fact that his grandfather's ward had blossomed into a woman of astounding beauty. It had to be her coloring, Anna had decided upon giving the matter serious thought, for no one of her acquaintance possessed quite the same fiery red hair China

Warrick did or could boast wide, tilted eyes that were far greener than any Kentish garden.

In an age when the standards of beauty were measured against the ideal of a buxom girl with soft blue eyes and golden ringlets, China's attributes fell hopelessly short. Yet she had been blessed (or cursed, Anna was wont to think bitterly these days) with a small, graceful form and a bewitching face dominated by a generous mouth that was far too tempting for the likes of any man, let alone one of Freddy Linville's inclinations.

"China," Anna said abruptly, "have you given any thought to going back to Badajan now that His Lordship is dead?"

"Back to Badajan?" China echoed softly. "No, I haven't. Not really."

In truth she had thought of little else since her great-uncle's death, but she had been afraid to admit as much to Anna, hating the thought of abandoning her and hating, worse, the thought of turning to Cassie for assistance, especially in the matter of borrowing money to pay her passage home. She regarded Anna with eyes that were filled with sadness, for she was thinking not only of the loss of her great-uncle, but also of the desolate years that had been her legacy ever since she had left Indonesia to obtain what her mother had termed a "proper Western education."

For a moment the silence between them was broken only by the hiss and crackle of the leaping flames, then China said slowly, "Even if I wanted to go back I couldn't. I simply haven't got the money." It was a painful admission for her to make, but she had always been straightforward and scrupulously honest and there was no sense in lying— not to Anna, who had been a loyal companion and friend for as long as China could remember.

"Oh, my dear, of course you do!" Anna exclaimed with considerable surprise. "Lord Linville doubtless provided very well for you in his will. At the very least he would have left enough money to pay for your passage."

Unexpected hope flared in China's eyes. "Do you honestly think so?"

"Do you honestly think he'd forget you?"

China smiled at Anna's vehemence. It was true, of course. Great-uncle Esmund would not have forgotten her. Though he had tried his best to make her happy, he had known from the first that Badajan would always be home to her. But for his unfailing love and his efforts to make her happy, the long years of exile would have been intolerable.

How slowly the time had crawled, the weeks seeming like months and the months like years! No matter how hard she tried to forget, it seemed to China that she had spent every waking moment dreaming of the island of her birth, visualizing its hot white beaches and steaming jungles, and trying not to permit the damp and chilly English climate to become a mocking reminder of the warmth and sunshine she had left behind.

Worse still had been the years she had spent enrolled in Mrs. Crenshawe's Seminary for Young Ladies, a finishing school in the heart of Kent whose glowing reputation and charmingly polished graduates bore no trace of the misery suffered by its inmates behind those thick, ivy-covered walls, China Warrick in particular.

She had been ostracized from the first for her bright red hair and unfashionably brown skin, and for the fact that her paternal great-grandfather had been Sir Kingston Warrick, a notorious blackguard forced to flee England because he had—as rumor went—once bludgeoned a man to death. Furthermore, China had been born on an island in pagan Indonesia, which made her both a novelty and an outcast and held her up for ridicule in the eyes of her scornful classmates.

Nor did her natural warmth and fiery beauty endear her to the headmistress, for Olivia Crenshawe was a woman of strict Victorian convictions, prim, prudish, and thoroughly humorless, who had set about with grimly self-righteous intent to break the unacceptable high spirits of this odd little creature with the riotous red hair and outlandish green eyes. Raised under the loving though hardly responsible wing of a father who had seen no wrong in teaching his daughter to swim and shoot, to forgo the habit of wearing shoes, and to curse in languages as diverse as Greek and Mandarin Chinese, China had proven difficult to tame, and yet Olivia Crenshawe had persevered—and triumphed in the end.

Grueling hours spent on rote lessons in an airless classroom while the rest of the girls were permitted to stroll through the blossom-covered Kentish countryside had taught twelve-year-old China Warrick the meaning of discipline and the bitter unfairness of being hapless enough to find disfavor in the headmistress's eyes. The treasured mementos she had brought with her from home—an exotic seashell she had scooped from the sand on the morning of her departure and the string of coral beads the elderly munshi Tan Ri had given her to ward off evil spirits— were confiscated until her enthusiasm for lessons was deemed "satisfactory." The cool silk frocks she had brought with her from home, regarded as shockingly heathen, were promptly taken away, and in their stead China was forced to wear stifling pantaloons and pinafores, and underclothing that pinched and itched unbearably.

Appalled by the fact that the girl saw nothing wrong with doffing her shoes or rolling up her sleeves whenever the springtime temperature climbed, Mrs. Crenshawe had seen to it that China's wardrobe was altered to include impossibly high collars that must remain buttoned to the chin, and leather boots that were laced far too tight for comfort and were never, never to be removed. The rich red gold hair that China had worn in thick plaited ropes or allowed to swing freely to her hips was confined with countless pins into a chignon that was far too heavy for her slender neck. She was soon plagued by headaches and grew listless and pale, and Mrs. Crenshawe congratulated herself on her success in converting this troublesome barbarian into a picture of chaste Victorian modesty.

At the age of sixteen China had graduated from Olivia Crenshawe's seminary, her "education" complete, yet her plans to return home to Badajan had been shattered by a stroke the Earl had suffered shortly after her return to Broadhurst. Left partially paralyzed and confined to a chair, he was completely dependent on her, and China could not bring herself to abandon him to her cousins' care. She had never been fooled by their apparent devotion to their grandfather and had shuddered at the thought of what they would do to the now-helpless old man once she was gone....

"China, do pay attention when I speak to you!" Anna Sidney's voice seemed to cut across those interminable years, dispersing the wretched memories that had momentarily held her in their thrall, making her shiver with cold and grief and reminding her that she was free forever of Olivia Crenshawe's autocratic cruelty and no longer bound to Broadhurst by a sense of love or duty to a man who was dead.

"Whatever were you thinking of, child? I don't believe you've heard a word I've said! Don't you want to talk about going home?"

"I'm sorry." An oddly bitter smile twisted China's lips. "Do you suppose my parents even want me to come back?"

"What makes you say such a thing?" Anna gasped. "Your parents didn't intend for you to remain in England for the rest of your life! Oh, my dear girl, there's no reason for you to stay now that your great-uncle is dead, and though I shall miss you terribly, I don't see why you shouldn't go."

"I imagine you're right," China said doubtfully.

"Of course I am," Anna said firmly, and lifted her head at the far-off slamming of a door and the utterance of a string of vile curses. It was quite obvious from the little she could hear that Freddy was once again losing badly at cards.

"If his present luck continues," China said slowly and with the ghost of a smile, "there'll be little enough of Lord Linville's inheritance left by the time the will is read."

The gilded bronze clock in the Long Gallery had long since chimed the hour of four o'clock before the last of the guests who had declined to spend the night stumbled down the steps to their waiting coaches. Awakened by the noise they made, China slipped quietly out of bed and watched from the window as the procession rumbled out of sight in the chilly darkness. Assuming that the rest of the household had finally gone to sleep, she drew on a silk wrapper and reluctantly left her room in order to assess the damage. Judging from the noise they had made, she felt certain that it was considerable.

It had been shortly after midnight when she had first been awakened by the sound of gunshots from the garden below and had scrambled to the window, her heart thumping against her ribs. Long minutes had passed before she realized that Freddy and some of his friends were staging a mock duel for the amusement of the ladies, cavorting amid the rose bushes with pistols brandished. Fortunately no one had been hurt, and after tiring of the game they had returned to the library where their laughter and the shrieks of a particularly boisterous young lady had made it impossible for China to fall into anything but a fitful sleep.

The house was cold and menacing in the darkness, and China shivered as she descended the winding staircase to the Great Hall. The candle she carried flickered in the draft and in its smoking light the portraits of Linville ancestors seemed to frown down at her from their height on the wainscotted walls. For some reason their sightless eyes made China uneasy, and it annoyed her that she should feel so, for she had often wandered alone at night through the enormous house and had never had cause to feel afraid.

This time, however, she couldn't help but experience a profound sense of relief as she stepped into the library to find a cheerful fire still burning in the grate. Stretching her hands to its warmth, China cast an apprehensive glance around her and was grateful to discover that, apart from an overturned chair and several empty bottles scattered on the rug, little damage seemed to have been done. She breathed a sigh of relief and in the next moment gave a cry of alarm as a slurred voice addressed her from the shadows: "You must have been expecting something bloody awful when you came in, coz. Never seen that look on your face before."

China whirled about and her heart plummeted as she saw Freddy Linville slumped in an armchair near the door, his cravat askew and the front of his vest dribbled with wine. An unhealthy pallor tinged his high cheekbones, and his eyes were bloodshot.

"I was afraid something might have been broken," she admitted.

The buckram- and leather-bound books lining the paneled walls were valuable first editions, and the tall, glass-fronted cabinet behind the elegant Louis XIV escritoire was filled with rare porcelain and crystal, among them a thirteenth-century Cristallo goblet of which only three were known to exist: one here at Broadhurst, one in the Doge's Palace in Venice, and the other in the private collection of María Cristina de Borbón, mother of King Ferdinand IV of Spain. China had been worrying most of the night over what might have happened to it in the clumsy and uncaring hands of a band of drunken revelers.

"Oh, I made certain they behaved themselves this time," Freddy assured her, rising unsteadily to his feet and tottering closer. "Can't afford to have another piece of Limoges smashed, eh? Or worse, one of Grandpapa's ruby vases. Broken glassware don't fetch much on the market, I'm afraid."

China gasped. "Surely you're not thinking of selling them!"

"Why not? I'm planning on renovating Broadhurst now dear Grandpapa's dead and gone. Place is too bloody spartan for my tastes, and I can't abide the ghastly antiques he kept about. They'll be far better off converted to cash, don't you think?"

"You can't possibly be serious!"

"Now, now, love, no need to look so shocked," Freddy responded with a lopsided grin, and wagged an unsteady finger in her face. "This way they're bound to wind up in a museum someday to the benefit of the public good. Daresay they'll be more appreciated there than they ever were here." He belched loudly and indelicately and added, "Same goes for Grandpapa's collection of dreary Jacobean furniture. Don't give a bloody farthing how long it's been in the family. It's tasteless and boring and I want it out of my house."

China's lips tightened, and she turned back to the fire without speaking, knowing how useless it would be to try to argue with him. Neither Freddy nor Cassie had ever appreciated the beauty of the priceless *objets* or the historic significance of the imposing collection of oils and watercolors by Dutch and Italian masters that were housed in

Broadhurst's rooms. It had always been and would always
be the actual value in pounds sterling each item could
fetch at auction that mattered to them, and perhaps that
was why the Earl had come to feel so much closer to her,
his grandniece, who had genuinely shared his love of ar-
tistic beauty.

"I wonder if the old man will turn in his grave when
we have the appraisers in for tea?" Freddy mused unkindly. "Should be an interesting affair, don't you think,
coz?"

He laughed and staggered a little as he wiped the back
of his hand across his mouth, for he was drunker than he
cared to admit and feeling reckless and untouchable in his
role as the new Earl Linville. Nine insufferable years had
passed since the day his parents had perished in a theater
fire in London, to the end that Freddy had quite unexpectedly found himself next in line to wear the Linville
mantle.

To his annoyance his aged grandfather had stubbornly
refused to die from the injuries he had sustained in that
same fire, and had lingered on for what seemed an eternity,
amusing himself solely (or so it had seemed to Freddy) by
keeping his grandchildren dancing like puppets on a
string—especially over matters concerning money, of which
Freddy never seemed to have enough. And every year the
Earl seemed to grow older but no frailer, for even the stroke
he had suffered last year had failed to finish him off. It
was not until pneumonia, with the aid of an unusually
cold and damp summer, finally put an end to him that the
long wait was over at last.

Freddy and Cassiopeia had been both surprised and
profoundly pleased to learn what those nine insufferable
years had won them. By Freddy's own calculations Esmund Louis Harcomb Linville had amassed a fortune of
well over twenty thousand pounds, a sum that didn't even
take into consideration the priceless artworks, and *objets*,
nor the considerable shares in the Honorable, the East
India Company, which provided the estate with considerable yearly income.

Now that Freddy was lord of Broadhurst and everything
in it, he took infinite pleasure in the knowledge that he

had also become temporary but quite legal guardian of his dear cousin China.

Standing with her hands stretched toward the warmth of the lapis-inlaid fireplace, she seemed unaware of Freddy's heavy-lidded scrutiny. In the glow of the fire she was breathtaking to behold, the leaping flames revealing golden highlights in her red hair and dancing across the graceful white column of her throat. Her lashes were thick and curling, fringing eyes that were far darker than the haunting green of emeralds, and a faint frown pulled at the corners of her warm, pink mouth, emphasizing the unconsciously seductive fullness of her lower lip.

To the watching Freddy she seemed irresistibly alluring, a slender goddess as fragile and enchanting as a delicate rose, and, best of all, a virgin still, her untutored body awaiting the caresses of a man's experienced hands. Freddy licked his lips, noticing how the folds of her silk wrapper fell from her hips and revealed all too clearly the tempting outline of her breasts.

What a brooding, unhappy child she had been when she had first appeared on their doorstep from faraway Badajan! Freddy, six years older and, in his grandfather's words, rapidly growing into an "unbearable little prig," had found her outlandish red hair and forward manner thoroughly objectionable and had been greatly relieved when she had been packed off to finishing school. Her visits to Broadhurst, encompassing holidays and summer terms, had thankfully been short, and China had obligingly kept to her rooms for the most part, so that one could easily forget she even existed.

Freddy had never bothered to pay his younger cousin any mind at all until the fall of 1845 when he had returned from a two-year tour of the Continent to find his grandfather's plain little ward transformed into an impossibly bewitching beauty. Yet somehow, and much to his bitter anger, the vixen had managed in his absence to ingratiate herself so completely into the old Earl's affections that Freddy, who might otherwise have seduced her without a second thought, was forced to hold himself on a tight rein in order not to incur his grandfather's wrath.

But now, of course, the old man was dead and China,

who would have celebrated her seventeenth birthday with a debut ball next month, was bound to her cousin by virtue of the fact that she was not yet of legal age. It was a pleasing thought and, considering it, Freddy chuckled aloud, causing China to turn her head and regard him questioningly.

The neckline of her silk wrapper opened inadvertently as she did so, providing him with a tempting view of her shadowed cleavage, and Freddy, emboldened by drink, reached out without warning and pulled her into his arms.

"Can't help m'self, m'dear," he said in a hot, panting whisper as she cried out in alarm. "So damnably beautiful. Must have you." His wet lips fastened themselves upon hers, and China Warrick suddenly found herself being kissed for the first time in her life.

It was not at all what she had imagined a kiss to be, nor did it even remotely resemble the impassioned and stirring embraces described by the starry-eyed girls at the Seminary who had confessed in whispers to having experienced them. It was, quite frankly, nothing short of repulsive, for Freddy's personal grooming habits had always been poor, and with the smell of stale wine and sweat filling her nostrils, China was overcome with revulsion.

"Let me go!" she said, gasping, but to no avail, for he hadn't even heard her and wouldn't have been able to help himself even if he had. His pulse was pounding and his hands worked feverishly at the lacing of her wrapper, and he was aware of nothing but his fierce need to possess her, this small but enchantingly slender creature who was, he had realized the moment he touched her, a woman made for loving.

Forced backward by the pressure of Freddy's seeking hands, China cried out as she heard the delicate wrapper tear in his grasp. It had been a gift from her parents and China, who had treasured it for that reason alone and not because it was spun from costly Badajan silk, reacted with blind panic.

Striking out at him with her fists, she managed to twist out of his grasp, and as she backed away from him she stumbled unexpectedly against a brass stand that stood near the fireplace. Without hesitating, she snatched up a heavy poker and whirled about, bringing it down on Freddy's skull—and letting it clatter to the floor with a horrified gasp as he sagged without a sound.

China's hands flew to her cheeks and in the sudden silence the hiss of the fire and the rattle and tap of the wind against the panes seemed a menacing whisper. Long minutes passed and still Freddy did not stir, and China was forced to come to the frightening conclusion that he was dead.

"I've killed him," she whispered, her hands pressed to her lips, the knuckles showing white. "Dear God, I've killed him!"

She backed to the door, unable to tear her gaze away, afraid that if she turned even for an instant he would rise like some ghostly specter and grab the hem of her wrapper, smearing it with a blood-stained hand.... She uttered a strangled gasp and fled, her bare feet making no sound on the thick rugs and her hair whipping like a red banner behind her. A door banged shut in the draft of her passing, but China scarcely noticed, for she was intent upon one thing only: to escape before anyone could discover what she had done.

Several minutes later Bayard, Broadhurst's ancient and ill-tempered mastiff, was awakened from a sound sleep by the rusty creaking of the hinges on the stable door. Hackles rising, he emerged from the rose bushes and trotted stiffly across the frost-brittle lawn. A growl rumbled low in his throat, and he sniffed suspiciously at the musky odor of manure and horses drifting from the warm interior of the low stone building. His lips drew back from his teeth as a small cloaked figure emerged from within.

Halting, China spoke to him coaxingly and reached out a gloved hand to pat his massive head, aware that his thunderous barks would instantly awaken the grooms. She drew a quivering sigh of relief as the tip of his tail gave a conciliatory wag. Turning, he lumbered off in the direction of the house and China wasted no time in leading her mount to the block.

Her fingers were stiff with the cold and she was shivering uncontrollably by the time she had succeeded in tying her valise to the saddle and swinging herself onto the gray gelding's back. The clopping of hooves echoed hollowly on the cobblestones, and ghostly bands of fog drifted across the courtyard to bead like pearls in China's hair. She cast an anxious glance up at the soaring walls of the house, and though the windows remained tightly shuttered and dark, she could feel her courage begin to falter.

"I mustn't run away," she whispered to herself, her conscience presenting her with an image of Freddy lying face down on the library floor, blood seeping from his head. She knew that it was inexcusably cowardly to run away and that they would surely catch her before she had gone very far. But the thought of returning to confront Freddy's lifeless body brought the bile to her throat. Swallowing hard, she urged the gray to a trot, and once the turreted roof with its countless chimney pots had disappeared from view behind a barren stand of elms, she brought the whip down hard on his muscular flank.

Startled by the stinging lash, the big animal leaped away, and even if China had suddenly changed her mind about turning back, she could not have diverted him from his flight. A chill wind stung her cheeks and she shivered in response, for deep in her heart she knew that she did not possess the courage to face trial for Freddy's murder.

A rosy glow was beginning to pale the eastern heavens, dimming the stars and touching the frost-covered fields with a wash of shimmering pearl, but China was oblivious to the beauty of the coming dawn. The rolling Kentish hills, the tidy cottages with their sleeping gardens and neatly thatched roofs went unnoticed in her whirlwind passage. She could think of nothing save the distant city of London and pray that among the ships lying anchored in the Thames she would find one that was due to sail east on the tide.

Chapter Two

Ethan Bloodwell, captain-owner of the Portsmouth-registered brigantine _Kowloon Star,_ opened a bloodshot eye and groaned aloud as an annoying shaft of sunlight, falling from the shuttered stern windows onto the pillow near his head, all but blinded him. His vision swam unpleasantly, and when he peered at the French traveling clock ticking on the dressing table, he found he had to squint in order to see its gilded face. Half past eight? What the devil—?

Abruptly he came up on one elbow, unmindful of the sickening throbbing in his head, and stared in growing disbelief at the disorder that had been his well-organized cabin the night before. Swearing softly, he regarded the contents of the dresser drawers lying strewn about the colorful Persian carpet; the sleeve of one of his fine Holland shirts splattered with wine from a carelessly overturned bottle. His seaman's chest had been opened and his shaving kit tossed aside, and the costly rice paper he had brought back from Japan had been carelessly removed and lay in a crumpled pile beneath his desk.

Ethan Bloodwell's frankly sensuous mouth twisted

wryly. God's blood, surely he hadn't been that drunk last night? Not enough to have rampaged through his belongings like some maddened bull! His pale blue eyes narrowed as they fell on a box of inlaid sandalwood which had originally lain at the bottom of the sea chest and was now on the floor, its hinged lid broken, the guineas locked within it mysteriously gone.

Mysteriously?

"You bloody, drunken fool," Ethan Bloodwell cursed to himself, enraged that he had been tumbled like some beardless boy on his first brothel visit. It was true that the black-haired wench had been appealing, but he should have known better than to let her spend the night in his bed rather than pressing a few coins into her hand and sending her on her way.

"Serves you bloody right," he muttered, rising naked from the bed and splashing water from a nearby ewer onto his face. He grimaced as he toweled himself dry, deciding that he must be growing old indeed if an uneducated Cheapside whore could rob him blind in his own quarters. Prowling with restless animal grace to the stern windows, he threw back the shutters and let the early morning sun fall full on the planes of his face.

Rajiid Ali, the *Kowloon Star*'s first mate, would have no trouble finding her if he were told to do so, Ethan reflected, for the Arab was a master at ferreting out missing persons. Yet what was the use in dragging her back to his ship? It was doubtful that he would recover so much as a penny of his money, and Ethan didn't particularly relish the thought of making his foibles known to his crew. Besides, the wench had been accommodating—and certainly clever. Perhaps she deserved to keep the gold she'd managed to lift from him.

Ethan Bloodwell hinged the shutters back into place. The sunlight, which continued to fall through the wooden shafts, was muted and played with golden fingers across the length of his body, revealing the whipcord leanness of his muscular limbs and the hard, flat lines of his buttocks and belly. Pulling on his breeches, he stooped to gather the scattered pieces of rice paper and brush away with an impatient hand the lock of sun-bleached chestnut hair falling across his scowling brow.

A knock on the door heralded the arrival of his steward with breakfast, and in an uncharitable tone of voice the captain bade him enter.

"What are you playing at, Nappy?" he inquired irritably when the door remained discreetly closed. A curious silence reigned in the corridor outside and Ethan, his temper snapping, threw it open and demanded harshly, "What the devil do you want?"

"C-Captain Bloodwell?"

Ethan's anger was abruptly checked by the unexpected sight of a pair of large and translucent green eyes that were framed by the fur-trimmed hood of a black traveling cloak. They were staring up at him with a similar measure of blank astonishment until the young woman they belonged to dropped her gaze inadvertently to the wide expanse of his sun-bronzed chest. Becoming aware of the extent of his nakedness, she turned without warning and bolted for the stairs.

"Just a moment there."

Seizing her wrists, Ethan jerked her inside, where she surprised him by giving vent to all the fury of a wildcat, her booted feet drumming against his shins as she struck out at him in an effort to twist herself free. The hood of her cloak fell back from her face and his eyes were drawn immediately to the rich red color of her hair. His interest caught, he released her abruptly, and she backed away from him, rubbing her bruised wrists and gazing up at him with compressed and mutinous lips.

"Who are you? What are you doing here?" Ethan inquired into the accusing silence.

She made no reply, and without taking her eyes from him, dragged the hood back over her curls. Ethan was struck by her beauty: her smooth magnolia-petal skin, the perfection of her small, straight nose, and the intriguing tilt of her reddish gold brows. His wandering eyes came to rest on a crimson strand of hair that curled about her throat where a pulse beat rapidly with fright, and abruptly Ethan felt his annoyance return. His throbbing head and rifled cabin were the fault, after all, of a woman, and even though this one was not even remotely responsible, he found himself feeling extremely uncharitable toward her sex as a whole.

"Would you kindly explain to me what you're doing aboard my ship?" he demanded disagreeably.

Through quickly lowered eyes, China Warrick found herself staring at a pair of worn buckskin breeches that seemed molded to muscular thighs. She dared not look any higher: at his naked chest with its rippling muscles that disconcerted her thoroughly and made her aware for the first time in her life of the vast and bewildering difference between women and men. She had never seen a naked man before or even imagined that one day she'd find herself alone in his private quarters, and she couldn't for the life of her understand why he made no move to cover himself in her presence.

"I'm sorry," she said in a strained and awkward whisper. "I shouldn't have...I've made a terrible mistake."

His smile was more than a little unpleasant. "Were you hoping to find me asleep so you could try your own hand at lifting a few trifles? Surely the talk in the streets must have it by now that the captain of the *Kowloon Star* is an easy pinch?" The pale blue eyes were suddenly close. "I will warn you, my dear, it won't fare as well for you as it did for your companion."

China felt her throat constrict at the menacing heat that radiated from him. Although she had no idea what he was talking about or why he should be so angry with her, she had witnessed enough of Cousin Freddy's bacchanalian misconduct during the past two nights to recognize the fact that the captain was deplorably drunk.

The discovery brought with it a suffocating feeling of panic. It had taken every ounce of her courage to leave her horse Bastian behind and make her way on foot down the deserted wharves that stretched for mile after mile along the foggy, murmuring waterfront. Nor had she found it an easy matter to descend alone into the dank holds of the *Kowloon Star* to speak to her captain; she who had never traveled beyond the front gate of Broadhurst without a proper escort.

"Perhaps I'd better go," she said in a breathless whisper and began edging for the door.

Fingers like a steel trap closed about her arm and in a deceptively silky tone Captain Bloodwell said, "I think not."

The fear that leaped into the wide green eyes irritated him. Good God, he wasn't about to ravage the cunning brat here and now! He'd quite had his fill of female companionship for the moment, thank you, and furthermore this one looked altogether too young and fragile for his tastes.

"You still haven't answered my question," he reminded her impatiently, and his fingers tightened in an unmistakable warning.

China, having already suffered enough humiliation at his hands, and who was by now sufficiently unwilling to tolerate any more, said simply: "I need passage to Singapore, Captain. The harbormaster told me your ship sails on Thursday."

"That may well be true," Ethan acknowledged readily, "but the *Kowloon Star* is not a passenger ship, and I've no intention of making her one. Now, then, is that all you wished to say to me?"

China could feel her heart thumping uncomfortably against her ribs. Never in all her sheltered life had she met anyone quite like Ethan Bloodwell, whose ill temper awed her and whose aggressive masculinity was both overwhelming and thoroughly frightening. Accustomed to Freddy's foppish affectations and to the frail, soft-spoken man who had been her great-uncle, China's experience with men was lamentably limited, and she did not know enough about the power of a flirtatious smile or an archly promising glance to attempt to utilize either one of them in extricating herself from the captain's bruising grip.

Yet womanly instinct, which she could not help but possess despite the fact that she was unaware of its existence, came to her rescue, for looking into his harsh, unyielding face she had a sudden inkling of where Captain Bloodwell's loyalties might lie. Taking a deep breath, she stared boldly into his eyes and said, "I must leave for Singapore at once, Captain, and yours is the only ship scheduled to sail before the end of the month. Perhaps you haven't taken on paying passengers before simply because the fare wasn't lucrative enough. I am prepared to pay you one hundred pounds for safe passage to Indonesia."

Captain Bloodwell appeared outwardly unimpressed despite the fact that the usual fare was less than a fifth of the sum she had mentioned. "Will that be in paper or bullion?" he inquired blandly.

China hesitated, unwilling to lie. She possessed no money of her own and had been hoping to barter for the price of a ticket with her dressing gown of Badajan silk. The fabric, she knew, was worth a great deal of money, despite the fact that Freddy had torn it.

"My dear young lady," Captain Bloodwell resumed, taking her silence for confirmation that she could not, in truth, afford to pay him such a sum. "I'm afraid one hundred pounds isn't worth the trouble of escorting a tiresome female and her gaggle of chaperones halfway around the world. Worse still is the intolerable thought of having to endure the wrath of your relations were the fact to come to light that you are a runaway, or worse, a bluestocking thirsting for adventure."

With grim amusement he saw the telltale color flare from her white throat to her hairline. "You must admit," he added unkindly, "that your presence here smacks royally of the clandestine."

China could feel the sting of tears in her eyes. She didn't want to spend another moment in this unpleasant person's presence, yet what was she supposed to do? Give up her only chance of freedom and openly return to Broadhurst in order to be imprisoned for murder?

"I'm willing to raise my offer to two hundred pounds," she said tremulously.

To her astonishment Ethan Bloodwell threw back his head and gave vent to a hearty burst of laughter. "You're a persistent chit," he admitted with a certain grudging admiration. "Tell me, is it a family tiff you're escaping or the bleak likelihood of marriage to an elderly and unattractive suitor?"

It occurred to him as he spoke that she was far too young and innocent, not to mention lovely, to suffer such a fate, yet he was perfectly aware that it was common practice of ambitious parents to foist their marriageable daughters off on the richest, most eligible husbands they could find. A pity if this were indeed the case, yet what did this green-eyed wench's domestic worries matter to him?

Looking down at her and seeing that she had responded to his inquiry with a haughty stare and tight lips, Ethan was betrayed into a grin, which did nothing at all to endear himself to China Warrick. She, in fact, was far too angry by now to notice how disarming Captain Bloodwell could appear when he smiled. She didn't care at all for his insolent manner, and found his square jaw and lean, sun-browned countenance not at all to her liking.

"I believe I'll be going now," she started frostily, but Captain Bloodwell was not about to let this intriguing, red-haired enigma slip from his grasp. It did not trouble him in the least that she was running away from home. Two hundred pounds was well worth the price of being her abettor, and he was unscrupulous enough—and certainly drunk enough—to consider her offer quite seriously.

Folding his arms across his chest, he regarded her with interest. "If I did agree to take you with me, where would you come by those two hundred pounds?"

Bewildered by this abrupt change in attitude, China could only stare.

"Well, girl? Do you intend to sail with me or not?"

China swallowed. The fact that he had suddenly agreed to help her and that she had no one but this intimidating man to turn to was nearly as frightening as the thought of returning to confront the corpse she had left behind in Broadhurst's elegant library.

"Are you really going to take me with you?"

Ethan grinned. "No need to look so wary. I will, but only if you can assure me those two hundred pounds will be paid."

"I have some money that belonged to my great-uncle," China admitted in a reluctant whisper. Was it true, as Anna had claimed, that Great-uncle Esmund had left her enough money to pay her way home? And would Anna, she wondered, ever forgive her for what she had done to

Freddy and what she was doing now? "When he died he left it to me."

"Ah, so you're an heiress."

China looked away, unable to meet those mocking eyes. The way Captain Bloodwell said it made it sound extremely vulgar.

"And who was this great-uncle of yours? Perhaps I was fortunate enough to have known him."

But China was not at all willing to tell him. Wasn't it bad enough that she had brought dishonor to the Earl's name by murdering his grandson and heir? She could not shame him further by speaking his name to a drunken and disreputable man who had nothing but profit in mind.

"I'm beginning to wonder about you," Ethan Bloodwell said thoughtfully as a weighty silence lengthened between them. Reaching out his hand, he touched a fiery curl that tumbled over the shoulder of her cloak and was startled when a crimson strand entwined itself without warning about his finger as though in possession of a life of its own. Winding it about his knuckles, he pulled China closer until she came to a halt with her upturned face nearly touching his.

"What is it you're frightened of?" he inquired softly, seeing the panic in her eyes. "The unspeakable secret you're running away from ... or me?"

Never in her life had China found herself in such proximity to a man, discounting, of course, that horrible episode with Freddy in the library. The folds of her cloak were tangled between Ethan Bloodwell's legs, and he was standing so close that she could see the faint stubble of a beard across his jaw and smell the not-unpleasant odor of manly sweat that clung to him.

"Well, little firebrand?"

China made no answer. In that moment she wasn't sure herself, and in her ignorance she attributed the mad pounding of her heart to revulsion. Nostrils flaring, she jerked herself free of his grasp and, lifting up the trailing ends of her skirts, turned and ran. Cursing, Ethan lunged for her and briefly managed to grab the hem of her cloak before it slipped from his fingers and she was gone, vanishing like a fleeing doe up the staircase and out into the harsh light of day.

During the past half hour the wharves below had come alive with activity. The *Kowloon Star,* moored at the East India Docks, was no longer riding isolated at anchor, but shared her narrow docking with numerous ships newly arrived from the sea routes. Storm-battered and weary, a half-dozen jaded East Indiamen jammed the wharves around her, their weathered decks swarming with men unloading their massive holds. Fleet schooners nosed into berths between them to disgorge casks of French spirits and bolts of delicate Bruges lace, and on the sun-baked docks below, horses, wagons, and cursing men pushed and shoved and fought one another for room. Luggers riding low with bulky cargoes of iron ore and coal moved ponderously down the shipping lanes, gulls wheeling in their wake, and China, disoriented by the chaos, did not at first know which way to turn.

"'Ere, lass, ye'll get yerself 'urt!" a ruddy-faced seaman warned, almost knocking her down with a barrel he deposited, grunting, on the planking beside her. "Best take yerself 'ome."

China was only too happy to comply, yet she found it all but impossible to push her way through the jostling, shouting gangs of dock workers and the horses that sweated and strained to pull the heavily loaded drays away.

"Look lively, there, girl, look lively!"

Gasping, China leaped aside as a muscular Suffolk punch nearly ran her down, its iron-shod hoof catching the hem of her cloak and ripping it. Dust whirled in her face and she pressed herself, coughing and panting, against a nearby stack of crates.

"Miss China! Miss China, over here!"

China looked up, startled at the sound of her name, and blinked in disbelief as she spotted Weston, Broadhurst's elderly butler, pushing his way toward her through the teeming crowd. The world spun dizzily before her eyes, and she stumbled and would have fallen if he hadn't applied his walking stick energetically to the shins of passing roustabouts and managed to free a path to her side.

Taking her by the arm he inquired anxiously, "Are you all right?"

"I'm ... I'm fine, Weston, thank you."

"I'd just about given up hope of finding you! You shouldn't have come here alone, miss!"

It was not surprising that there should be an uncharacteristic edge to Weston's voice, for he was well aware that the girl knew London only from the sheltered elegance of His Lordship's Mayfair town house and was entirely ignorant of the dangers that could befall any young woman wandering unescorted along the waterfront.

His hold on her arm tightened. "What in God's name are you doing here, miss? Surely you can't be running away from home? Mrs. Broyles said as much, but I wouldn't believe it."

"I had to leave," China told him with pain-darkened eyes, her voice dropping to a whisper. "Because of Freddy."

"What about him?" Weston prompted.

China could not frame the horrible truth into words. Why was Weston making it so difficult for her to explain? Surely he knew what had happened? He must! Why else would he have come all this way if not to fetch her home? She lifted her face, which was very white and vulnerable in the harsh light of day, and asked tremulously, "How did you know where to find me?"

"Chauncey saw you take Bastian down the Tunbridge Road. Both of us assumed you were on your way to London." A worried crease appeared between his eyes. "Though I must say I cannot for the life of me understand why you'd do such a thing, miss! I know it's been difficult for you since His Lordship died," he added kindly, "but surely there are other, and safer, ways to arrange for your return to Badajan? When I think of what might have happened! It's fortunate I found you before something dreadful occurred!"

China could not believe that he really seemed to have no idea what had prompted her to flee the house. "Oh, Weston, surely you must know what I did to Freddy?"

"Lord Freddy? Why you've done naught to him, miss!" Weston was regarding her with genuine astonishment. "Granted he isn't in the best of spirits at present. When I came downstairs this morning I found him lying on the sofa in the library suffering a most evil headache. Said he must have fallen and hit his head on the corner of the reading table, which isn't surprising considering the amount of—" He broke off with a dry cough and after a moment resumed: "It was a proper bump, I'll tell you that, miss, but I daresay he's none the worse for it. Did you happen to know something about it?" he inquired curiously.

China's breath caught painfully in her throat. "Are you saying that my cousin—that Freddy isn't dead?"

The absurdity of the notion betrayed Weston into a wheezing chuckle. "Dead? The very idea! No, not at all, miss, though I imagine he wishes he were. A bumped head and a hangover can't be the most pleasant afflictions to endure together."

China suddenly felt as if her knees had turned to water and she clung weakly to Weston's arm, staring up into his face with such a dazed expression that he felt his heart twist with concern. "Please, Miss China, let's take you home," he urged. "I convinced Lord Freddy to go back to bed, and it would be better if you returned to Broadhurst before either he or Lady Cassie awaken. Once they find you gone I'm afraid we'll have the devil of a time explaining where you've been. I've brought the carriage round so you won't have to ride. Now, wherever did you leave poor Bastian?"

China leaned her head tiredly against the elderly butler's shoulder and closed her eyes, allowing his affectionate prattle to soothe her ravaged nerves. She was glad, so very glad that Freddy wasn't dead and that no one suspected her of having tried to kill him, and she was ever so glad, too, that she was going home.

Perhaps it was due to her profound relief and the exhaustion that followed in its wake, but China forgot entirely about the captain of the brigantine *Kowloon Star* and the desperate offer she had made him. She was aware of nothing at the moment save an overwhelming need to sleep, and sinking wearily onto the padded leather cushions of the enormous black coach bearing the Linville coat of arms, she fell at once into a deep and exhausted slumber.

* * *

Lady Cassiopeia Linville, tapering fingers drumming on the carved oak arms of her chair, scowled at the visitor who had just been ushered into her private salon. A tea service and several tempting pieces of puffed pastry stood untouched on the small table at her elbow, and although the thin and unhealthily sallow young man eyed them with obvious hunger she did not offer him one. Indeed, she had no intention of doing so, and even though it was clear to her that the freckle-faced youth was nervous, she was not about to waste precious time putting him at ease. Dismissing the footman with a curt nod, she regarded him impatiently.

"Well, Mr. Browne? Did you find it?"

Arthur Browne, newly hired clerk of the distinguished legal firm of Biggs and Kenilworth of Brighton, Dover, and London, scuffed his worn shoes on the elegant Moorish rug. "Aye, mum," he murmured with downcast eyes. There was something oddly unnerving about Lady Cassiopeia Linville, and though he couldn't exactly put his finger on what it was, he found it unquestionably difficult to meet her coldly scrutinizing stare.

She was certainly a handsome woman, despite the prominent black mole that marred her imperious chin. Her features were gracefully patrician, her figure excellent for her three-and-thirty years, and her carefully arranged hair was a rare and glossy auburn in color. Like all Linvilles she was tall and carried herself with straight-backed grace, but the interminable years of waiting for her brother to come into his inheritance had left deep creases in her smooth face and a mulish set to her mouth. Hers was an intractable nature, her heart incapable of love, and she had always been forced to go to great pains to hide her spiteful ways from her grandfather, a man who had abhorred unkindness in any form.

Spoiled and petted as a child, Cassie Linville had found her world altered overnight by the arrival of her infant brother Freddy. It had galled her that the attention that had always been lavished upon her could possibly be transferred to this reddened, colicky creature, and her bitterness had increased as the years went by and Freddy grew into a handsome boy with the uncanny knack of ingratiating himself into the affections of the doting grown-ups around him. Cassie wholeheartedly despised him and dreamed of the day when she could flee her father's house and leave the obsequious Freddy forever behind.

It was not until she was nearly twenty-five, an old maid in the eyes of London society, that Cassie finally received what she had been waiting for: an offer of marriage. Yet Sir Lionel Edgewater, her intended, was a man some thirty years her senior and a most disreputable roué; a match between them was promptly forbidden by both her parents and Lord Linville. Cassie, however, was adamant. She would be Lady Edgewater, she would have a house of her own and twenty-six servants at her command and she would put an end at last to the scoffing whispers of those who claimed that Cassie Linville was too coldly proud and tart-tongued to find a husband.

Being of age, she had entered into the marriage without her parents' consent only to find herself widowed after four short months, Sir Lionel having choked to death on a chicken bone while dining at his club one evening. Because he had died without issue, the sum of his estates went automatically to some pimpled nephew from Groton, and the furious Cassie had had no choice but to return home and resign herself to the likelihood that no new offers would be coming her way.

Four months later her parents and grandmother perished in a theater fire, and Cassie pronounced it immeasurably regrettable that little Freddy had not lost his life in a similar fashion. Yet she soon found herself beginning to look at her brother with new eyes. As the heir to a considerable fortune, he was suddenly no longer the irksome creature she despised, and she had set about at once to flatter him and work her way into his good graces so that when the elderly Earl invited the boy to live with him at Broadhurst, Freddy had insisted that Cassie accompany him.

Neither of them had known at the time that they would have to wait nearly a decade for Freddy to come into his inheritance, but Cassie, who had grown surprisingly fond of her brother in the interim, had schooled herself to be patient. She had never been blind to Freddy's faults, and knowing that he would need a firm hand in administering his grandfather's wealth once the old man died, she could well afford to wait....

"Ma'am? Excuse me. Did you hear what I said?"

Cassie Linville started visibly as her eyes fell on the nervous young man before her, and for a moment she had no idea who he was. Then her vision cleared and with an effort she recalled herself to the present. What on earth had she been thinking of? This fellow here, this Arthur Browne, was he really the best Freddy had been able to come up with? He was not at all what she would term capable and trustworthy, yet that was exactly how Freddy had described him. Her lips thinned. Spineless little toady was far more like it!

"Well?" she inquired frostily, deciding there was little she could do about it now. "Did you manage to see my grandfather's will? What did it say?"

Every trace of color fled from Arthur's face, leaving the sallow skin a queer and pasty white. "I didn't have the chance to read it all, ma'am. I'm rarely alone in the office, you see, and I had quite a bit of trouble getting the safe open."

Doubtless because his hands had been shaking too much, Cassie thought with disgust. "Go on, go on."

"I barely had time for a quick look," Arthur stammered. "There were so many pages and I was afraid someone might come in and—"

"For God's sake, you were paid to find out who inherited my grandfather's estate, not to read every clause in the document!"

Arthur's Adam's apple bobbed spasmodically and he said unhappily, "Yes, ma'am, I know."

Cassie's expression was one of outward calm though her fingers had tightened convulsively about the arms of her chair. "Well, Mr. Browne? Who inherited? It was my brother, Lord Linville, wasn't it?"

He coughed self-consciously, certain that Her Ladyship would not take the news well. From the look of her she was an ill-tempered and vengeful dragon who didn't take kindly to being told one thing when she'd clearly been expecting to hear another. And though Arthur might despise himself and regret the impulse that had prompted him to accept Lord Freddy Linville's handsome bribe, he could not lie to her, for he was wretchedly aware that he would be caught in that lie as soon as Mr. Biggs returned form East Anglia and the will was officially read.

Drawing a deep breath he said miserably, "It was Miss China Warrick, ma'am."

When nothing but silence greeted his disclosure he cast a fearful glance at her and his heart seemed to skid to a halt when he saw that her skin had taken on the color of old parchment, drawn tightly across the bones of her face so that the mole on her chin stood out in livid contrast. Her long, bejeweled fingers had curled like claws about the arms of her chair, and Arthur, retreating a step without being aware that he did so, could feel the nervous sweat trickle down his back.

"Ma'am? Did you hear me? I said—"

Colorless eyes that glittered like a bird of prey's riveted themselves upon his face. "I heard you perfectly well, Mr. Browne."

Arthur hesitated, finding himself unable to turn away, fascinated and repelled by the almost inhuman baring of her yellowed teeth. Looking up and catching him staring, Cassie demanded furiously, "Whatever are you waiting for? We require nothing else from you. Get out!"

Ten minutes later a hastily summoned Freddy was shown into his sister's elegantly furnished salon. With his eyes deeply hooded and red, his left temple violently bruised, and his dressing gown wrinkled, he did not look at all like the handsome young dandy who had accosted his innocent cousin the night before. And indeed his manners were more those of a drunk and disorderly barbermonger than a civilized gentleman or a peer of the realm.

"I'll have you know my head aches abominably," he complained as soon as Cassie shut the door behind him. "I shouldn't be out of bed, much less scrambling about at ungodly hours to oblige m'lady. It's been one bloody—What the devil's wrong with you?"

Cassie had resumed her frantic pacing. "What's wrong with me?" she echoed, regarding him with open scorn. "You should be asking the same of dear, departed Grandpapa! I vow he must have been perfectly mad when he died!"

"Calm yourself, Cass," Freddy begged, anxious to spare his throbbing head the hammerblows inflicted by her shrill voice.

"Calm myself? How can I? Do you know what that simpleminded ass has done? He's made you heir to a worthless title!"

She laughed bitterly when she saw the confusion on his dissipated face. "Don't look so bewildered, my dear little brother! I just received a visit from Mr. Arthur Browne, a whimpering milksop if ever there was one, and he was kind enough to inform me that we are as poor as titmice. It's China who inherited everything! Everything, do you hear? It all belongs to China!"

Freddy paled at her words. "But that can't be! I knew the old man was fond of her—"

"Fond of her?" Cassie shrilled. "He practically doted on the conniving creature! How could he not when she used every wile she knew to worm her way into his affections? Pretending interest in those ridiculous hobbies of his and keeping him company for hours on end when you know what a perfectly unendurable bore he was! Oh, God, I vow I could kill the scheming brat!" Her voice shook and she collapsed onto the brocade-upholstered armchair.

Freddy, running his hands through his tousled hair and finding that they were shaking uncontrollably, scowled and said hoarsely, "We should have seen to it that she was sent back to Badajan as soon as her schooling was completed."

"If you'll recall, it was Grandpapa who refused to let her go after he'd suffered his stroke. And China agreed to stay and take care of him, ostensibly out of the goodness of her heart." Cassie's eyes narrowed with venom. "Doubtless she already knew or suspected that he intended to leave her his fortune."

"There is one thing working to our advantage," Freddy pointed out in a conversational drawl.

She regarded him contemptuously. "Oh, really? And that is...?"

"The fact that Biggs ain't expected at Broadhurst for

another two days. As far as he or anyone else is concerned the contents of Grandpapa's will are known only to God. That gives us plenty of time in which to act."

Cassie's eyebrows lifted. "To act? What do you mean? What do you intend to do?"

Freddy's mouth twisted into an ugly line. "I'm sure you agree that we're not about to spend the rest of our lives depending on China for charity. I expect she'll be equally as tightfisted as Grandpapa was, perhaps even worse. You do remember the scene she made on her birthday last year when I took away that bolt of Badajan silk she'd received, and gave it to Lord Staverton's wife?"

"Lud, yes," Cassie agreed, recalling China's silent withdrawal and her grandfather's towering rage. Both of them had simply refused to see how utterly wasteful it would have been to allow China to keep the entire length of the priceless material for herself. Grandfather, at least, should have realized, inasmuch as Lord Staverton possessed a powerful voice in Parliament, that Freddy's political ambitions could only have been enhanced by the generosity of the gift—even though, if the truth must be told, he had been hoping to raise nothing more than his own personal esteem in Sophie Staverton's bright blue eyes.

The value of Badajan silk, as both Cassie and Freddy well knew, was such that only the wealthiest of European aristocracy could afford it, and just because China Warrick's father produced it it didn't mean that China had the right to squander yards and yards of it for her own selfish use. At least that was how Cassie and her brother had seen it, though their grandfather had not.

"Do you remember, Freddy, how Sophie Staverton refused to part with it?" Cassie recalled now with a malicious chuckle. "Though Grandpapa did manage to talk her into selling some of it back. There was enough left over for a dressing gown for China, I believe."

Freddy made an impatient gesture. "Yes, yes, I remember, but that's all in the past now, Cass. What matters at the moment is the fact that I refuse to crawl to China for handouts—provided she even sees fit to give them to us. The situation must be handled promptly, before Roland Biggs arrives."

Cassie's eyes widened and she regarded her brother with appalled comprehension. "Surely you aren't planning to get rid of her? You can't be serious! No matter how carefully we arranged every detail, we could never convince anyone that China happened to meet with an accident just two days before she was to inherit a fortune! Besides, how do you propose to go about it? We've dabbled in unscrupulous schemes before, my dear brother, but murder requires some very clever planning."

"Oh, good Lord, Cassie!" Freddy snorted incredulously. "What sort of fool do you think I am? Even a senile old addlepate like Roland Biggs would suspect foul play the instant something happened to her! And I, my dear sister, am not about to end my days dangling from a hangman's rope."

"Very well," Cassie said tartly, "what then?"

Freddy threw her a smug and condescending glance. "It's quite simple, actually. I'm going to marry her."

"What?"

"Why not? As her lawful wedded husband I'd have complete and legal administrative control of the estate, and since we're not first cousins, but cousins once removed, no one would think to protest."

"Suppose she doesn't agree?"

Turning his head to regard his reflection in the floor-length mirror hanging across the room, Freddy allowed a satisfied smile to curve his lips. Despite the multicolored bruise that disfigured it, his was an inordinately handsome face and he knew that no woman, least of all his young and impressionable cousin, would be able to resist it.

"Don't worry, Cass," he said, yawning. "She'll agree, and quite eagerly so, I might add. Now if you'll excuse me? I'm going back to bed. Be a luv and leave orders that I'm not to be disturbed, hmm?"

_____ *Chapter Three* _____

Broadhurst, a gift from the boy king Edward VI to the first of the Linville lords, was an imposing estate whose boundaried walls ran for mile after mile along the fertile Kentish countryside. The manor house, a massive and heavily turreted structure of native gray stone, sat square on the site of a Norman castle destroyed by the Roundheads in 1645. Rebuilt after the Restoration and remodeled by the fifth Earl Linville to its present Georgian style, it boasted forty rooms of state, the elaborate friezework and burnished paneling in each adorned with an impressive collection of sixteenth-century Flemish tapestries. Tiered gardens, laid down by a team of Italian architects, surrounded the central block of the house, and terraced lawns sloped gracefully to an artificial lake where tame swans paddled amid the lily pads. Beyond the extensive rose garden lay greenhouses and stables, the grassy paddocks bordered by cherry orchards, oasthouses, and fields of ripening hops belonging to Broadhurst's vast working farms.

Freddy Thurston Linville stepped from the gold-appointed Morning Room onto a small, walled terrace, allowing his gaze to rove possessively over the manicured beauty of the parkland below him. He gave a gleeful laugh as his eyes fell on the small stone and oak chapel nestled amid a copse of copper-crowned beeches on the far side of the lake where, two days ago, the old Earl's remains had been laid to rest.

"Did you think to deny me what by right has always been mine?" he demanded aloud. "You were a devilish nuisance alive, dear old Grandpapa, but now that you're dead you haven't the power to prevent me from doing as I please!"

A feeling of exhilaration swept over him. Had his grandfather truly expected him to stand by and allow the Linville fortune to fall into the hands of a mere child like China Warrick, whose only lawful claim to the family name was the fact that her grandmother, Lady Delia Linville, had been the Earl's adopted sister?

Sipping tea laced with cherry brandy, Freddy wandered back into the Morning Room, pausing to admire the Vandyke hanging over the rose marble mantel and wondering idly how much the appraisers would assess its worth to be. Plenty of time for that later, Freddy decided lazily, days and days, in fact, for at the moment his thoughts were taken up with other and more pertinent matters: his marriage to his cousin, for one thing.

Though he'd spent most of yesterday languishing in bed, he hadn't exactly been idle. Rather, he had given a great deal of thought to his future bride and deciding how best to present his suit. While he had no qualms on the score of being accepted, he was well aware that China was genuinely grieving for the loss of her great-uncle. And although Freddy was not about to tolerate any tiresome demurring on her part on the grounds that the Earl was but three days in his grave, he knew better than to handle a feisty thoroughbred the likes of his cousin with a heavy and impatient hand. Better to gentle her with tender words and assurances of his devotion and so extract a promise from her, for it didn't really matter one way or the other if they were married or not by the time the will was read. The engagement and its formal announcement would be binding enough.

Hearing the rustle of crinolines in the hallway outside, Freddy whirled about to see China withdrawing hastily from the threshold at the sight of him.

"In a hurry, coz?" he drawled.

She hesitated a moment before stepping inside, his appearance having taken her entirely by surprise, for it was not Freddy's usual habit to arise so early. And since he had spent all of yesterday abed, she had been hoping to find herself spared a confrontation with him until afternoon at least. But as luck seemed not to have favored her there was nothing for it but to square her shoulders and say good morning in a tone she hoped was pleasant enough and above all suspicion and reproach.

"You seem deuced eager to avoid me this morning," Freddy observed, turning to face her, and was considerably annoyed when she reacted with a smothered gasp to the sight of the purple bruise discoloring his temple.

Perhaps it was the fact that this simple gesture pricked his vanity that prompted him to throw his carefully laid plans to the wind; or perhaps a measure of his sincere belief that no woman could resist his Byronic good looks that forced the words impulsively and unwisely from him. And certainly it had something to do with the sight of China standing slim and impossibly lovely before him, a small, red-haired creature in deep mourning black, whose parted lips made it impossible to resist her.

Whatever the reasons, the fact remained that Freddy was quite suddenly unable to help himself from seizing China's hands in his and incautiously pressing his suit— to the end that he found himself promptly refused.

Because he had never for a moment entertained the notion that China might say no, and because she had done so in a hesitant manner suggesting maidenly modesty (and not, as was the case, because shock had robbed her of the ability to speak), he asked again—and was similarly and far more firmly turned down.

"I'm sorry, Freddy," China said clearly, though her face was very white. "It's kind of you to wish to look after me, but I intend to return home to Badajan. There's really no reason for me to stay now."

"No reason? China, my dear! Am I not reason enough?"

She detached herself as unobtrusively as possible from his grasp. "No, Freddy," she said decisively, "I'm sorry, truly I am. But it wouldn't be right. Surely you must see that?"

"Oh, hang it all!" he burst out. "If it's because of what happened the other night, I can assure you that I'll not force my attentions on you again. It was a gross and unforgivable gesture on my part. Why in hell are you looking like that?"

"You knew?" China whispered, shocked.

"Of course! Do you honestly think I'd admit to that insufferably humorless Weston—or anyone else—that you were responsible for laying me to the floor? Or the reasons behind it?"

China was regarding him with horrified eyes. Freddy's answering smile was as appeased as a well-fed tiger's—and equally as dangerous. "I could have had you arrested for attempted murder, my dear, but after some reflection I decided I'd frightened you unfairly and that you couldn't be blamed for overreacting."

"That was very kind of you, Freddy."

"Yes, wasn't it? And after you've agreed to marry me I don't see why we can't forget the unpleasant incident ever happened."

"But I'm not going to marry you," China stated firmly.

He laughed lightly and unconcernedly. "Have you forgotten that you're not yet of age and that you're in no position to make that decision?"

"No, I haven't," China said, and her eyes began to flash in a manner that would have discouraged anyone who knew her better. "But apparently you have forgotten that my parents are still alive and even if I did wish to marry you—which I do not—I could not do so without their consent."

"That may well be true," Freddy conceded after a moment, nettled because he had, in truth, forgotten. China, who had had enough of this undesirable interview, put an end to it by nodding stiffly and withdrawing without another word.

It couldn't be possible! she was thinking furiously to herself. Freddy must have taken leave of his senses to think that she would ever marry him. His behavior only strengthened her belief that Anna was right and the sooner she left England the better. And until such a time as her return to Badajan could be arranged, she could only hope that she had made it clear to Freddy that there was no sense in continuing to press for a match between them and that nothing more should be said or done on that score by either of them.

In that respect she was sorely mistaken. Freddy withdrew to his rooms to nurse his wounded pride and to plan. A half hour later, he appeared downstairs and brusquely ordered the carriage brought round. Giving the coachman a series of terse instructions, he settled back against the cushions with a sigh, and set off to spend the afternoon in Tunbridge Wells in the company of a surly-looking fellow by the name of Jack Weir, an inmate recently released from Newgate Prison. Their meeting, held in a deserted inn far from the main posting roads, was brief, and after the furtive exchange of a bulging sack of coins, both men left by way of different roads.

"Going riding, are you?" Freddy inquired interestedly, passing his cousin in the vaulted foyer of the Great Hall late the following morning. Intent on the gazette in his hands, he had not at first seen her, and it was the rustle of velvet on stone that had brought his head around. His pulse quickened on seeing that she was once again wearing the full-skirted habit with its trim, black-beribboned jacket that she had not donned since the old man had taken ill and died.

"I thought I'd gallop Bastian a bit," China told him.

"Enjoy yourself, coz," he said in a familiar and unaffected drawl and turned to his paper. China, feeling happier than she had in days, lifted her skirts and ran outside. If Freddy could put yesterday's embarrassing interview out of mind and behave as though it had never happened, then so could she!

"Mornin' miss." A white-haired man in an age-stained leather apron stood at the mounting block holding firmly to Bastian's bridle. Touching his blunt and oil-darkened fingers respectfully to his thinning forelocks, he remarked with a grin, "'Is 'ighness be ready enow. No worse the wear for bein' rode t' London Town these two days past."

"Thank you, Chauncey," China responded warmly, for she was greatly fond of Broadhurst's elderly stablemaster.

Pulling on her gloves, she swung herself into the saddle and allowed Chauncey to adjust the stirrup. She touched Bastian's flank with the tip of a bone-handled whip and sent him trotting off in the direction of the park. Moments later they had vanished over a grassy rise, Bastian's hooves leaving a trail of sparkling rainbows across the morning dew.

With the cool autumn wind caressing her cheeks and the perfume of late-blooming summer flowers heavy in the air, China felt as if an enormous weight had eased from her shoulders. It was as if she had been set free for the first time from the funereal atmosphere of the great house and from the bleak unhappiness that had marked her existence since the day Esmund Linville had taken to his bed, never to leave it again.

The pale October sun was surprisingly warm, burning through the lingering mist and dancing with rippling fingers across the wind-ruffled surface of the lake. Turning Bastian down the neatly edged gravel path leading to its grassy banks, China shielded her eyes and rose up in the stirrup to watch a flock of wild ducks take off from the water amid an explosion of scarlet wings. She had allowed her grasp on the reins to slacken for a moment, and was caught entirely off guard when Bastian, perhaps spooked by the whirring, whistling creatures that swooped over his head, reared unexpectedly and backed away in snorting terror. Reaching out to pat his neck in a soothing gesture, China was nearly unseated when he bolted, his ears flattened against his head as he whirled on his haunches and lengthened his stride to a panic-stricken gallop.

Frightened as she was, China knew better than to try to stop him. He had taken the bit between his teeth and she was well aware that she lacked the physical strength to bring him to a halt. Indeed, there was nothing she could do but wait for him to slow of his own accord—and hope that she could remain in the saddle and that he wouldn't stumble or, worse, put his foot in a badger hole.

Clods of turf flew beneath his drumming hooves and the hard-packed ground passed in a blur of flashing brown and gray. China's derby tumbled from her head and her hair, escaping its seed-pearl netting, whipped in crimson strands against her smarting cheeks. In no time at all they had crossed the length of the western park, Bastian pounding up one hill and down another, narrowly skirting the damp and dangerously slippery hollows and the low-hanging branches of the towering oaks. His maddened flight quickly took them across the long, furrowed fields of harvested rye and on toward the ancient, moss-grown wall that marked the end of Broadhurst's fertile farmland and the boundaries of the estate.

It was an extremely high wall of crumbling stone, running at right angles to the land and separating the wild Kentish moor from Broadhurst's cultivated acres. The terrain on the opposite side was rough, China knew, the ground boggy and low-lying, and littered with rocks. Her throat went dry, and she pulled sharply on the reins in a quite useless effort to make the big animal swerve, well aware that Bastian could easily break his leg landing on the uneven footing and crush her beneath him when he fell.

The off-side rein slipped from her grasp as she leaned forward to secure it and China, knowing she could no longer do anything to make Bastian change course, braced herself for a fall.

The crack of a pistol, discharged amid a stand of chestnut trees not ten yards away, startled both the runaway horse and the girl clinging to his back. Swerving wildly, Bastian skidded to a halt only inches from the wall, his hind legs tucked up beneath him, while China, who had risen in the stirrup in anticipation of the jump, was caught totally unprepared and went catapulting over his head to land in a crumpled heap on the far side.

"Hello there! Are you hurt?"

Thankfully she was not, for after lying for a moment on her back staring dazed and dizzy into the robin's egg blue of the sky, she came stiffly to her feet. Her habit was torn and streaked with mud, and a smudge of the same dirtied her cheek, but China scarcely noticed, for she had turned her head and froze, finding herself staring into the

sun-weathered face of none other than Captain Ethan
Bloodwell.

He was sitting astride a roan mare on the opposite side
of the wall, studying her with a similar expression of utter
disbelief. For a moment they regarded one another in
shocked silence, then Captain Bloodwell threw back his
head and abruptly broke into a gale of hearty laughter.

"Will you kindly explain what could possibly be so
amusing about a near-fatal accident?" China demanded,
quivering with indignation.

"My apologies, Miss Warrick," Ethan Bloodwell obliged,
the amusement vanishing from his face. "I didn't expect
to meet you again under—er—under such unusual circumstances."

"How do you know my name?" China countered, remembering quite distinctly that she had deliberately refrained from introducing herself during their thoroughly
unpleasant meeting. She was certain, too, despite how absurd it might seem, that he hadn't been quite this tall or
arrogantly handsome the first time they had met—had
he?

Given his shocking state of dishabille and the appalling
disorder of his cabin, she would never have believed him
capable of presenting even a moderately respectable appearance. Yet here he was, turned out like any gentleman
of leisure, in a well-tailored coat of dove gray superfine
and matching calfskin knee breeches. The stock about his
neck, stark white against his darkly tanned face, was meticulously pressed, and the chestnut hair she remembered
as being raked negligently across his brow was now neatly
combed.

Despite his air of refinement, Captain Bloodwell seemed
to exude some untamed quality that was curiously at odds
with the standards of fashion set by the London dandies
of his day and whose often absurdly overruffled and frilly
costumes his simple attire seemed intended to mock. Disconcerted by the fact that he could cross with such apparent ease from his world into theirs, China demanded
suspiciously, "Who is it you've come to see? Someone here
at Broadhurst?"

Dismounting, Ethan vaulted the boundary wall and

peered without answering into her dirty face. Whipping a cambric handkerchief from the breast pocket of his coat, he dabbed away the mud, then turned over her hands and examined the angry red scratches on her palms.

"I'm quite unhurt," China assured him, snatching her hands free and retreating a safe distance. She was shaken by the odd jolt that had traveled through her at his touch and credited the light-headedness caused by her fall as being responsible. "If you would please answer my question, Captain? What are you doing here at Broadhurst? And how did you know my name?"

"Suppose you tell me first how you managed to come so close to breaking your neck on this intractable creature," he suggested, indicating Bastian, who had recovered his wind and stood cropping grass a short distance away.

"If you must know," China said in a tone that suggested clearly that he had little right to, "he was spooked by a flock of ducks."

Intent on finding her boot, which had slipped off during her fall, she did not see the frown that pulled at the corners of Captain Bloodwell's mouth or the sudden, attentive stillness about him. When she lifted her head to regard him curiously, alerted at last by his unexpected silence, he turned away and bent quickly to retrieve a small leather boot that lay near him in the grass.

"Is this what you're after?" he inquired politely.

China's face cleared. "Yes, thank you. I cannot imagine how it came off." She held out her hand for it, but Captain Bloodwell made no move to relinquish it and waved her instead to a nearby tree stump. She opened her mouth to protest, but when his amused gaze told her clearly that he was well aware of her discomfiture, she compressed her lips tightly and seated herself. She was not about to provide him with another excuse for laughing!

Lifting aside the skirts of her habit, she extended her foot and deliberately looked away from the scandalous length of stockinged calf she was forced to reveal, hoping that Captain Bloodwell would be gentleman enough to do the same. On bended knee Ethan obligingly slipped the boot back on, and as his head bent close to hers China couldn't help but notice how his thick chestnut hair had a tendency to curl boyishly about his ears. A wave of heat suffused her cheeks and she looked quickly away, aware that this was not the sort of discovery anyone in her position ought to be making.

"Thank you," she said with as much dignity as she could muster once he had helped her upright. Shaking out her skirts, she lifted her chin and regarded him sharply. "Now, would you please be so kind as to answer my question?"

"Certainly. I didn't come here to see you," he told her bluntly. "I came to speak to Lord Linville."

China's brows rose. "My cousin?"

She stiffened as he lifted her without warning onto the back of his mare, and his lips curved devilishly.

"Is there a reason for this, Captain Bloodwell?" China asked frostily.

"I thought perhaps you would prefer to ride back to the house rather than walk," he said obligingly, though he was thinking as he looked at her that he hadn't expected her to weigh so little or to possess a waist that was slim enough to be spanned with his hands.

"I am thoroughly capable of handling my own horse," she informed him crisply. "There's no need for us to trade mounts."

An insolent gleam appeared in his eyes. "My dear Miss Warrick, who said anything about trading mounts?"

"You did! You said—"

"I said you would doubtless prefer to ride, as it's a long walk back."

China's brows rose. "And just why should I have to walk?"

He grinned at her in a maddening fashion. "Perhaps I forgot to mention that your horse has gone lame. It would appear he pulled a tendon crossing that boggy field."

China's anger dissipated instantly. For the first time she noticed that Bastian, who stood with trailing reins a short distance away, was favoring his left hind leg. Uttering a dismayed gasp she started to slide from the saddle only to feel Captain Bloodwell's hard, detaining fingers close about her wrist.

"No need for concern, my dear child. It can wait until he's back in his stall."

His blue eyes locked with hers and China had the distinct and thoroughly unnerving impression that he would physically restrain her if she tried to dismount. What was he hiding from her? she wondered anxiously. Was Bastian's injury so serious?

"I assure you he'll mend good as new given a few days' rest," he pronounced. "Now, are you going to permit me to ride with you, Miss Warrick, or will you condemn me to the distance on foot?"

China's lips tightened. Put that way he made it impossible for her to refuse without appearing rude. It was his horse, after all, and she averted her face in order to hide her annoyance from him.

Chuckling softly, Captain Bloodwell swung himself into the saddle behind her. China's cheeks burned as she felt the pressure of his thighs come to rest intimately against her, but she forgot her embarrassment the moment she saw him pull a long-barreled pistol from the pocket of his breeches and tuck it casually into the saddlebag behind him.

"Was it you who fired the shot that made Bastian stop?"

"It was, and you were fortunate I was able to," Ethan replied grimly. "There was no other way to prevent him taking that wall."

China's eyes lifted to him and he noticed for the first time that the upswept lashes which framed them were lightly dusted with gold. "Then I must thank you for saving me from what might have been a serious injury." Her expression was suddenly grave and he found himself wondering if she ever smiled or laughed.

"It's odd that I was unable to stop him myself," she continued thoughtfully, "for he's quite accustomed to the waterfowl on the pond and usually pays them no mind. Still, I'm grateful you intervened. Thank you."

Ethan inclined his head politely and was inwardly angered by the unexpected tug at his heart when he looked into her proud face. God's blood, she was young! A child still, and he should have realized even before he set out for Kent that he would be openly courting disaster by entangling himself in her affairs. Regrettably it was too late to extricate himself now. His fired pistol and that haughty and yet oddly compelling look on her face had seen to that.

China was not ignorant of the fact that Ethan Bloodwell was in superb physical condition, yet she didn't care to be reminded of it once he kicked his mare into a trot and she landed time and again against the hard muscles of his chest. Though the air was decidedly cool he had left his coat unbuttoned and China was dismayed at the unwanted intimacy of hearing the steady beat of his heart in her ear, and tried determinedly to inch away from the uncomfortable warmth of his body.

"This would be far more pleasant for both of us if you'd stop your squirming," he remarked at last, his amused voice sounding directly in her ear.

China stiffened in response but was distracted from replying by the sight of several mounted men galloping hard across the plowed fields some distance below them. She immediately recognized her cousin Freddy, several Broadhurst footmen, and Gilfrey, the head groom.

"They must be looking for me," she exclaimed.

"What makes you think so?" Ethan asked.

"Freddy would never have accompanied them otherwise. He cannot abide horses! He must have seen Bastian run away with me and volunteered to help."

"*Ecce signum*," Ethan said softly. "There goes proof."

She threw him a startled look. "What do you mean?"

He ignored her question. "Your cousin doesn't ride, Miss Warrick?"

"Seldom. He prefers to drive, though he has hunted on occasion. Where are you going? Shouldn't we try to intercept them?"

"I think not," Ethan responded tersely and turned the mare down a narrow footpath leading in the opposite direction where they were instantly concealed by the shadows of a dense cluster of oaks, the faithful Bastian limping behind. Broadhurst's sprawling rooftop with its numerous gables and chimney pots was visible above the glade of barren trees and Ethan set the mare trotting toward it, blatantly ignoring China's protests until she was simmering with indignation.

"I hope you realize you're being impossibly rude," she

told him sharply. "How can I inform my cousin I've come to no harm when you insist—"

She broke off, aware that he was not listening to her, but was staring intently off into the trees to the right of the path. Hearing the sound of drumming hooves coming from that direction, she craned her neck and was astonished to see Eli Chauncey, Broadhurst's stablemaster, burst through the thickets astride one of the Earl's long-legged hunters.

Startled at the sight of them, he drew rein sharply and flung himself out of the saddle, moving swiftly for a man of his age and size, and crossed the path at a run. "Are yer 'armed, miss?" he called out anxiously.

"It might be wise to call your bloodhound off before he comes any closer," came Ethan's quiet warning in her ear.

China's eyes widened as she saw that Chauncey was carrying a firearm, an outdated but meticulously preserved flintlock that obviously stemmed from an age when Chauncey, as a young groom, had hunted deer in Broadhurst's extensive private forests with the youthful Esmund Linville.

"I'm fine, Chauncey," she said hastily. "I took a spill, but it wasn't at all serious. Whatever is going on?"

"Lord Freddy were on't terrace when 'e saw Bastian run away wi' ye, miss." Coming to a breathless halt at the mare's side, Chauncey reached out to take her bridle. "All of us come lookin' for ye and John 'Olm said 'e thoughts 'e saw a strange fellow o'er by t' West Gate. Well, I wents to 'ave a look and couldn't find no one. Now, that wouldn't 'appen to 'ave been ye, sir?" he added, addressing Ethan with an unmistakably hostile glower.

"It might have been," Ethan allowed unperturbed. "I cannot say for certain that I came through the West Gate, but as I missed the turnoff in Tunbridge it is likely I did not enter the property through the front entrance." His eyes narrowed. "As my business with Lord Linville is legitimate, however, I should like to ask that you stop fingering your weapon."

"Most people what 'as business with 'Is Lordship don't steal round the property," Chauncey countered suspiciously, not caring for the captain's lean, hard face or for the fact that he had seen fit to take Miss China up on his horse—or her for allowing it! "They takes the drive to the front door and waits properlike for Mr. Weston to announce 'em."

Ethan sighed and, affecting to put an end to the tiresome interview, said in a bored and disaffected drawl, "I've already told you, my good man—"

"Be a decent chap," Chauncey interrupted in a tone suggesting he were speaking to a recalcitrant child rather than a man of obviously worldly experience. "Set Miss China down and give me t' pistol I sees there in your pouch."

Opening his mouth to deliver a suitable retort, Ethan was startled into silence when he felt China's slim body beginning to shake uncontrollably against him. For a moment he was mystified, but when he leaned forward in the stirrups to peer into her face he was at first dumbfounded and then outraged to see that her eyes were crinkled at the corners and that breathless little gasps were coming from her parted lips. Even then he could scarcely believe the evidence presented him: The little bitch was laughing!

"See here," he began through clenched teeth, but China's uncontrollable laughter interrupted him.

"It's—it's all right, Chauncey," she said between smothered giggles. "It's true Bastian ran away with me, but Captain Bloodwell arrived in time to prevent a serious accident. He isn't a trespasser or any other sort of interloper, but if you feel the need to disarm and arrest him, perhaps you should."

Damn her! Ethan thought uncharitably and scowled darkly as she burst into renewed peals of helpless laughter. This was the thanks he got for intervening on her behalf? Being held up as a source of amusement by some impertinent, half-grown chit and trading insults with an insolent fellow brandishing a popgun that, from the look of it, should have been donated long since to the British Museum's Department of Antiquities?

Dismounting, he turned to assist China to the ground, his expression a thundercloud of annoyance, but when she reached out her gloved hands to him he was astounded by the transformation he saw in her face. Perhaps it was because the laughter had served to set those incredibly green eyes ablaze or because the pale magnolia skin was suddenly flushed with a warm and astonishingly beautiful color, but Ethan was rendered quite speechless, finding himself confronted with a flash of spirit he hadn't known she possessed.

There was something gay and free of cares in that young, innocent face which Ethan found inexplicably infectious, and to his considerable annoyance he was unable to keep his lips from twitching as he put his hands about her waist and lowered her to the ground.

"There, I've turned her over peacefully," he said, addressing her glowering warden, and crossed his arms casually before his chest. "Are you still interested in trying to subdue me?"

"Eh ... could be I were bein' a bit 'asty," Chauncey said reflectively, for it seemed likely that the arrogant gent had had ample opportunity to do Miss China harm long before this had that truly been his intent. "I 'opes ye won't be takin' me ill, sir."

Ethan brushed the apology aside with a brusque shake of his head. "I quite understand."

Indeed, it was perfectly obvious to him that the grizzly stablemaster was fiercely fond of his young mistress, but Ethan suddenly and quite simply decided that he had had enough of both of them and that he no longer had any wish to entangle himself in the affairs of this strangely disturbing young girl. And, just as quickly, he had changed his mind about seeking out an audience with Lord Freddy Linville and decided further that it would be greatly advisable to make his exit before that redoubtable gentleman arrived on the scene.

Perhaps he might have escaped with his conscience intact and China Warrick's fate left in the indifferent hands of the gods but for the fact that Eli Chauncey bent at that moment to examine Bastian's legs and Ethan saw the broad shoulders stiffen as the probing fingers slid along the foam-flecked flesh of the animal's flank.

Few men, in looking back over the course of their lives, can claim awareness at a time when a particular decision or choice is being made that they are turning down a path

that will forever alter the direction of their days. Only in
retrospect is such vision ever clear, yet Ethan Bloodwell,
peering speculatively from Chauncey's leathery countenance into China Warrick's questioning young face, felt a
twinge of uncharacteristic pity and knew without a shadow
of doubt that he was blundering down a dangerous path
with his eyes wide open. It was a course that could quite
easily put an end to the freedom and lawlessness of his
own existence, but only, he argued with himself, for the
time being.

Moving quickly to place himself between China and the
dejectedly drooping head of her lamed horse, he said intently to the stablemaster, "Miss Warrick believes her
mount was spooked by a flock of waterfowl on the lake.
I've no doubt they were the cause of his reckless behavior."

Still kneeling with his hands roving Bastian's swollen
leg, Chauncey swiveled his grizzled head around, and for
a long moment he regarded the captain's set face in silence.
His own expression was uncertain and fraught with a great
many unsaid things, and it was not until his gaze swung
past him to China's white, anxious face that the silence
was broken and he came stiffly to his feet.

"'Aven't I warned ye time and again," he scolded, "about
takin' 'im out when 'e's fresh, miss? Like as not those ducks
wouldn't 'ave scared 'im if ye'd let Gilfrey run the spark
out of 'im first."

"How badly is he hurt?" China inquired worriedly.

"'E'll mend," Chauncey said shortly and cast a relieved
and quite meaningful glance at the captain. "Ahem—Now
why don't yer let the Cap'n 'ere take yer back t' 'ouse?"

Before China could answer, the thickets behind them
snapped and quivered violently and a red-faced young
gentleman in scarlet coat and tailored breeches burst onto
the scene astride a foam-flecked chestnut hunter.

Checking his mount with a heavy hand that left the
poor animal tossing its head in pain, he regarded the stout
stablemaster with open hostility. "What the devil is the
meaning of this, Chauncey? I thought I told you—*China!*"

Every trace of color drained from his face as he caught
sight of the small, mud-splattered figure standing at
Chauncey's side. His gloved hands tightened convulsively

about the reins, and the hunter snorted and sidled uneasily as the bit sawed into its sensitive mouth.

It was almost as if he'd seen a ghost, Ethan thought to himself, suddenly alert. With open interest he studied the younger man's pallor and the rapid rise and fall of his Adam's apple as he breathed with the quick, panting breaths of someone who has just suffered a most unpleasant shock.

"I take it this is your cousin," Ethan remarked in an affable undertone to China, yet his voice had the unfortunate effect of resounding loudly in the stillness.

Instantly the shock on Freddy Linville's white face vanished and was replaced by anger, and since he found it easier to vent his spleen on this impertinent stranger than to look again at China, he said curtly: "You there! What in blazes are you doing on my land?"

If Freddy had hoped to collect his scattered wits by verbally abusing Captain Ethan Bloodwell, he was sorely mistaken, for the expression that passed across the hard countenance in response checked him as effectually as a slap across the mouth. No one uttered a word, and in the tense silence the jangling of bridle trappings and the stamping of the nervous hunter's hoofs were unnaturally loud.

"This is Captain Bloodwell, Freddy," China said at last, affecting to put an end to this oddly bewildering and unpleasant scene. She was frightened by the rigid lines of Ethan Bloodwell's long body and embarrassed by the craven expression on her cousin's flushed face.

"I am quite capable of making my own introduction, Miss Warrick," Ethan told her blandly. "I take it you are the new Lord Linville?"

"I am." The title was a soothing balm to Freddy's shattered nerves, and he was relieved to find that his composure was rapidly returning. "May I ask again what you're doing here, sir?"

"Certainly. But I should like to speak with you in private," Ethan replied in a tone that, for all its affability, would have given those who knew him just cause to feel uneasy. "I trust it's not inconvenient?"

"See here, my good fellow," Freddy said irritably. "I

haven't time to play games. As you can see my cousin has met with an accident."

"It is precisely because of Miss Warrick's . . . accident that I am here," Ethan continued, giving the word unmistakable emphasis. Ah, that served to wipe the smug look from that insipidly handsome face!—which, Ethan decided idly, was not going to age well considering the lines of dissipation already etched about the too-full mouth, and the excess flesh above the tightly knotted cravat that hinted at encroaching jowls.

"I'm afraid I don't understand. What is it you want with my cousin, sir?"

Ethan was not particularly willing to take up the matter with both Miss Warrick and a Broadhurst servant listening in, yet Freddy Linville's blustering uncertainty angered him unaccountably and it was grimly clear by now that the fellow deserved every qualm he was suffering—and more. Looking the bemused young man squarely in the eye, he said crisply, "It concerns the two hundred pounds Miss Warrick offered me several days ago for her safe transportation to Badajan."

_____ *Chapter Four* _____

"Your drink, sir."

With a suitably inscrutable façade, John Weston set a fluted glass of swirling amber onto the small octagonal table at Captain Bloodwell's elbow. Stealing a surreptitious glance into that deeply browned face, he found the pale blue eyes roving over the watercolor sketches adorning the walls of the East Wing's private drawing room. Weston found he didn't particularly care for the look in those hard eyes or the disrespect with which their owner lounged in the velvet-upholstered Jacobean armchair, and said as much to Lydia Broyles upon his hurried return to the kitchen.

"'S a nasty lookin' bloke," the portly cook agreed, wiping a dab of flour from her cheek. "Saw him come in with Lord Freddy, and I'll tells you, Mr. Weston, I knowed right away there was trouble brewin'."

Doubtless the woman was right, Weston reflected, for Lord Freddy and his sister had all but abandoned their visitor in the drawing room and were currently engaged

57

in some sort of argument in the library down the hall, a gross breach of conduct that was to him most curious.

"Lord Freddy were lookin' proper anxious," Lydia added with a shake of her unkempt head and, kneading a misshapen lump of dough with capable hands, added direly and with a concern that was to prove only too well founded, "I only hopes no harm'll come of it."

"It's out of the question!" Lord Freddy Linville was at that very moment saying furiously to his sister. "Allow China to sail East with some arrogant sea captain we know nothing about? And pay him two hundred pounds in the bargain? I refuse to consider it!"

"Be quiet, Freddy," Cassie said impatiently, pacing with considerable agitation back and forth before the stone-mullioned windows. "I need to think."

Freddy Linville passed a shaking hand across his eyes. "I cannot understand," he said as though he hadn't heard her, "how she could possibly offer him such a monstrous sum! It's—it's preposterous!"

"And I'd like to know what on earth prompted the foolish girl to ride to London in the first place?" Cassie wondered furiously.

Freddy, who suspected quite accurately why his young cousin had attempted to run away, blushed uncomfortably and made an impatient gesture. "It doesn't really matter, does it? Just tell me how the bloody devil we're supposed to get rid of that fellow when I'm convinced he suspects us of mischief."

"That's another thing," Cassie interrupted wrathfully, whirling to confront him with an agitated rustle of silk. "How dare you—how *dare* you plan something so—so— blatantly and unforgivably stupid without consulting me first? Why didn't you tell me China had refused to marry you? Surely we could have discussed the matter and come up with a better solution than arranging for her to break her neck on her horse!"

"I didn't intend to have her killed," Freddy said stiffly.

"What then? Were you hoping to injure her sufficiently so that in a weakened state you could readily break down her resistance?"

Freddy's sulky expression told her exactly how close

her words had hit the mark, and Cassie was forced to keep her fury in tight check, aware that it would accomplish nothing. Taking a deep breath, she strove to calm herself, and after a moment she resumed with commendable composure. "I have no idea how this Bloodwell fellow came to suspect what you were about, but I agree that he clearly suspects something, and unless you wish him to turn us in for attempted murder you'd better content yourself with letting China go home."

"Letting China—Cassie, are you mad?" Freddy's face was a study of blank astonishment.

Cassie said coldly, "No, I am not. But since you saw fit to undertake this outrageous, this unbelievably addled scheme behind my back and then tell me nothing about it until you were caught—purely by chance and by a man who appears just as clever as he is dangerous—then I have no recourse but to act as *I* see fit. And that means sending China home with this unmentionable Captain Bloodwell, despite the fact that she promised to pay him two hundred pounds for her passage."

"But Cassie—"

She cut him off with an intractable shake of her head. "No, my dear brother, you've galloped head-on into the noose, and the only way to extract yourself is to behave as though nothing untoward exists between the two of us and our dear little cousin." She nibbled delicately at the tip of a fingernail, her fury abating. "Surely you must agree that Captain Bloodwell will be forced to abandon his suspicions if we acquiesced quite willingly to China's wishes?"

"Of course," Freddy agreed irritably. "For one thing he has no proof to back his suspicions and I was most discreet with Weir, but you're overlooking the most important point, Cass." Abruptly he beat his fist on the desktop. "Damn, what a bloody muddle this is! Have you forgotten that China will still inherit Grandpapa's fortune whether she's living in England or not?" His expression was suddenly haggard and his hand shook uncontrollably as he reached for the snifter and splashed brandy into it.

"Of course I haven't forgotten," Cassie said reasonably, "but will she, Freddy? Will she really inherit what has always been yours by right?" There was a smile playing on her bold red lips that reminded Freddy of a sated lioness purring over her kill.

"I don't know what you mean," he said uneasily.

"It's quite simple, actually. Badajan is half a world away and anything could happen to her once she arrives there—anything at all."

Freddy snorted contemptuously. "What was it you were saying earlier about bungled accidents, my dear?"

"We're talking about the East, Freddy, and Indonesia in particular, where a certain measure of risk governs the lives of any European who resides there. In a world as lawless and desperately poor as Southeastern Asia I'm certain the Linville wealth could wield considerable influence—enough, say, to arrange for any number of successful accidents?"

There was suddenly an excited gleam in Freddy's eyes and once again his hands were shaking, but this time not with fear or despair. "Riots, insurrections, howling mobs of dark-skinned natives—what a colorful picture you paint, Cassie love, and how very clever of you to think of it!"

"Poor China has lived such an isolated existence here at Broadhurst," Cassie agreed sweetly, "that I seriously doubt she realizes what an uncivilized part of the world she's going back to." She heaved a dramatic sigh. "And as her loving family, I suppose we'll have to let her go without a fuss."

It would have given her considerable anxiety and just cause to rethink her strategy had she known that Ethan Bloodwell, familiar enough with human vices, had been able to guess with a fair amount of accuracy what topics lay under discussion beyond the bolted library door. Freddy and Cassie Linville hadn't fooled him in the least. Despite their gushing sentiments and the fuss Cassie had made over China when she had returned to the house, her manner had been as coldly calculating as any Araby trader dealing in ivory and gold, whose affable smile hid the treachery of a serpent as surely as the dagger in the folds of his cloak.

Ethan rose and prowled with the feline grace peculiar to a man of the sea across the Aubusson rug, its colors of cream, gold, and blue softening the intense saffron yellow of the elegant salon. Drawing back the long hangings covering the window, he peered idly into the garden. Clouds had gathered from the west, scuttling dark and menacing across a lowering sky in which the sun would soon be blotted out, and the leafless boughs of the elms and the clipped yew hedges quivered beneath a freshening wind.

There will be rain tonight, Ethan thought, and a nor'easter to fill the *Kowloon Star*'s sails when she turned her bow toward Asia.

A restless hunger filled him and he found himself yearning for the sun-baked deck beneath his feet, to feel the salty spindrift in his face and a rebellious tide astern. It was the sea that had called to him from the first, ever since he had taken to climbing over the walls of Mother O'Shaughnessy's Asylum for Orphans and Foundlings and stealing by night to the shipyards of Cork, fascinated by the half-completed hulls that loomed in the darkness and dreaming of their future ports of call in faraway Africa, Zanzibar, Persia, forbidden Japan.

Incredibly, he had managed to fulfill his boyhood dream and see for himself those mysterious, alluring Eastern lands. He had become intimately acquainted with the spice-scented cities of Ceylon, the colorful bazaars of Aden, even the imperial splendor of the Forbidden City; and once, years ago, he had commanded a clipper even more impressive than the brigs and barkentines he had admired as a boy in Ireland—the fleet and unbeatable *Lotus Star*.

Then he had lost her, through fate, foolishness, and incalculable treachery, and if he was ever to make her his again he would need a hell of a lot of money and the devil's own luck. Two hundred pounds would go a long way toward seeing the *Lotus Star* freed from impoundment, and returning an insignificant young woman to Indonesia was certainly easier and far more lucrative than running a humdrum trade route between Malaysia and England. His eyes narrowed. Hell, it would take a year or more of that kind of insufferably dull work to earn him the same money!

It was his unwillingness to let those two hundred pounds slip through his fingers that had prompted Ethan to inquire after the identity of the young lady who had made

him that startling offer. And it had been childishly simple
to do so since the coat of arms on her coach had been seen
by half a dozen tars who had watched it rumble from the
docks. A brief visit to an old friend in Mayfair, a woman
who was herself a knowledgeable paragon of British aristocracy, had instantly linked its description to the Linville name. And everyone, Ethan had discovered, was eager
to talk about the Linvilles....

"He was quite, quite the gentleman, the old Lord Linville was, and handsome, too," said a dowager duchess
whose youngest son, a friend from Ethan's youth, had served
in India in the Horse Guides until his death in Kabul in
1843. "You should have seen the young girls making
ninnyhammers of themselves with their mooncalf eyes
and wistful moues whenever he walked into a room!"

"I take it you were immune to his charms?" Ethan
grinned, sipping Turkish coffee and reclining on satin
cushions in a boudoir crammed with memorabilia of a long
and fully savored life.

"Dear me, no! I'd have given my eyeteeth to win him,
and yet he never remarried after he lost his wife and family
in the Grosvenor Theater fire. Do you remember it, dear?
No? Oh, it was a tragedy, a terrible tragedy! So many good
friends lost. I expect the Earl must have been quite lonely
living in that gloomy old house once his wife and Reginald
and Sarah died, because I cannot imagine why else he
would have invited those reprehensible grandchildren of
his to live with him. Orphans, mind you, are not always
the pitiable little creatures one imagines them to be."

"No, they are not," Ethan agreed wryly.

"Thank goodness," the duchess resumed, "there was the
girl, China, to bless the last years of his life, for she was
gentle and kind and I'm convinced he truly loved her."

Ethan would have liked to have learned more, for he
placed a great deal of value on Her Grace's opinion, but it
appeared that she could shed little light on that particular
subject as, regrettably, she knew the Earl's grandniece
only from hearsay.

"Of course it was out of the question for her to attend
parties or balls before she made her debut," the duchess
explained, "and as His Lordship cared little for socializing

himself, the two of them rarely left Kent. I have heard that she's quite beautiful though somewhat unusual. But then it's always the odd ones who have a way of making themselves unforgettable, eh?"

A similar opinion had been offered by Ethan's lady friend in Mayfair, though she was not the least inclined to be as charitable as the dowager duchess had been.

"China Warrick? Pooh!" she had said with an indifferent shrug of her ivory shoulders. "Such a curious creature. All eyes and pointed chin! One must consider, too, that her great-grandfather was Kingston Warrick, a most reprehensible man—a rake and a murderer, as rumor has it—and you know what they say about bad blood being—"

Ethan had interrupted her words with a grin. "Retract your claws, Amanda, my dear. I've no personal interest in the chit."

Lady Collier regarded him with ill-humored suspicion. "Then why all these questions?"

"Money," Ethan had answered lightly and truthfully. "I stand to make a considerable sum from the child and want to be certain she can afford it."

"Oh, I assure you she can," Lady Collier had answered curtly and with growing annoyance. Knowing Ethan as well as she did, she was also aware of the futility of plying him with questions of her own. "I imagine the old Earl left her quite a fortune when he died, and of course there's the Warrick plantation on Badajan which she will doubtless inherit."

"Plantation?" Ethan's interest quickened though his expression remained bland. Badajan, if he remembered correctly, was one of the countless jungle-infested islands of Indonesia, and though he was familiar with that particular corner of the globe he could not honestly say that he had ever been within twenty leagues of it. "What do the Warricks produce—teak?"

Amanda's generous red mouth curved and she ran a caressing finger down the length of his jaw. "You may be a worldly man, Captain Bloodwell, but you don't know a thing about attire—or silk, to be exact. That is what the Warrick name is famous for."

Her cool brown eyes warmed as they roved the long

lines of his body while Ethan lounged completely at home
in faded calfskin breeches and a much-worn muslin shirt
on the sofa in the refined elegance of her withdrawing
room. Browned and muscular where her poor husband was
pale and inclined toward pudginess, Ethan Bloodwell was,
in Amanda's breathless opinion, a magnificent specimen
of manhood whose visits to England were too vexingly
infrequent for her liking.

"The plantation produces silk, perhaps the finest in the
world," she continued grudgingly when he made an impatient gesture with his glass. Oh, how it annoyed her to
be wasting their valuable time talking about this! "It's
frightfully expensive because they only produce a small
amount every year, which puts it in great demand—especially among the nobilities of Europe. I'm told the color
is a very rare gold, and I believe the Queen herself pos-
sesses a shawl of it."

"Is this family of hers still living?"

Amanda frowned. "I've no idea. But I do know they sent
the girl to England in order to attend Olivia Crenshawe's
Seminary. Lord Linville's sister, Lady Delia, was the child's
maternal grandmother, but one can't claim blood relationship as Lady Delia was adopted. I wouldn't be at all
surprised, however, if— Where are you going?"

"I'm afraid I have another engagement in Belgrave
Square. My thanks, Amanda. You've been most helpful."

Amusement glinted in Ethan's eyes as he bent to kiss
her, for he had seen the flash of ire on her lovely face that
she hadn't been able to conceal. Regrettably there wasn't
time to savor Lady Collier's infinite charms; the gentleman
awaiting him in the elegant town house, with its corner
towers and mansard roof, was an impatient one, with only
a few minutes to spare even an old acquaintance like himself.

"Hrrumpf! Had no choice but to turn respectable, m'boy,"
the gout-ridden gentleman grumbled when Ethan com-
mented with a grin on the grandeur of the house and the
fussy neatness of the majordomo who had shown him in.
"'S all part o' the game if you want to garner votes. Aye,
votes! Parliament, didn't I tell you?" His eyes twinkled.
"I'll warrant you never expected that from a wily cur-

mudgeon who used to race contraband from one end of the globe to t'other, eh?"

"I rather pictured you drawing your last breath at the end of a hangman's rope," Ethan agreed solemnly, though his lips twitched with affection as he gazed down at the graying head of the former captain-owner of the *Elias Matiste,* the huge fighting merchant ship upon which sixteen-year-old Ethan had served as third mate.

"You taught me everything I know," he added with an easy grin, but Captain Sir Geoffrey Reade waved that away with a limp paw and a snort of disgust.

"From what I hear you've managed to make a name for yourself without me—and raised plenty of eyebrows in the process." He chuckled and wheezed and helped himself to an enormous pinch of snuff. "Can't say it surprises me any. You were always the wild one. Now, then, I'm a busy man. What is it you want from me?"

Ethan's request was precise and to the point.

"Fellow by the name o' Roland Biggs handles the estate, I believe," Sir Geoffrey said promptly. "His mother died up Ely way last week and my guess is good he ain't read 'em the will yet." A beetled white brow cocked in the younger man's direction. "You're not thinking of moving in on the family fortune by wooing that sourpuss granddaughter of his? By all that's holy, I thought you had better taste in women than that, boy!"

"I do," Ethan had assured him and, whistling softly, had collected his cloak and gloves and taken his leave.

Now, as he recalled everything he had learned about the Linvilles in the course of that single afternoon, Ethan decided that there must be something about their wealth and the magnificence of their ancestral seat that could not help but arouse admiration and envy. Broadhurst was unquestionably an imposing edifice—crammed with priceless heirlooms and gardens so extensive that one could walk for hours on end without reaching their boundaries. But Ethan, who had idled away many pleasant hours in Eastern palaces and zenanas more awe-inspiring than Broadhurst could ever hope to be, did not find himself particularly impressed.

It was the rustling of crinolines in the corridor outside

that brought his attention round, and he turned his head to see China Warrick standing on the threshold. Ethan blinked, for he wasn't exactly sure in that moment if he recognized her or not. He had been deplorably hung over the first time he had seen her, and smeared with mud, she had not painted a particularly attractive picture when he had rescued her from the bogs less than an hour ago. Yet he saw now that she had discarded the torn, muddied habit for a satin frock and ruffled petticoats, and though the color was a severe and unrelieved black, the cut was such that it did nothing to hide the slimness of her form; the tailored bodice, with its row of black pearl buttons, displayed her slender waist to perfection. Her disheveled red curls had been plaited into a chignon which, though heavy and far too dignified, gave an appealing maturity to her face.

All the unkind things Lady Collier had said about her came back to Ethan's mind, and he could understand quite clearly the older woman's jealousy. China Warrick's sloping green eyes and bright red hair, coupled with an unpretentious innocence curiously at odds with her wanton looks, were unique in a culture where beauty was measured by colorless virgins with quivering, touch-me-not attitudes. Accustomed to the dark-eyed beauties of the East, Ethan had come to think all Englishwomen cold and undesirable, yet here was living proof of the old adage that exceptions existed to every rule.

"Where are my cousins?" China's question brought his musings to an end. Enchanting she may be, yet someone, and he strongly suspected those scheming cousins of hers, wanted her dead. And money, in the form of the Linville fortune, seemed to be the reason behind it.

"Your cousins," Ethan said curtly, uncharacteristically disgusted with himself as he recalled that money had been the same reprehensible motive that had brought him to Broadhurst, "are currently engaged in an argument in the library over the question of your leaving."

China stared at him blankly for a moment before her expression cleared. "Oh, but there's no need for that! I've decided to stay in England, at least for the time being."

"You've decided to stay?" Ethan inquired disbelievingly.

China nodded. "Yes, why not? It was foolish of me to have approached you as I did, particularly because I hadn't discussed the matter with my family first. Since then I've decided that it simply wouldn't be proper of me to leave so soon after my great-uncle's death. It wouldn't be right to abandon my cousins so unexpectedly."

"My dear young woman, I hope you aren't serious!"

"Why shouldn't I be?" she asked, confused.

Captain Bloodwell regarded her with a frown that held more than a trace of impatience. China found herself thinking suddenly how out of place he looked in the drawing room with its delicate hand-flocked wallpaper and lovely glass *objets*. Far too...too...She searched about for the proper word and was surprised when she came up with "savage," and yet it was true. There was something about him that reminded her of a wild animal: restless, untamed, possibly dangerous. And something in the way he was looking at her gave her pause, forcing her to resist a sudden impulse to retreat a step, the pulse in her throat quickening despite herself.

"Two days ago," he observed when it was clear to him that she intended to remain silent, "you were willing to pay me an exorbitant sum to take you away from here. You came to my ship unescorted and, quite obviously, without the permission or even the knowledge of your cousin, Lord Freddy Linville."

He saw the color stain her hollow cheeks. "That may well be true, Captain, but that was two days ago. As I've already told you, I've since changed my mind. I don't want to sail to Badajan. Not with—Well, it doesn't matter."

"Not with me?"

She looked away and he was seized with the sudden desire to laugh. How very young she was and so utterly, charmingly transparent! But there was the two hundred pounds to think of, and something else: the prickling of a long forgotten and ill-abused conscience.

"You were frightened when you came to see me, Miss Warrick," he said bluntly. "And you made no effort to deny the charge that you were running away from home. Will you tell me what it was that compelled you to travel alone to London? I can see that it troubles you no longer, but I confess that the discovery leaves me curious."

"I had no intention of running away!" The color in China's cheeks deepened. She wanted no one, least of all an unmentionable opportunist like Captain Bloodwell, to learn what she had done to Freddy. Yet how was she to get rid of this man to whom she had given her word? Certainly she wanted to go home to Badajan, but not with him and definitely not without Freddy or Cassie's open approval!

Ethan was watching her intently, and he was not at all surprised when she lifted her chin and said with a trace of hauteur, "My reasons for traveling to London are personal, Captain, and as the cause behind them no longer exists, I see no need for you to pressure me into revealing them. I am sorry I misled you into believing you were in a position to earn two hundred pounds, but as we signed no agreement I cannot see how—"

"You little fool!" Ethan burst out. "Is that honestly what you think is at stake?"

"What else could it be?" she asked, startled.

Ethan could feel his temper growing short. Why did she persist in gazing at him with those damnably wide and innocent eyes? She was like a sheep being led off to slaughter, or worse, an ignorant child, helpless and abandoned and about to be manipulated by exploitive guardians who cared not a whit for her welfare.

The image was too disturbingly familiar for Captain Ethan Bloodwell, and in a moment of uncontrollable ire he said harshly, "In God's name, can't you admit that your cousins want you dead? That's why you tried to run away from them, isn't it?"

He knew the instant he saw the color drain from her face that he had been mistaken, for no one could credibly feign the shock that stiffened her at his words.

"I would never have believed anyone, even you, capable of such a crude, preposterous statement!" China whispered through rigid lips when she could speak. "If you think to frighten me into sailing with you so that you can collect—"

"Good God, woman!" Ethan exclaimed in utter frustration. "You really had no inkling, did you?"

China's face was so pale that her eyes seemed to take up every inch of it and she was trembling with fury. "How dare you persist in perpetrating such an outrageous claim?"

Without mincing his words Ethan told her, and she listened in stony silence. When he finished speaking, she said simply and with quiet dignity, "I'm sorry, Captain, but I refuse to believe such a vulgar lie."

Upon which his face suddenly changed and for the first time China found herself feeling genuinely afraid of him. Wordlessly he took her arm and yanked her out to the stables, ignoring her feeble protests and chasing out the grooms with a curt command. China was thrust without ceremony into Bastian's stall where she had no choice but to view with her own eyes the indisputable evidence in the form of an ugly red welt on his glossy gray coat. And still she would not believe.

"You haven't the faintest idea what you're talking about! It looks to me like a bee sting or—or—"

"Or what?"

The tone of his voice infuriated her. "It could be anything! A scratch from the briars or the mark of my whip!"

"Oh, come, Miss Warrick, surely you don't believe that? A bee sting wouldn't bleed that way and I doubt you possess sufficient strength or the unkindness to whip your mount that hard."

"Then what is it?" she demanded accusingly, turning the tables on him, her eyes blazing.

"My guess would be a stone, fired from a slingshot by someone hiding in the shrubbery near the pond. You said Bastian was spooked by a flock of ducks, but why would he suddenly be afraid of something he is normally quite accustomed to? Furthermore, you'll recall that the stable-master saw someone hurrying off the grounds shortly after Bastian bolted. Who do you expect it was? A poacher? A villager making use of a shortcut into town? Come, come, Miss Warrick, you must face the truth. It was a man hired by Lord Linville to see that you met with an accident."

"No! No! No!" China said frantically. "You're inventing tales! You're still after those two hundred pounds I promised!"

"This has nothing whatsoever to do with money," Ethan told her savagely.

"Even if such an outrageous claim were true," China said breathlessly, "why would my cousin wish to have me killed? Do you have an answer to that, Captain?"

"Certainly," Ethan said heartlessly. "Money. Suppose your cousin somehow discovered that you, and not he or his sister Cassie, had inherited your great-uncle's fortune? Wouldn't he try his desperate best to get rid of you?"

"Now I know that you're mad!" China said. "My great-uncle would never have left Broadhurst to me! Both the estate and the earldom are entitled property, and as my paternal grandfather was a Warrick, there isn't the least chance that I could have inherited! And why would Freddy want to kill me if only yesterday he asked me to marry him?"

Ethan's eyes narrowed. "What did you tell him?"

"I turned him down, of course," China said frigidly, "though I don't see that it's any business of yours."

"I suppose he'd been courting you openly for quite some time?" Ethan inquired, ignoring her.

"No, actually—" She broke off and regarded him with barely restrained fury. "I can see clearly how someone of your objectionable morals could twist something like that around until it seemed dirty and premeditated."

"I'd advise you to consider the matter most carefully, Miss Warrick. It's quite likely that your cousin was forced to resort to violence when his chance to win both your hand and your fortune was lost when you refused him."

The palm that cracked sharply across Ethan's sun-browned cheek left an angry red mark, but China didn't wait long enough to see it. Lifting her skirts she stumbled out of the stall, slamming the door behind her while breathless sobs tore from her throat. "It can't be true!" she said to herself. "It simply can't be true!"

Chapter Five

Captain Ethan Bloodwell, standing on the aft deck of the east-bound brigantine _Kowloon Star_, glanced at the barometer and frowned.

"Still falling, sir," the coxswain reported briskly.

"I've eyes in my head, lad," Captain Bloodwell reminded him and turned his narrowed gaze to the hot, hazy sky. He had been hoping for a break in the weather ever since the _Kowloon Star_ had found herself becalmed in the glass-still waters south of Algoa Bay, but the prospect of a storm was not an appealing alternative. Not, at any rate, with a half-dozen women on board who had proven themselves immeasurably poor sailors from the moment the ship had slid into the wind-chopped waters of the English Channel.

Ethan's eyes turned to the main cabin where an awning had been erected against the wall to provide shade for his passengers' comfort. Every afternoon, when the air below decks grew insufferably hot, they would gather beneath it to fan themselves and seek what little relief they could from the unrelenting African sun. Decorum had been abandoned with the rising of the mercury, and even the absurdly prudish Mrs. Lucinda Harrleson had permitted her daughters to exchange their heavy, high-necked gowns and crinolines for cooler muslins and wide-brimmed chip straw hats.

At the moment Bella and Dottie Harrleson were busy with their embroidering needles though Ethan noticed that their gazes strayed constantly to his young coxswain, one of the few Englishmen numbered among his polyglot crew. Their mother would have been aghast had she been aware of her daughters' interest, for young Thatcher was undeniably not of acceptable social rank, despite being handsome and quite personable.

"Captain?"

Ethan turned questioningly as his coxswain addressed him and then was startled to see that China Warrick had ascended the steps and was staring across the hot, sullen water waiting politely for him to acknowledge her. She was dressed in the unrelieved black of mourning, yet despite the heat she somehow managed to look cool and unapproachable.

"Did you wish to see me, Miss Warrick?" Ethan inquired somewhat curiously, for she had been avoiding him assiduously ever since the *Kowloon Star* had slipped her berth in London weeks ago. Not that he could honestly blame her, given the heartless manner with which he had presented her with the evidence of her cousins' perfidy. And of course it was perfectly obvious to him that she would gladly have waited until the end of the month to take any other ship than the *Kowloon Star* if the news of her father's tragic death hadn't arrived at Broadhurst the very same day Ethan had come to see her.

Obviously desperate, China had swallowed her pride and calmly asked him to take her, and Ethan, who would probably have refused had she begged and pleaded and wept, had found it bloody impossible to ignore those solemn, grief-ravaged eyes. Furthermore, he would have been the first to deny that it was pity that had prompted him to order the *Kowloon Star* readied for immediate departure, and although he remembered perfectly well having once told China Warrick that the *Kowloon Star* was not a passenger ship, he himself had arranged for Lucinda

Harrleson and her daughters to be taken aboard in order to provide the girl with appropriate female companionship.

Allowing his gaze to fall on the group of chattering women on the deck below him, Ethan was forced to ask himself, certainly not for the first time, why in hell he had bothered to go to so much trouble on China Warrick's behalf? He was not the sort to do favors for anyone, particularly prickly little creatures with sad green eyes, and in truth it shouldn't have given him a single qualm to leave her behind in England to await the next passenger ship from the P & O Line scheduled to depart for the Orient. Perhaps the two hundred pounds he was to collect from her brother Damon Warrick had had something to do with it?

"How may I help you, Miss Warrick?" he inquired once again, his courteous tone bringing a look of surprise to his coxswain's face.

China regarded him accusingly, as though he alone were responsible for the oppressive heat, and said tartly: "You told us last night that the wind would pick up today, Captain. I haven't seen the least indication of it."

Ethan grinned. "Apparently you haven't looked at the glass, Miss Warrick."

China gave him no more than a chilling glance before bending to examine it.

"You can see that it's falling," Captain Bloodwell continued helpfully, "which means—"

"I am not ignorant as to how a barometer works," China interrupted. "I would expect," she added, shielding her eyes as she lifted her gaze to the hot, brassy sky, "that inclement weather is brewing. Do you anticipate a storm, Captain?"

His grin widened. "Are you frightened by the possibility?"

She did not rise to his bait as expected, but cast an apprehensive glance below where the Harrlesons were gathered in the shade of the brightly striped awning. "Actually I'm worried about Louisa. She's not a very good sailor."

Captain Bloodwell's gaze followed hers to the child who was playing with her doll on the sun-baked deck, unmindful of her mother's entreaties to remain with the others in the shade. Her dark brown hair was tied with ribbons and a spotless pinafore covered her flounced yellow dress. Feeling their eyes upon her, she lifted her hand and waved, and a cheerful smile lit her wan little face.

"Louisa is not a good sailor, no," Captain Bloodwell agreed.

"I'd hate to see her grow any thinner than she already is. Goodness knows Mr. Quarles has been doing his best to feed her," China went on, referring to the brigantine's tough steward Nappy Quarles, who had, to his captain's considerable surprise, adopted both the winsome child and Miss Warrick as his personal charges. "She seems to be eating well, but I cannot imagine what another bout of seasickness will do to her."

Captain Bloodwell's brows rose, thinking that he would never understand her or have suspected that she was the sort of woman to be governed by maternal instinct. Yet ten-year-old Louisa Harrleson, of delicate health and obviously neglected by her mother and indifferent older sisters, was the sort of child who could touch even the coldest of hearts. She seemed to have taken to China from the start, and often as not could be found listening with rapt attention to the spellbinding tales of her girlhood on Badajan.

"You make a most admirable champion, Miss Warrick," he observed blandly, finding himself unaccountably annoyed. "Few women would welcome without complaint the task of emptying tins of vomit and spoon-feeding children with weak stomachs."

"I fail to see anything amusing about Louisa's lack of seamanship," China said frostily, refraining with difficulty from adding that Mrs. Julia Clayton, a personable young widow who numbered among the brigantine's female passengers, possessed an equally weak stomach and that Captain Bloodwell didn't think to condemn *her* for it.

"My apologies," Ethan replied with a mocking bow in her direction. "It was not my intent to make fun of Louisa. I was merely reflecting on your apparent fondness for the child and how well you cared for her when the seas were rough."

"And who wouldn't be fond of Louisa?" China asked crisply. "She hasn't a friend in the world and her mother is far too absorbed in those spoiled older sisters of hers to care what happens to her. Furthermore Louisa has never been away from home, much less on a ship bound for India, and no one seems the least bit interested in allaying her fears. I know exactly how—" She broke off, biting her lip and staring up into the captain's sun-browned face with wide, dismayed eyes.

"You know exactly how she feels?" Captain Bloodwell finished, and though his voice was of a sudden no longer mocking, China could not permit him to probe into such a painful part of her being. She had vowed to herself after that awful encounter in Bastian's stall never to deal with him on a personal level again.

"I was going to say that I know exactly how to treat people suffering from seasickness," she said, recovering with admirable ease and thinking of poor Anna Sidney whom she had nursed during the stormy voyage from Badajan six long years ago.

"I believe," Captain Bloodwell said, regarding her sharply before turning to scan the sultry sky, "that your talents will come in handy before the day is out."

"Then you really think there will be a storm?"

"My dear Miss Warrick, read the glass. If you know so much about atmospheric variables then surely you'll find the answer there."

China whirled with an indignant rustle of flounces and descended to the main deck without another word.

"What did he say, China? Is it going to get cooler soon?"

China smiled into Louisa Harrleson's expectant face. "The captain assured me it would. By evening, perhaps, or even sooner."

"How does he know?" the little girl asked doubtfully.

China was tempted to laugh. Of all the worshipping females Captain Bloodwell had taken aboard his ship, Louisa seemed to be the only one who thought to question his omnipotence. "He let me have a look at his barometer," she explained. "The glass was falling, which means the weather should be breaking."

"Such a dear, patient man," Lucinda Harrleson remarked, overhearing her words. "I cannot imagine how he manages to remain civil with all of us constantly underfoot!"

It was because he was being paid a considerable sum to tolerate their presence, China reflected uncharitably, but refrained from saying as much to plump Mrs. Harrleson, who appeared quite fond of the captain though China couldn't for the life of her imagine why. And as for being civil—she shuddered at the very thought of applying the term to him.

"Captain Bloodwell seems reasonably certain we're in for rough weather," she added, not wanting to spare them any illusions. "There's a storm brewing that should reach us by evening."

"He was probably teasing you, China, dear," Mrs. Harrleson said brightly. "Do look at the sky. Not a cloud to be seen!"

"Or a breath of cool air, either," brown-eyed Dottie added with a gasp, fanning herself vigorously. Damp patches darkened the armpits and back of her gown and China, peering sympathetically into her reddened face, was intensely grateful for having been born in Indonesia, for despite the oppressive thickness of her black bombazine gown, she seemed to tolerate the heat far better than her companions. Then again it might be because the Harrlesons were all so plump, but, no, China recalled, Mrs. Clayton suffered from the heat just as much as they did and one certainly could not consider her overweight.

Actually she was far too thin, China corrected herself unkindly, glancing from beneath lowered lashes at the woman reading in a nearby cane chair with a wide-brimmed straw hat covering her glossy black hair. She had no illusions about the sort of woman Julia Clayton was. Ostensibly widowed several months ago, she was on her way to India to collect the remains of her dear, departed William, who died in the line of duty serving Queen and Country as a major in the 70th Foot. But China had noticed the first day out to sea tht Julia wore no wedding ring, and as time went by she began to suspect that the young "widow" was actually traveling to Calcutta, the *Kowloon*

Star's first port of call, to escape some sort of scandalous liaison she had forged in England.

The fact that Julia Clayton had taken an immediate fancy to Captain Ethan Bloodwell was obvious to China as well. In fact, all of them, Mrs. Harrleson included, seemed to worship the very ground upon which he stood, and China was at an utter loss to understand why. She couldn't in all fairness credit him with any endearing virtues apart from being good-looking. He was tall, it was true, and sun-browned and lean, had blue eyes and a square, clefted chin that some women might consider appealing, but what about his objectionable character? Didn't rudeness, arrogance, and the inability to take anything seriously count in judging him as a man?

China scowled as she watched Dottie and Arabella turn yearning eyes to the aft deck where Captain Bloodwell stood by the binnacle with his hands propped casually on his hips. Would they continue to worship him, she wondered, if they knew that he had been deplorably drunk the first time she'd seen him and that his cabin had looked as though a typhoon had swept through it? And what about the greed that had prompted him to track her all the way to Broadhurst?

China sighed, aware that she wasn't exactly being fair. At least he had been honest enough to admit his motives, and his behavior toward her since the *Kowloon Star* had set sail had been exemplary. She supposed it was because he had played a part in something she wanted desperately to forget, or because she knew that he felt sorry for her in view of her bereavements, but China had always despised pity in any form. At least she could soothe herself with the knowledge that she need never lay eyes on him again once the journey was over!

Not until the sun had vanished beneath the motionless sea did the breathless air shiver with the first faint gusts of wind. It was a spectacular sunset, the sky scarlet like the slashed underbelly of some great beast, and heat lightning played in a fantastic array of colors across the darkening water. China, who had come up from the saloon after supper, lifted her face gratefully to the welcoming puffs of wind that were beginning to ripple the glassy water.

"Isn't it marvelous, Mr. Quarles?" she inquired, addressing the steward hurrying by on some unknown task, his arms filled with an assortment of tools.

"Marvelous? I'd just as soon 'ave the 'eat than the storm wot we're expectin'! Got to batten down t' ship an' board the port'oles an' clean up the galley like bleedin' women—beggin' yer pardon, Miss China—so's we can blow by in safety!" He spat disgustedly into the scuppers. "And you calls it marvelous, you do!"

China took no offense at Nappy's dour words. She had already learned that he complained a great deal but that little attention should be paid to the nature of his ramblings. She had grown fond of Nappy Quarles, which was surprising given that Captain Bloodwell's crew consisted of little better than a motley collection of cutthroats and thieves.

Nappy, however, was a gentle-hearted old soul who would have spluttered with indignation had anyone dared suggest as much. Just over five feet tall and perpetually unshaven, he wore a patch over his left eye which made him look, China thought, exactly like a miniature pirate. He had lost the eye, he had told her, during a typhoon off the Great Barrier Reef when the Dutch freighter on which he had been serving struck a shoal and went down.

"The wind tore 'er masts clean away, miss, an' the spars an' blocks came rainin' down on the decks, killin' 'arf the men 'oo wasn't drowned an' maimin' the rest, myself included."

He had been knocked unconscious by a block that had hit him on the head and whose metal hinges had gouged out his eye, and there was no doubt in his mind that he would have gone down with the ship had Providence not revived him long enough to climb into a jolly boat and make for shore with the rest of the crew. The blow to his head had not only cost him an eye but had left him with the curious predilection of falling asleep without warning regardless of the time of day or the activity he was engaged in.

"Thort be 'ow I got the name Nappy," he had told her.

"Never knows from one minute to next when I'll be fallin'
asleep, and if it wasn't for Cap'n Ethan I'd not 'ave a berth
ter ship out in. 'E's a first-rate fellow, 'e is," Nappy continued loyally. "Not many'd take on a steward 'oo falls
asleep in 'is stew, but Cap'n Ethan gave me a chance. I
owes 'im, I do."

Privately China found it difficult to believe that charitable inclinations had led Captain Bloodwell to offer the
one-eyed steward a berth on the *Kowloon Star*. More likely
than not Nappy worked cheap and China had already come
to realize, given the dilapidated state of the brigantine,
that Captain Bloodwell and his pirate crew survived strictly
hand-to-mouth. Small wonder he had been so anxious to
avail himself of her two hundred pounds!

Yet to be fair, the *Kowloon Star* was kept in immaculate
condition, every inch of brass polished to a dazzling gleam,
the ropes and oft-patched sails never permitted to become
torn or frayed. Yet meals aboard ship were meager compared to the lavish feasts China recalled having eaten on
the clipper *Honoria,* which had brought her to England so
many years ago, and the bunks in the sparsely furnished
cabins were narrow and covered with uncomfortably rough
blankets.

"Best go below, Miss China, an' make sure yer things
be stowed," Nappy said to her, glancing with lowered brows
at the darkening sky. "Marvelous weather, indeed," he
muttered, and growling beneath his breath, hurried off to
carry out his chores.

Negotiating the gloomy companionway, China realized
at once what had not been apparent to her on the wide
deck above: that the seas had already begun to rise, and
she found it difficult indeed to maintain her footing on the
uneven flooring.

"Poor Louisa," she murmured, reaching her cabin to
find the little girl lying forlornly in bed, her small face
white and pinched. "I'm afraid it's only going to get worse."

"I don't mind, China. Not if you're with me."

They had been sharing a cabin together ever since the
Kowloon Star had encountered rough seas in the English
Channel, when Louisa's mother and sisters had found
themselves too ill to look after the girl. China had per-

suaded Nappy to string up a hammock for her, and though
the narrow confines had proven extremely cramped, Louisa
had begged to remain once the weather cleared, a request
to which her mother had gladly given permission. Thank
goodness, Lucinda had said often since then, that dear Miss
Warrick had taken it upon herself to look after Louisa until
the *Kowloon Star* brought them to Calcutta where Colin
awaited them with an army of servants to see to his off-
springs' every need. Children could be so dreadfully *difficult* when one paused to consider it!

"Mama's in bed, too," Louisa said in response to China's
query. "I don't think she's feeling well, either. Is it very
bad outside?"

"Actually it was still quite nice a few minutes ago." A
glance out of the heaving porthole told China that the
situation had worsened considerably even during the short
space of time since she had come below. A faint glow lingered on the western horizon, casting sufficient light for
her to see the black clouds roiling beyond the darkening
hills of Africa. Waves capped with wind-whipped foam broke
sullenly against the hull, the sound mingling with the
hollow reverberations of approaching thunder.

"Won't you tell me a story, China?" Louisa pleaded.

"Which one would you like to hear?" China inquired,
reaching up to light the lantern.

"The one about your great-grandfather," Louisa replied
promptly.

China's lips twitched. "Haven't you heard that one
enough?"

An impish grin lit Louisa's pale face. "No."

"Great-grandfather Kingston Warrick was a very
wealthy aristocrat," China began obligingly, seating herself on the edge of the bunk and smoothing out her skirts.
"He owned a beautiful estate in Sussex which he'd inherited from his father, and several town houses in London.
He was a Member of Parliament, belonged to the Corin-
thian Club, and drove a four-in-hand better than any fashionable gentleman of his day."

"He was an outlaw, too," Louisa piped in, wiggling with
excitement despite the fact that she knew every detail of
the story.

"Not an outlaw exactly," China said, "but a rake, which I suppose isn't really much better. He was fond of gambling, at any rate, and being young and foolish, squandered his fortune by disreputable means until he found himself with nothing but a mountain of debts to show for his troubles."

China had never made any attempt to hide her great-grandfather's objectionable past from anyone. If the truth must be told, she was rather proud of his exploits and was not inclined, as should have been sensible, to refrain from mentioning them in polite company. One shouldn't run away from what one was, China firmly believed, and it was utter nonsense for the Warricks to hide behind sanctimonious claims of untainted blood when Kingston Warrick's story was no secret to the world. This view had never endeared her to her cousin Cassiopeia, who had reacted with horror whenever she was reminded that the Linvilles were connected, thankfully only by marriage, to that most notorious renegade.

"They were going to hang him, weren't they, China?" Louisa asked, round-eyed at the prospect. "For stealing or for killing somebody even though nobody really remembers what he did?"

"That's right. But instead of sending him to the gallows, the prime minister convinced the king to spare him, and he was transported by convict ship to Botany Bay."

Though this sordid fact would have brought exclamations of horror from her mother and sisters, Louisa found it far more intriguing than any fairy tale Bella had ever told her. "Except that he never made it to Botany Bay, did he? He escaped during a storm just like this one," she recited eagerly, "and rowed away in a boat with one of his friends."

"Why, I believe you tell the story far better than I do, dear."

"Oh, but I like listening to you!" Louisa protested. "Please tell the rest!"

"All right, then: The island upon which Sir Kingston and his friend Mr. Stepkyne washed ashore was totally uninhabited unless one counts the monkeys and parrots and a few wild boars. It had several extinct volcanoes and was virtually covered with jungle. Sir Kingston saw flowers and petals as big around as he was tall, exotic birds with long, feathered tails, and on the beach he found shells that were far prettier than a sunset."

"He liked it so much that he decided to keep it and build his house there," Louisa put in happily, for this was her favorite part of the tale. "Tell me how he got the silkworms, China, and how he started to make silk on his island."

China smiled. This, too, was the part she liked best. "After Great-grandfather finished clearing the jungle and moving into his house, he built himself a ship and sailed to China. There he made friends with a powerful mandarin warlord who invited him to stay in Canton, even though no European had ever set foot beyond the walls dividing the Chinese mainland from the sea. Like Great-grandfather, the warlord was a man who loved to gamble."

Her narrative was interrupted as the *Kowloon Star* plunged headlong into a trough of water, upsetting the lantern on the small writing table and bringing a frightened look to Louisa's face.

"Are you all right, dear?" China asked worriedly.

"I think so. Please... finish the story, China."

It would be prudent to keep Louisa's attention away from the nauseatingly canting deck, China decided, and her voice rose briskly above the howling of the wind. "No one knows what the final wager between Kingston Warrick and the warlord was all about. There aren't any references in his journal and he never bothered to tell anyone, even my grandfather." (Which was a lie because China knew perfectly well it had involved the virtue of a certain palace lady both men had coveted, though she was not about to say as much to Louisa.)

"Your great-grandfather won," Louisa remembered.

"He did, and in payment the warlord was forced to give him whatever cargo lay in the hold of the first of his ships to reach Macao that month, regardless of its worth. Great-grandfather could have won a shipment of silver bullion or tea or... or even pigs," China continued. "Instead he won a shipment of silkworm larvae, which delighted the old warlord no end because he was certain Great-grandfather wouldn't have the least idea what to do with them."

"He was wrong, wasn't he? Sir Kingston took them back to Badajan and grew them and made silk and got frightfully rich."

"To make a long story short, yes he did." China laughed. "And soon he'd made friends with important people like the Sultan of Jahore who owned Singapore Harbor. He persuaded the Sultan to give Singapore Harbor to Sir Stamford Raffles of the British East India Company," China went on, hoping her voice would lull Louisa to sleep. "In return he received a full pardon for his crimes, and even though he could have gone back to England to live he decided to stay on Badajan. It was wise of him, because when the Dutch gave all of Singapore to the British five years later, immigrants began to pour into Malaysia. And because Badajan lay less than twenty miles across the Singapore Strait in Indonesia, Great-grandfather was able to hire a great many workers to help him and his friend Rudyard Stepkyne grow their silkworms. Soon he was rich enough to take a trip to England where he met and fell in love with my great-grandmother, who agreed to return with him to Indonesia to live."

"Just like Mama and . . . and Papa," Louisa murmured sleepily. "Only she's going to India, not Badajan. Do you suppose we could come visit you sometime, China?"

"Of course you can," China assured her, and fondly smoothed the child's hot brow.

"Could I have some water, please?" Louisa whispered. Her face was little more than a pale oval against the pillows, and China, who had been sitting beside her, feet splayed against the deck as she struggled to maintain her balance, gazed at her with concern.

"Do you think you can keep it down?"

"I—I think so."

Unfortunately the ewer was empty. China threw a cloak over her shoulders and stepped out into the companionway. "I'll be back as soon as I can," she promised. "Stay in bed until then. Don't try to get up."

"I won't."

It took China far longer than she had anticipated to reach the narrow steps leading topside where the water barrels were stored. Pummeled by towering waves, the

Kowloon Star was being tossed about like a stick on the tide, and China was badly bruised by the time she managed to force open the outer door. No sooner had she stepped out into the darkness than the wind caught her, tearing the pins from her chignon and roaring through her skirts. Rain buffeted her, not the cool, gentle rain of an English shower, but icy torrents that drenched her thoroughly and flung gusty splatters into her face.

The ewer flew from her grasp as China reached for a better handhold, skittering crazily across the heaving deck before being swept overboard. A rush of seawater crashed over the railing in its wake, sucking greedily at China's skirts, and she gasped as she felt her hold on the frame of the cabin door slip and she was thrown with bruising force against a nearby bulkhead. She knew then that it had been utter madness to leave her cabin.

Groping her way blindly back to the door, she was knocked off her feet by a wall of surging water that swept her toward the heaving rail as though she weighed no more than the ewer. She screamed in panic and clawed desperately for a handhold only to find her fingers slipping from the wet wood so that she was grasping nothing but thin air. She screamed again, knowing she was about to be swept overboard.

Without warning someone came hurling out of the darkness, snatching at her arms and managing to catch her hair instead. China groaned in pain as the rushing water and her unseen rescuer fought a relentless tug-of-war until, coughing feebly and half-blinded by stinging salt, she was hauled to her feet to find herself staring into Captain Ethan Bloodwell's rage-contorted face.

"You fool! Are you mad? What in hell are you doing on deck?"

He gave her no time at all in which to reply. Pushing her toward the ladder, he fought grimly to maintain his footing, and they had just managed to reach the companionway door when a rush of white water caught them and slammed them brutally against the rail. China groaned aloud as she felt her ribs crack against the unyielding wood, and she staggered and nearly fell.

"Hold on!" she heard Captain Bloodwell shout, and she

clung to him blindly, his arms coming around her to hold her fast. Her skirts were tangled about his legs and she could feel the wild drumming of his heart against her cheek. Icy seawater dashed over them and the wild plunging of the deck brought her harder against him where she could feel the heat of his body even through his soaking oilskins, and an odd tremor fled through her that was neither terror nor cold.

Incredibly the water receded without plucking them loose, and China felt herself being lifted against Ethan's hard body. Coughing and gasping, she struggled to keep from fainting with the pain of the ribs that must surely have been shattered when she hit the wooden rail.

"You bloody mindless little fool!"

They had reached the protective interior of the companionway, the appalling furies behind them, and suddenly China could see and breathe again, and hear the shocking words falling from Ethan's lips.

"In God's name where did you come by such blatant stupidity? Even a child has more bloody sense than to think of doing what you did!"

China remained silent not only because she was too exhausted to speak but because she had suddenly realized that everything he said was true. She could easily have been drowned just then, plucked from the deck and hurled into the black maelstrom like so much spindrift in the wind. Still coughing, her left side seared with white-hot pain, she was too numb to be scandalized at finding herself in Captain Bloodwell's arms, her cheek resting against the soaking front of his oilskins while a torrent of shocking epithets continued to rain on her hapless head.

"This isn't my cabin," she protested as he kicked the door open and she found herself in the spacious aft quarters she recognized as his own.

"Ever observant, aren't you, my dear child?"

"I am not your child," she retorted, then bit her lip to keep from crying out as he laid her down on the bed.

"Your quarters are notoriously narrow and you can't be properly tended there." He straightened as he spoke and regarded her with considerable impatience, his dark, dripping face filled with anger. "I expect you've broken a rib or two and they'll have to be bandaged. It will be somewhat painful, but under the circumstances you should be grateful you're still alive."

"I'm sorry," China whispered and scarcely recognized the hoarse voice as her own. "I suppose it was foolish of me to venture topside, but I wanted to fetch water for Louisa and I didn't realize it would prove so dangerous."

Ethan's expression changed to one of startled disbelief, and he pushed her back none too gently as she attempted to rise. "I should have realized that you wouldn't come topside merely for a taste of adventure," he said coldly. "I'll see to the child myself, Miss Warrick. Meanwhile you're to lie here until Nappy's had a look at you. And in the future I'd suggest that you try to govern your charitable instincts with at least a modicum of common sense."

She wanted to argue with him but every breath hurt unbearably and the beams above were beginning to swim hazily before her eyes. She was shivering uncontrollably and scarcely heard Captain Bloodwell curse in sudden annoyance.

"What—what are you doing?" she demanded thickly, feeling his hands at the bodice of her gown.

"You're going to have to come out of those wet things before you ruin my mattress, Miss Warrick. I'd also prefer it if you didn't catch your death of cold while under my care."

"I can do that myself!" she protested but found that her limbs seemed weighted with lead when she tried to lift them.

Observing her feeble efforts Ethan laughed, that hateful, arrogant laugh she had heard so often before. "Would you rather have Nappy do it or me?"

"Neither!"

"Come now, Miss Warrick. Under the circumstances there's no reason to cling to silly virtues. I could send for Mrs. Harrleson, but I seriously doubt the poor woman is in any condition to leave her own bunk even if it means saving you from scandal." China thought she saw his white grin flash through the misty haze that surrounded her. "Besides, to coin an ancient adage: It's nothing I haven't seen before."

"You're a shame...shameless—" She coughed and tried to struggle upright only to feel those hard fingers propel her back again into the blankets. "Let me go at once, do you hear?"

"My dear young woman, I have no intention of doing so."

His callous disregard for her modesty infuriated China and she lifted her hand to slap him, yet succeeded only in shaking a feeble fist into his grinning face. Captain Bloodwell burst into hearty laughter, amused by the contradictions in nature that seemed China Warrick's alone. The acerbic tongue and quick wit of a tiresome bluestocking could yield instantly to the shy blushes of a painfully prim Victorian maiden, and he wasn't exactly sure which of them he preferred.

Neither one, actually, he decided, suddenly impatient to have done with her and return to the quarterdeck. Seeing that she had drifted into an exhausted sleep he quickly stripped the wet garments from her shivering body and covered her with blankets.

A disquieting frown drew his brows together when he finished, for Ethan Bloodwell did not care to admit to himself that China Warrick possessed a body of damnably feminine allure, all curves and unblemished ivory softness. He disliked finding himself thinking of her in terms other than the two hundred pounds she represented, and was annoyed at the fact that she could mean anything more to him.

"Was you needin' me, Cap'n?" Nappy Quarles inquired from the doorway. Unmindful of the elements that seemed prepared to shake the ship to pieces, he grinned cheerfully at the tall Irishman, though his mouth dropped open as he gazed past the captain's wide shoulders to the still figure on the bed. "Blood an' thunder! Wot's 'appened to Miss China?"

"She was stupid enough to come topside," Captain Bloodwell said unkindly. "I imagine she's broken a rib or two, though it's the least she deserves. Can you patch her up, Nappy?"

The little steward eyed him suspiciously. "Wot in blazes were she doing on deck?"

"Now, don't go blaming me, old man," Captain Blood-well said tersely. "I'm not in the least responsible. The foolish creature wanted to fetch water for Louisa. Which reminds me—"

"I already brought the poor mite a drink," Nappy interrupted. "And I'll takes care o' Miss China, too. You can leave 'er to me an' go back to the 'elm."

Ethan turned heel without another word. Miss Warrick was in as good hands as any, he reflected, and it would serve her right if she awakened in time to find Nappy binding her ribs when she wasn't wearing a scrap of clothing to protect her modesty. That should teach her the foolishness of leaving her quarters in rough seas, even if unselfish tendencies had motivated her to do so.

He shook his head with lingering disbelief. God's blood, at first he'd thought he'd been dreaming seeing her up on deck battling seas that even his men hadn't dared to challenge! Fortunately for both of them Miss Warrick had possessed enough sense not to struggle when he had grabbed her hair to prevent her being swept overboard. And she had obeyed instantly when he had ordered her to hold still against the rail, where any false move might have caused them to lose their footing on the soaking, slippery planks and send them plunging into the roiling sea.

Aye, she had held on to him, and Ethan's lips tightened as he was presented with the unwanted memory of the slim arms that had wound themselves about his neck and the warm body that had been pressed intimately close. Cursing beneath his breath, he thrust the image away, for it only served to remind him of the unpleasant fact that what he had just seen of Miss Warrick's body had made it clear to him that it also happened to put to shame any others he had ever had the pleasure of viewing.

Shrugging into his oilskins, Ethan threw open the companionway door and stepped out into the roaring tempest, issuing orders to his first mate in a voice that was as malevolent as the furies surrounding him.

_____ *Chapter Six* _____

China awoke with the uneasy feeling that all was not
as it should be. No sooner had her eyelids opened than she
realized at once that her suspicions were correct, for she
found herself gazing not at the beams of her own familiar
cabin but the paneled teak walls belonging to the elegant
quarters of the captain of the *Kowloon Star*.

"How dare he!" she said with a gasp. Struggling to push
aside the blankets, she fell back against the pillows as a
stabbing pain shot through her left side. Touching her rib
cage gingerly, China found it bound with a wide strip of
cloth that seemed intended to serve as support, though it
was doing little better at the moment than hurting her
abominably. Her probing fingers stilled suddenly and a
wave of color suffused her face. There didn't seem to be
anything underneath the bandage or anywhere else on her
body.

China Warrick lay perfectly still, trying to cope with
the knowledge that she was lying naked in Ethan Bloodwell's wide bed, and trying not to imagine who had removed her soaking gown and crinolines the night before.

But of course she remembered, remembered all too well, in fact, and she stumbled blindly to her feet, ignoring the pain.

Her ire increased as she hunted about wildly for her clothes and was unable to find them. With tightly compressed lips she helped herself at last to a chambray shirt she found in the bottom drawer of the teak dresser, her breathing labored as she shrugged into it and rolled back the sleeves, though it was difficult to say whether her agitation stemmed from lingering outrage or the pain of her bandaged side.

"You oughtn't to be out o' bed, Miss China, not wiv them ribs needin' ter mend."

China whirled about to find a disapproving Nappy Quarles on the threshold with a breakfast tray in his gnarled hands. "They wasn't broke, lucky for you, but bruised 'arf proper and you'll be better orf if yer stay abed a while."

"Where are my clothes, Mr. Quarles?" she inquired with as much dignity as she could muster.

Nappy's single eye twinkled as he became aware of her heightened color. "I'll bring 'em back soon's they're dry. Meantime sit and 'ave some vittles. You're lookin' a slight too pale for my likin'."

It irritated China that Nappy seemed to take it for granted that she should remain where she was. It was almost as if he were quite accustomed to serving breakfast to unmarried females occupying Captain Bloodwell's bed!

"Go on and eat, miss," he suggested kindly, setting his tray on the table. "No need t' blame the cap'n for wot 'appened."

Struggling for composure, China drew a long, shaky breath. She had no desire at the moment to discuss the reprehensible captain of the *Kowloon Star* or his unforgivable behavior. "How is Louisa?" she inquired.

Nappy beamed. "Chipper as a crow pickin' leavins off a dung 'eap."

"I . . . see. Then the storm's blown over?" Actually there was no need to ask, not with proof in the form of a silver-studded wake frothing beneath a brilliant blue sky just beyond the stern windows.

"Prettiest weather you could wish for. Now go on and eats yer breakfast," Nappy advised. "I'll be back later wiv 'ot water for washin'.'"

China found herself too hungry to argue. Seating herself at the table she spread a liberal helping from the condiment jar onto a freshly baked biscuit and stuffed the entire thing into her mouth. The sound of laughter coming unexpectedly from behind her caused her to whirl about and then sink back, flushing, into her seat.

Ethan Bloodwell stood in the doorway with the sunlight glinting on his chestnut hair and grinning at her in a most disconcerting manner. Determined to give him no further cause to laugh, China lifted her chin and fixed him with a withering glance, defying him to comment on her state of undress.

"Hunger seems to have done away with your restraint, Miss Warrick," Captain Bloodwell said gravely, though his lips twitched suspiciously. "Still, I won't be boorish enough to berate you for it. I realize it's almost noon and that you haven't eaten a bite since your misadventures of the night before."

China's own lips quivered dangerously, but Ethan was not at all surprised when she said with admirable calm: "I am indebted to you for what you did, Captain. I would have been swept overboard but for your timely intervention."

"And once again you are forced to thank me when you would prefer to dispatch me into hell." He grinned again and strolled inside. "You are quite welcome, though I've the feeling you'd sooner bite off your tongue than feel grateful toward me for anything."

"I can assure you, Captain," China began with frosty dignity, though these were her own sentiments exactly, "that I—"

"Spare me your protests, little firebrand. I've never come across a more transparent face than yours."

He paused before the table where she sat, and it seemed to China as if the roomy quarters had suddenly become quite hot and close. She bowed her head, unwilling to look at him, yet despite herself she found her eyes drawn to his strong, sun-browned hands. She grew still as she remembered how carelessly they had undressed her the night before.

Grimacing, she looked up again only to surprise an expression on Ethan's face that somehow made her aware that he, too, was remembering the same thing. She wet her dry lips and wanted to tell him how angry she was at the liberties he had taken with her despite the fact that she had been injured, yet found her throat so tight that she was unable to utter a sound. The silence in the room deepened until it seemed to become a tangible thing, whispering with taut emotions and, for Ethan, watching the sunlight from the stern windows torch China's hair with a halo of burnished gold, with an odd feeling of regret.

"Perhaps you would be so kind as to leave me in privacy," China whispered at last. "Mr. Quarles informed me that my clothes were still wet, and I didn't think to ask him to fetch others."

"Yes, I can see that you were forced to avail yourself of my belongings," Captain Bloodwell said heartlessly, studying without the least trace of self-consciousness the length of white calf that was visible beneath the tails of the shirt she wore. "I'm relieved to see you were able to find something suitable."

The collar of her shirt was opened at the throat and, despite China's efforts to button it, was wide enough to reveal the shadowed hollow between her breasts. She could feel her skin burn where his gaze had fallen.

"Captain Bloodwell, I—Oh, my goodness! *Miss Warrick!* Whatever are you doing here?"

China went rigid at the sight of Julia Clayton standing in the open doorway, and in the shocked silence that descended, Ethan's face grew hard, knowing there was no suitable explanation to account for the girl's presence in his quarters. Not, at any rate, one that would serve to wipe away the look of disbelief from Julia Clayton's face or convince her that nothing untoward had happened between them.

"Please come in, Mrs. Clayton," he invited blandly, but before he could say anything more China rose from the table, calmly ignoring the fact that her attire was no more lacking in refinement than a bawdy Cheapside doxy's.

Turning her head, she regarded the staring Julia with a boldly tilted chin and said coolly, "There's no reason to look so shocked, Mrs. Clayton. Captain Bloodwell was kind enough to permit me the use of his cabin after I injured myself during the storm last night. Now if you'll excuse me, please? I was just leaving."

The creaking of the beams as the ship listed in response to the varying wind seemed unusually loud as she paused before the captain. Though her upturned face was white and strained she regarded him with no less dignity than a dowager duchess in silken regalia attending the Queen's birthday ball, and Ethan found himself suddenly thinking that he would never again view her as a mindless chit without a scrap of courage.

"Thank you once again, Captain Bloodwell."

He sketched a brief bow and had the audacity to say, "My pleasure, Miss Warrick," though surely he must have been well aware that his meaning would be entirely misconstrued by the listening Julia. The grin that crossed his dark face was equally infuriating, and China, her courage failing at last, fled without another word.

She spent the morning in the privacy of her cabin, washing the salt from her hair and resting her bruised and aching body on the bunk, though it was at best a fitful rest, for every time she closed her eyes she was forced to relive the thoroughly demeaning scene she had endured in Captain Bloodwell's cabin. As the afternoon waned, however, she found herself growing restless, and because she had no more excuses to remain below, she decided at last to make an appearance on deck. After all, she argued with herself, there was no reason to hide below as though she had something to be ashamed of!

Yet no sooner had China emerged from the companionway than she was pounced upon by Lucinda Harrleson, her ample chins quivering with outrage.

"There you are, Miss Warrick! I must confess that I am at a total loss to express my feelings on this sad affair! I told Mrs. Clayton that she must have been mistaken, but she assured me—Oh, I cannot believe what she said! To think that Captain Bloodwell arranged for me to travel as your chaperone aboard this ship when in truth—in truth—" Her plump little hands were clasped beseechingly to her bosom. "Tell me it isn't true, child!"

"I'm afraid it is," China said clearly, assuming that Julia Clayton hadn't wasted a moment in telling Mrs. Harrleson that she had spent the night in Captain Bloodwell's quarters. "If you'll allow me to explain," she went on, her voice low with painful embarrassment yet knowing that the subject must be brought into the open, "it isn't what you think."

"There's no need to explain, child, truly there isn't!"

"But I'm afraid there is," China insisted. "Mrs. Clayton is quite mistaken about what she saw. It was not my decision to be taken to Captain Bloodwell's quarters."

"Merciful heaven!" Lucinda gasped, her worst fears realized. "I knew you couldn't have gone to him of your own accord! I suspected at once that he must have—Oh, my dear, this is absolutely dreadful! I hope you realize there is only one recourse!"

"And what might that be, Mrs. Harrleson?"

The poor woman fell silent at the unexpected arrival of Captain Bloodwell himself, who had been drawn from the quarterdeck by the sound of her piercing voice. His blue eyes were unnervingly cold as they regarded her, yet Mrs. Harrleson recovered quickly, her sense of outrage fully fired.

"Mrs. Clayton was sensible enough to inform me of the shocking circumstances which took place in your quarters last night, Captain Bloodwell. As dear China's appointed guardian I intend to see that you are brought to account for your deplorable actions."

Captain Bloodwell grinned. "And what might these 'deplorable actions' be, madame?"

Mrs. Harrleson's eyes grew round, and fiery color rose to her cheeks. "Why—why—you're perfectly aware of what I'm referring to! I was just about to explain to China that no recourse exists other than that the two of you are married at once. At once!"

Ethan was tempted to roar with laughter, but the sight of China Warrick's white face sobered him sufficiently to check his amusement. "And just how do you propose to

carry out the wedding ceremony, Mrs. Harrleson? I'm afraid
we won't be making landfall for several weeks."

The thought did not seem to deter Lucinda Harrleson,
who had obviously mapped out her course of action quite
thoroughly. "You are captain of this ship, sir," she reminded him frostily, plump shoulders quivering with determination. "You have the authority to perform the
ceremony yourself."

"Ah, but I have no intention of doing so," he pointed
out blandly. "Nor, I expect, will you be able to force me
into it."

Mrs. Harrleson stared up at him with disbelieving eyes,
her image of him as a romantic hero cruelly shattered.
How thoroughly uncooperative and unpleasant he was
being! It galled her to think that she had actually entertained the notion of permitting one of her own darlings to
marry him. "You are no gentleman, Captain Bloodwell!"

His humorous grin was faintly self-deprecating. "I'm
afraid I've never had any illusions on that score, madame."

Mrs. Harrleson's hands twisted nervously, for her interview with Captain Bloodwell was not going well, not
well at all. She had expected him to agree without condition to marry China, which was the only proper thing
to do under the circumstances, and instead he was behaving in the most appalling manner imaginable! Furthermore there was something entirely unsettling in those cold
blue eyes she had never noticed before and she was beginning to wonder if perhaps she hadn't misjudged him
altogether.

"Then what's to be done about China?" she persisted,
realizing that her young charge hadn't spoken a single
word since Captain Bloodwell had arrived. "Surely you
must see that her reputation—"

"Has suffered no damage," China said clearly, regarding Mrs. Harrleson with level green eyes. "I have no intention of marrying Captain Bloodwell," she continued
shortly, her brief glance at the tall Irishman speaking
volumes concerning her feelings on the subject. "You must
understand that all of my life people have been forcing me
to abide by their decisions and sparing no consideration
as to how I might feel. While I appreciate your concern,

Mrs. Harrleson, I cannot allow you to manipulate me like that." Her eyes hardened as she saw Captain Bloodwell's lips twitch. "Especially not this time!"

She withdrew with an angry rustle of flounced satin petticoats, leaving Lucinda to stare openmouthed into Captain Bloodwell's lean face. Had those rude words really come from dear, sweet China, who never raised her voice at anyone? The poor child must be frantic with shame!

"Now see what you've done!" she accused.

"My dear woman, will you please permit me to explain?" Captain Bloodwell asked irritably.

"I am afraid, sir," pronounced Mrs. Harrleson with magnificent aplomb, "that we have nothing further to say to one another." And with her ample chins quivering, she swept imperiously away.

"What in God's name," Ethan inquired, lifting his bemused gaze to the vast sky above him, "have I done to deserve this?"

"'China' sure is an odd name for a woman, ain't it? What prompted your ma to call you that, Miss Warrick?"

The question, uttered by the portly captain of the American clipper *Birmingham,* was accompanied by a raised hand to signal the hovering steward for another glass of wine. "Damned fine Canary you've got here, Bloodwell. Never had better vintage. Ahem...Excuse me, Miss Warrick, you were saying—?"

"Actually it was my father who named me," China responded slowly, regarding Captain Terence Aloysius with carefully concealed disgust. Was it possible that all Americans drank this much and swore so loudly? Not only did he possess deplorable table manners but China had actually seen him pinch Arabella Harrleson's bottom in the companionway earlier this evening and then laugh heartily at the girl's startled squeals. Though Bella had ended up blushing and giggling, China had decided that she would have slapped him resoundingly had he dared do the same to her.

"Damned unlikely name," Captain Aloysius muttered, belching thoughtfully.

"On the contrary, it seems rather apt," Ethan Bloodwell

remarked, lounging negligently at the head of the table. The barely discernible drawl in his voice had deepened in the past hour or so as he had watched the heavyset clipper captain consume almost two bottles of his rarest Canary. "What else would one name a daughter with eyes the color of jade and hair as red as the Emperor's Imperial robes?"

Startled, China was betrayed into sending him a glance although she had been snubbing him deliberately ever since they had gathered in his quarters. How had he known? His heavy-lidded eyes revealed nothing save polite interest and China looked quickly away again. It vexed her suddenly that she knew so little about Captain Ethan Bloodwell, and she wondered how he had managed to guess with such accuracy the origins behind her name?

It was only for the Harrlesons' sake that she had made an appearance tonight, though regrettably her relationship with Mrs. Harrleson had been decidedly strained since their awkward encounter on the main deck several weeks ago. And China was rather ashamed of the relief she felt knowing that after their farewell dinner in Captain Bloodwell's quarters, the Harrleson women would be rowed across to the *Birmingham* in order to sail north with Captain Aloysius to Calcutta.

The thought of saying goodbye to Louisa genuinely saddened her, yet China reminded herself that the little girl would soon be reunited with her adored father and that the *Kowloon Star*, able to forgo her scheduled call in India, would reach Singapore far sooner than anticipated. It was actually quite fortunate that the big clipper had hailed them in the Bay of Bengal and Captain Aloysius had volunteered to take the Harrlesons along.

"I take it your pa's been to China, Miss Warrick?"

The American sea captain, having lost interest in Arabella's silly simpers and shying away from Julia Clayton who, in his experienced opinion, had her tentacles poised to ensnare the first unsuspecting man she could find, had turned his attention at last to China.

"Both my father and grandfather traveled extensively throughout Kwangtung," China answered obligingly, "and I believe my great-grandfather was the first European to set foot in Canton."

"Your great-grandfather?" Captain Aloysius found his interest aroused. Knowing his history admirably well and being far less gone in his cups than one would tend to believe, he was able to make the logical connection between China's casual remark and her well-known surname.

"Kingston Warrick? Your great-grandaddy wasn't Kingston Warrick, was he? Well, bless my soul, it's a small world, ain't it, missy? I knew your pa pretty well, you know. My ship, the one I had afore the *Birmingham,* carried consignments of Badajan silk to New York for him one year. Hell of a man, your pa. I heard tell he'd drowned last summer."

He seemed not to notice the spasm of sorrow that crossed China's face at the mention of her father. The arrival of her mother's letter bearing the news of Race Warrick's death had been a blow from which she had yet to recover. It wasn't fair! she couldn't help thinking. It wasn't fair that he had died so shortly before she was due to return home and after she had waited for what had seemed a lifetime to see him again!

"He was a good man, your pa," the clipper captain was saying, propping his elbows comfortably on the table. "Most of the captains what carried goods for him sure did respect him. And I never heard a sorry word said about him 'cept by those who envied his money."

Chuckling, he scrubbed his lips with a napkin. "Heard King's Wheal Plantation ain't been doin' too good since he died. Talk has it that stepson of his just don't know what he's doing."

"I believe it's growing late," Captain Bloodwell said abruptly, snapping shut the watch he had drawn from the pocket of his satin waistcoat.

"Wait a moment, please. Are you referring to my brother Damon?" China inquired. "Is there trouble at the plantation?"

But Captain Terence Aloysius was not a half-wit and had been quick to understand the warning on Ethan Bloodwell's lean face. "By God, it is late," he agreed, hearing the muted clanging of the ship's bell from the deck above.

Lumbering to his feet, he herded his new passengers to the door and urged them to fetch their belongings.

"We'll have India off the starboard bow by mornin'," he promised heartily. "And don't you worry none about that brother of yours, Miss Warrick," he added for good measure, feeling a stab of remorse when he saw the worried frown that lingered on her face. "I heard tell from a seafarin' friend of mine put into Boston just before we left that he had a bit of trouble steppin' into his daddy's shoes. I'd imagine that's all behind him now."

A faint line drew China's brows together and she wished she could see what lay behind the captain's hearty bluster. Was there really something wrong at King's Wheal Plantation? Did she have a reason to feel uneasy or was she simply reading more into Captain Aloysius's harmless gossip than was actually there?

Thankfully she forgot all about Badajan in the disorder that accompanied the Harrlesons' leave-taking, finding herself rather surprised by the fact that Captain Bloodwell could remain so patient with the chaos that descended upon his ship. His expression was benign as he duly kissed the plump hands held out to him in farewell and personally assisted the portly Mrs. Harrleson into the waiting launch. Little Louisa clung tightly to his neck as he stooped to bid her farewell, and China was astonished by the gentleness in his face as he lifted her into the bow of the boat. Their eyes met when he straightened and he grinned at her.

"You were thinking, no doubt, that you would not consider me the sort of person to demonstrate a fondness for children?"

"As a matter of fact I was," China admitted, nettled that he had once again been able to read her mind.

"I'm not as callow as you would like to believe, Miss Warrick," he said as he took his place at her side.

"No?"

His sun-browned hands tightened unexpectedly about the railing. "No. Regrettably you are not the only one who understands the suffering an abandoned child is capable of feeling."

China gazed curiously into his face but the profile presented in the flickering light of the port lanterns was unrelentingly harsh. Hearing Louisa's piping voice calling her name in farewell, she turned and waved until the jolly boat had drawn alongside the *Birmingham* and its passengers hauled safely aboard.

"I can't believe they're really gone," she remarked with a sigh.

"Yes, it's a blessing, isn't it?" Captain Bloodwell inquired.

"That isn't what I meant," China protested, though she couldn't help laughing, and was somewhat taken aback when he chose to join her before both of them lapsed into an oddly companionable silence.

Although the sun had set several hours ago, a faint orange glow lingered on the horizon and the first stars twinkled in a lavender sky high above the soaring mastheads. The evening breeze was warm and slight and the blocks overhead tapped softly in response. After the Harrlesons' noisy departure, the tranquil beauty of the evening became apparent to the young woman and the tall sea captain standing together at the rail. They were alone on deck, the seamen on watch having withdrawn, and Julia Clayton, who had generously volunteered to continue on to Singapore as "dear China's chaperone," had retired to her cabin, professing a headache.

China was uncharitably inclined to believe that Julia's malaise had been caused by eyestrain from simpering askance at Captain Bloodwell all evening. Nonetheless, she was profoundly relieved to have escaped Julia's company, for she was still furious at having been used as a pawn in the young widow's scheme to remain aboard the *Kowloon Star* where she might continue her blatant pursuit of its handsome captain.

"A proper escort indeed!" China sniffed, and was unaware that she had spoken aloud until Captain Bloodwell turned to her with his brows inquiringly raised.

"Were you offering an opinion on my morals, Miss Warrick, or merely letting your thoughts wander at random?"

"Neither," she responded with that directness he illogically found both tiresome and curiously refreshing. "I was thinking about Mrs. Clayton and her reasons for remaining on board your ship."

"Surely you aren't questioning the sincerity of the good woman's motives?" Captain Bloodwell chided. "How uncharitable of you."

Having seen the glint of amusement in his eyes, China was not at all fooled by the seriousness of his tone.

"Surely you must realize, my dear Miss Warrick," he continued as though lecturing her, "that Lucinda Harrleson could not have sailed with the *Birmingham* if it meant you were to be the only female left aboard my ship. By volunteering to remain behind, Mrs. Clayton made it possible for them to be reunited with Colonel Harrleson all the more quickly."

China said tartly, "I recall Julia saying that in all likelihood her own husband's remains had not been transported from Lahore as yet and that she had no desire to languish in Calcutta until they arrived."

Captain Bloodwell laughed, and it occurred to China that he, too, doubted the existence of the mysterious Major Clayton. "I'm afraid she won't find Singapore an exciting alternative."

"How does she propose to return to India?" China wondered curiously. "And where will she stay while she awaits passage? As I recall, Singapore has but a few private residences and certainly no rooms for rent."

The expression in the blue eyes was almost pitying as Ethan Bloodwell gazed down into China's profile. "My dear child, you have a great deal to learn about the city you left six years ago. Singapore is now the gateway of Far East trade, and its European community has doubled in the past five years alone. There's even a new hotel going up in the British quarter which rivals anything that stands on the fringes of Mayfair."

"When was the last time you were there?" China inquired curiously.

"Shortly before we returned to England."

"Were you carrying goods?" Ethan Bloodwell did not strike China as the sort of person to indulge in the admittedly dull profession of foreign trade.

"Well, well," he said, grinning. "I see you've finally grown curious enough about me to probe into my affairs."

China's lips tightened. "I was not probing. I was simply wondering, and if you find my question offensive—"

"Not in the least," he assured her with a laugh. "We were carrying consigned goods from Java to a brokerage house in London, a lackluster mission, I confess, but one that financial circumstances necessitated."

"I recall my father telling me when I was very young that Badajan silk was always shipped via clippers because they alone were capable of turning a profit due to their hold capacity and the speed with which they traveled."

Captain Bloodwell's expression was suddenly enigmatic as he lifted his head to stare up at the soaring masts barely visible against the darkening sky, the yards of canvas bellying taut as the sails filled with a freshening gust of wind. "Your father was right, Miss Warrick. The *Kowloon Star* isn't cut out for the competition existing between the modern clipper fleets roving the Far East. I owned a clipper once myself, and I daresay she was the fastest afloat. Regrettably I lost her through sheer youthful recklessness."

"That doesn't surprise me in the least," China said impulsively, and earned herself a hearty laugh from the captain.

"No, I imagine it doesn't."

Both of them fell silent, for there seemed nothing else to say, and it was at that moment that the moon chose to rise above the water, a fantastic, bloodred orb sagging in the darkened sky like a ripened fruit and scattering a wake of scarlet jewels on the shivering sea. The wind that came on its heels carried with it the intoxicating scent of the Orient, lifting the hems of China's skirts and brushing them lightly against Ethan's boots.

He looked down to find her staring across the rippling water, her face pale in the moonlight, her hair touched with its brilliant opal glow, and it occurred to him that she was achingly, impossibly lovely and that he should give in to impulse and kiss her.

China turned her head, perhaps because she felt his eyes upon her, perhaps because she intended to remark upon the beauty of the night, and as the slim line of her jaw came out of the shadows, the flickering glow of the lanterns clearly revealed the curve of her soft, full mouth.

She grew still as her eyes lifted to his, and a breathless expectancy settled over them, as sultry and heavy with promise as the warm, scented wind that blew from the coastline of India.

But Ethan did not kiss her. Instead he turned away abruptly and observed with a harshness that was curiously at odds with the innocuous nature of his comment: "I'll be needed at the helm now the wind has freshened. If you'll excuse me, Miss Warrick?"

China wanted to make a suitably flippant retort, yet found that she was seized of a sudden with the inability to speak at all. And so she could only nod her head and watch as Ethan strode away in the darkness, and her small hands twisted convulsively in the folds of her skirts.

"I don't care that he didn't kiss me!" she whispered indignantly to herself, womanly instinct having told her he had been considering just that. "I vow I don't care at all!"

Chapter Seven

"Are you scared, miss?"

China turned from the rail to look inquiringly at Nappy Quarles. "Scared? Of what?"

"'Ow should I know?" The little steward shrugged. "Of goin' 'ome, maybe. Things ain't gonna be like they was when you left. Ain't that wot's troublin' you?"

China pondered the question for a moment, then shook her head. "I suppose I'm a little nervous," she admitted, "but not frightened. What made you think I was?"

Nappy grinned, and his single eye twinkled. "Got me glancin' over me shoulder 'arf the time, you do, starin' off t' coast that way. What do you expect to see?"

This time China had no answer, for she didn't really know herself. Land had been spotted with the setting of the sun the night before and when she came on deck this morning she had seen for herself the thin strip of emerald coastline across the dazzling water. Under the urging of a brisk wind, the _Kowloon Star_ was eating up the distance, and the Arab mate Rajiid had predicted docking by four bells. Fascinated, uneasy, and, in truth, somewhat afraid,

China found her gaze drawn time and again beyond the
dipping rail to the island of Singapore which marked the
end of her journey and six long years of exile. Badajan lay
beyond the shimmering strait that separated Singapore
from the mountainous islands of Indonesia, but it was in
Singapore's sheltered harbor that the *Kowloon Star* would
drop anchor at last and China would bid farewell to her
captain and crew.

Lying directly south of the Malay Peninsula, Singapore
possessed a deep-water dock that stretched for miles along
a palm-choked coast. Ships flying the flags of uncountable
nations jammed the wharves, ancient sampans and Chinese
junks flitting between lumbering East Indiamen and the
fleeter schooners and brigs. Clipper captains waited with
bristling impatience as their crews worked feverishly to
load cargoes of tea, raw silk, and mahogany before fleeing
homeward with the winds of the northeast monsoons at
their heels. Fortunes could be made and lost in a single
day, and none of them could afford so much as an hour's
delay.

Slipping into her berth some two hours later, her lines
neatly shored, the *Kowloon Star* seemed ponderously old-
fashioned in comparison to the sleek clippers fluttering
the well-known red-and-blue pennants of the Americas
line. China, standing at the rail, surveying a teeming wharf
that held no memories for her at all, was aware of nothing
but the incredible din: the blend of a dozen foreign tongues
as sailors and native Malay roustabouts scurried to load
and unload the waiting ships.

Palm trees, church spires, and mosques topped with the
curved moon symbol of Islam were crowded against the
skyline and from the city itself came the swelling murmur
of countless thousands of voices and the cries of goats and
children and the barking of pariah dogs. It was a sound
China had all but forgotten and which few Westerners had
ever heard: the exotic song of an Eastern city.

"Changed a bit since you was 'ere last, eh, miss?"

"I don't recognize a thing, Nappy, not a thing! They've
cut down so much of the jungle, and I don't think any of
those buildings were here when I left!"

"Been putting up a lot since the blokes back 'ome started

minist'ring the island as part of India. Lots of the old Company johns've settled 'ere, bringin' their families wiv 'em. Still a frontier town, though," Nappy observed with a shake of his grizzled head. "Plenty of ruffians to be found 'ere, and not all of 'em Malays and Chinese neither."

"Then you've been to Singapore before! Why didn't you mention it to me?"

"You never asked is why!" Nappy's bushy brows were drawn together and he cast a disapproving glance at Captain Bloodwell, who was issuing orders on the aft deck as preparations were made to lower the anchor and furl the enormous sails. "Used to run a trade route between 'Ong Kong and British Bengal years ago an' we always nosed by 'ere to take on water an' the like. Cap'n Ethan were cap'n-owner of the fastest clipper ever took to the sea. 'Ad it right cosy, we did, until the cap'n decided we wasn't making enough money to suit 'im so 'e up and let John Company license 'is ship. Do yer know what that means? Being licensed by John Company?"

China did. John Company, a sobriquet for the powerful British East India Company, the firm which owned a monopoly on all Indian and Asian trade, often issued licenses to the owners of independent ships to carry goods in its name. Usually the cargo consisted of tea and silk, but China had been born on the island of Badajan, not some isolated English estate, and she remembered perfectly well the discussions her father and his manager Darwin Stepkyne had held on the subject of the huge clippers and merchantmen that sailed on clandestine missions from Calcutta to Whampoa and back again.

"Captain Bloodwell was not by any chance a China trader?" she inquired frostily, already certain that he was.

Nappy's walnut face reddened. "Now what can you know about them, Miss China?" he asked uncomfortably.

Her chin lifted. "I know all about them, I'm afraid. China traders were unscrupulous men who indulged in illegal activity for the sake of profit, most noticeably in the smuggling of opium that was made in British Bengal and sold on the Chinese mainland."

"You'll not be believing that, Miss China!" Nappy protested, genuinely scandalized. In his firm opinion young ladies were to be kept totally ignorant of such ignoble activities as contraband smuggling, and it thoroughly disconcerted him to have Miss Warrick look him straight in the eye and mention it as casually as discussing the weather!

"Oh, but I do believe it," China assured him in no uncertain terms, golden brows haughtily raised. "I also happen to know that although opium is considered contraband in China, it was nonetheless purchased secretly by the Chinese Guild of Merchants who resold it on the mainland—for huge profits, of course." She regarded him coolly. "Not many British subjects are aware of that, but I happen to have heard it from my father and he was not one to fabricate tales."

"On my 'onor, miss—"

"My father said that payment for opium was made in silver bullion," China continued as though lecturing a schoolboy remiss in his lessons, "and that the traders used it in India to purchase tea and silk which they sold in turn on the Western markets. In that manner they managed to convert their illegal profits into legitimate cash. Isn't that so, Mr. Quarles?"

"Now, Miss China, Cap'n Bloodwell wasn't—"

"There's no sense in hiding the truth from me," China interrupted, her indignation growing as she was handed further evidence of what an unscrupulous rogue the Irishman was proving to be. "From what you've said I'm quite certain Captain Bloodwell smuggled Bengal opium for a living and lost his ship like the rest of the traders when China and Britain went to war over it. That would explain the evidence of penury aboard the *Kowloon Star* and—and I say it's the very least he deserves!"

"Quite a harsh judgment from a supposedly softhearted young woman, isn't it?" Captain Bloodwell observed from behind them.

China whirled about, her cheeks flushing with righteous indignation. "Then you don't deny it?"

He grinned. "There'd be no sense in that now, would there?"

"Oh!" China burst out. "I should have realized you'd be proud of it!"

His grin did not falter. "Not proud, Miss Warrick. I considered it a necessary means of survival at the time."

"Other men earn quite respectable livings without stooping to dishonesty."

"Ah, but I am not 'other men,' Miss Warrick."

"You needn't remind me of that!" The green eyes surveyed him as though he were a particularly loathsome specimen of crawling insect.

"China traders," Captain Bloodwell pointed out helpfully, "stood to make more money in a single opium run than a respectable clerk in a London bank could collect after forty years of devoted labor."

"At least that clerk was not a lawbreaker!" China retorted. Exasperated, she added, "Didn't your parents ever teach you the meaning of the law?"

"I have no parents."

"Oh." She was disconcerted by the flat tone with which the last remark had been uttered. "You are an orphan, then?"

"Not at all, Miss Warrick. I was nurtured at the ample bosom of dear Mother O'Shaughnessy, the kindest director ever to bless the sacred halls of the Cork Asylum for Orphans and Foundlings. I enjoyed my stay so much, in fact, that I was twelve years old before I thought to run away to sea."

There was an unpleasant gleam in the hard blue eyes that told China she would achieve nothing pursuing the topic of Captain Bloodwell's past. Yet his casual reference to his childhood made a great number of things clear to her that had heretofore been beyond her understanding. His kindness toward little Louisa Harrleson, for one thing, and his odd remark—which she had pondered at length without enlightenment—concerning his sentiments on the loneliness of an abandoned child. Surely a boy denied the loving comforts of a home, without parents to steer him properly down the path of good, could easily grow into a man who shunned the righteous and embraced the lawless existence of a smuggler.

"Spare me your tiresome lectures, Miss Warrick," Captain Bloodwell said as though she had spoken her thoughts aloud, "and don't waste time convincing yourself that loneliness or deprivation drove me to the wrong side of the law. I doubt my life would have been very much different had I been raised in the home of a devout clergyman rather than in an orphanage."

"I am quite prepared to agree with that," China said so earnestly that both Captain Bloodwell and his steward broke into hearty laughter.

Naturally neither of them would think to take their deplorable pasts seriously, China thought with a frown, and experienced a pang of utter vexation recalling that she herself had agreed to place two hundred pounds into the hands of a former China trader. God alone knew for what sordid purposes it was intended!

Captain Bloodwell's amusement faded and he stood regarding her with a trace of impatience. "I came to inform you that you may disembark as soon as your belongings are packed, Miss Warrick. Your trunks will be taken wherever you direct, and Rajiid will see that a message is delivered to Badajan announcing your arrival."

China stared at him incredulously. "You aren't thinking of simply leaving me here in Singapore, are you?"

"My dear Miss Warrick," he said unkindly, "my schedule is already ruined because I agreed to bring you here rather than dropping you off in Djakarta. If you feel the need for companionship, you can always stay with Mrs. Clayton until someone from King's Wheal comes for you."

"And what about payment for my passage? Don't tell me you've had a change of heart and decided not to collect it?"

"My dear girl, the foolishness of that statement should be quite obvious to you," Captain Bloodwell observed. "It so happens that I have pressing business in Djakarta, but I assure you I'll be back."

"Suppose I tell my brother not to pay you?" China threatened, annoyed that he could be unfeeling enough to simply abandon her here.

"You won't," Captain Bloodwell said with an impudent grin, "because you gave me your word, and I distinctly recall your telling me that a Warrick's word is honor-bound."

China colored angrily. "What can a thief possibly know about honor?"

"I make it my business to know about everything, Miss Warrick. Now, Nappy, would you please collect both Miss Warrick's and Mrs. Clayton's belongings and make certain Rajiid sees them safely to the Raffles Hotel?" He turned back to China. "It's no great distance to undertake on foot and you'll find yourselves most comfortable there. Goodbye, Miss Warrick."

"I'm afraid 'e ain't much on ceremony, our cap'n," Nappy said by way of apology as Captain Bloodwell strode away.

"I'm not in the least surprised at his rudeness," China said stiffly.

"Go on and pack yer things, miss. I'll take you t' Raffles myself. No sense troublin' that rascal Rajiid."

When China descended to the wharf a half hour later she spared no further thought to the captain who stood on the deck high above her, for a sense of profound relief washed over her the moment she left the *Kowloon Star* behind. She was free at last, free of the tyrannical rule of Cassie and Freddy Linville, free of the stifling rigidity of Victorian life, free of Captain Ethan Bloodwell and the last link to England he represented. She took a deep breath, savoring the moment, and scarcely noticed Nappy's urging hand beneath her elbow.

The streets were crowded with foreign seamen, native Malays, Indians and Chinese, and only a few Europeans shopped amid the tiny stalls flanking the enormous rows of warehouses. The air was warm and breathless; without a wind the sulphurous smell of the tidal swamps was thick and objectionable.

Yet despite the heat the City of the Lion seethed with activity, and countless rickshaws drawn by shouting Malaysian boys jolted down the deeply rutted streets, passing so close to the curb that China walked with her crinolines pressed aside for fear that the high wooden wheels would brush against them. The eating hour had begun and cooliehatted natives crowded into the food stalls while little boys with clacking sticks announced the arrival of the *mee* man selling his noodles and prawn gravy.

A noisy Chinese funeral procession replete with professional mourners and dancing priests clogged the street and forced Nappy to steer the two women down a dark, twisted alley, past Buddhist temples and storehouses hung with laundry. Ancient storytellers squatted on woven mats in many of the doorways, regaling their wide-eyed audiences with singsong chants as they smoked on their waterpipes.

"Shouldn't we have hired a carriage?" Julia Clayton inquired, looking somewhat nervously about her. "There don't seem to be many women walking about in the streets."

Nappy shook his head. "Bain't too many of 'em 'ere to begin with, ma'am. Town's too rough for 'em. Not many want to live 'ere even wiv their mates, and those that do don't come down to the waterfront."

"I don't recall Singapore having had such a bad reputation," China said.

"Probably because you've always been safe wiv the Warrick name so well known 'ere," Nappy suggested, and his hand tightened unconsciously about the hilt of the knife he carried well out of sight in his breeches. He couldn't be sure if Miss China's bright red hair was earning her the attention of many of the passersby or if it was because they happened to recognize in her small face some distinctive feature that unquestionably marked her a Warrick. Either way, he wasn't going to take chances with her safety. The Clayton bint had been right: They should've traveled in a carriage instead of on foot, despite the fact Cap'n Ethan would've scoffed. Well, maybe he didn't seem to think Miss China's welfare a cause for concern, but Nappy certainly did.

"Is it very much farther, Mr. Quarles? I vow the heat is most oppressive." Julia's dark hair was limp beneath her wide-brimmed bonnet and her petticoats and skirts hung heavy over their wide whalebone hoop. Unlike China, who had been sensible enough to dress in a gown of cool muslin, she had donned her finest silk walking dress with long, ruffled sleeves and matching gloves. Hoping to cause a stir among the populace of Singapore, Julia was extremely disconcerted to find that no one was paying her the least bit of attention, with the exception of the sailors who eyed her rudely from the doorways of the waterfront brothels and saloons.

"'Ere we are, ladies," Nappy Quarles announced cheerfully, emerging from the dark alley into the humid sunshine of a pleasantly deserted street lined with palms. "Nicer down this way, ain't it?"

The Raffles Hotel stood a short distance below them, an imposing white building with a sloping, red-tiled roof and tended gardens flanked by tall white houses with numerous porticos and arching windows facing out to sea.

"Why, it's lovely!" Julia Clayton exclaimed with considerable surprise. "I hadn't expected—Mr. Quarles!" She gasped as the little steward thrust her without warning into the doorway of a nearby building. "Whatever are you doing?" She screamed, seeing that he had pulled a knife from amid his clothing, and her bewildered gaze followed his to the alley from which they had just emerged. "Please put that weapon away at once!" she ordered hotly, seeing nothing but three innocuous-looking youths engaged in animated conversation before a nearby shop window. "Surely you don't think those boys mean us harm?"

But China, who could read their dark, inscrutable faces as well as Nappy, put a restraining hand on Julia's arm. "Let's go to the hotel," she suggested levelly, though her throat was suddenly dry.

"Really, China!" Julia said in exasperation. "Is all of this necessary?"

"Do wot she says, Mrs. Clayton," Nappy instructed. "'Urry, now."

The hotel was less than a block away, but no sooner had China taken the protesting Julia by the arm and started quickly up the street than the three young men burst out of the alley and leaped without warning upon them. Nappy, who had brawled his way through countless waterfront dens from London to Macao, countered fearlessly with his knife although he was clearly no match for the viciousness of a trio of attackers trained in the martial arts. Hearing an agonized grunt behind her, China halted in midstride, and gasped as she saw Nappy collapse beneath half a dozen hands and feet, each one capable of breaking bones with a single blow.

"Stop that! Leave him alone!" she cried, and was totally unaware that she had spoken in Cantonese.

Startled, the three men turned to stare, and the brief

diversion gave Nappy the chance he needed to scramble to his feet. "Go on, miss!" he shouted. "Get on t' 'otel!"

A heel caught him full in the belly and he doubled over and collapsed. China raced out into the street to help him, but she stumbled over the hem of her skirts and went sprawling against a tunic-covered chest. Instantly, iron fingers wrapped themselves about her throat, squeezing relentlessly.

"China!"

The scream seemed to come from a great distance, and China caught a glimpse of Julia's terrified face as she struggled to free herself, her hands flailing, twisting, and clawing at the face of her attacker. Without warning there was a sharp pain between her shoulder blades and a rush of something warm and sticky that soaked her gown and left her gasping for air as the world spun dizzily before her eyes.

"China!"

Julia's voice again, and an Oriental face that appeared through a gray, swirling mist only to vanish as a tall man in the flowing robes of an Arab filled her dimming field of vision. Rajiid, China thought with breathless relief. Abruptly the strangling hold about her throat was gone and China, slumping to the street, allowed the welcome blackness to claim her.

"What a dreadful thing to happen!"

"And in broad daylight, too! Whatever is the world coming to when one isn't even safe on the streets anymore?"

"Has someone notified her family?"

"I believe one of the clerks was sent to Badajan with a message for Damon Warrick. Though one can never trust those Malaysian creatures. You know how lazy they are."

The whispered voices became muffled and indistinct and eventually died away, and China, who had opened her eyes at the sound of them, shut them gratefully again. There was a hot, throbbing pain between her shoulder blades and at the moment she wanted to be left entirely alone. She assumed that she had been brought to the Raffles Hotel and that someone, perhaps a local doctor, had bound her wound, for she could feel a thick padding of bandages across her back and middle, and smell the lingering odor of some soothing ointment.

"Just a moment, please! Whatever are you doing? You cannot go in there!"

A woman's voice again, well-bred and British but thoroughly unfamiliar.

"Will you please explain to me, madame, why I cannot?"

"Why, because it simply isn't decent! Miss Warrick is in a state of undress."

China's eyes flew open, for she had no trouble at all recognizing that faintly mocking drawl, and she turned her head just as Ethan Bloodwell stepped into the pleasantly furnished, cream-painted room and shut the door on two thoroughly scandalized faces in the corridor. A faint frown appeared between his eyes as his gaze met hers. For a moment silence descended between them, and it was so still that China could hear the muted din of traffic beyond the shuttered windows.

"I hope you realize that your foolish heroics have once again very nearly cost you your life," Ethan said at last.

"How is Nappy?" she inquired, turning her face away, for she was far too weary to endure the blistering lecture she sensed was forthcoming.

"Cut and bruised, and I daresay he'll mend. As for those Amazons outside your door—"

"I've no idea who they are," China whispered.

"Mrs. Clayton says they're friends of your mother's who've volunteered to look after you. A Mrs. Charlotte Aldridge and her sister Agnes."

"Yes," China said slowly. "I think I remember them."

Crossing his arms before his chest, Ethan leaned his shoulder against the wall and frowned down into her drawn face. Because China had closed her eyes once again he couldn't help but notice how the long, silky lashes curled against her smooth cheeks, and how translucent was the skin beneath them.

"Where am I? Is this the Raffles Hotel?" China inquired after a moment. It was odd that she should not feel the least bit embarrassed at finding herself alone with him, and perhaps it was because she felt so terribly tired and in pain, but it almost seemed to her as if she derived a measure of comfort from his presence. Which was absurd, of course.

"It is. Rajiid brought you here after he dispensed with your attackers. I might add that you were extremely fortunate, Miss Warrick." An edge crept into his voice. "If he hadn't been following close behind with your luggage..."

"I know," she whispered. "I'm very grateful to him."

"The knife, by the way, glanced off a rib and thereby missed anything vital, but you've lost a considerable amount of blood. Would you mind telling me what in blazes—"

"Captain Bloodwell, I'm afraid you'll have to leave at once! Mrs. Aldridge is positively scandalized by your behavior and it won't do to have people talking any more than they already are! Besides, this is not the time to be lecturing poor China on what she should have done!" It was Julia Clayton's authoritative voice coming from the corridor, and China heard Ethan chuckle as he obligingly opened the door.

"There's no need to upset yourself, Mrs. Clayton. I merely wanted to make certain Miss Warrick was in no danger of dying, and I see that she is not. I understand her brother has been sent for?"

"I believe he has. The desk clerk arranged for a message to be delivered to Badajan."

"Excellent.... It would seem you're in adequate hands, Miss Warrick, so I might as well take my leave. Is there anything I can do for you before I go? No? Good day to you, then."

"Oh, China!" Julia said on a breathless sob once he had gone. "Can you ever forgive me for treating you so unfairly? I know I've been horrible and underhand, and when you were so brave and that—that terrible man stabbed you with his knife I realized I'd been so terribly unfair to you! I had no right to dislike you simply because you had everything I wanted!"

China regarded her blankly. "Why, Julia, what could I possibly have that you want?"

"Your fortune, for one thing," Julia confessed shamefacedly. "Everyone knows your great-uncle was simply made of money, and your looks and your sweetness. You're so innocent, China, not jaded at all, like I am. Oh, I wish I had my life to live all over again!"

She rose with a pained little gasp and began to pace the room, her handkerchief pressed to her lips. "I've had many men in my life, China," she confessed unhappily. "Too many, in fact, to remember them all. There, that shocks you, doesn't it? But I just couldn't seem to help myself, if you can understand that." She uttered a bitter laugh. "No, I see you cannot, but I suppose it doesn't really matter. You might as well know that I was forced to leave England in order to avoid an unpleasant scene with the wife of a man I had been...indiscreet with. There really wasn't anywhere else for me to turn. That's why I decided India would be as good a place as any to begin anew."

"Then there never was a Major Clayton?"

Julia's laugh was brittle. "My poor innocent! Of course not! I've never been married. At any rate, I've set my cap for Ethan Bloodwell, and while I beg your forgiveness, China, I intend to win him in spite of you."

"But Julia," China said with wide, uncomprehending eyes, "why should I be standing in your way?"

A measure of scorn and envy crept into Julia Clayton's voice. "Oh, come, China, surely you don't think I've forgotten about that morning when I found the two of you together. Surely you know I'm not as gullible as Lucinda Harrleson!"

A wave of color suffused China's face and she struggled weakly onto one elbow. "Oh, no, Julia, you're mistaken! I told Mrs. Harrleson the truth!"

"Are you saying that you don't care for him?"

"Care for him!" China's color deepened. "How utterly absurd! I cannot think how anyone could possibly find him the least appealing!"

"Can't you?"

China's gaze dropped. "No."

"Then apparently you know very little about men," Julia said quietly. "My, but you look tired, dear," she added in the next breath. "How selfish of me to keep you from your rest! They've given me the room next to yours and you have only to call if you need anything." She stooped to kiss the girl's pale cheek and then moved hastily to shut the door behind her.

Collapsing against the pillows, China found that, tired as she was, she could not sleep. Her room was hot and very bright despite the shutters drawn across the windows, and no matter how many times she changed position on the narrow bed, she could not make herself comfortable without hurting her wounded back. And try as she might she could not forget the disturbing things that Julia had said to her.

Nappy Quarles was also disturbed—by his captain. When Ethan Bloodwell returned to the ship a short time later, afternoon was waning and from the crowded rooftops of the city the muezzins were calling the faithful to prayer. Ominous thunderheads were gathering over the mainland of Malaysia, and on the docks and in the wooden go-downs the workers kept apace, sorting and storing cargo and hoping to finish before the rains began.

"Well, did you see 'er?" Nappy demanded impatiently. "'Ow bad is she?"

"The doctor was just leaving when I arrived," Ethan said briefly, "and I spoke to him in the lobby. She seemed in pain, but I think she'll mend by the by. What about you, old man?" He frowned as he regarded the rainbow-hued bruises that darkened Nappy's leathery face.

"I been worse," Nappy said with a shrug.

"Did you describe those fellows to Rajiid?"

"Yus," Nappy growled. "'E's still out lookin'. Now, about Miss China?"

"There's really no need for concern, Nappy. Her brother has already been notified, and it's probable she'll be on Badajan come evening."

"Well, I'd likes to know 'oo'd dare 'urt 'er!" Nappy persisted, stumping after the captain to the aft companionway. "She's never meant no 'arm to anyone!"

"She tried to defend you, didn't she?" Ethan inquired dryly over his shoulder.

"That be different! She weren't armed and—and she's a woman!"

Ethan laughed harshly. "You know perfectly well that

female lives matter little indeed to riffraff like that. You say Rajiid is still making inquiries?"

Nappy nodded. "'E went arfter 'em once 'e 'elped bring Miss China t' 'otel, but I don't think 'e'll be finding 'em. Sure as I'm standin' 'ere they be on a ship bound for 'Ong Kong by now! Gutter rats, nothin' but gutter rats. Bah!" he spat contemptuously into the scuppers.

"No different than the rest of the populace here," Captain Bloodwell observed mildly and turned away. "Send Rajiid to me when he returns."

"Wait a minute, Cap'n, I been thinkin'."

Ethan's eyes narrowed. "About what?"

"Them barstids 'oo attacked us," Nappy confessed. "Maybe I'm a foolish old man, but I can't help thinkin' they was waitin' deliberate for us to come down that alley."

"For you? Or just any likely victims?"

"I ain't sure. It's just a feeling I 'as. I knows 'ow them barstids work, and they don't usually loiter round 'otel doors waitin' to pop an old man an' a pair o' wimmen 'oo ain't carryin' no luggage."

"That may be," Captain Bloodwell conceded thoughtfully, "but the *Kowloon Star* docked less than an hour before the incident occurred. No one, least of all three Cantonese thugs, could possibly know who we were. And why should they hold a grudge against an innocent girl and an old man like you?"

"Maybe they wasn't arfter me," Nappy said carefully. "You got more enemies than friends in these parts and that old pal o' yers Wang Toh Chen-Arn put a price on your 'ead just afore you lost the *Lotus Star* and all the opium in 'er 'olds. Just maybe," he continued angrily, seeing that Captain Bloodwell appeared unimpressed by the likelihood, "somebody 'oo recognized the colors on our masthead decided 'e'd earn 'isself a tidy reward for bringing you in."

"It's possible," Ethan allowed after a moment, "though highly improbable. Wang Toh hasn't shown his face for the past five years, and furthermore why would anyone wishing to collect the price on my head attack you or Miss Warrick instead of me? I think you're seeing ghosts in dark corners."

"It's rum curious you be, Cap'n!" Nappy burst out indignantly. "We was set on just an arf 'our arfter we docks, an' Miss China fetched a knife in t' back an' 'ere you're actin' like it's no more than a bitty raincloud in't sky! Miss China don't deserve—"

"Miss Warrick," Ethan interrupted brusquely, "needs to learn to curb her impulsive nature now that she has returned to the East. What one would have considered spirited behavior back in England would be labeled nothing short of reckless here. She is fortunate to have escaped with the few injuries she did."

"Is that all you 'as to say?" Nappy inquired incredulously.

Ethan's lips thinned. "It is. Now leave me in peace, Nappy. I've wasted enough time as it is running over to the Raffles at your behest."

"Barstid!" Nappy said furiously as the captain vanished below. "Muck-eatin' barstid! Don't care an 'arf-penny wot 'appens to 'er, does 'e?"

And grumbling beneath his breath he returned to his vigil by the entry port in the hopes that Rajiid would be returning soon and bringing those Cantonese ruffians with him.

_____ *Chapter Eight* _____

"Ever sorry, mistress. There can be no sailing without payment."

China Warrick, hot, tired, and in considerable pain, struggled to maintain a grip on her temper. If only she could remember enough of the Malaysian tongue to roundly curse the wiry boatman in a manner he understood! It wasn't fair of him to refuse to take her across the Singapore Strait simply because she couldn't pay him until they arrived!

"I haven't any money with me," China explained calmly, doing her best not to let her frustration show. Yet it was difficult not to, for although the afternoon had long since waned, the sun continued to glare down on her bare head and she could feel the heat from the wooden dock burn through the thin soles of her slippers. The night wind had not yet begun to blow, and the stench of refuse wafting from the quay was strong.

China had walked most of the distance to the outskirts of the city on foot. Here, far from the busy shipping lanes and the crowded docks, the jungle seemed to tumble down to the waterline itself, and the mosquitoes whined incessantly about her head. The tide was out and the water gurgled softly against the wharf, setting the fisherman's battered sampan rising and falling in response.

"Ever sorry, mistress," he repeated with a respectful bow. "My boat does not leave until money crosses hands."

China compressed her lips in utter vexation. Oh, why hadn't she sought passage somewhere along the harborfront instead of seeking out the people of the Orang Laut, the Malay boat dwellers, who lived a mile or so beyond the sprawling city limits on platforms made of stilts high above the tidal floods? And yet these were the same people she remembered from her childhood as always being eager to ferry you anywhere you wished to go without question or argument in exchange for a few coins at the end of the trip. What made this particular fellow so deuced reluctant to help her?

"You'll be paid as soon as we arrive," China persisted. "I've explained to you who I am and why I cannot pay you at present. Surely my word is good enough?"

The expression on the dark-skinned face remained bland. "I am sorry, Mistress China Warrick. For certain you are a lady of honor, but I do not know you."

"But surely you must have known my father?" China protested.

"Once the Warrick name meant honor," the boatman said carefully, "and the Warrick word trust. Yet that is no longer. I am a poor man, mistress, and will go hungry if my sampan does not return tonight with a load of fish."

China felt her heart skip a beat. This was not the first time she had heard someone imply that all was not well at King's Wheal Plantation. Was that the reason behind the message Damon had sent saying that he could not possibly come for her until the day after tomorrow? Something about the skiff being in need of repair, China remembered Julia having told her.

It was the pity in Julia Clayton's eyes more than anything else that had prompted China to leave the hotel in order to seek out her own transportation to Badajan. She wasn't about to wait another day to get home, and furthermore, she couldn't tolerate the thought that Julia or—

or anyone might begin to suspect that no one on Badajan wanted her back!

"Won't you reconsider?" she inquired crossly. Her wounded back was aching and it was very hot on the pier and she didn't care to spend the rest of the evening arguing with a local fisherman. The distant mountains of Indonesia were clearly visible across the glittering water, and Badajan lay no more than three hours away. If only this obstinate fellow would see that he stood to earn a tidy sum for such a small amount of work!

"I am sorry, mistress."

He was polite but adamant, and China was unable to convince him to change his mind. And because there were no other boats to be seen along the length of the wharf, she gave up at last and resigned herself to returning to the hotel and waiting for Damon after all.

"Do you realize, Miss Warrick," a quiet voice remarked unexpectedly from behind her, "that you have once again behaved in an utterly inexcusable manner?"

China whirled about with a gasp to find Ethan Bloodwell's disconcertingly cold eyes boring into hers. "How did you find me?" she whispered, involuntarily retreating a step.

"With difficulty since you didn't leave word at the Raffles as to your intentions," he stated unpleasantly. "Mrs. Clayton was beside herself when she informed my steward you had disappeared." He grimaced, thinking back on the distasteful conversation with Nappy that had followed Julia's visit, Nappy who had incredibly seen fit to hold him responsible....

"So you've finally done it, 'ave yer?" the little steward had demanded, confronting his captain on the aft deck, his bruised face reddened with agitation. "I 'opes you're satisfied, you great, bloody, misguided barstid!"

Ethan had straightened from his charts with a scowl and had asked quietly, "Whatever are you talking about, old man?"

"The Clayton bint were just 'ere. Says the girl packed 'er things an' disappeared from t' 'otel arfter you been to see 'er. Well, I mightn't be clever, but I can adds two an' two an' figure you went and drove 'er orf! I 'opes yer 'appy wiv yourself!"

"Whatever are you babbling about?" Ethan had demanded impatiently.

"Miss China, that's 'oo! Run orf, she 'as, an' I'll bet m' last shillin' you drove 'er to it wiv yer bloody unkind tongue! I 'eard about wots you said to 'er at t' Raffles this mornin'! Blamin' 'er for wot she done."

"Are you telling me that Miss Warrick left the Raffles on her own?" Ethan had interrupted disbelievingly.

"Don't I speak t' Queen's good English?" Nappy demanded furiously. "You 'eard wot I said! Left wivout a word to anyone and no tellin' where she's at!" He gestured frantically to the crowded rooftops that were visible beyond the rows of wooden warehouses. "I vow she's out 'untin' up passage to 'er blamed island this minute and maybe gettin' 'erself stabbed again in the process! You can't dangle no better bait afore the riffraff of this town than a English lady wot's out on 'er own! An' wot about them barstids 'oo attacked us?"

At this point Ethan had roughly shouldered Nappy aside, and issuing terse orders to the hovering watch, had strode down the gangplank in pursuit of the wayward Miss Warrick himself. Fortunately it hadn't proven difficult to find her, for as Nappy had said, a lone female in black sarsenet mourning was wont to attract considerable attention. He was only relieved that the foolish chit hadn't succumbed to the attack Nappy had feared.

"How did you happen to find me?" the chit in question was at that moment asking, and the sound of her voice served to return Ethan's angry thoughts to the present.

"It was quite easy," he told her curtly. "Few women would have the temerity, or perhaps the stupidity, to come this way unescorted. You seemed to have attracted a considerable amount of attention, and I had only to ask. Now, Miss Warrick, I would suggest that we return to my ship before you succumb to heatstroke." He scrutinized her rudely. "You appear wilted enough as it is."

China lifted her chin, determined to overlook his unkind words and the fact that her hair hung limply down her back and that the hem of her gown was coated with

dust. "It was kind of you to come after me, Captain," she
said with admirable dignity, "but I'm afraid I must refuse.
I intend to go home immediately."

An unpleasant light appeared in the narrowed blue
eyes. "Aboard that?" Ethan inquired, indicating the sun-
blistered sampan, which did indeed appear in danger of
springing a leak at any moment. Fortunately he spoke in
English so that its owner was spared offense, but when
China opened her mouth to hotly defend her decision she
was given no opportunity of doing so.

"You have no choice but to return with me," Captain
Bloodwell pointed out brusquely. "It's almost dark, and
you've no money to pay for your passage."

China's eyes flashed. "That may well be true, sir, but I
certainly do not intend to go anywhere with you. If I do
decide to spend the night in Singapore, then it will be at
the Raffles Hotel."

"I think not," Ethan countered in a tone that was deceptively mild. "For it has dawned on me—quite belatedly,
I might add—that unless I keep a closer eye on you, I
stand in genuine danger of losing my two hundred pounds."

"Did you think I intended to run away without honoring
our agreement?" China asked indignantly.

Ethan's mouth was suddenly a hard, slashing line. "My
dear young woman, I was referring to the fact that you
could easily have fallen victim to another robbery traipsing about the waterfront alone. And I seriously doubt your
brother would have agreed to settle your debt were I to
deliver a lifeless corpse to his door."

"Oh!" China gasped, her eyes filled with anger. "I cannot imagine how Julia Clayton can possibly fancy herself
in love with you," she was stung into retorting. "I happen
to think that you are the most exasperating man I've ever
met!"

"I'm perfectly aware of your sentiments, Miss Warrick,
and need no additional reminders, thank you. Now could
we please continue our argument elsewhere than on this
confounded wharf? I vow the smell of sewage is beginning
to seep into my clothes."

China did not reply, and there was something oddly

defeated in her bowed head that moved Ethan to remember Nappy's charges concerning his earlier unkindness.

"I apologize for my harsh words, Miss Warrick," he said unexpectedly, "both here and in your hotel room earlier. I understand your brother sent word that he was unable to come for you. If you return to the ship with me, I promise to give the order to depart for Badajan in the morning. Do you consider that fair enough?"

China's head came up and those astonishingly translucent eyes were suddenly upon him, bringing to mind the disturbing memory of the time he had found himself gazing into them and wondering what it would be like to kiss her.

"Would you really?"

Ethan was forced to laugh at the scowling distrust on her face, and abruptly the moment was gone and she was once again nothing more to him than the troublesome means of attaining those coveted two hundred pounds. "I give you my word as a gentleman."

China found herself laughing, too, amusement lending animation to her wan features and bringing Ethan to the startled realization that he had never given her cause to laugh before.

"Your word as a gentleman? I don't believe I've ever heard such a black-faced lie. Still, I suppose I shall have to accept it as I have no other choice."

"Indeed," said Ethan blandly and offered her his arm.

It was dark by the time they returned to the ship, night having fallen with the swiftness peculiar to the tropics. The go-downs were dark and the stalls along the waterfront tightly shuttered, and their footsteps echoed hollowly on the weathered planking. Stars flared and glittered in the black sky above and on the water the Chinese tong-kangs flitted silently to and fro, their running lights scattering a gleaming wake behind them.

Ethan had placed a hand beneath China's elbow, and though she disliked being touched by him, she found herself leaning gratefully against it. Both Nappy and Julia met them by the entry port, and such was China's weariness that she tolerated their scolding without a murmur and did not think to question Julia's presence on board the ship or even object as she was whisked below and put to bed like a child. She fell at once into an exhausted slumber from which she did not awaken until the following morning when the green headland of her beloved island lay just beyond the brigantine's bow.

"Oh, Nappy!" she cried joyously, coming topside and running lightly to the rail. "It's every bit as beautiful as I remember!"

The *Kowloon Star* was sailing through a stretch of dazzling blue water, her canvas reflecting blinding white on the glass-clear surface. The ship was drawing well, running above shoals of brilliant coral in which schools of rainbow-colored fish darted to and fro. Across the aquamarine water Badajan's lush green mountains soared into a sky of crystalline blue, every jagged contour achingly familiar to China's eyes.

She pointed eagerly. "Do you see the volcano there between those mountains? My grandfather was alive the last time it erupted, and in his journal he described how the lava flowed down to the shore and—Oh, do look, there's the beach where my brother Brandon and I used to swim! Do you see it there to the right of those rocks?" She could not take her eyes off that white stretch of sand with its swaying palms and lapping tide.

Privately Nappy was of the opinion that there was little to distinguish Badajan from most of the other islands flung like a chain of dusky jewels across the transparent water, yet he could not help but respond with a grin to China's enthusiasm.

"Where's the 'ouse at?" he queried, seeing no break at all in the dense jungle before him.

"It's on the leeward side of the island, above the deepwater dock that my great-grandfather built." China's eyes sparkled as she recalled the excitement that had surrounded the arrival of the schooners that called once a month with mail and goods from the mainland. How like a holiday it had seemed, and she could remember scurrying down to the docks with Brandon at her heels to collect the candy and honeyed coconut awaiting them in the charthouse.

"It seems a beautiful place," Julia Clayton said with a sigh, drawn to the rail by the sound of China's happy chatter. Badajan seemed a sun-drenched paradise to her, the product of working-class parents born and raised amid the soot-blackened houses of Sheffield. "I do so wish I was going ashore with you," she said wistfully, then added brightly, "but I'm afraid I simply can't." Her eyes had come to rest possessively on the tall man standing at his customary place near the helm. "Captain Bloodwell has agreed to take me with him to Djakarta."

China grew still at her casual words but Julia, not noticing, continued gaily: "From the captain's description I gather Java will be far more civilized than Singapore, and certainly much less lonely, since he has promised to introduce me to some of his friends. It was kind of him to offer to do so, don't you think?"

China nodded. Julia had warned her clearly that she intended to pursue the captain, hadn't she? And it wasn't as if she herself was in the least enamored of him! On the contrary, she couldn't tolerate the man, and yet Julia's scandalous disclosure had, oddly enough, served to dampen the happiness of her homecoming.

"Now 'oo in 'ell can that be?" Nappy mused, and China, grateful for the diversion, shaded her eyes to peer across the water at a sleek white skiff beating toward them from around the headland, taut sails cracking in the wind.

"Why, it's the *Tempus!*" she cried excitedly. "My father's yacht!"

Leaning over the rail she watched eagerly as the skiff dropped sail and drew alongside the brigantine's salt-blistered hull, the dark-headed young man at the helm receiving prompt permission to come aboard. Scrambling up the boarding nets, he drew himself erect, and it was a commendable facet of his character that he did not so much as blink an eye as he found himself confronted by a dozen hostile-eyed seamen whose raffish appearances served to underscore the unscrupulous name the *Kowloon Star* had earned for herself in these waters.

"Good afternoon," said Captain Bloodwell, striding forward to greet him. "I take it you've come for Miss Warrick?"

"I have." Darwin Stepkyne, several years younger and considerably shorter than Ethan Bloodwell, regarded the sea captain with ill-concealed disapproval. He had never stood face-to-face with the man before, but knew enough of his character—mostly from hearsay—to decide that his appearance, like his reputation, did nothing to commend him.

"Mr. Damon Warrick has charged me with seeing his sister safely home," he said coolly. "May I ask where she might be?" His tone indicated that he would not be at all surprised if the unscrupulous captain had kept her clapped in irons in the rat-infested steerage.

"Certainly," Ethan said obligingly. "She's over there by the railing."

Darwin Stepkyne turned and found himself staring into a pair of eyes that all but took his breath away. He would never have believed that anyone could possess eyes quite so wide and green or that they could slope at the corners in the mysterious manner of a Balinese temple cat.

"Miss—Miss Warrick?" he gulped.

"Oh, Darwin, have I really changed that much?" China inquired with a soft laugh.

He stammered an affirmative, unable to believe that this was the same little girl who had wept silent tears on the morning she and her father had sailed for Singapore, her pinafore crumpled, the ribbons in her bright red hair drooping in the heat. There was a portrait of China Warrick in the study at the plantation house, but she had been a child then, baby-faced and petulant. Though the angular planes of her cheekbones and the long, expressive fingers caressing the marmoset on her lap gave evidence to the beauty she would one day become, few observers looked far enough beyond the boyish crop of red curls to notice.

Darwin Stepkyne had certainly never bothered to. As manager of King's Wheal Plantation, his vision rarely extended beyond the pages of his ledgers. He remembered China Warrick only as a disconcertingly precocious child determined to learn the secrets of silk-making in order that she might help her adored father run the plantation when she was old enough.

Race Warrick had indulged her, of course, at first because it amused him to humor his daughter and later, realizing she had been born with the same passion for silk as Warrick men, had studiously begun teaching her the intricacies of the art. Darwin, recently returned from university and struggling to fill his own father's shoes, had viewed the child as little more than an annoyance. Eventually he became so accustomed to her presence that he rarely gave her a second thought, yet this grown-up China Warrick warranted more than a casual look, and Darwin couldn't help staring. He was convinced that none of the young ladies residing in Singapore's European community could possibly rival this dramatic creature.

China was quite unaware of his spellbound expression, for she was guilty of an equally forward perusal, remembering Darwin only as an awkward, bookish youth who lived in constant terror of her father. He had grown older since she'd been away, of course, but still appeared just as pleasantly dull as he had been then, his thin legs too long for the cotton trousers he wore, the ink stain on his lower lip giving evidence to the fact that he still liked to nibble his ink pens.

Captain Bloodwell, who had by this time grown thoroughly bored with Darwin's openmouthed staring and China's pensive silence, put an end to their encounter by chiding, "I'm afraid you've neglected to introduce us, Miss Warrick."

China blushed painfully, yet her heightened color merely served to enhance her incredible loveliness in Darwin's eyes, and he paid scant attention to the names she supplied in response. "If you would see to Miss Warrick's luggage, Captain," he said briskly, making no attempt to hide the fact that he was eager to depart with his prize.

"Hafiz, ready a launch for Miss Warrick and see that her trunks are safely stowed," Ethan Bloodwell ordered, and his narrowed eyes regarded Darwin closely. "We were given to understand that no one would come for Miss Warrick until tomorrow."

"We had thought the same," Darwin said agreeably, "but the repairs to the skiff were completed sooner than anticipated." He cleared his throat and added with an uncomfortable glance in China's direction, "Ever since the *Bonne Heure* went down with Master Warrick last summer we've had only the one. She snapped a line with Master Damon yesterday, and it's been the devil itself to fix."

"Then the *Bonne Heure* was never recovered?" China inquired.

"I'm afraid not. Nor Master Warrick, either."

"I see. I didn't know. Mother's letter was so vexingly uninformative."

"He was on his way to Singapore when a squall blew up," Darwin told her, deciding she might as well hear the tragic details from him. "You know how quickly they can swoop down from the north."

China remembered clearly that the fickle Asian winds were a force to be reckoned with, and she could well imagine how the *Bonne Heure* had been smashed to pieces on the coral shoals, making it impossible for her father's body to be recovered. And even if he hadn't gone down with the skiff, there must surely have been sharks.

"I believe the launch is ready, Miss Warrick," Ethan said briskly. "Rajiid, will you see Miss Warrick to the skiff?" he inquired of the dark-eyed Arab who stood silently nearby.

"Really, Captain, there's no need—" Darwin began frostily, only to fall silent as he saw something in those hard blue eyes that was far from pleasant. Turning back to China to manfully escort her himself, he was annoyed to find that she had abandoned him in order to bid farewell—fondly, no less—to the unsavory members of Captain Bloodwell's crew.

He witnessed this unheard-of spectacle in silence, but when China went so far as to actually return the awkward embrace of a noisome little fellow with a hideously bruised face and an eyepatch, his sensibilities got the better of him and he moved forward to intervene. Instantly an iron arm barred his way and he found himself looking into a pair of eyes as cold and blue as eternal ice. Not a word passed between them, and after a moment Captain Bloodwell released him, inquiring affably over his shoulder if Miss Warrick was ready to depart.

China nodded and offered him her hand, but he made no move to take it. "There's no need to say farewell, Miss Warrick, at least not yet." He grinned impudently into her startled eyes. "Have you forgotten that I intend to pay a call on your brother when I return from Djakarta?"

In truth China had, and it was an unpleasant reminder at a time when she was feeling apprehensive about the homecoming she had dreamed of for years. She murmured an assurance that her brother would welcome him upon his return, and allowed the hovering Darwin to help her into the boat.

Amid the whirring of well-oiled pulleys, the two of them were lowered into the water, and those gathered at the rail were granted a brief glimpse of China's red hair before the weathered launch deposited her at the Warrick yacht. Though she must have felt their eyes upon her as she stepped aboard, China did not turn, and only Ethan Blood-well's eyesight was keen enough to detect the oddly defeated droop of her small shoulders.

Chapter Nine

There had never been need for either carriages or roads on the mountainous island of Badajan, as its inhabitants traveled on foot along the overgrown jungle paths or astride the superb Arabian horses Race Warrick had bred since his youth. Silks and supplies were transported to and from the enormous dock via drays so that the drive leading to the house was little more than a narrow strip of sand. The green-shaded jungle pressed close on either side, held at bay by ranks of stately palms whose fronds stirred restlessly in the muggy air as China and Darwin ascended the moss-grown watersteps.

China could feel her dress clinging uncomfortably to her back and she could hardly wait to shed her muslin gown for the coolness of native silk. She wished that Darwin would cease his endless prattle about market fluctuations and profit percentiles as it was only making her feel cross. There would be plenty of time to discuss the family business later; at the moment, she was interested only in the tall white house that was visible above the blossom-covered crowns of the frangipani trees ahead.

Undaunted by the fierce winds of the monsoon season, Sir Kingston Warrick had built his house high on an unprotected knoll overlooking the docks and the dazzling sea beyond. The white-plastered walls of the three-story structure were lined with terraces and arching windows, and a rambling veranda wrapped itself about the main block and along the tiered wings that ran in either direction to be lost amid the sprawling gardens. The imposing front door was framed with glass and studded in brass in the manner of houses built along the Persian Gulf, and flanked by soaring white columns distinctly at odds with this singularly Eastern affectation.

Its appearance, perhaps intentionally so, brought to mind the pleasant country houses of Sir Kingston's native Sussex, and ungracious visitors were wont to describe it as an apt symbol of the arrogance of the Warrick dynasty. And yet it was reassuring to see that little had changed during the long years of China's absence. The plantain palms in the flower-choked garden were perhaps a bit larger, and fragrant purple creepers had wrapped themselves over the veranda railing and edged onto the gabled roof. Otherwise, there was nothing in its appearance to distinguish this day from a blistering hot morning six years ago when China had hurried down the path at her father's side, taking two running steps to his one long stride, her lower lip caught between her teeth as she willed herself not to cry.

"Has it changed very much?" Darwin asked.

"No, not really." China's voice quavered despite herself, for she had been thinking that however familiar everything might appear on the outside, it could never be the same now that her father was gone. His death had not seemed quite real to her in England, and somehow she had managed to push away her gnawing grief during the time at sea. Yet here, remembering how his laughing presence had filled the high-ceilinged rooms and made them seem so cosy, it was impossible to continue the pretense any longer.

"Is my mother at home?"

"Mrs. Warrick is presently in Djakarta." Darwin cleared his throat and added hesitantly, "It was something of a shock for us to learn that you had sailed from England aboard the *Kowloon Star*. Captain Bloodwell doesn't usually make it a habit of transporting passengers." He regarded her curiously, but China offered him nothing in the way of explanation.

She didn't say anything at all, in fact, for she hadn't even been listening. A hot, hard lump had formed in her throat as they crossed the arching cypress bridge leading from the footpath to the entrance of the house, and she was aware of nothing but the confusion of emotions that overwhelmed her. Pink water hyacinths choked the pond beneath them and the water was so clear that China could see the ornamental Japanese carp feeding among the polished pebbles. She found herself wondering if Brandon had kept his promise to look after them in her absence.

Her skirts rustled softly as she ascended the steps and crossed the wide front porch. The lump in her throat had grown larger, and she found herself breathless, her hand shaking as she reached for the bell pull.

"Psst! China!"

She drew back, startled. "What—? Brandon?" Her head came around. "Where are you?"

"Over here!"

The bougainvillea tumbling over the veranda rail quivered and suddenly a round, mischievous face with enormous green eyes was peering out at her. Mulberry juice stained the front of what had once been a clean white shirt, and the boy's dark red hair was covered with twigs and dried leaves. China's breath caught in her throat as she looked down at him. Brandon's uncanny resemblance to his father made her heart turn over, and she wasn't at first certain what she should make of this grinning twelve-year-old who had been little more than a baby when she had gone away.

"Brandon?" she asked hesitantly. Would he remember her at all?

The creepers snapped loudly as he wiggled through them and China was almost knocked from her feet as his sturdy little body hurled against her skirts and clung there.

"Oh, China, I'm so glad you're home! I didn't think you'd ever come back!"

"I promised I would, didn't I?" she chided softly.

"Yes, but—"

"Shouldn't you be at your lessons, Brandon?" Darwin interrupted, feeling rather like an intruder as he watched China hug the little boy to her.

"I wanted to wait for China to come," Brandon confessed unashamedly. "I overheard Damon telling Al-Haj you had gone to fetch her."

"You shouldn't eavesdrop," China reproved, her arms still about him.

He grinned at her, revealing a raffish gap between his front teeth. "I'm sorry. I didn't mean to."

Looking down at him, China couldn't find it in her heart to rebuke him. He was not particularly tall for his age, for Warrick men were shorter than average, though very strong, but he was handsome and bright, and obviously possessed a great deal of the swaggering Warrick charm.

"Damon was hopping mad about your coming home, China. I think it was because you sailed from England on Ethan Bloodwell's ship. He said Captain Bloodwell was a cad and a bloody womanizer and that you would have been better off—"

"Brandon! You mustn't repeat such things!"

"I know, but that's what he said. What's a womanizer, China?"

"Someone who is rude and objectionable," she replied, shaking out her rumpled skirts without giving the matter further thought.

Darwin uttered a strangled cough, and reddened when China glanced at him questioningly. "Perhaps we should go inside," he suggested. "Master Damon will be waiting."

"I'll take you, China," Brandon offered, sliding his small hand into hers. "He's in the study writing letters. Philippa's still in the schoolroom. She hates 'rithmetic but Mr. Lim won't let her go 'til she gets her sums right."

"Mr. Lim?"

"He's our new tutor. Mr. Tenyon went back to India when Papa died, so Damon asked Mr. Lim to teach us because he can speak Malay and English just as good as Chinese. I don't like him very much. Are you home for good, China?"

"Yes, I am."

"Damon's been awfully busy since Papa died, you know. He hasn't had any time for us at all. We haven't been to Singapore in ages, but Mama promised she'd take us when she got back from Java. Now that you're here you can go with us, too, can't you, China?"

She couldn't help but smile. "I don't see why not. Does Philippa—"

"Well, well, if it isn't Great-uncle Esmund's little starveling! Though I must confess you certainly aren't the skinny chit who left here six long years ago!"

China whirled about, her petticoats belling. "Damon!"

"What's this?" he inquired, crossing the porch to embrace her and seeing her wince in response. "Not happy to see me?"

Laughing and crying all at once, China assured him she was delighted although his careless handling had hurt her wounded back. She was relieved that he didn't seem to notice the thick bandage wrapped about her shoulder which the tufted sleeves of her gown helped conceal.

"You've grown into a hell of a beauty, hasn't she, Win?" Damon inquired, holding her at arm's length and surveying her critically. "I'm convinced you'll have every pretty piece in Singapore turning green with envy. Egad, that hair! There'll be talk of witches in the kampongs once the natives catch a glimpse of you."

"Witches!" China echoed.

Damon laughed at her startled expression. "Welcome back to the East, my love, where witchcraft and superstition vie for supremacy with the white man's notion of progress and enlightenment! Race may have had red hair," he added thoughtfully, "but not in the least like yours. What a pity he died before he had the chance to see what a fiery little creature he'd sired!"

China could feel the tight band of anxiety around her heart begin to ease. This was Damon as she remembered him: cryptic, outspoken, and exasperating, yet always the endearing rogue. He had been fifteen when she went away, a solemn boy wavering on the brink of manhood, and handsome beyond belief with his mother's brown eyes and proud, dark features, always at odds with her father and anyone else who represented authority.

He was twenty-one now, a grown man, and taller than she had expected him to be. How handsome he appeared in his casually turned up shirtsleeves and loose trousers, browned by the sun and grinning at her with familiar impudence! China could think of at least a dozen fellow inmates at Miss Crenshawe's Seminary who would have swooned at the mere sight of him.

"Let's have refreshments," Damon suggested, tucking her arm beneath his. "Win's probably told you that Mother isn't here. I expect her back tomorrow. Come inside, Darwin, and Brandon, fetch your sister. We'll have sherbet in the courtyard."

Brandon brightened. "Honeyed almonds, too?"

"If Al-Haj can be persuaded to part with them."

"I'm so anxious to meet Philippa," China confessed as Damon held open the door for her. "Though she's written me diligently over the last two years, and such amusing letters, it isn't quite the same as confronting someone face-to-face. I've never really grown accustomed to the fact that I have a sister I've never seen!"

"She was born less than a month after you left," Damon said briefly, dismissing the event as though it had been a mere oversight on his mother and stepfather's part, which, if the truth must be told, it had. "She's seven now, and a quiet little thing, shy and extremely fragile."

An invalid, China remembered from one of Malvina Warrick's rare letters. The child's arrival had come as a surprise to everyone, and not a wholly welcome one at that. Even her father, China had surmised from missives received in later years, had been rather disappointed with the sickly little girl his wife had borne him.

She herself had not preconceived notions about her younger sister, only the vague impression of a precocious, warm-hearted person dwelling in the drawings and later the brief letters written in a peculiar, childish scrawl that had poured with astonishing regularity into the old Earl's home. She could scarcely wait to tell Philippa how much they had brightened her own existence.

"Come, sit down," Damon invited.

Having grown accustomed to the dark, overstuffed furniture crowding the rooms at Broadhurst, China had forgotten the spare splendor that permeated a tropical plantation house. On the outside King's Wheal might rival an English country manor, but heat, humidity, and the preference of Sir Kingston himself had decreed the cool, uncluttered decor of an Eastern palace. The rooms were large and high-ceilinged, lined with open windows to take advantage of the cooling ocean breezes, and fitted with painted shutters that could be barred against the blinding heat or the driving power of the monsoon rains.

The coral-toned receiving room into which Damon led her was decorated with gilded mirrors and priceless Persian rugs and separated by high, wrought-iron gates from a central courtyard that was opened to the sky and in which a fountain murmured softly. Terraces leading to private sitting rooms and bedchambers were situated beneath its arching plaster walls, the tall glass doors flanked by massive stone containers planted with orchids. A pair of cockatoos preened on ornate stands in one of the arching doorways while a female bearer in a gold-embroidered sarong fed them seeds and dried fruit from a shallow glass bowl.

China seated herself on a tassled cushion and accepted with a smile of thanks the eggshell-thin cup she was offered. "It feels wonderful to be home," she said, sighing. "I cannot believe all those years of waiting are finally over!"

"It's been a long time, hasn't it?" Damon agreed, smiling at her over the rim of his glass.

"I think I'll ride down to the village once my trunks have been unpacked and visit Tan Ri and Tonna's grandmother," China added. Her earlier apprehension and the feeling of strangeness had fled and she was eager to visit the friends she had dreamed of seeing for so long.

"I'm afraid most of the old guard isn't here anymore," Damon told her apologetically, accepting another brandy from the hovering servant. "We've less than a dozen groundskeepers nowadays and an even smaller household staff."

"But surely Tonna is still here?" China protested, referring to the Indonesian woman who had raised her from birth.

Damon shook his head. "She went to Macasar not long after you left. Come, now, don't look so stricken! Race gave her ample compensation."

"And Tan Ri?"

"He's been dead for . . . hmm . . . two or three years now. You have to remember he was old even before you went away."

"Yes, I suppose he was."

"How like softhearted China to mourn her servants," Damon remarked not unkindly. "You haven't changed an iota, have you? It's one of the reasons Mother decided to send you away. You were becoming too much like them, spending your time down in the kampongs picking up all of that Taoist claptrap about sacrifices, demon gods, and the like. I imagine those stuffy women at Mrs. Crenshawe's Seminary had quite a task screwing your head on properly, eh?"

He chuckled and stretched his long legs more comfortably before him. "At any rate, I'm deuced glad you're back."

"I am, too," China said with a smile. Taking a sip of the fragrant Arabic coffee, she asked hesitantly, "Has it been very difficult for you since Father died?"

"We've managed," Damon said with a shrug, "though I daresay it's far easier now than it was at first. Why don't you tell us something about England?"

Before China could answer, the tapping of sticks across the stone floor could be heard, and China looked around to see a little girl of some six or seven years lurching toward her on crutches, her face glowing with excitement. Auburn ringlets fell to the shoulders of her crinkly white pinafore and there was a smattering of freckles across her small, upturned nose.

"Oh, Brandon, I was right!" she cried, addressing the boy beside her. "She's as pretty as a fairy princess!"

"Hello, Philippa," China said warmly and stooped to pull the little girl into her arms.

Unaccustomed to displays of affection, Philippa stiffened, but only for a moment, for China's embrace was warm and soft. A subtle scent of roses clung to her gown and Philippa breathed deeply of it as she wiggled timidly closer.

"You're not going to go away anymore, are you?"

"No, I'm not," China said firmly and her throat ached in response to Philippa's contented sigh.

"Tell us the truth," Damon prodded, leaning back against the cushions. "Was it so very awful?"

"Not all of it," China admitted, thinking fondly of the sweeping lawns and gracious reception rooms of Broadhurst.

While Brandon and Philippa listened round-eyed, she spoke of her great-uncle and his courtly ancestral home, of Lyddie Broyles, Weston, and dear, grizzled Chauncey. Freddy and Cassie were dismissed with little more than a terse acknowledgment, for China had resolved to speak to Damon privately concerning her reason for fleeing England and why she had had no other choice than to do so aboard Ethan Bloodwell's *Kowloon Star*. There would be time for that later, plenty of time. Right now she wanted to savor her homecoming and enjoy the companionship of her family and forget that her scheming cousins even existed.

It came as something of a surprise to all of them when a servant interrupted to announce that tiffin had been prepared, a light meal of subtle Indian flavor that, as was Warrick tradition, was taken on the veranda every afternoon. Darwin turned down the invitation to dine and hastened back to the sheds, certain that he had neglected the workers long enough.

"We'll take a tour of the plantation tomorrow before the heat rises," Damon said to China, and lifting Philippa to her feet, he herded them out to the veranda where a table had been laid in the cool, blossom-scented shade.

The sea sparkled through the rustling green leaves of the breadfruit trees, and a refreshing breeze dispersed the heavy rainclouds that had gathered from the north. A wind chime tinkled pleasantly and China paused for a moment near the steps, drinking in the beauty of the garden with its enormous Bodhi trees, flowering orchids, and carefully tended oyster-shell walks.

"Would you like to ride down to the village with me

after lunch?" she inquired of Philippa, dismissing in her eagerness the possibility that her wound might make it impossible for her to ride herself.

Philippa's pretty face crumpled. "I can't."

"Why not? Surely those sticks don't prevent you?"

"It's because she hasn't got a pony of her own," Brandon explained. "There's only Serab left in the stable and he's too big and wild."

China's startled eyes went to her half-brother, who had seated himself at the head of the table. "What happened to Father's horses?"

"I sold them."

"You sold them! Why?"

Damon shrugged. "I didn't see the need to keep them any longer. You and Race were the only ones who ever rode, not to mention that their upkeep was getting extremely costly."

"We don't have to keep blood ponies," China protested. "And what about Brandon and Philippa? It's important that they learn to ride. What could a new pair of hacks possibly cost?"

Damon frowned, looking every bit as stubborn as his mother. "Too much, I'm afraid. You mustn't forget that this is Indonesia, not England. You can't send a servant into the nearest city for the luxuries you lack. The ponies would have to come from Calcutta or perhaps even farther—Oman or Aden—and the cost of transportation is high."

In her father's time, things like cost had never been considered, and China found herself wondering uneasily if financial woes had beset King's Wheal since Race's death. Could this be what the American clipper captain had meant when he spoke of troubles on Badajan?

China took a bite of honeyed fruit though she scarcely tasted its sweetness. If this was indeed true, what was Damon going to say when she told him that she owed Captain Ethan Bloodwell two hundred pounds?

"No need to scowl so, love," Damon chided, catching sight of her expression. "If a pony really means that much to you, I'll speak to Mother about it."

"That would be kind of you," China said glumly, knowing perfectly well that the money would end up going to settle her debt to Ethan Bloodwell. Oh, it was all so vexing! Why had she ever promised that reprehensible man so much money?

When Malvina Warrick returned from Djakarta the following morning it was to find her eldest daughter unexpectedly in residence and apparently up to her old tricks: making friends with the servants. Hurrying upstairs, Malvina was taken aback to find her daughter engaged in lively conversation with three dark-headed Malaysian girls who were pressing and packing away the heavy winter gowns China had brought with her from England.

Possessing a nimble command of languages and drawing on the words she remembered from her youth, China was in the act of describing to her giggling audience the Western custom of lacing oneself into painfully tight corsets and stays of leather-bound whalebone, and laughing unaffectedly with them as she sorted through the billowing piles of crinolines and petticoats thrown across her bed. The high-ceilinged bedchamber was lined with rows of tall windows that opened on one side onto the cool of the courtyard and provided a dazzling view of the sea on the other. Malvina, stepping through the curtained arch leading from the outer salon, was startled by the sight of the four young women, three brown and one white, chattering comfortably together, their laughter rising softly above the tinkling of silver bracelets and ankle chains.

"I should have suspected!" she exclaimed, her words bringing an abrupt end to their merriment. "Who else but you, China, could possibly be at the bottom of this undignified horseplay?"

Clapping her hands, she sent the serving girls scurrying away and stood regarding her daughter with fondness and a trace of resignation. Despite the unrelieved severity of her dark green taffeta gown she was a handsome woman, her thick brown hair pinned in a dignified chignon at the base of a long, slender neck. Tall and somewhat mannish in deportment, Malvina Warrick possessed a heart-shaped face of astonishing beauty despite the lines that time had etched from the proudly flaring nostrils to her stern lips.

"You haven't changed a bit, have you, child?" she inquired with exasperation. "Damon told me as much, but I was inclined to believe your years in England had cured you of such inappropriate behavior. Didn't Livvy Crenshawe teach you that it simply isn't proper to consort with servants? It does nothing but breed contempt, though I daresay it was your father's fault; stuffing your head with nonsense about making friends with the natives and teaching you unladylike pursuits like swimming and shooting."

She had come forward as she spoke, to take China's chin in her cupped palm. "At any rate you've grown into a beauty," she decided approvingly. "I'm afraid the hair won't do—far too red it is, though I imagine what's to thank is the fact that you didn't bother wearing a bonnet on the voyage home. The tropical sun—"

She broke off abruptly and a faint smile touched her lips. "I believe those are the same words I said to you when you went away, aren't they?"

"Yes, Mother. You said I should be certain to wear a bonnet so I wouldn't arrive in England burned a shocking brown. You were afraid Great-uncle Esmund would mistake me for a native."

Malvina gave a soft laugh and her face was suddenly smooth and youthful. "I did say that, didn't I? How odd! I suppose things haven't changed much after all. Welcome home, dear."

Her embrace was fleeting, but China, accustomed to her mother's undemonstrative mannerisms, returned it gladly. In her own way, she sensed, Malvina was pleased to see her.

"You must be careful about becoming too familiar with the servants," Malvina resumed, her gaze falling to the partially filled trunks on the rug before her. "You're not a child anymore, and it simply isn't becoming."

"I'm sorry," China apologized, though she was thinking with dismay that her mother had grown considerably older in her absence, the once-smooth skin about her eyes lined with wrinkles, a slight stoop to her normally proud shoulders. Would her father, she wondered, have aged this much, too?

It was unpleasant to discover that one's parents, the pedestal of permanence in one's life, could be so painfully mortal, and China was consumed with a rush of tenderness for the woman who had at one time garnered nothing but resentment within her. "I suppose I shouldn't have coaxed them into talking with me," she admitted. "It won't happen again."

"It will doubtless take time to reaccustom yourself to Eastern ways," Malvina allowed before dismissing the topic in favor of another. "You seem to have applied yourself quite diligently to your studies. Mrs. Crenshawe was extremely complimentary in her reports to me."

That had been in thanks, mainly, to the generous monthly stipends her father had established for her, China thought uncharitably, and not because Olivia Crenshawe had been overly impressed with her accomplishments. Oh, how she had loathed the emphasis on deportment, ballroom dancing, and needlepoint that had dominated the daily curriculum! Fluent in Malay, Cantonese, and Greek and well versed in the classics by the time she was enrolled in the fashionable seminary, China had quickly grown bored with her studies. And boredom, coupled with loneliness and the discovery that she had nothing in common with the other girls, who dreamed of debuts and the beaux they would conquer, had served to make her a thoroughly indifferent student.

"Now that you're here I plan to put your education to good use," Malvina added, pleased with the practical aspects of having a carefully polished daughter in the house. "You may begin by acting as hostess whenever your brother entertains clients. Doubtless you'll be far better at it than I am."

"Why, thank you, Mother," China said with considerable surprise. "I'd be delighted. I wasn't aware that we entertained our buyers."

"It's a custom Damon started after your father's death," Malvina explained, "and I'm pleased to say he's been doing rather well in that respect. Race was never one to lavish attention on his guests, but we consider it most important."

"I'd be happy to help," China said again, though the sudden tilt of her chin was one even Ethan Bloodwell, in such a short space of time, had learned to view with a jaundiced eye. Though China did not object to pouring tea and engaging in polite conversation with Damon's guests, she had no intention of spending all of her time thusly occupied! She wanted to help Darwin produce silk, to take the shimmering material in her hands and work with it as her father had taught her.

"I want to help in the sheds, too," she told her mother, seating herself on the edge of the daybed and watching as Malvina sorted through the gowns she had been folding away.

"I'm afraid you'll be far too busy for that," Malvina objected. "We've people coming continuously nowadays. Oh, China, these gowns are lovely! You'll have everyone pea green with envy!"

"About helping Damon in the sheds—" China resumed.

"Perhaps you should wait and discuss that with Damon," Malvina suggested. "Though you should be forewarned that your duties as hostess will take considerable time. Oh, China, this moiré antique is magnificent! I've never seen such elaborate embroidery! Why don't you wear it when the Sandringhams come next week?" Turning, Malvina favored her daughter with a critical glance. "Mourning black does not become you, child, and it only makes the heat seem far more unendurable. You should pack all of that away now that you're home." She shook out the wide skirt of the beautiful ballgown and held it aloft. "I've never seen anything like it!" she repeated with a sigh. "You'll wear this when the Sandringhams come, won't you?"

"Of course, Mother," China said automatically, though she was not about to let the matter of working with Damon drop simply because her mother did not profess enthusiasm for the idea.

"Why, certainly, you're welcome to help," Damon assured her when they met for coffee later that morning. "I'm just wondering if you remember how difficult the work actually is."

"I'm not at all certain I approve of your spending time in the sheds, child. I'd far rather you remained indoors," Malvina said.

China might have acquiesced to her mother's wishes had those not been the exact words Malvina had uttered, though in considerably frostier tones, years ago when China had first professed an interest in silk. Recalling how her father had laughed in response, pointing out with pride that his daughter was "all Warrick" and not the least afraid of heat, dust, scorpions, or spiders, China's resolve held firm. And Malvina, recognizing the all-too-familiar look that crossed her daughter's face, threw up her hands in defeat.

"Very well, child, do as you wish. I can see you're every bit as stubborn as your father was!"

China smiled. "Thank you, Mother. And I promise I won't let my work in the sheds interfere with entertaining Damon's guests."

"What's this?" Damon inquired, startled. Swiveling about in his chair he fixed his mother with a curious glance.

"China has agreed to act as hostess for me," Malvina informed him proudly. "Though of course there are certain clients I intend to keep for myself. I'm sure you know the ones I mean, dear."

"It seems an excellent idea," Damon allowed, his thoughtful gaze falling on the slim, muslin-clad form of his half-sister. "And as for working in the sheds, China," he resumed, "it would probably be advisable to pay them a visit before making your decision. It may be that things are quite different from the way you remember them." He glanced at his pocket watch. "Darwin should be there by now, and I'm certain he'd be happy to take you on a tour. I'm afraid I won't be able to join you as I've already neglected my paperwork long enough."

China brightened. "May I take Serab in that case?"

"Of course. Wait a moment and I'll ring for your gloves."

She thanked him with a warm smile and hurried upstairs to change into her habit. Hearing the door on the landing slam in an unladylike fashion behind her, Damon sought his mother's eyes, and he grinned.

"Contrary to what anyone might think, I'm deuced glad to have her back!"

"You know, I think you're right, love," Malvina said, and she began to hum as she poured herself coffee from the nearby cart.

Chapter Ten

China Warrick's green eyes glowed with excitement as she emerged from a dense stand of jungle below the plantation house astride her brother's coal black Arabian stallion. Her wounded back was healing well, and only the slight stiffness of her posture gave evidence to the fact that it continued to pain her. Keeping Serab to a decorous trot, though she would have dearly enjoyed a gallop, she drew rein at last in the shade of a towering catalpa in order to watch a group of Malay laborers stripping mulberry trees in the sandy orchard below her. The leaves that were being placed into their waiting baskets were intended, she knew, for the soy concoction her great-grandfather had formulated years ago to sate the ravenous appetites of his newly hatched worms.

The laborers, wearing coolie hats to protect themselves from the scorching sun, bowed respectfully in China's direction, and she inclined her head to acknowledge their greeting. They were paid workers, for slavery was not tolerated on the island, and the custom of kowtowing to one's superiors to demonstrate obeisance was strictly for-

bidden. No Warrick, Sir Kingston had once said, should
ever permit another human being to grovel at his feet,
and his word, like all others he uttered, had become ir-
revocable law.

Setting her restless mount trotting into the clearing,
China found herself comparing the chattering workers with
the wretchedly paid and poorly fed scullery maids and
bootblacks at Broadhurst. Great-uncle Esmund had tolerated no abuse of his servants, yet the stroke he had
suffered the year before his death had left him too infirm
to maintain the household alone, forcing him reluctantly
to give the upper hand to his granddaughter. And it hadn't
taken long for Cassie's tyrannical manner to instill terror
into the hearts of his loyal staff.

Dismissal without compensation had followed on the
heels of even the slightest infractions, and Cassie's volatile
temper had all too often been piqued by the most trivial
of offenses. China had often seen her slap the overworked
maids for not obeying orders quickly enough, and had chafed
at being forced to hold her silence, aware that her great-
uncle's health would only suffer were she to burden him
with the truth. What had become of the poor creatures
since she had sailed away on the *Kowloon Star?* Had Lyddie Broyles given notice as she had so often threatened to
do, and had Anna, in Freddy's unkind words, promptly
been "sacked"? And where was she now if that were indeed
the case? Without references it would be all but impossible
for her to find another post.

Jerking savagely on Serab's off-side rein, China told
herself that she mustn't feel guilty at having been forced
to abandon them. Especially not when one considered the
circumstances surrounding her own departure! Her lips
tightened. It would serve no purpose to dwell on the misery
that had compromised her last few days in England. Like
the rest of her life, it lay in the past and was better off
forgotten.

China turned down the sandy footpath leading toward
Badajan's extinct volcano, whose shelving, tree-choked base
formed a natural clearing, offering ideal protection from
the monsoon storms that raged twice annually across the
island. Here, inside a cluster of thatched-roof sheds, Ba-

dajan silk was produced in time-honored fashion, the silk-worm cocoons that had been culled from egg production being steamed to kill the pupae developing inside and then unraveled into the filaments of thread that, once woven, would yield the shimmering golden beauty of Badajan silk.

The surrounding jungle steamed in the aftermath of an earlier rain, and the jade green darkness was alive with the screaming of birds and the shrilling of insects. The scent of frangipani hung heavy in the humid air and China breathed deeply, thinking to herself that even the most fragrant roses in an English garden could not possibly rival their sweetness. Mountains rose sharply before her, their peaks lost in misting clouds, and amid the dripping lobes of the breadfruit leaves China could see patches of hot blue sky. Wild orchids entwined themselves about the serpentine trunks of liana trees and the air was alive with the cooing of doves feasting on soybeans ripening in the rich volcanic soil.

Leaving Serab tied outside the first of a half-dozen rambling, single-story buildings, China lifted her skirts and stepped into the warm, musty darkness. She had not forgotten that utmost cleanliness was vital in keeping the silkworms free of disease, and paused inside the door to trade her tiny boots for a pair of wooden clogs. As her eyes adjusted to the dimness, she made her way from the narrow anteroom into the first of the sheds.

Here a stout Chinese silk mother stood silent vigil before the countless rows of trays containing the growing worms and their endless rations of mulberry fodder. In her hand she carried a tail feather plucked from one of the peacocks roaming wild on the island. Sharp black eyes narrowed in concentration, she wandered back and forth among the trays, pausing here and there to prod a sluggish worm with an expert flick of her feather. The more the silkworms ate, of course, the faster they grew and the sooner they would spin themselves into their fat white cocoons of raw silk fiber.

"Our joss good, very good," she said in response to China's query. "We burn joss sticks many nights after your honorable father's death. Our vigilance was rewarded greatly."

"Greatly, greatly," a companion echoed, smiling tooth-
ily. Reaching into the front of her voluminous apron she
drew out a small scrap of cloth. "Ever see such lustrous
yarn, hey?"

Letting the filmy threads run through her fingers, China
agreed that it was beautiful beyond compare, her words
earning her the giggling approval of both women.

Moving into the weaving room, China waved to Darwin
Stepkyne who stood amid the clacking looms inspecting
the cloth as it spilled in pale golden strands into the waiting baskets. He brightened at the sight of her and hastened
to her side, mopping his brow and observing that it was
deuced humid this time of year and hoped that she was
not uncomfortable?

"Not at all," China assured him. Darwin stood en-
tranced by the enchanting face that smiled up into his.
With cream-colored ribbons tied beneath her chin and
wearing an ivory jacket that flared gently over her hips,
China looked impossibly fresh and lovely, her tilted green
eyes and rosy cheeks a welcome change for a young man
accustomed to the dark-skinned similarity of the native
girls.

"Very little has been altered since your father's death,"
he remarked in response to China's observations, though
he was wounded by the fact that she seemed more interested in the weaving process than in carrying on a conversation with him. "It would be foolish to tamper with
tried-and-true methods, wouldn't it? And your father's were
certainly the best."

"I see you've kept the work force here all Chinese,"
China added, peering beyond the looms into the next room,
where a group of young girls ranging in ages from ten to
thirteen were busily spinning silk from the fibers of pierced
cocoons that rested in woven baskets beside them.

"Oh, we wouldn't dare mix them!" Darwin was aghast
at the idea. "We've never had problems thanks to your
great-grandfather's foresight, though how he ever guessed
there would be friction between the Moslem Malays and
the Buddhist Chinese is beyond my ken. Fortunately the
Malays seem content in their role as farmers and they do
a crack job harvesting mulberry trees and growing soy-

beans. The Chinese, on the other hand, have proven time and again their skill at nurturing silkworms. They're very delicate creatures, you know. Temperamental, even," he added with a grin.

"Yes, I remember," China said, gazing with interest about her. There were perhaps a dozen looms set up in the long length of the weaving shed, each one operated by a Chinese woman whose features were hidden by a colorful silk kerchief. Hand weaving required utmost concentration, and none of them had been able to acknowledge her presence with more than a brief nod before they were forced to bend over their work once more.

"The Malay kampongs are still located on the far shore of the island," Darwin continued, hoping China wouldn't turn her head just yet and catch him admiring her charming profile. He knew that it was inexcusably rude of him to stare, but he couldn't seem to help himself. It was doubtful that he had ever seen anything quite as lovely as the smooth line of Miss Warrick's brow visible beneath the shadow made by the wide brim of her chip straw hat, or her small, straight nose or the disturbing fullness of her lower lip.

"I'm sure you remember that the Malaysians tend to keep well away from their Chinese co-workers," he added, "though we do employ an increasing number of immigrants who seem a bit more tolerant."

His voice dropped to a whisper despite the fact that the sound of the looms effectively drowned out his words. "Privately I don't mind telling you that I prefer the indigenous ones, Miss Warrick. You can investigate their personal histories more easily than those who show up asking for work and who might have committed any number of crimes in their native lands."

China nodded gravely though inwardly she was tempted to laugh. Darwin, she recalled, had always been afraid of the natives, whose dark faces, he was convinced, hid all sorts of unmentionable secrets. Of course there was nothing whatsoever to fear, for the tolerance Kingston Warrick had fostered among the first Malay and Chinese laborers employed at King's Wheal had not been weakened even after so many years. It was, as Sir Kingston had written in his journal, simply a matter of keeping the islanders' differing religious beliefs strictly separate while taking pains to accord each an equal amount of respect.

A naïve principle, perhaps, yet one that had worked well in Sir Kingston's time and which had been upheld by his son and grandson after him. Ignorance and intolerance, Race Warrick himself had believed, was responsible for a great deal of the racial tensions that plagued Singapore, Malaysia, and the other islands of Indonesia, and he had been adamant on the score that his own children should be raised to understand and appreciate the rich cultural heritages surrounding them. To that end China had been taught from childhood never to interrupt the faithful when they knelt and faced east to say their daily prayers, and to understand the legends and beliefs that prompted the sometimes frightening practices surrounding demon worship. She had been taught to speak both Cantonese and Malaysian, the predominant languages on Badajan, and the teachings of the *Tao-teh-king* had been required reading in the Warrick schoolroom.

"I'm certain you'll be pleased to know that your brother Damon has been doing rather well for himself," Darwin was saying as they strolled back to the packing sheds where young girls in colorful sarongs rolled bolts of silk in preparation for shipment. "He seems to have a flair for entertaining guests, which was certainly never your father's way."

"No, my father never had patience for that sort of thing," China agreed with a smile. "He was always far too busy here in the sheds to worry about exhorting buyers. And since there was always a greater demand for our silk than we could fulfill, there was never any need to tempt them with food and drink." She was silent as she pulled on her gloves, then lifted her eyes to Darwin's and inquired bluntly, "Has anything changed since his death?"

"It was quite difficult getting used to working without him," Darwin admitted. "His death was so sudden, after all. Fortunately the laborers were already accustomed to taking orders from me, as your father had always given me an appreciably free rein in dealing with them." He hesitated and then added, "I think things might have been far more difficult had Master Damon decided to start spending more time here in the sheds. The workers aren't used to dealing with him and they might have resented his intrusion. Fortunately he's always been content to handle the paperwork and the buyers and rarely comes down here at all."

"It would seem Mother sent the wrong offspring to England," China observed wryly, thinking that Damon would have enjoyed the teeming social life the Linvilles had led far better than she ever had. "I vow Damon would have succeeded splendidly as a London dandy."

Inwardly she was pleased by Darwin's implied vote of confidence in her brother. The doubts Captain Terence Aloysius of the clipper ship *Birmingham* had instilled within her were resolved, and she told herself that he must have been drunk, or perhaps being deliberately unkind, in hinting that Damon had been unable to run the plantation without her father's help. This precursory tour had made it clear to her that Badajan silk was still being produced in the same efficient manner and that an excellent yield was being anticipated from the latest harvest of silkworms that were at this moment being dried on racks in the adjoining room. And it pleased her, too, secretly, to learn that Damon showed no interest in working here in the sheds, for that would mean that there would doubtless be plenty for her to do.

"Do you intend to take an active part in the business?" Darwin inquired curiously, opening the weaving-room door for her.

China brushed past him, her cream-colored skirts held aloft, and said with a laugh, "Yes I do, and don't you dare lecture me or try to talk me out of it! I haven't forgotten a thing Father taught me."

"Oh, but I wouldn't dream of it, Miss China! Your brother and I would be very gratified if you would spend some of your time with us."

"Are you certain there's work for me to do?"

"Oh, any number of things! Your command of Cantonese, for example, would prove most helpful in dealing with the weavers who, you may recall," he added, his voice dropping once again to a conspiratorial whisper, "require constant supervision. And then there are the reelers, though perhaps it would be better if you stayed away from them. It's a rather foul-smelling and quite dirty task washing and unraveling cocoons, and I don't believe you'd care for it."

He looked at her expectantly, but China made no reply, for she hadn't even been listening to him. Her attention had been caught by a basket left on the earthen floor near the doorway, a basket she hadn't noticed before from which an odd cooing came to her above the clatter and whir of the looms.

"Why, it's a baby!" she exclaimed, stooping to peer inside. A tiny Chinese girl wrapped in raw silk swaddling, as enchanting as a porcelain doll, regarded her with curious green eyes.

"Miss China! You mustn't touch her!"

The horror in Darwin Stepkyne's voice made her whirl in alarm, the hand that had reached out to caress the petal-smooth cheek falling to her side. "Whyever not?"

Darwin's jaw worked nervously. "She—she's—Oh, blast! I'm afraid I'm not at liberty to explain."

"Why not? Is she ill?"

"No, she isn't ill."

Gazing impatiently into Darwin's reddened face, China waited for him to continue, yet when he showed no inclination of doing so, she glanced imperiously at the woman seated before the loom nearest them. "Is anything wrong with your daughter?" she queried in Cantonese and earned herself a blank look and a shake of the head in response.

"Let's forget I ever said anything at all," Darwin suggested uncomfortably. "There's nothing wrong with the child, really."

After a moment China said, "Very well," and, stepping around the basket without another word, went out into the hot sunshine.

Darwin, following close on her heels, was perfectly aware that any other woman, given the innate curiosity of her sex, would have pestered him in a most persistent manner. Miss Warrick, on the other hand, made no more mention of the child and merely observed as she replaced her wooden clogs with a pair of boots that she ought to be getting back to the house. Darwin found himself admiring her for the cool indifference with which she had chosen to handle his admittedly odd behavior, liking her in a way one would a very good and trusted male friend. And because he had never found himself actually liking a woman before, he lost all sense of proportion and promptly fell in love.

It was not astonishing that he should do so. His experience with women was, after all, limited to an occasional dinner party in the European quarter of Singapore in which he had proved himself far too shy to engage in clever conversation and too exceedingly clumsy to dance. Furthermore the only appreciable length of time he had spent away from Indonesia had been his years in Cambridge, where his fellow classmates had labeled him pleasant enough though a thoroughly unmitigated bore. His reclusive nature did not encourage social mingling, and while his connections to the Badajan Warricks might have opened a great number of doors for him had he desired it, Darwin had not. To the end result that he was lamentably unsure of himself in dealing with the fairer sex and knew nothing at all about comporting himself properly in their presence.

Today, however, he found himself seized with a reckless confidence heretofore unknown to him. Though China's striking beauty put her in a class of women whose very presence never failed to make him stammer and blush, he found himself of a sudden unable to curb his buoyancy, and chattered gaily as he accompanied her to the post where she had tethered her mount.

Unaware of the emotions roiling within him, China responded cheerfully to his banter and remarked politely that she had enjoyed their tour and hoped he would find her a useful asset to the family business. "After all, I may prove more of a hindrance than anything else," she admitted ruefully.

Consumed with longing as he gazed down into her pointed little face, Darwin assured her that any help she offered would be more than welcome. His pulse raced as she rewarded him with a smile, and he would have been sorely wounded to learn that she forgot him the moment her horse trotted off amid the trees.

It was over the Chinese infant that China brooded, and

Darwin's curious actions were still on her mind when she
joined her mother for tea in her elegant boudoir later that
afternoon. As Malvina dressed, China described to her
mother the plantation manager's odd behavior.

"I cannot imagine what was troubling him," she finished, leaning forward to set her teacup on a dainty table
of brass-inlaid teak. "He said I mustn't touch her and then
refused to tell me why." Her face paled as a sudden thought
struck her. "You don't suppose cholera has cropped up in
the kampongs, do you?"

"Oh, heavens, no!" Clipping on a pair of diamond ear-
bobs, Malvina stooped to examine the results in the
weather-dimmed reflection of the looking glass. "That must
have been Lien Chin's daughter you saw and Darwin didn't
want to tell you who she was. Such a blushing prig, that
boy!"

"Who is Lien Chin? One of the villagers?"

"She was the infant's mother though I believe she died
in childbirth." Malvina reached for the rouge and began
to apply it carefully to the hollows of her cheeks. Visitors
were expected at King's Wheal that evening and she wanted
to look her best. One of them, a wealthy Chinese mandarin
with a reportedly insatiable passion for silk, had traveled
all the way from Canton to place an order, and Malvina
intended to perform the time-honored ritual of serving the
refreshments herself.

"I'm afraid I don't remember the child's name," she said,
speaking to the reflection of her daughter that shimmered
in the mirror before her. "It's rather long and utterly silly.
Black Pearl of the Orient? I believe that may be it."

"But why on earth would Darwin treat her so oddly if
there isn't anything wrong with her?" China wondered.
"She's such a harmless little creature!"

"Probably because she's your half-sister." The long white
fingers never faltered in their application of facial powder.

"My *half-sister*? You must be mistaken, Mother. How
can she possibly—"

"Oh, really, child, don't be obtuse," Malvina said tartly.
"Lien Chin was one of your father's mistresses, and Black
Pearl his bastard daughter. She was born several months
after he died. I don't believe he ever knew of her existence."

She shrugged her bare shoulders and added sourly, "It's a wonder he never sired more of those half-caste creatures, being as promiscuous as he was. But then again one never knows how many red-headed Warrick brats are scampering about these islands."

The abrupt silence that followed her words was oppressive, and weighed down on China's chest like lead. The shutters in her mother's boudoir had been opened and a fresh, southwesterly wind blew inside, bringing with it the damp fragrance of frangipani from the garden. It was a smell that would remind China for the rest of her life of that particular moment, when the fragile fabric of her life was torn asunder and her innocence lay destroyed like the petals of a rose crushed by savage rain.

Rising woodenly to her feet she stumbled to the door and fled the sound of her mother's laughter: bitter and pitying and thus unkind beyond belief. Her slippers made no sound as she hurled down the long gallery that ran the length of the inner courtyard, and burst through the front door and into the hazy sunshine.

Tears streamed down her cheeks and hot, aching sobs tore from her throat. She ran blindly over the arching footbridge that spanned the placid pond and, tripping over her skirts as she reached the far side, would have fallen had she not landed sprawling in the arms of a man who had hastened across the grass to intercept her, startled by the crazed look on her face.

"China! What's happened?" He was shaking her, his fingers biting into her arms. "Are you hurt?"

China looked up, her vision blurred, into a hard face that for the first time in her memory was neither mocking nor unkind. She tried to speak but found she could not, and laying her head against Ethan Bloodwell's shoulder, she began to weep.

Chapter Eleven

Thick with tears, China's words were nearly impossible to understand, yet by the time she had spilled out her misery Ethan was seized with the unfortunate desire to laugh. Looking down at her bowed head, however, his amusement vanished and, unaccountably, anger stirred in its stead.

"Good God, Miss Warrick, is that all?"

China jerked away from him as though he had struck her, and he was forced to steel himself against the bitter betrayal he saw in her eyes. He was not about to let himself feel sorry for her, nor acknowledge the surprising warmth that had flowed through him when her slim body had been pressed against his.

"I imagine it was quite a shock to discover what sort of man your father was," he observed after a moment, folding his arms across his chest. "And having the evidence flung without warning into your face is doubly unpleasant."

"You seem to be quite familiar with the experience," China said stiffly, scrubbing furiously at her eyes.

"I've never met one of my offspring face-to-face," he allowed with considerable amusement, "or even caught wind of the fact that I have any, but I can assure you I would feel the same were one of them to knock upon my door."

"Would you?" she inquired, yet it was a listless question, for she had turned her back on him and her shoulders had drooped.

Ethan studied her for a moment in silence. She was standing before a cluster of hibiscus shrubs whose riotous white blossoms framed her unruly red curls. Butterflies bobbed and fluttered in iridescent colors about her, and the unexpected thought occurred to him that the beauty he had found so unusual when he had first seen her in the refined surroundings of Broadhurst was somehow far more disturbing here in this exotic and overgrown tropical garden. The thought filled him with an odd surge of anger and he frowned and said curtly, "Your father was human, Miss Warrick, with needs like any other man."

"That didn't give him the right to have Chinese mistresses," she accused.

"I'm not defending him," Ethan said mildly. "I'm merely suggesting that perhaps he was not particularly happy. Badajan is very remote, and with the exception of the work force, none but you Warricks reside upon it. It's entirely possible that he was a lonely man."

China's lips tightened. "He didn't have to be. He had me, and yet he allowed my mother to send me away!"

Ah, there was the rub, Ethan Bloodwell thought, gazing almost pityingly into her tear-stained face. It would seem that Race Warrick had failed his daughter on two counts; first by sending her away and then by dying before she could return, and worsening the bitter proof of his mortality was the damning presence of his bastard child.

"You know very well," he said brusquely, "that transposed Englishmen always send their daughters home to be educated until they come of age."

"I'm not a child you can pacify with simple words, Captain," China said frostily, refusing to see the truth of his statement. Bella and Dottie Harrleson had been sent home for the same reason, she knew, though Lucinda had insisted that it was only because children were so very vulnerable to the illnesses that flourished in the Indian climate. No one, it seemed, was honest enough to admit that competition for eligible husbands in the Crown Colonies was fierce and that polish and refinement were essential if an offspring was to make a successful match.

The disturbing notion that Malvina might have had similar designs in mind occurred to China with the suddenness of an unexpected blow between the eyes. Surely she hadn't endured those insufferable years at Olivia Crenshawe's seminary simply because her mother hoped it would improve her chances of finding a husband?

"I'm not the least surprised that you prefer to defend my father's adulterous behavior rather than condemn it for the ignoble rutting it was," China informed the captain with a fine show of temper. "Men! You are every one of you egotistical and pompous beyond belief! And as for the child—she—she—Oh, whatever are we going to do with her?" she asked, her face crumpling unexpectedly.

Ethan regarded her callously as he leaned his hip against a low stone wall. "Why don't you simply throw her into the sea? Most of the natives get rid of their unwanted children that way. If drowning doesn't take care of her the sharks certainly will."

China's face paled and she took an involuntary step backward. "Oh!" she cried. "How can you say such a thing? How can you even joke about something so horrid? We have to help her, don't you see? She's being raised by weavers and spends the entire day shut up in those musty sheds. She needs sunshine and proper food."

Ethan found himself unable to control the laughter that burst from him without warning. Would he ever come to understand this red-headed enigma? Did he even want to?

"What a curious creature you are," he remarked with a grin, unmindful of her indignant expression. "One moment you're damning the image of a man I believe you loved more than anyone, and the next you're prepared to gather his bastard child to your bosom."

"You'll not call her that word! Mother said her name is—" China scowled, thinking that "Black Pearl of the Orient" was clearly as unsuitable as the child's Chinese name. A better translation would have to be found, especially if she was to be brought up in an English household where foreign sobriquets would never, never serve.

"Her name is Gem," she said stiffly, deciding upon it at the last moment, "and I intend to see that she's raised as a Warrick."

"Do you?" The amusement vanished from Ethan's face. "Have you considered what your mother may say about that?"

China's mouth became a thin, stubborn line. "I know my father wouldn't have wanted her growing up as a peasant. He wouldn't have neglected her that way."

"You're quick to take up the cause of a man you recently denounced as a rutting boar," Ethan pointed out unkindly, deciding it would be better for everyone concerned if he could change her mind before Malvina Warrick caught wind of her intentions.

China's eyes lifted to his, and she said firmly, "It was wrong of me to say that about him, especially since it isn't true. It doesn't matter what sort of man he was." Her eyes narrowed suddenly and she regarded him with considerable hostility. "Why should I justify myself to you? It's none of your business!"

"You were the one who brought up the matter in the first place," he reminded her blandly.

It might be wise, China reflected with compressed lips, to change the subject before she was goaded into further losing her temper. "What are you doing here on Badajan, Captain?" she inquired frostily. "I thought you had business in Djakarta?"

"And so I did," he replied with a grin, "until I chanced to discover that the man I was to see had died unexpectedly several months ago."

"How unfortunate," China remarked acidly. "I imagine he was found floating in the sewer with a knife in his back?"

"As a matter of fact he was," Ethan said, and suddenly there was something in his eyes that gave her pause. She cautioned herself to remember that Ethan Bloodwell's life was as far removed from her own as Badajan was from the mountains of the moon. She was a person who respected the law while Captain Bloodwell would have none of it. She longed for nothing more than to live a simple life here on the island of her birth while he seemed content to rove the seas and make his fortune however he pleased. There was a dark side to Ethan Bloodwell, and China, looking up into those pale blue eyes, decided uncomfortably that she didn't care to ever come into contact with it.

"If you must know," he resumed, speaking as though she were a tiresome child who had pestered him persistently, "I spent the last two nights on Barindi, an island below Sarawak, as the houseguest of Prince Azar bin Shaweh. We played pachisi, of which His Highness is inordinately fond, but because he lost badly and has a tendency to take his losses sorely, I thought it wise to cut my visit short. Surely you must realize why I came here?"

A feeling of panic swept over China, who hadn't expected him back so soon. What in heaven's name was she going to tell Damon?

"I trust your brother is prepared to pay me?"

"Of course he is," China responded stiffly, hating him for the laughter lurking in his eyes. "Why shouldn't he be?"

"Two hundred pounds is a large sum, Miss Warrick. I only wanted to make certain your brother had been duly forewarned."

China felt a telltale wave of heat rush to her face. "Damon fully intends to settle the debt," she assured him stubbornly.

"Good, then please be so kind as to take me to him."

"Very well, Captain," China said stiffly. "If you'll come this way?"

With an angry swish of her skirts, she led him across the lawn and into the house, nodding to the elderly Al-Haj, who opened the door for her. As she crossed the courtyard she squared her shoulders, determined to exhibit an outward calm that would betray none of the apprehension she felt within. God's blood! If only she had made it a point to speak to Damon sooner! Not that it would have made any difference, she decided glumly. Hopefully Captain Bloodwell would remain civil instead of being his usual impertinent self, but that, China decided with a grimace, was like wishing the moon were made of cheese!

Damon Warrick was visibly startled when his sister swept into the study with the reputed renegade Ethan Bloodwell behind her, yet he rose quickly to greet the latter with a firm handshake. "It was kind of you to come, sir," he said formally. "I've been wanting to thank you for bringing China back to Asia. Please, won't you sit down? China, ring for refreshments, would you?"

"I'm afraid I haven't come to pay a social call," Captain Bloodwell said mildly, his words checking China's hand on the bell pull.

Damon gestured to an armchair which faced his cluttered desk. "If this is a business call, I imagine it has something to do with my sister's passage from England?"

Ethan sat down. "As a matter of fact, it does."

Lowering herself into a chair near the door, China gritted her teeth and willed herself to say nothing.

"To be exact," Ethan continued blandly, "it concerns the payment of Miss Warrick's fare from London to Singapore."

Damon's brows rose. "Surely her cousin saw to that before she sailed?"

Ethan shook his head. "There were certain unavoidable circumstances preventing his doing so."

"Is this true, China?" Damon inquired.

"I'm afraid it is," she said with admirable calm considering the captain's pale, mocking eyes were upon her, wreaking havoc with her determination not to lose her temper. "I received Mother's letter concerning Father's death on the day Captain Bloodwell's ship was scheduled to sail. There simply wasn't time."

"I understand," Damon said, and shifted restlessly. A delegation of Chinese merchants was expected to call on him within the hour and he didn't care to be engaged until then bickering over the disposition of a few paltry pounds. "Will you accept a draft, Captain Bloodwell?" he inquired, reaching into the top drawer of his desk while China relaxed visibly and leaned back in her chair. "I'm afraid I don't keep an appreciable amount of cash here on the island. No reason to, you understand. How much is it I owe you? Ten pounds?"

"I'm afraid it's more than that," Ethan said blandly.

Damon frowned. "How much, then? Twenty? Thirty? *Forty?*"

"Two hundred."

Hot color rose to Damon Warrick's face, washing over his angular cheekbones and up to the prominent widow's peak at the roots of his hair. "You must be mad!"

"That is the sum Miss Warrick gave me to understand would be paid upon her arrival."

Damon's mouth tightened and Ethan found himself thinking idly that he must have inherited his looks from his mother, for there seemed to be very little Warrick blood in him. That flaccid chin and those thin white hands spoke of a weak and easily influenced character, and Ethan wondered to himself why the spirit and fire that burned in the young woman sitting restlessly near him should be lacking in her brother.

"I'm afraid I don't understand," Damon protested, gazing inquiringly into the still face of his sister.

Ethan grinned obligingly. "Allow me to explain."

"No, please," China interrupted hastily. Her petticoats rustled stiffly as she approached her brother's desk. "I'm afraid it's true, Damon. I was terribly anxious to get home. It didn't seem an unreasonable sum at the time."

"Is that all you have to say?" Damon demanded incredulously as she lapsed into silence.

She bit her lip and nodded.

"Now, see here," Damon began, but was interrupted by the captain, who had risen smoothly to his feet.

"Excuse me, sir, but it's obvious that the two of you have a great deal to discuss." Indeed, it was quite clear to him that China had said nothing yet concerning Freddy Linville's cruelty toward her. And because he was not about to permit any stirring of sympathy to prompt him to settle for a lesser sum of money, he knew better than to remain behind to witness her pained confession.

"Perhaps," he said curtly, "I should call again when the time is more convenient?" Glancing down at China's bowed head he looked away quickly, his lips tightening as he felt an annoyingly familiar tug at his conscience. "No need to

ring for a servant," he added tersely. "I can show myself
out."

A strained silence followed on the heels of his departure,
and Damon, who had risen to pace the floor like a caged
animal, halted at last behind the chair into which China
had lowered herself.

"I'd like to know what madness possessed you to offer
that man two hundred pounds?" he said coldly. "Twenty
pounds I could understand given your anxiety to return
home after Race's death, but two hundred? Where on earth
did you expect me to come by such a sum?"

China's heartbeat checked. "Do you mean to say that
you won't pay him?"

"Of course not! How bloody stupid do you think I am?"

"But Damon, I gave him my word!"

"It's out of the question!" Damon said harshly. "That
man is nothing but a scheming opportunist! No one but
an unmitigated blackguard would take advantage of the
fact that you obviously had no concept of the sum you were
offering him. Two hundred pounds, China! Two hundred!
A London gentleman could survive comfortably for a year
off money like that, perhaps even longer! You didn't sign
anything, did you?"

"No," China said clearly. "I considered it unnecessary.
Surely you must see that the issue here is one of honor."

"Honor?" Damon snorted. "Either you're deaf and blind
or spending six years locked away in a seminary has rendered you totally witless! Didn't anyone ever tell you what
sort of man Ethan Bloodwell is? Didn't you listen to the
gossip aboard his ship?"

"I do remember hearing something about a clipper he
once owned," she allowed reluctantly, aware that Damon
expected an answer. Yet she didn't care to tell him that
Ethan Bloodwell had also been a China trader, though her
reticence did nothing to help her, for Damon was apparently quite familiar with the captain's past, and the things
he told China in the course of the next few minutes made
her long to cover her ears and flee. Arms running? Murder?
Instigating a coup d'état against a harmless despot who
ruled one of the island kingdoms off the African coast and

whose disposal had resulted in the deaths of scores of innocent people?

Surely Damon was mistaken! Even a man of Ethan Bloodwell's dubious morals couldn't possibly have been responsible for such dreadful things!

"I'm afraid he was," Damon assured her grimly. "And I'm certain he's committed a number of other outrageous crimes we simply haven't heard about."

"Perhaps he decided to become respectable after he lost his ship?" China suggested hopefully. "His voyage to England seemed to have involved honest trade."

"In this particular instance it might have been," Damon allowed, "but what about the rest? I've heard rumors that he'll carry anything if the price is right, from smuggled arms and stolen artifacts to slaves. He's been boarded and searched by Navy ships on numerous occasions though he's too goddamned clever to get caught. Now do you understand," he added not unkindly, "why I can't believe you promised him so much money?"

China nodded miserably. Lifting her troubled gaze to Damon's she asked, "What are we going to do? I'm afraid Captain Bloodwell will insist on being paid. He's not a very patient man and from what you've told me it's entirely possible that he'll stoop to anything to collect his money." She swallowed hard. "Suppose he becomes ugly about it?"

"Oh, I'm certain he will," Damon said darkly.

China bit her lip. "What do you think he'll do?"

"Probably take a lien against the family if I refuse to honor the debt."

China paled. "He can't do that! Can he?"

"I imagine we could take it to the courts and win," Damon said bitterly, "but it would probably take years and cost a small fortune. I don't believe Bloodwell is going to wait that long either, the bastard." Savagely he raked his fingers through his hair. "A fine kettle of fish this is, by God!"

"Perhaps it would be wisest to simply pay him what we owe him," China said slowly. "You say we haven't got the money, but surely Father must have left *some* provisions, or at least a small stipend for me?"

"I'm sorry, China, Race left no will at all. Why should

he? He couldn't have known that he was going to die so soon!"

"But there must be some kind of trust," China persisted.

Damon shook his head. "Sorry, love, but all our money is tied up in the plantation, and at the moment we happen to be badly short. It's to be expected with Race having died so unexpectedly. His creditors all but panicked when word got out. They were fairly killing one another to be the first to call in their debts, and Mother and I had no choice but to pay them. So much for so-called gentlemen and their codes of honor!" He shook his head and after a moment added darkly, "And as for Ethan Bloodwell, I'm afraid he's got us over the ropes, and he damned well knows it."

"Then what will you do?" China asked hopelessly.

Damon scowled and massaged the back of his neck. "Do? I suppose I'll have to fight him as best I can. Through legal channels, of course, though I doubt he knows the meaning of the word."

China's hands clenched into fists. "I can't believe he'd actually do this to us."

"Can't you?" Damon asked unkindly. "Did you see him as some sort of hero, China? A knight in shining armor who rescued you from your years of exile in England? I'm afraid he turned your head with foolish fantasies. Ethan Bloodwell is a notorious blackguard and an unspeakable cad and the only things in life that matter to him are those with price tags attached."

"I suppose you're right," China said bleakly, knowing it would no longer serve any purpose to explain to Damon why she had been so desperate to leave England. It wouldn't change a thing and Damon would only point out, justifiably so, that acting under those particular circumstances, Ethan Bloodwell had been even more unscrupulous than he had originally thought.

"I'm sorry," she whispered.

Damon patted her shoulder reassuringly. "Now, now, you mustn't blame yourself. I have it on good authority that Ethan Bloodwell has cheated plenty of people over the years who were not only more clever than you are but thoroughly knowledgeable as to his character and thus forewarned. We'll find a way out of this muddle, I promise.

Perhaps he'll prove a reasonable fellow after all and accept
a lesser sum for your passage."

"I hope you're right," China said unhappily, though she
doubted it.

Seeing the harassed look on her brother's face, she felt
her heart go out to him. It wasn't fair that Damon should
have to pay for her mistake, and it wasn't right of her to
drive King's Wheal further into debt by taking money out
of the beleaguered family finances. China resolved in that
moment to deal with Ethan Bloodwell on her own. She
had blundered into his trap without anyone's help, and
the least she could do was to make every effort to extricate
herself from it alone.

She had learned at an early age to fend for herself, and
upon considering the matter for a moment in silence she
decided she would have to speak to the captain as soon as
possible and see if she couldn't convince him to give her
a little more time. Perhaps she might catch him now, before his ship weighed anchor.

"Where the devil are you going?" Damon demanded as
she hastened toward the door, yet nothing answered him
save the rustle of her petticoats and the sound of her footsteps fading on the hot tile floor.

The *Kowloon Star* had not yet gone, for Ethan had lingered for an appreciable length of time on the terrace that
ran along the back of the house, held there by a dazzling
view of Badajan's soaring mountains and the neighboring
islands of emerald green lying in the sea beyond. Through
the palm fronds he could see strips of brilliant turquoise
water, the later afternoon sun filtering them with rippling
bands of silver. Surf foamed against the sandy shore shelving the headland, and towering thunderheads were stacked
in the hot sky above, promising more rain by evening.

Whistling tunelessly, Ethan descended to the lawn and
nodded amiably to the ancient Chinese gardener smoothing the crushed shell walks with a wooden rake. Hearing
the sound of high-pitched laughter from the far banks of
a small pond hemmed by dark, flowering creepers, he
strolled over to investigate, and reached the grassy banks
in time to hear the young, exasperated voice of a child.

"I told you you weren't going to be any good at it! Girls are so stupid!"

"Let me try again, Brandon, please?"

"Oh, all right. Take this one. It'll probably work better."

Despite himself Ethan had to laugh as he caught sight of the pair of children who were skipping pebbles across the weed-choked water. He knew at once that they were Warricks though their unruly red mops tended more toward auburn and not the burnished gold of China's fiery tresses. Both of them had whirled at the sound of his voice, and the girl, who could not have been more than six or seven, saw him first. Paling, her hands flew to her lips, and though she was hampered by a pair of crutches she plunged like a startled fawn into the thickets.

"Philippa! Where are you going?" The boy's eyes widened as they slid from the blossoming shrubs behind which his sister had vanished to the tall man in nankeen breeches standing farther down the path. "What are you doing there?" he demanded warily, and admirably held his ground as Ethan approached.

"I've been visiting with your brother," Ethan told him obligingly, and grinned. "My name is Ethan Bloodwell."

Brandon's mouth dropped. "The captain of the *Kowloon Star?* The one that brought China from England?"

His hostility dissipated at Ethan's nod and was replaced with undisguised admiration. Unlike Horatio Creel, who sailed Warrick schooners between Badajan and Hong Kong, Captain Bloodwell fit exactly Brandon's ideal of a seafaring man. Where Captain Creel was portly and growing old, Captain Bloodwell was lean and strong, and quite young, in Brandon's critical opinion, for a grown-up. He especially liked the rakish way the captain wore his holland shirt opened at the collar and wondered if, like the pirates he'd read about, he kept a pistol hidden in his waistband and a knife in his boot?

"Did you bring her with you? The *Kowloon Star?* I asked China if you'd take us to England the next time you went but she said no. Why not?"

"I'm afraid your family wouldn't approve your choice of ships," Ethan said, grinning.

"How come? I'd really like to go with you. Philippa

wants to meet the Queen and I want to see Broadhurst.
China's told me all about the wine cellars. She says they
have tunnels in them that our ancestors used when they
had to hide from the Roundheads. Do you suppose they're
still there?"

"The Roundheads or the tunnels?"

Brandon looked confused for a moment, then his eyes
began to dance in a manner that reminded Ethan all too
annoyingly of his sister. "The tunnels, of course. There
aren't any Roundheads anymore!"

"Brandon! Brandon, where are you?"

Having been on her way down to the docks in the hopes
of intercepting Ethan before he departed for Singapore,
China had stumbled upon a tearful Philippa scurrying
back to the house and claiming that she and Brandon had
been spied on by a stranger in the thickets near the pond.
Knowing that strangers were rare on Badajan, rarer still
those who wandered about the grounds unescorted, China
had hurried to investigate, never pausing to think that it
might have been Captain Bloodwell himself Philippa had
seen.

"Brandon!" she cried again.

"Over here, China!" she heard him call. "I'm down by
the pond!"

A moment later Ethan saw her emerge pale, disheveled,
and out of breath on the far banks, where she froze abruptly
at the sight of him, her skirts swirling about her; the fear
on her face giving way to startled recognition.

"Look, China!" Brandon cried before she could speak,
gesturing eagerly. "It's the captain of the ship that brought
you here!" In his excitement he had forgotten Ethan's name,
but with childish temerity plunged on undaunted: "Don't
you remember? He's the one you called a bloody womanizer!"

A painful wave of heat flared from China's throat to
her hairline and her hands twisted convulsively in the
folds of her skirts. Unable to think of anything to say,
knowing that any apologies she cared to make would sound
feeble at best, she could only meet the captain's amused
gaze squarely. Standing there with her red hair spilling
down her back, small chest heaving from the exertion of

running, she regarded him with an outwardly unruffled calm, and in that one brief moment Ethan knew, with the startling clarity that came so rarely to his rough, unorderly life, that he loved her.

The discovery shocked him profoundly, for he was not the sort of man to fall in love with a woman a dozen years his junior, nor with this one in particular, an opinionated, temperamental, and thoroughly troublesome creature who by rights should have sent him fleeing for the far corners of the earth. Yet the fact remained that he did, and he should have realized as much days ago given the irrational fear that had driven him to the Raffles Hotel when Nappy had brought him the chilling news that China Warrick had fallen victim to a brutal stabbing.

Trying to remind himself of the trouble China Warrick had caused him ever since she had first appeared in his life, he found himself thinking instead of her damnably courageous nature: of the time she had accompanied him without complaint to London after fleeing the cruelty of her cousins and the shattering news of her father's death, of the time she had braved a savage storm to bring water to a sick child, of the manner in which she had been prepared to endure the wrath of her own mother so that a bastard infant might have a name... China laughing, China weeping, China lecturing him tirelessly on the countless riches a virtuous life might bring him....

"What are you doing in the garden, Captain?" China asked coolly, coming down the path to stand before him. She was immeasurably annoyed that he had dared to take it upon himself to wander at leisure about her property. She chafed to give him the dressing down he deserved, yet knew that she could not possibly be rude to him in view of the insulting thing Brandon had inadvertently said.

"Captain?" she prompted, wondering suspiciously why he was standing there regarding her with a strangely unsettling frown between his eyes. What devilment was he planning now?

Apparently none, for after a moment he grinned at her in that impudent manner she knew far too well and said, "No need to look so distrustful, Miss Warrick. I was merely taking a stroll through the garden before returning to my ship."

"I see." She appeared to be on the verge of saying something else, but in the end remained silent, for she found herself oddly disconcerted by his presence although she was at a loss to explain why.

"Since you seem to resent my presence here," Ethan was saying affably, "I suppose I should be taking my leave." His lips twitched at the patent relief that crossed her face, and he added lightly, "Pray remember it's only for the time being."

"Oh? And just when do you intend to return?"

"My dear Miss Warrick, you surprise me! I'd come to believe you were not the type to succumb to idle curiosity." His eyes glinted as he saw the bright anger in her own, and he made a half-bow over her hand. "Until we meet again."

Turning heel, he strode away, the oyster shells crunching beneath his boots, and Philippa, who had hobbled up behind them, peered cautiously around China's skirts and said earnestly, "I don't like him."

"That makes two of us," China stated, and guided them back to the house with a toss of her head.

The brigantine *Kowloon Star* lay anchored a quarter mile beyond the Warrick docks, the furled canvas of her sails flapping in the breeze as she idled gently with the tide. Though Ethan was whistling softly between his teeth as he came aboard, an indication that he was pleased with himself, it did nothing to soothe his one-eyed steward, who had been watching anxiously for his return.

"Well, was 'e there? Did yer see 'im?" Nappy demanded, confronting Ethan as the jolly boat was made fast.

"Do you mean Damon Warrick?" Ethan inquired absently, tilting back his head to watch the sails thundering into place as his men clawed their way out onto the yards in response to the order to weigh anchor. The clouds above the raking masts had been driven away by a brisk wind, taking with them the promise of rain and leaving the sun to beat relentlessly upon the unprotected decks. Pitch bubbled between the sun-blistered planks as the temperature soared, but Ethan did not notice. This was Asia and he was accustomed to its simmering heat.

"Not 'im!" Nappy said. "That 'eathen barstid Wang Toh! There was a lorcha wiv 'is purple dragon crest come sailin' round the point bold as daylight an 'arf 'our ago and put orf near shore. Don't know if 'e's aboard because nobody's showed their faces yet."

Ethan's face had grown still. "Well, I didn't see him, though Warrick mentioned he was expecting visitors. Are you sure about that crest?"

Nappy's grizzled jaw quivered with affront. "It ain't changed in the past five years so I don't see 'ow I could mistakes it! Now what would that rascally Chinaman want wiv the Warricks, I wonder?"

"Even warlords have a fondness for Badajan silk," Ethan said softly. Staring off across the shimmering water he pondered the significance of Nappy's discovery.

"Did yer make trouble wiv Miss China's brother?" the little steward inquired suspiciously.

Ethan's keen eyes had picked out the lorcha lying at anchor beyond an outcropping of wind-honed coral to the east of the island. It rode calmly with the tide, the waves lapping against the salt-crusted hull, and there was no mistaking the silk banner that flapped aggressively in the breeze.

"No, I didn't," he said after a moment, hands clasped behind his back. "I merely informed him that I'm holding him accountable for the two hundred pounds he owes me and that I intend to use whatever means necessary to collect it."

"Yer threatened 'im."

"On the contrary, I was most amiable. It was young Warrick who lost his temper."

"You shouldn't 'ave agreed on that kind o' money in the first place," Nappy said uncomfortably. "It waren't right to do that to Miss China."

"She made the offer, Nappy, I merely accepted it."

"You still oughtn't to've done it. It waren't no trouble bringin' 'er 'ere, after all."

Ethan uttered a crack of laughter. "No trouble? Have you lost your mind? If Miss China Warrick and her dra-

matic escapades weren't trouble enough, what about Lucinda Harrleson's self-righteous trumpetings or those
simpering daughters of hers? And as for Julia Clayton—"

"You was the one wanted to take 'er to Java," Nappy
reminded him dourly, though he had been secretly pleased
when the captain had opted for a trip to Barindi instead
and had left the lovely widow behind in Singapore.

"Don't remind me," Ethan said dryly, and shook his
head. "No fortune on earth could tempt me to repeat that
voyage again."

"It still ain't right," Nappy said mutinously. "You
could've asked for a few guineas from that brother of 'ers
and called yerself satisfied."

The blue eyes nailed into his. "Why are you so fond of
her anyway, old man? Even if Miss Warrick were buxom
and blond, the kind I know you prefer, you're far too old
to be chasing skirts, so it can't be that."

"No, it ain't," Nappy agreed, his tone making it clear
that Ethan was treading dangerous ground to dare suggest
as much. "She ain't like the 'arpys I've known in my day.
She's a gentle sort wiv a good 'eart, and anyone wot's got
eyes in 'is 'ead can see she's 'urtin' and needin' a friend."

Ethan's brows rose, for he had never heard sentiments
of that nature uttered by his taciturn steward before. And
yet he could not make a single mocking rejoinder, for annoyingly enough he had fallen under a similar spell, he
who had always kept a cool head and an unequivocally
hard heart where women were concerned.

"I have no intention of settling on a lesser sum for Miss
Warrick's fare," he said at last, his tone so unexpectedly
harsh that Nappy looked up at him in surprise. "Two
hundred pounds, my good fellow, will not even begin to
make restitution for what this voyage has cost me."

"So what do you mean to do?" Nappy inquired. "Toy
wiv Master Damon like a cat wiv a mouse? It's a game I
knows you likes t'play."

"I haven't decided yet," Ethan said shortly.

"And yon pulin' foreigner?" Nappy's head jerked in the
direction of the lorcha.

"As for Wang Toh," the captain responded slowly, "I

believe I'll pay a call on a few acquaintances in Macao and see what he's been up to these past few years and why his name suddenly seems to be cropping up wherever I turn." Ethan swore beneath his breath, wishing he had been granted the opportunity of confronting Wang Toh Chen-Arn in the elegant ambience of Damon Warrick's study. It would have saved him a considerable amount of trouble to speak to the mandarin face-to-face.

"'E swore 'e'd kill yer next time 'e laid eyes on you," Nappy reminded him uneasily.

"So have at least a dozen other equally determined individuals over the past ten years," Ethan pointed out with a shrug. "And as you can see, I am quite alive."

"There's always tomorrow," Nappy countered. "Why don't we go on t' Singapore an' forgets we saw 'im, eh?" He glanced hopefully into Ethan's intractable face and then spat raucously over the rail. "Bah! Ain't no reasoning wiv you! Never was and never will be! You've made yer bed, Cap'n Ethan, go on an' lie in't!"

"I'm afraid I haven't any choice," Ethan replied, but Nappy, stumping disgustedly to the galley, didn't hear him.

"Hafiz," Ethan said after a moment, addressing the passing Persian, "my spyglass, please."

Despite himself he felt his heartbeat quicken as he lifted the glass to his eye and saw a small boat cast off from the lorcha several minutes later, its oars dipping vigorously as it sped away in the direction of the Warrick docks. Training his gaze upon it, Ethan studied the tall, emaciated individual sitting rigidly in the bow. Sunlight glinted on his oiled queue, and on his sleeve he bore the embroidered purple dragon that proclaimed his fealty to the house of Wang Toh. There was a ledger clutched to his chest, and Ethan guessed that he was one of the mandarin's accountants.

The telescope's circular field of vision presented him with the unreadable faces of three other men, also Chinese, but whose elaborately embroidered robes indicated that they were merchants in their own right and not in Wang Toh's employ. Seeing this, the steel-edged excitement churning in Ethan's gut turned to bitter disappointment.

"The Imperial One is not here," came the soft voice of

Rajiid Ali from behind him. He spoke in Arabic, and his remark was not a question.

Ethan answered it nonetheless. "No." The glass shut with a snap. "I wouldn't be suprised if he's grown too fat to leave Canton. His flunky there has obviously been sent to purchase silk."

"The Imperial One was always fond of finery."

Ethan uttered a short laugh, envisioning the silk-draped immenseness of Wang Toh Chen-Arn, the powerful mandarin whose oily fingers dabbled in nearly every lucrative business deal between mainland China and the "barbarian West." There was not a throw of the die that did not yield him gain, nor a secret society in which his spies were not active, and though he was loathed by Chinese and Europeans alike, his wealth and power were such to prevent any of them from contemplating a move without his approval.

"I am certain they have seen your colors, just as we have spotted theirs," Rajiid added, referring to the black field with its scarlet lotus flower that flew on the masthead of the *Kowloon Star* and informed all but the uninitiated that bloodshed and vengeance, for which its colors stood, were not unfamiliar companions to the men who served her. "Wang Toh will wonder what business you have with the Warrick family."

"Perhaps he already knows," Ethan said, and the thought made him frown.

"Truly I believe this meeting was not intended," Rajiid countered softly.

Ethan sent him a mocking glance. "Have you forgotten the teachings of the Koran? Does it not tell us that encounters such as these are never left to chance?"

A flicker of something very like amusement fled across Rajiid Ali's hawkish face. "Perhaps that is so, but it lies in your own heart, not in the stars, to choose what you will do."

"Predestination be damned!" Ethan said cheerfully, tucking the glass into his belt. "I'm not going to do a bloody thing!"

The Arab was visibly startled. "And what of Wang Toh? He will not dismiss so quickly the claim that you are merely passing through these waters. By Allah, he is like a pariah dog, and will sniff out any hint of profit that can be made from the news his spies will soon bring of your dealings with Damon Warrick."

There was suddenly something on Ethan's lean face that was not at all pleasant; a brief lifting of the civilized façade to reveal the hard brutality of the man beneath it. Seeing it, Rajiid nodded contentedly.

"The Imperial One would not be wise to scratch at wounds better left to heal," he observed.

"No," Ethan agreed. Turning, he allowed his gaze to travel across the blinding stretch of blue-green water to the roof of the plantation house nestled amid a canopy of dark trees on the side of a steep mountain. "It would be most unwise of him."

"Captain Bloodwell? We're awaiting your orders, sir."

Ethan's expression was thoughtful as he turned to regard his coxswain. He had mentioned to Nappy that he intended to sail to Macao, but was he really considering snatching up the gauntlet Wang Toh Chen-Arn might or might not decide to fling into his face? If his years as a China trader had taught him anything, it was to strike first, ruthlessly and without warning, and withdraw before first blood had been spilled. But he was older now, and wiser, or was it perhaps that the rashness of youth had given way to other considerations, unforeseen complications in particular, that cautioned restraint?

Perhaps Nappy was right in claiming that the past should be left for dead. And it was entirely possible, even probable, that Wang Toh had forgotten him and was not in the least interested in resurrecting an old enmity that would prove more troublesome to him than it was worth.

"Plot a course for Singapore, lad," he instructed Quentin Thatcher, his decision made.

"Aye, sir."

As the coxswain moved away, Ethan's gaze fell on Rajiid, who had been studying him with dark, expressionless eyes.

"We have business in Singapore?" the Arab inquired politely.

"Indeed we do," Ethan said with a laugh, and suddenly

he knew what he intended to do. "Prince Azar bin Shaweh has presented me with a house on the outskirts of the city and it might prove beneficial to take a look at it."

Rajiid's dark face remained bland. "It would seem your nights in Barindi were fruitful. I take it you beat him neatly?"

"Nothing of the kind. Shaweh's an inexcusably poor pachisi player."

"Yet you have won from him a house?"

Ethan's grin was wolfish. "It was either that or the choice of a half a dozen concubines."

"By Allah, that is tempting fruit indeed! Would you have been permitted to pick them yourself?"

Ethan laughed, and suddenly the tension eased from his face. "No. That's why I opted for the house. He's a crafty bastard and I had no desire to take up with the unmanageable Amazons he would doubtless have presented me. I understand it's a rather impressive dwelling once reserved for visiting British residents. I suppose we ought to take a look at it."

"I fear that owning a house will turn you respectable," Rajiid protested, though his black eyes twinkled. "Once you take up lodgings there you will find yourself longing not only for a wife but sons to fill your footsteps."

Ethan's burst of laughter held an unmistakable note of derision. "If that is truly the case, my friend, I was a fool not to have chosen the concubines."

_____ *Chapter Twelve* _____

His Highness, Prince Azar bin Shaweh, had been true
to his word, for the servants residing in the three-story
coral-colored house at the end of a wide street near the
waterfront had already been warned to expect a new master, and Ethan was somewhat disconcerted by the effusive
kowtowing that greeted his arrival. It was a pleasant house,
well-sashed and painstakingly maintained, its red-tiled
roof flanked by octagonal towers. The upper floors were
lined with porticos permitting the cooling sea breezes to
flow throughout the bedrooms, and offered a sweeping view
of the cloud-covered mountains of Indonesia.

Though a small house by Eastern standards, it rambled
across several acres of ground with lush gardens sloping
to a secluded beach where the surf lapped gently against
the sand and the jumbled masts and rigging of the ships
crowding Singapore's teeming harbor could be seen across
the humid stretch of water known as the Inner Roads.

"I didn't realize I'd inherited the whole bloody staff,"
Ethan said to Nappy, surveying the bowing servants that
had gathered on the outer patio to greet them.

"Not a bad deal by 'arf," Nappy pronounced with obvious delight. "It'll please me proper to rest my bones in a real 'ouse for a change. This ain't no Battersea rat-'ole, that's for sure," he added, surveying the crenellated sea wall that soared high above the rustling palms. "Could've been some Indian rana's palace by the look of it. 'Ave that toff there show us inside." He indicated the beaming Malay who had identified himself as Lal Sri, Ethan's new houseboy. "Might as well take a look 'round the place."

It was easy to understand why the house had been a favorite with visiting British diplomats. The cream-colored receiving rooms were furnished in pleasing style with dainty inlaid tables and a profusion of cushions upon which to sit. A collection of musical instruments hung on the wall in one room, including the Malay gulingtangan, a set of bronze gongs in a rough-hewn wooden frame. In broken English Lal Sri gave them to understand that the girls of the household had been taught to dance and that he himself would be happy to accompany them on the instrument.

"For your pleasure, yes?" he said, beaming.

Nappy could not contain his laughter. "Eager barstid, ain't 'e? 'Ow'd yer 'appen t'pick this jool orf the Prince's crown, eh?"

Ethan's lips twitched. "I believe it was growing into something of a liability for him now that so many British women have settled in the community. It seems they objected strongly to their husbands' habits of taking ease with the young ladies who resided here."

Nappy chuckled. "So you've won yerself an 'ouse of ill-repute, 'ave you? Can't say as I'm surprised."

"Officially it was never used for that purpose," Ethan told him with a grin. "As a matter of fact Prince Shaweh presented it to the British Resident in commiseration for the deaths of the *Baldoin*'s crew."

"'Oo? Oh, yer means them Navy gobs what was killed by 'ead 'unters when they was marooned on Barindi a few years back? I remember the blokes in Parliament 'owlin' for vengeance. All set to send a fleet of 'Er Majesty's warships to blow the island orf the map."

"To soothe their ruffled feelings Prince Shaweh apparently made several generous gifts to the British Queen, including unlimited use of this house to government officials whenever they were in residence."

"'Oo ain't been usin' it since their wimmenfolk caught wind of what was goin' on," Nappy guessed.

"Exactly. And to rescind his offer without losing face, His Highness decided to turn ownership over to someone else—neatly enough, to me, which takes a great load off his mind, I imagine. I'm also certain the administering body of India will accept with sighs of relief the news that the house will no longer be available to visiting dignitaries."

"And trouble's been avoided afore it got to be embarrassing. Well, well." Nappy hooked his thumbs into the waistband of his trousers. "Let's 'ave a look around, eh?"

There were over a dozen bedrooms in the upper two stories of the house, each with a generous-sized bed whose satin sheets were changed daily to thwart the mildew that plagued the humid coast. The ground floor was given over to reception rooms, libraries, and formal salons, blending quite pleasingly the delicacy of Chinese art with dark, heavy furnishings of English origin. Ethan was amused to find the library crammed with classic literature, though the stiff bindings of the volumes he took down indicated that few, if any, had ever been read.

Dismissing the hovering Lal Sri, he and Nappy stepped onto a terrace that ran along the rear of the house where a cool breeze eased the fierce heat of the early afternoon. Shading his eyes, Ethan peered across the dancing water at the Chinese lightermen in their battered tongkangs who scurried to unload ships anchored in the Outer Road.

"A place like this'd fetch a pretty penny," Nappy remarked presently, returning from a tour of the fountains and ornamental pools that dotted the gardens.

Ethan's brows rose. "What makes you think I mean to sell it?"

"Well, why not? Wiv the money you'd make you could forget about them two hundred pounds Miss China owes."

"Ah, I suspected as much."

Nappy's brow darkened. "Well, it ain't a bad idea! You'd earn yourself enough t'get the *Lotus Star* back from them buggers wot tooks 'er away, and Miss China wouldn't need to pay you at all."

The look on Ethan's face made him realize instantly the futility of his argument. "I still say it ain't right," he muttered beneath his breath.

"I have every intention of keeping the place," Ethan informed him curtly. "Not only because it happens to appeal to me, but because it provides a better view of the Inner Road than any other house along the waterfront. A lookout posted in one of those towers there could keep accurate count of the ships coming in."

"And you'd be the first to know if one o' them ships 'appened to be strikin' the purple dragon, eh?"

"The thought did cross my mind," Ethan admitted.

"You're not thinkin' of stirrin' up trouble wiv a cove the likes of Wang Toh?"

The blue eyes were suddenly hard. "And if I am? You've never been one to question my decisions."

"Maybe not, but this time it's different," Nappy said darkly, and the seriousness of his tone caused Ethan to regard him with considerable surprise.

"What makes you think anything's changed?" he inquired suspiciously.

"For one thing, I know you've been 'appy wiv the *Kowloon Star,* and we've been doin' good for ourselves of late. It ain't been like them first years after we lost the *Lotus Star.*"

"Praise Allah for that," Ethan said dryly.

"And now you're wantin' to risk everything on some pig'eaded notion of revenge! Why? Five years is gone by and all of a sudden you're eager for a reckoning! Wot's changed, eh? Wang Toh waren't at fault that 'Is Perishin' Majesty's Imperial Navy broke you an' impounded your ship! 'E lost as much as you did, may'ap more! Can't yer leave it be?"

Thrusting his hands into his pockets Ethan stared off across the water, the slight easterly breeze ruffling his hair and stirring the fronds of the plantains in the garden behind him. From the riverfront came the muted clanging of a ship's bell and a whiff of the acrid smell of refuse before the wind shifted and the air was clean and sweet once again.

"I suppose I'll have to," he said at last. "We stand to gain little by tugging the Imperial One's robes after all this time."

"That's the first piece of sense you've bloody well ever showed," Nappy said with considerable relief.

"It doesn't mean I'll turn tail if Wang Toh comes looking for trouble," Ethan warned. "Nor," he added curtly, "do I intend to sell this house." Turning, he regarded its imposing seaward façade in silence, and after a moment he said, "I've discovered myself afflicted of late with a curious yearning to settle down. And now that I've been presented with such a pleasing abode, I might as well try my hand at becoming a respectable citizen." His grin and the fact that Nappy knew him far too well snuffed any rising hope that he might be serious.

"What you really means is that you plans t' keep your eye on the comings and goings in t'arbor while playin' at bein' a gentleman. Just for the benefit of anyone 'oo might be suspicioning yer motives," the one-eyed steward observed. "'Oo is it you're arfter now? Wang Toh or the Warricks? I don't 'old for it, Cap'n Ethan. Not one perishin' bit."

"Duly noted, Mr. Quarles," Ethan said mildly. "Now, if you'd be so kind as to send Hafiz back to the ship? We might as well get the men installed in their new quarters."

The prospect of taking up residence in Prince Azar bin Shaweh's rambling house pleased the members of the brigantine's crew, as Ethan knew it would. After the long weeks at sea and the stifling humidity of the past few days they were only too eager to idle away the hours in the cool, high-ceilinged rooms and enjoy the entertainment provided by the dark-skinned beauties residing in the women's quarters.

Even the dubious Nappy had to admit that it proved pleasant to recline on satin cushions during the hottest hours of the day and sip iced concoctions while engaging in no more strenuous tasks than playing chess with Rajiid. "A man could get soft livin' like this," he said with a sigh, munching fried coconut from a tray that a saronged maiden placed before him.

"The Malays believe that relaxation is imperative to the well-being of a man's soul," Ethan told him with a grin. "Possessions are unimportant, wealth unnecessary, and work of any sort considered ridiculous."

"And 'oo's to say they ain't right? Why don't you take orf them 'ot togs an' join me, Cap'n?" Nappy invited, but Ethan graciously declined. Unlike his men he had no desire to indulge in the desultory lifestyle that marked the passage of the hours within the coral-toned walls of the enormous house. And he soon found himself far too busy for idleness as word of his arrival spread throughout the city and he was inundated with invitations and calls from Singapore's curious residents.

"It looks as though I've become the latest diversion," Ethan remarked with a laugh, sifting through the cards that Lal Sri brought to the table the following evening. "No one seems to care that I've a reputation not worth thinking about and reside in a house once known for its unsavory activities."

"All the more reason to welcome you to Singapore," his dinner companion assured him with a grin. "You're a novelty in a town where nothing's secret. And you're not half bad-looking, which means eager mamas will be trampling all over themselves to get a closer look at you."

"Heaven forbid!" Ethan made a face and helped himself to another serving of the soy-glazed duckling prepared by his affable Chinese cook. "I suppose I should be thankful that I'm not exactly the sort one would wish one's daughter to marry."

"Oh, on the contrary, my friend! You're male and unmarried, a rare species in the tropics, not to mention that you happen to be surrounded by an aura of danger and intrigue—just the sort of rogue to fuel any young girl's dreams."

"And prompt the city fathers to bar their doors against me."

His companion gave a hearty laugh. "That may happen eventually, but I assure you that at the moment you have piqued their interest favorably and they will pick you over

carefully with their fine-tooth combs before declaring you
unsuitable for decent company. You're in for a very trying
ordeal." He laughed at the prospect and took a noisy gulp
of wine.

Captain Tyler Crewe was an enormous man with powerful forearms and bushy blond brows arching over a pair
of shrewd eyes in an expression of perpetual surprise. Yet
there was nothing in the least innocent about the burly
American or, for that matter, did much remain on the face
of the earth that still could surprise him.

Tyler had known Ethan for the past twelve years, both
men having begun their sea careers in the highly com-
petitive and often violent trade of ivory and pearls that
flourished in the ancient ports of the Persian Gulf. Tyler
Crewe had been twenty-eight at the time, six years older
than Ethan, and captain-owner of a schooner known for
its ruthlessness. Ethan and a young Arab by the name of
Rajiid Ali had dogged his heels in a battered felucca, joining forces with him when it proved advantageous or beating him at his own game when the profits were high. Soon
both of them had grown wealthy enough to parlay their
fortunes into more ambitious ventures and trade their
modest ships for the fighting merchant clippers that were
the undisputed sovereigns of the sea.

Their rivalry had been further honed when both made
bids for the fabulous wealth awaiting those who traded
Bengal opium, and it was the *Lotus Star* that had pulled
Tyler Crewe from the water when his ill-fated clipper had
been smashed to tinder by Imperial warships. Eventually
the Opium War had broken Ethan as well, yet their friendship—if such it could be called—had endured, as had their
driving ambition, which had seen both men return swiftly
to power when other China traders had fallen by the way-
side or been crushed by the vengeful boot of John Company.

Like Ethan, Tyler Crewe had spent the last five years
clawing his way back from nothing, and because he could
be far more devious and devoid of honor when he chose,
he had managed to gain possession of another clipper, the
rake-masted *Orion*, of which he was inordinately proud.
There was also a modest house in Djakarta and an adoring
almond-eyed mistress or two, and though the cloth trade

in which he was now engaged was nowhere near as lucrative as dealing opium and silver bullion, Tyler considered himself content.

He was quite curious to see what sort of business had
brought Ethan Bloodwell to Singapore, knowing full well
that this house and its tropical setting were far too dull
and confining for a man of his tastes. Not for a moment
did Tyler believe that Ethan had simply decided it was
time to cool his heels after roving the high seas for so
many years, especially not with that sly yellow bastard
Wang Toh stirring up new trouble after five years of silence.

Tyler, too, hated Wang Toh Chen-Arn, but only because
he envied him his power and wealth and not because of
the fact that his greedy insistence on loading the *Lotus
Star*'s holds to capacity with opium—a delay that had cost
them three days in port—had ultimately resulted in the
seizure of Ethan Bloodwell's treasured ship.

"I heard tell Wang Toh's men have been boarding and
searching merchant ships on the Pearl River," he said
innocently. "Claims he's got an imperial edict from the
viceroy though he's being damned careful not to touch the
British. What d'you suppose he's looking for?"

"Illicit cargoes, I'd imagine, as a 'service' to the Emperor," Ethan answered with a shrug. "Though his motives
are doubtless far from exemplary. By impounding illicit
commodities he can assure his own monopoly on the market and charge the highest prices. It's perfectly legal, though
he'd better watch his hide if he continues, because he's
going to ruffle a blasted sight too many feathers."

"Especially if he inadvertently happens to seize a vessel
engaged in peaceful trade for the British Empire," Tyler
added.

"Lal Sri, more prawns," Ethan commanded, seeing Tyler's plate was empty, and effectively bringing an end to
the conversation. "And take these damned cards away, will
you? From now on tell anyone delivering them that I am
not at present disposed—Hold on there, what's this?"

It was an ostentatious vermilion seal that had caught
his eye. Taking it from the bowing Lal Sri, he unfolded
the expensive Chinese-made paper and burst into laugh-

ter. "Well, Tyler, it would seem you were right. I have been deemed respectable by the locals."

"How's that?" Captain Crewe inquired.

"It's an invitation to a party, one that will obviously be frequented by the most discriminating of Singapore's *grand monde*. Here, Lal Sri, I'll reply to this one personally. The rest you can return with my regrets."

"Who's it from?" Tyler asked, not particularly interested.

"A friend," Ethan responded with a grin. "Just a friend."

It was Nappy Quarles to whom Ethan showed the invitation later that night as the two of them relaxed on an upper-story balcony. A hot breeze ruffled the palm fronds in the garden and the violet sky overhead was awash with the pale glimmer of stars. The sounds of the city were muted and far away, and only the gurgle of the tide and the distant yapping of a scavenging mongrel came to them on the wind.

"What be it?" Nappy inquired curiously, squinting in the dim light to read the words printed in a bold Western hand on the embossed piece of foolscap.

"I have been invited," came Ethan's amused voice, "to a very formal party at King's Wheal Plantation honoring the return of Miss China Warrick to the bosom of her family."

"Ah!"

Ethan gave a quiet chuckle and presently Nappy saw his long shadow rise and wander to the edge of the balcony where fragrant jasmine creepers tumbled over the balustrade, showering the stones with a carpet of white petals. "It would seem that despite my differences with her son, Malvina Warrick wishes to have me present in appreciation for returning her daughter to Badajan."

"I'll be damned," Nappy said wonderingly. "And arfter all the grief you've caused 'em. 'Ard to believe the Warrick woman'd dream of welcoming you to 'er 'ouse." He fell silent and after a thoughtful pause he added, "She's tryin' t' buy you, ain't she?"

"Of course. How could you doubt as much? Little does she realize that it will take more than breaking bread with them to sway me from my purpose."

"Are you still plannin' to make trouble for Miss China? She don't deserve that, even from you."

Ethan turned his head to regard his steward with a look that was as dark and enigmatic as the night. "I'm going to collect those two hundred pounds no matter how much you may disapprove, Nappy. If Miss Warrick is smart enough she'll convince her brother to uphold his end of the bargain."

"And if they was tellin' the truth? Wot if they don't 'ave enough money left to pay you?"

"Nonsense," Ethan said impatiently. "Prince Shaweh assured me the Warricks are as wealthy as pashas. And I don't intend to let a mere boy the likes of Damon Warrick cheat me out of what I'm owed."

"It's a rum curious cove you've become, Cap'n Ethan."

"Now, why would you say that? In the old days you never raised objections if we were forced to bash a few heads or slit someone's throat to achieve our ends."

"In the old days," Nappy growled, "we never 'armed no one 'oo didn't ask for't, and you always took a care not to involve no wimmin. 'Ow come you can't leave Miss China be, eh?"

"It's precisely because of China Warrick and her broken promises that I find myself in this annoying situation," Ethan responded shortly. "Believe me, I'd just as soon wash my hands of her, but as I refuse to do so until I've been payed I may as well make it worth my while."

"Then you'll be goin' to the party?" Nappy inquired unhappily.

It was impossible for him to misconstrue the gleam in those hard blue eyes.

"Wild horses," Ethan pronounced blandly, "couldn't keep me away."

"I were afraid o' that." Nappy sighed in defeat.

Inasmuch as he now found himself in possession of an embossed invitation to King's Wheal Plantation, Ethan could see no harm in putting it to use by taking a covert tour of the island prior to the commencement of the evening's festivities. He was particularly interested in the layout of Badajan's production sheds and suspected that he would find them deserted as it seemed likely that Darwin Stepkyne would shut them down early in order to attend the party. In all likelihood the natives, who were ever wary of strangers, would also be absent, and Ethan doubted that he would ever again be presented with a better opportunity of doing some exploring. There could be no harm in learning what he could about the Warricks' way of life, for such information might prove quite useful, and he was extremely surprised when the announcement of his plans was greeted by loud protestations from his steward.

"It's askin' for trouble you be, pokin' round that island like you was friends wiv Damon Warrick! 'E'll 'ave you carted orf to gaol 'e will!" Nappy predicted direly, dropping the razor with which he had just finished shaving his captain into a wash bowl on the dresser.

It had been raining steadily since dawn and the windows in the spacious bedroom were barred against the slanting downpour that drummed against the glass. Accustomed to the unending seasonal rains, neither man took the least notice of the muted roar or of the fact that they were forced to raise their voices in order to be heard above it.

"He'll have to catch me first," Ethan said mildly, drying his jaw with a towel. "Not a bad job, Nappy," he added, examining himself in the floor-length glass that took up one corner of his dressing room. He was naked to the waist, and the lamp glowing softly on the nearby table reflected the sheen on his chest as he shrugged into a clean shirt and adjusted the cuffs.

"I decided to leaves it ter Damon Warrick to slit yer throat," Nappy growled.

Ethan's tone was amused. "My dear Nappy, you're behaving as though I were a simpleminded schoolboy. Do you honestly believe Damon Warrick poses the least little threat to me? I merely want to take a look around the island, a harmless bit of reconnoitering even you shouldn't find objectionable."

But Nappy took a dim view of his captain's plans, stating dourly that just because Damon Warrick owed him money didn't mean he had to go about stirring up more trouble for Miss China. Moreover he was seized with the suspicion that Ethan had other reasons for prying into the Warrick business, and Damon's connections with Wang Toh sprang uneasily to mind.

"It ain't that 'eathen Chinerman, is it?" he demanded bluntly. "Ever since that flunky of 'is called on Badajan to buy silk for 'im you've been actin' cagey as a tiger."

"Just the fact that Warrick entertained the man in his house makes me uneasy," Ethan admitted. "I wouldn't put it past Wang Toh to make a bid for King's Wheal now that Race Warrick is dead."

"That ain't no reason for you to get involved," Nappy pointed out angrily.

"Not even to protect Miss Warrick's interests?"

"I wouldn't want 'er involved wiv the 'eathen barstid," Nappy conceded reluctantly. "I fancy 'er brother don't 'ave the same experience 'is pappy did, and that'll make 'im fair game for the likes of Wang Toh." His expression grew troubled. "King's Wheal'd make a pretty jool in that barstid's crown."

"My own thoughts precisely," Ethan said. "And if Wang Toh Chen-Arn manages to wrest King's Wheal out of Damon Warrick's grasp it will give him a monopoly on all the silk produced between Whampoa and Singapore. I, for one, am not about to let him grow that powerful. That's why it's important for me to take a look around the island tomorrow night."

"I still don't like it."

Grinning, Ethan turned from the mirror and folded a clean white stock about his neck. "Stop looking so miserable, you wretched goat. I only want to have a look around! You act as if I mean to descend upon the heathens and foment a rising."

"I knows you, Cap'n Ethan," Nappy countered, refusing to be humored. "I knows you better than yer think, and where you go there's allus trouble!"

Shrugging into a gray coat that contrasted superbly with the snowy whiteness of the knotted stock, Ethan gave his steward a mocking laugh. "Enough of your fearful bleatings, old woman. I refuse to pass up the opportunity, and as I am late for an interview with the British High

Commissioner we might as well end our—What is it, Lal Sri?"

"Excuse, please, Bloodwell Captain." The little man was in an obvious state of agitation, bobbing his head and begging a thousand pardons for the intrusion.

"What is it?" Ethan repeated.

"It a woman here to see you, Bloodwell Captain," Lal Sri explained hastily. "I told her you make ready to go out, but she would not leave."

"Did she give her name?"

"She would not say. She only ask for you."

Ethan sighed. "Very well, show her in."

"She already in. When I try to close door she come past me. She would not wait. That why I thought it best to call you."

"It would seem," Ethan remarked with a sigh, "that Julia Clayton has finally discovered my whereabouts."

Nappy's brows rose. "I thort she were stayin' in them rooms she rented orf Geylang Road? She were going to wait there 'til the *Steengraffe* sailed."

"That won't be for another week," Ethan said dourly. "And if all Singapore knows I'm here why shouldn't Mrs. Clayton have heard of it? Damn! What a blasted nuisance! Lal Sri, tell Rajiid Ali I've been delayed. I should be joining him shortly."

It was not Julia Clayton who awaited Ethan in the mahogany-paneled salon but a young woman in a dark blue cape, a dripping hood pulled over her face, whose presence caused him to check sharply on the threshold.

"Well, well, Miss Warrick," he said, recovering himself admirably and strolling inside. "I must admit this is an unexpected surprise. Surely you didn't come across the Strait in this weather?" He eyed the pool of water spreading beneath her feet with distaste.

The plaintive wailing of an infant stopped China's reply, and Ethan's eyes narrowed as he noticed the bundle she had concealed in the folds of her cloak.

"What the devil is that?" he inquired rudely.

China dragged off the hood that had heretofore obscured her features, and Ethan was startled by the expression on her face. "What is it?" he demanded. "What's wrong?"

"It's Gem."

"Who?"

"The baby."

"Ah, yes. Your father's—er—your half-sister."

"I'm afraid she's ill," China said tremulously, brushing a sodden curl from her face and clutching the infant tightly against her.

"So you brought her here to me?"

"I didn't know what else to do! Mother refused to let her into the house and the old woman caring for her wasn't doing anything to help her except burning joss sticks to chase away demons. Anyone can see she needs proper medical attention."

"That may well be true," Ethan admitted curtly, "but I'm not a doctor."

China lifted her chin. "I know, but Darwin Stepkyne told me there was a doctor here in Singapore and I thought—"

"No, apparently you didn't think at all," Ethan interrupted harshly. "If you had, you wouldn't have come here in broad daylight with an infant in your arms. What do you suppose people are going to say about that?"

She regarded him blankly, her eyes seeming to take up every inch of her face. "I don't understand."

"My reputation is lamentably well known in these parts," Ethan pointed out ruthlessly, "as is the fact that you returned to Badajan aboard my ship. What obvious conclusion are people going to arrive at, seeing you enter my house unescorted, with a child?"

Scarlet color flared in China's cheeks as she realized what he was intimating. "Oh!" She gasped. "They wouldn't dare!"

"Poor Miss Warrick, how innocent you are!"

"It doesn't matter, does it? Surely Gem's health is much more important than idle gossip? Now, about the doctor Darwin mentioned?"

"I know who he means. A Frenchman by the name of Piaget who lives somewhere near the Sultan Mosque. Why don't you give her to me? And take off those soaking things. It won't do a bit of good if you come down with an illness yourself."

Ethan frowned as he took the whimpering bundle from her. It disturbed him that the child did indeed look ill, her breath rattling in her small chest and her cheeks flushed with fever. At least she had remained dry and warm during the crossing, for China had wrapped her securely in oilskins.

"I think it would be a good idea if you left as soon as possible," Ethan added, and his frown deepened. "You didn't by chance come alone?"

"No. I've got Lam Tan, one of the servants, waiting aboard the *Tempus* for me."

"Do your mother and brother know where you are?"

"I thought it best not to tell them."

"Well, I must say I'm relieved to discover that you can, on occasion, exercise commendable thinking," Ethan said grimly.

"That's exactly the sort of mockery I expected from you!" China retorted.

"My dear girl, then why did you come?" he asked, regarding her bedraggled form without a trace of sympathy.

"Because I had no idea where Doctor Piaget lived," China answered resentfully, "and I didn't care to wander the streets unescorted. I heard that you had acquired a house here in the city, and I thought perhaps you might permit Mr. Quarles to take me to him."

"Nappy?" Ethan was unaccountably annoyed. "Why didn't you think to ask me?"

There was no point in lying and China said stiffly, "In view of the things I've been told about you, Captain, I wasn't certain you would help."

"And what things were those?" The blue eyes were suddenly disconcertingly close. China looked away and was inordinately relieved when a loud voice from the doorway put an end to the silence that fell between them.

"Ah, my friend, so you are at home! I found the front door ajar and that obsequious houseboy of yours for once not in attendance, so I thought to myself that I'd— Hello! Who's this?"

China turned to find a blond bear of a man standing on the threshold of the salon regarding her with considerable interest. He was by far the largest man she had ever seen and no sooner had her startled gaze met his than he grinned and made a deep bow.

"Captain Tyler Crewe at your service, ma'am. May I add that the pleasure is all mine?"

So this is what had prompted Bloodwell to settle down, he thought shrewdly. A wife and child, uncommonly pretty ones at that.

"You're a lucky devil," he said to Ethan. "Where'd you find such a prize, eh?"

"Tyler, may I present Miss China Warrick of King's Wheal Plantation?" Ethan stated affably, hiding his own amusement behind a suitably poker-faced façade. "Miss Warrick is in Singapore seeking medical attention for her infant sister."

"Her sister?" Tyler gave a snort of laughter. "Surely you can do better than that, Ethan? I'm not some gullible Christian willing to believe the best about folks, especially when it's obvious they're lying!" He gave vent to another burst of laughter and tears of mirth rose to his eyes.

"It's true, sir," China said coolly. "Gem is my half-sister. She's ill, and Captain Bloodwell has kindly agreed to look after her for me."

Tyler Crewe fell silent at her words, and his narrowed gaze traveled from China to the infant in Ethan's arms. A closer look was all it took to reveal to him what he had missed before: the dark skin and midnight hair could only belong to a Eurasian, a child of mixed bloodline whose kind Tyler himself had spawned too lamentably often.

"I beg your pardon, Miss Warrick," he said sheepishly.

"It's quite all right," China assured him, though of course it was not. It was highly insulting, in fact, to be mistaken for the sort of woman who would entertain the notion of marrying a man like Ethan Bloodwell.

"Lal Sri," Ethan said to the houseboy who had entered the room, "send someone to Kallang Road to fetch Jacques Piaget, and be quick about it. Here, why don't you take Miss Warrick with you and see that she's returned safely to the harbor?"

"You can't send me away!" China protested. "What about Gem?"

"I assure you she'll be in good hands. Nappy can be

trusted to carry out Piaget's instructions, and I'll make certain we get a goat so that she'll have fresh milk."

"I'd still like to wait for the doctor."

"It would be wise, Miss Warrick, if you went with Lal Sri," Ethan said in a tone that brooked no argument.

"Oh, very well," China said with a scowl, realizing that she shouldn't have expected anything else from him.

Once out on the street she started quickly for the harbor, never noticing the dark Oriental who stood hidden behind a row of hibiscus growing in a nearby garden and who watched her departure from the coral-colored house with a great deal of interest.

___ *Chapter Thirteen* ___

Standing on the *Kowloon Star*'s main deck waiting for the sails to be reefed and listening to the gurgle of the outgoing tide, Nappy Quarles threw up his hands in disgust. "If you bloody well means to go, then you'll be takin' me wiv you. Somebody's got to watch you don't get your 'ead caved in puttin' yer nose where it ain't got business bein'!"

Captain Bloodwell, who had been leaning against the rail watching the setting sun draw fingers of scarlet across the rippling water, uttered a soft laugh. "You might have saved my hide on numerous occasions, Nappy, but I don't think you've much to worry about this time. I merely intend—"

"I knows what you intend," Nappy growled ill-temperedly. "It's greed, pure and simple."

Ethan shrugged, and turned to stare with his usual infuriating indifference across the darkening strait where the dim outline of the Warrick docks was visible through the swiftly descending darkness. As yet no boats had been made fast against the pilings, but Ethan could see a pair of servants, resplendent in white uniforms, lighting the rows of colored lanterns that had been strung along the pier. A new moon was rising from the sea, cresting the breakers along the shore in pale, iridescent opal.

"We might as well go. It'll be dark by the time we land," Ethan said curtly.

"What about your togs?" Nappy asked in a last and extremely futile attempt to sway the captain from his purpose. "You'll get filthy pokin' round in the dark."

"The Warricks will simply have to receive me as I am," Ethan said with a shrug, and Nappy gnashed his teeth in frustration, for the captain was wearing the same gray coat he had donned for his meeting with the British High Commissioner two days before, and in honor of this particular occasion had augmented it with a vest of burgundy silk. Tailored in Savile Row during his last visit to London, it suited his broad shoulders and lean frame superbly, and Nappy, careless though he might be of his own appearance, was fastidious to a fault with his captain's and couldn't bear to see it ruined in the swampy jungle.

"You could send Rajiid in your place," he began hopefully, but Ethan had had enough of his steward's meddlesome suggestions.

"I'm going myself and that's the end of it," he said brusquely. "Stay here if you're afraid of getting dirty." Nodding curtly to Hafiz, who waited at the winch, he stepped into the launch and Nappy had no choice but to follow, glowering and tugging angrily at his eyepatch.

Despite the little steward's fears, they encountered no one as they landed their boat on a narrow strip of sand hidden from the docks by thick ranks of mangrove roots growing out into the water. Wading ashore, Nappy made the lines fast and slapped irritably at the mosquitoes whose incessant whines blended with the shrieking of tree frogs in the surrounding darkness. The night was humid and the underbrush pressed close, filled with the acrid scent of damp, decaying organic matter. Though the distance they covered was no more than a mile, it was difficult to negotiate through the dense vegetation and Nappy was breathing heavily by the time they emerged into a moonlit clearing at the base of a craggy volcano. Wiping his perspiring brow with his sleeve, he regarded Ethan impatiently.

"Well, 'ave yer seen enough?" Looking over the halfdozen palm-thatched buildings clustered together in the moonlight, he failed to understand their significance. An elderly Chinese watchman shuffled aimlessly between them, his shadow long on the loamy ground.

"I believe I have," Ethan responded after a moment, much to Nappy's surprise.

"Let's go, then," he said quickly, not relishing the prospect of being caught prowling about the property like a thief.

"Why don't you take the launch and go on back to the ship?" Ethan suggested as they emerged from the footpath onto an overgrown stretch of shore near the docks. In the glow of the lanterns on the blackened water they could see an assortment of cutters, yachts, and launches crowding the pier and hear the laughter of their disembarking guests. "There's no need for you to wait."

"Oh, ain't there?" Nappy inquired darkly, seeing the number of Chinese and Asians who had joined the elegantly attired couples streaming up to the house. Like most devout Anglophiles of his day, Nappy had a healthy distrust of foreigners.

"Suit yourself," Ethan said with a grin, and took care to scrape the mud from his shoes and brush the twigs from his coat before sauntering away. It occurred to him as he crossed the picturesque footbridge leading to the brightly lit veranda of the plantation house that the number of guests hinted at an elaborate affair, and he found himself wondering what Malvina Warrick had in mind. She was a scheming creature, Prince Shaweh had claimed as the two men gossiped desultorily in the private rooms of Barindi's magnificent summer palace.

"She is like a tigress crouching in the reeds," the dissolute nobleman had complained, moving a playing piece on the pachisi board with a plump, bejeweled hand, "though it's money she's after, not a fattened calf. We haggled for many weeks over the price of an order, and by the time we reached an agreement and an envoy was sent to collect it, she claimed the delay had caused the price to rise once again. She was ungracious enough to demand an additional twenty thousand rupiahs!"

"Which you paid," Ethan presumed, having already observed that the Prince was wearing a new Arablike jubbah of exquisite gold, the unmistakable color of Badajan silk.

"Only under protest! I would have a wish," His Highness added with a sigh, "to see that disreputable son of hers assume the upper hand, for he is young and arrogant and therefore easily fooled, but he seems content to play the role of pasha, entertaining guests and spending his wealth unwisely."

"Not at all like Your Highness," Ethan had rejoindered with a grin, though it was a well-known fact that Azar bin Shaweh pursued his own extravagant lifestyle to excess.

Suspecting that he was being mocked, the Prince's heavy-lidded eyes narrowed, but he could see nothing untoward in the smiling countenance of his guest. "Ah, bah!" he said at last. "We will talk no more of white men, for their exploits bore me and I have enough silk in my coffers to clothe my wives and retainers a thousand times over. It is your move, my friend."

Ethan had obligingly returned to the game and beaten His Highness quite neatly. Now, as he strolled up the newly raked path to King's Wheal, he could not help but recall that Prince Shaweh had likened Malvina Warrick to a hunting tiger, and he was curious to meet her.

The humidity was quite tolerable and even the nightly din of the jungle was muted, a pleasant backdrop for the violins that played softly in the reception room. The doors to the central courtyard had all been thrown open and silk-clad servants were posted inside them. Armed with palm fronds, they stood prepared to whisk away any offensively large insects that might be lured inside by the fierce lights and the heady fragrance of the jasmine creepers decorating the ironwork.

Withdrawing to a shadowed corner of the veranda, Ethan leaned for a moment against the rail to study the arriving guests. He knew most of them by sight, noticeably Sir Joshua Boles, an overweight and thoroughly corrupt director of the powerful East India Company, and Claus Van

Ryde, a wealthy Djakarta planter who dealt mainly in spices and teak—and in the covert selling of African slaves. There were other merchants and businessmen of greater or lesser importance, the Chinese in their lavishly embroidered silk robes, the Occidentals turned out in proper European fashion escorting wives whose pale, listless faces were the products, Ethan knew, of unrelieved boredom and Asia's oppressive heat.

Sauntering inside, Ethan paused to exchange pleasantries with Malvina Warrick, whose greeting was every bit as effusive as he had expected it to be. What he had not expected was to find her an unusually handsome woman, her glossy chestnut hair arranged in a heavy chignon that lent dignity to her proud features. Tall and prepossessing, she placed a slim, gloved hand into Ethan's and assured him that she was honored by his presence.

"My son spoke very highly of you, Captain Bloodwell," she told him, and Ethan had to admire her for the cool audacity of the lie. "I trust we'll have time for a private chat later this evening?"

Ethan's expression was bland. "It would be a pleasure, madame."

He was quick to see the calculating light that sprang into her eyes and wondered if Prince Shaweh hadn't overestimated her after all. Ruthless and cunning? Not to him. In the final analysis she seemed equally as transparent and predictable as the rest of her sex.

Damon Warrick, on the other hand, made little effort to conceal his hostility as he and the captain shook hands. "Glad you could make it, Bloodwell," he murmured insincerely. "I understand you've gained possession of a house in Singapore?" His expression indicated clearly that he had never heard more unwelcome news.

"I have," Ethan said, "and I believe it should make life a good deal simpler for me."

"How do you mean?"

A faintly mocking light crept into the pale eyes. "Why, in the event I'm forced to delay my departure because of your—shall we say reluctance?—to conclude our business."

"Why, you—" Damon bristled, but Ethan had turned

away, and suddenly China was standing in the glittering entrance hall before him smiling up into Claus Van Ryde's fleshy face. Her crimson curls were drawn away from her small face and secured with a veil of gold netting, and her eyes gleamed jade green in the light, as sultry and mysterious as the eyes of the royal cats that had lolled on satin cushions in the palace of Barindi last week.

Instead of the accepted hoop skirt and stiff horsehair crinoline, she was wearing an Indian sari of dark green silk that was draped over her bare shoulders and fell in loose, shimmering folds to her ankles. Her feet were encased in gold-embroidered slippers, and a cluster of pigeon's-blood rubies were fastened about her throat with a delicate gold chain. She looked small and fragile and as impossibly lovely as a rare orchid. Cold, consuming anger washed over Ethan Bloodwell, anger at Malvina Warrick, who had chosen to dangle her daughter like an exotic jewel before lustful men like Claus Van Ryde.

Feeling the heat of Ethan's gaze upon her, China turned her head, and hot color flooded her cheeks as she met his black expression. The sari had been a gift from her father, yet something in the captain's look made her feel as though she were wearing something utterly shameful and unorthodox. The pleasure she had experienced in feeling the whispering fabric settle over the contours of her body vanished beneath those hard, condemning eyes, and she was suddenly consumed by an embarrassment more profound than any she might have felt had she appeared naked before him.

With an effort she quelled the desire to cover herself, and turned deliberately back to Van Ryde, her head lifted in a dignified manner. Ethan's jaw tightened in response, the virginal modesty behind China's embarrassment not having escaped him. In that one moment he knew with a clarity equal to the force of a blow that his anger had not been caused by his disgust at Malvina Warrick's scheming, but by the knowledge that he was at a sudden consumed by an almost savage desire to possess her beautiful daughter.

He heard the rustle of silk, smelled the faint fragrance of China's perfume as she swept past him on Van Ryde's

arm, and, looking after her, realized what every other male
in the room already knew: that China Warrick was not a
child but a passionately beautiful woman and that he would
be less than a man if he did not desire her.

Ethan looked quickly away, but there hadn't been time
to compose his features, and when he unwisely chanced to
meet Malvina Warrick's watchful gaze he saw a trium-
phant little smile curve her wide mouth and knew at once
that he had blundered badly by underestimating her. It
was for no one's sake but his own that Malvina had seen
fit to trick her daughter out like some houri of Moslem
paradise, hoping to ensnare him with her beauty and
thereby win the Warricks free of their debt. And he had
stepped into the trap as surely as a blind man.

Ethan took pleasure in the fleeting doubt that crossed
her face when he grinned at her brashly in return, but
when he turned away again his eyes were cold chips of
ice, and Claus Van Ryde, confronted in the courtyard moments later, was extremely disconcerted by them. Though
he was baffled as to why this savage-looking stranger had
suddenly seen fit to interrupt an intimate conversation
with the charming China Warrick, he wisely withdrew.

For a moment the captain and the young woman in the
glittering sari confronted one another in silence, oblivious
to the murmur of nearby conversations and the tinkling
of the fountain. China was acutely aware of the embarrassed flush that was once again creeping to her cheeks
and cast about despairingly for something to say.

"I wasn't aware that you had been invited this evening,
Captain," she said at last.

"What in hell are you wearing?" Ethan demanded as
though she hadn't spoken.

She caught at her lower lip and said in a tone of deliberate calm, "My father had intended to present this to me
upon my return from England. I'm wearing it tonight in
honor of his memory."

Something in her defiant face aroused Ethan's anger
even further, and with an effort he refrained from delivering a lecture that would surely have reduced her to tears.
It was maddeningly obvious to him that she had no idea
at all of the disturbing results she had achieved by draping

her slim body in shimmering green silk, nor could Race Warrick be blamed for having failed to consider that, in her absence, his daughter might have grown into a heart-stopping beauty who could unwittingly tempt the fates by cladding herself thusly.

"Don't you realize you're making a thorough spectacle of yourself?" he was nonetheless compelled to ask.

"Why? Because I'm not turned out in petticoats and corsets like the rest of Mother's guests?" China's eyes flashed. "I needn't remind you that you, more than anyone, have no right to judge those of us who choose to flout convention. I believe there's a term for that: something about a pot calling the kettle black?"

She could not help but experience a small shock as she looked up and saw the effect her stinging words had upon him. She cast a swift glance beyond his shoulder and was relieved to see that several young gentlemen, including her brother Damon, were conversing nearby. The sight did much to bolster her courage, and she reminded herself that Ethan Bloodwell had no right to treat her like some erring schoolgirl in need of discipline. This was her home and her party, after all, and he was nothing but a reprehensible opportunist whose presence was thoroughly unwelcome.

Then, suddenly, she remembered something that made it impossible for her to snub him. "How is Gem?" she asked breathlessly.

"Piaget diagnosed some harmless endemic ailment," Ethan said obligingly, "and predicted it would run its course uneventfully. He did say that you were wise to remove her from the village, and the care she's received from Nappy has assured a swift recovery."

China's sigh of relief annoyed him. "I needn't remind you that she'll be returned to you the moment she's well," he added coldly. "Tomorrow or the day after, I imagine, and it would be wise of you to decide in the meantime what's to be done with her."

China knew that her mother would not tolerate the half-caste child in the house, and yet she was not about to return Gem to the indifferent care of her elderly Chinese aunts and uncles. She should have realized that Captain Bloodwell, being an orphan himself and therefore incapable of understanding the strength of family ties, would not view her decision to help the child kindly. Still, given his own unhappy childhood, one would have thought that compassion for anyone in a similar predicament might have moved him to offer his assistance. China's lips thinned. The fact that it hadn't proved unquestionably that he possessed no conscience whatsoever.

"If you'll excuse me," she said frostily, "I must see to my guests." Her tone and the chill in her green-eyed glance made it obvious that he was not numbered among their ilk, and with a barely perceptible nod she left him.

Ethan watched as she threaded her way gracefully through the crowded courtyard. Though he normally had no taste for champagne, he cornered a passing servant and consumed several glasses of it in long, angry swallows. Bored by the idle chatter around him, he stepped onto the terrace where the nightly winds smelled pleasantly of the sea and not the stale odor of pommade and unwashed bodies. Breathing deeply, he allowed the throbbing anger to fade from his blood. Leaning against the rail, eyes brooding and enigmatic, he considered the possibility that Nappy Quarles had been right in insisting that he abandon his pursuit of those two hundred pounds. Surely no amount of money was worth the prospect of having China Warrick offered up to him like some palace concubine!

A rustling amid the orange trees growing in a row of stone planters near the edge of the terrace caught his attention and he moved quietly to investigate. "Who's there?" he rapped out once he was standing on the flat stone steps leading down to the lawn. The leaves of one of the miniature trees quivered furiously in response, and Ethan leaned down swiftly to seize the shadowed figure crouching behind it.

"What the devil—?" His grim expression gave way to one of astonishment as he surveyed the quarry he had dragged aloft by the seat of its trousers.

Brandon Warrick, finding himself dangling a good distance in the air in the grip of a very stern-looking Captain Bloodwell, quelled the desire to squawk loudly for help. Instead he said as politely as he could, "I wasn't spying, you know. Would you please put me down?"

Amusement crept into the pale eyes and Ethan's lips twitched as he obligingly lowered the boy to the ground. His smile deepened as he watched Brandon make a great show of dusting off his pants before staring up at him with a boldly tilted chin he knew only too well.

"What were you doing there in the shrubbery if not spying?"

Brandon sighed with relief, guessing quite accurately that he was not about to be betrayed. "Philippa wanted to come downstairs to watch the party. Mother said we couldn't, but China said she didn't think anyone would find out if we peeked through the windows."

"Somehow that doesn't surprise me," Ethan observed.

"Well, I thought it was a good idea. At least until you heard me. I couldn't run away, you know, not if it meant hurting the trees. They're a special kind of fruit tree Damon has been trying awfully hard to grow."

Moving to the edge of the terrace he called in a stage whisper, "You can come out now, Phil. It's only Captain Bloodwell and he won't tell on us. Will you?"

"I suppose I can be trusted to keep a secret."

"Oh, good! Philippa, I said you could come out now!"

"Can't," came a tiny whisper from somewhere in the thick of the bushes.

Brandon gave an exasperated sigh. "Why not? Don't tell me you're still scared?"

There was a long pause and then a gulp that sounded suspiciously like a sob. "I got my dress caught on something."

"Girls!" Brandon pronounced with all the wisdom of his twelve years, and rolled his eyes heavenward.

Ethan laughed heartily and swung himself over the wall to find Philippa Warrick crouching in the bushes, her night rail entangled in thorny creepers.

"I've a mind to turn both of you in," he informed them once he had freed the little girl and lifted her onto the terrace, his expression suitably forbidding. "You should know better than to leave your beds after dark."

"We're not scared of the dark," Philippa informed him haughtily, though her small hand slipped for reassurance into Brandon's as she leaned upon her sticks.

"We've been sneaking outside ever since Philippa was a baby," Brandon added. "And China used to take me swimming at night before she went away. Sometimes it was just too hot to sleep and China said we could do it as long as Mother didn't find out."

"I see." Privately Ethan did not. China Warrick had never struck him as the sort of frivolous girl who would defy a stern parent and risk treacherous currents for the sake of a moonlight swim. She seemed too prim and painfully conventional in that respect, and yet it was true that she had surprised him on numerous occasions with flashes of spirit he had considered totally uncharacteristic of her.

For the first time he was moved to consider what the repressive atmosphere of a British finishing school might have done to a young girl born on an island as wildly beautiful as this one. A seminary, Ethan knew, was no more civilized than an orphanage when one scraped away its imposing veneer, and now that he thought about it, was probably staffed by spinsters equally as ferocious as Maggie O'Shaughnessy.

Remembering how his own rebelliousness had earned him the enmity of that large-bosomed woman with the shrill, harping voice, Ethan was seized by a fresh wave of anger at Malvina Warrick who had deliberately cast her helpless daughter into a similar fate. As an orphan he had had no choice but to remain in Maggie O'Shaughnessy's care until he grew old enough to know better, but China, innocent China...

Blast it, Nappy was right! It was time to forget he had ever heard of China Warrick or those two hundred pounds, for it seemed impossible to gain them without entangling himself thoroughly in her life. He had already learned far more than he cared to about the unhappiness of her childhood and the cruelty of her greedy cousins and scheming mother. He had made it a point all his life to maintain strict avoidance of entanglements like these, and hadn't he deliberately sworn to himself at Broadhurst that his responsibility for China Warrick would end with the adjournment of the voyage?

Of course, no one could have anticipated the difficulties that had confronted him one after the other the moment his ship had sailed into Singapore Harbor. And how could he have known that he would be foolish, nay, utterly mad enough, to succumb to the thoroughly unwanted entrapment of falling in love with the proud redhead who was the very root of all his annoyance to begin with?

By God, Indonesia was growing far too uncomfortable for the likes of one Ethan Bloodwell! It boded ill indeed if he was starting to sympathize with the plight of China Warrick, who by rights had everything a young woman could want. And if he hadn't been blinded by greed, he probably could have seen it coming before it was too late.

Blood and fury, it wasn't too late yet! There were scores of money-making propositions awaiting the *Kowloon Star* elsewhere in the world. With luck they could still catch the heels of the southwest monsoons and sail tomorrow for Whampoa, put by a load of tea, and race the northeasterlies home to England. And if that seemed too tame for his crew, they could always set their sights for the Ivory Coast, take on coffee in Abidjan and trade it in the lively markets of—

"Ethan!"

He whirled about, the pair of children forgotten, and was taken aback by the sight of China running through the opened balcony door. Her slippers made no sound as she flew across the terrace, the sari whipping about her ankles. As she emerged into the moonlight he saw with a small shock that there was fear in her eyes, and he hastened to intercept her. She stumbled as he reached her and he moved swiftly to catch her in his arms, and suddenly it was as if everything surrounding them had faded away and nothing existed but the warmth of the body he drew close against his and the slim arms that wound themselves about his neck.

Lowering his head, he kissed her, fiercely and without awareness of the rest of creation, holding her as a drowning man might welcome a lifeline. He felt her quiver against him and her untutored lips opened beneath the pressure of his. Neither of them knew how long the kiss lasted, lost in the aching pleasure of the embrace until China uttered a breathless sob and struggled free of his grasp.

Instantly Ethan let her go and she retreated, gazing up

at him with her knuckles pressed to her mouth, her eyes
wide and alarmed and filled with a discovery she seemed
not to have wanted to make. She would have fled him
then, but Ethan took her roughly by the shoulders and
demanded to know what it was that had frightened her.

For a moment she stared at him blankly, then gasped.
"It—it was the tunics those men were wearing when they
came in!"

"What tunics? What men?"

China clasped her hands together to control their trembling and strove to answer calmly. "The tunics on the bodyguards inside. They were made of black silk with yellow
chrysanthemums embroidered on the sleeves."

"One of the guests brought his bodyguards with him?"
Ethan inquired. Though he knew it was common practice
for wealthy Chinese to employ them, he found it odd that
anyone would bring them to a private party since it was
considered bad manners to suggest that a guest was not
safe in the home of his host. "Who was it, China? Do you
know the man's name? I take it he was Chinese?"

She nodded. "I haven't any idea who they were, but I
think they are the same men who attacked me outside the
Raffles Hotel."

There was a moment of stunned silence, then, "Good
God! Are you certain?"

"Of course I am! Why shouldn't I be? I'd forgotten all
about them until now, but I assure you I saw those embroidered characters quite clearly."

"In that case I'd better take a look at them myself. Wait
here."

Ethan was gone before China could reply, and she was
forced to swallow her protests. Hands clasped to her breast,
she watched him stride into the house, and couldn't help
but experience a pang of relief. She was right after all in
having turned to Ethan for help. At the moment it didn't
matter to her that he was a thief and a murderer and
currently engaged in blackmailing her family. He alone
would know what to do if the bodyguards her mother and
brother had just openly welcomed into the house were
indeed the same ones who had so brutally attacked her.

China shivered. And of course it was only right that

Ethan had kissed her, for she had been nearly hysterical with fear. And since she had never been kissed before she mustn't make hasty judgments or allow herself to ponder even for a moment why it had felt so *right* to be in his arms or why the gesture had given her something more than simple comfort.

A shadow loomed on the stones before her and China looked up to see Ethan step through the curtained archway. Her heart began a nervous pounding as he crossed the terrace to the garden steps where she waited. Gazing into his hard face she wondered why he should look more puzzled than angry. Hadn't he believed her? She knew she hadn't been mistaken!

"Did you see them?" she inquired breathlessly.

Ethan nodded without speaking and she sensed at once that he was distracted and that his thoughts were not with her.

"What is it?" she demanded. "Did you recognize them?"

"No."

"Yet you had expected to?"

Ethan was forced to smile. "I'm afraid you've read my mind with unsettling accuracy."

"Who did you think they would be?"

She was rather surprised when Ethan obliged her with an answer.

"I had hoped they came to King's Wheal in the company of a Chinese official known by the name of Wang Toh Chen-Arn. He's a mandarin from Tientsin who, I daresay, is nearly as powerful as the Ch'ings and certainly far more cunning. Though he owns innumerable silk communes throughout the Middle Kingdom he apparently has an unquenchable appetite for Badajan silk. I believe he's purchased a good deal of it from your brother of late. Have you ever heard of him?"

China shook her head.

"It's fortunate you haven't," Ethan observed. "And I, for one, am relieved that those bodyguards you saw are not in his employ since it bears to reason that he did not order the attack on you and Nappy."

"Is that what you originally suspected?"

Ethan propped his hands on the terrace wall and stood

looking out into the darkness. The evening breeze carried
with it the sweet smell of frangipani and blended it with
the disturbing scent of China's perfume. Innumerable stars
winked in the blackness overhead and a crescent moon
hung suspended above the craggy peak of Badajan's soaring volcano. Its clear white light touched the sweeping
lawn of the plantation house far below and dusted it with
a glitter not unlike the hoar frost of an early English
winter.

It was a beautiful night, the crash and murmur of the
surf sounding dimly from the shore below, and Ethan gazed
into the garden with apparent absorption, knowing it would
be safer to look there, or anywhere else, than at China,
who stood quietly and achingly desirable beside him.

He did not answer her question directly but after a
moment said quietly, "Years ago I lost the *Lotus Star* to
an unscheduled delay in Kowloon that gave the Imperial
Navy ample time to sail up the Pearl River and capture
her. I confess that the mistake was mine, for I refused to
believe that they could be so close on my heels. As it turned
out my judgment was poor, and a pair of Chinese warships
ambushed us and put us out of commission."

But not without a fight, China suspected, and she wondered why she should feel none of the outrage that by
rights she ought to, considering that he had been breaking
the law, for she knew perfectly well that his cargo had
been opium. Furthermore it occurred to her that by re-
sisting arrest, Ethan Bloodwell had probably been responsible for numerous casualties among the Chinese
marines, who were guilty of no other crime than attempting to put a stop to the smuggling of such a dangerous
narcotic.

"It was Wang Toh Chen-Arn who insisted on the delay,"
Ethan continued after a moment, rather surprised himself
that China hadn't chosen to make some acid comment of
disapproval. "Our hold space had been consigned to him
on that particular voyage, and though they were nearly
full, he insisted we wait for his lorchas to bring additional
opium from Malwa. I didn't object to the plan since both
of us stood to make more money that way, and only afterward did I discover that Wang Toh had accepted a huge

bribe from the newly appointed viceroy in Canton to stall me. Apparently the viceroy knew that warships were advancing on Hong Kong and wanted to be assured that the *Lotus Star* would be captured."

China's brows knitted. "Why would he want to see that happen? My father said most of the officials appointed by the Emperor were thoroughly corrupt, which would mean that he was taking bribes from the Chinese Guild of Merchants to look the other way whenever opium was smuggled. By impounding your ship he was clearly destroying his own means of income. Why would he want to do anything so foolish?"

"Under other circumstances, he would have been harming himself," Ethan agreed, "but as he had been given an imperial edict to stop the smuggling he would have lost tremendous face, not to mention his exalted position, if he failed to offer up at least one China trader."

"So you were chosen as a sacrifice," China said, and gazing into the hawkish countenance presented her in the moonlight she experienced a curious sense of loss on his behalf. It was apparent that the *Lotus Star* had meant a great deal to him. The discovery took her aback, for she should have been profoundly pleased that the Chinese had taken it upon themselves to aim a blow at the China traders, whose illegal trafficking of opium was a crime she abhorred. Regrettably the drug trade had by no means been halted by that costly war, and China had seen for herself how insidious was the damage inflicted by the sticky brown substance, since many of the elderly men in Badajan's Chinese community had smoked it in their water pipes.

"The viceroy had no intention of risking the ire of the Guild of Merchants," Ethan was saying. "That's why he decided to turn his energy to the destruction of British and Portuguese traders instead. Like most Chinese he had a healthy hatred of foreigners and knew better than to attempt to bring his own people to heel."

"The bribe Wang Toh accepted from him must have been very large," China remarked thoughtfully. "Much more, I suppose, than the cost of the opium he lost?"

She saw Ethan's jaw tighten, and suddenly she felt afraid

of the savage anger burning within him. When he spoke, however, his tone was mild and tinged with a self-deprecating bitterness.

"Oh, yes, it was a healthy sum indeed. And no sooner was his cargo impounded than Wang Toh publicly bemoaned the fact that I, a barbarian from the hated West, had shamed him. As is Chinese custom, he placed a princely price on my head, but of course it was all a splendid farce since he had already pocketed the viceroy's bribe."

"How did you find out he betrayed you?"

"That," Ethan said, straightening abruptly, "is a long story." Having realized that he had already told her far more than he wished her to know, more, in fact, than he had ever told anyone of his past, he added harshly, "Perhaps we should concern ourselves instead with the identity of the men who attacked you in Singapore."

"What did you find out when you went inside?"

"That the bodyguards whose emblems you claim to recognize are employed by a merchant named Tse-Jin Woo who resides in Changi."

"That can't be! Tse-Jin Woo was an old and trusted friend of my father's. He's been doing business with my family for years and isn't the sort to carry grudges or try to collect a reward by turning you over to that Wang Toh person you mentioned. In fact, he has so much money that he hardly knows what to do with it. That's why he keeps bodyguards—because he's afraid he'll be kidnapped and held for ransom. Why would someone like that want to hurt Nappy or me?"

"I don't know. I've never heard of the man before tonight," Ethan admitted, and her question nagged at him. Of course it was entirely possible that three of Tse-Jin Woo's bodyguards had been retained secretly by an outsider eager to strike a blow against an old enemy—but who? It simply wasn't Wang Toh's way to bribe strangers he couldn't trust or to order an attack on Nappy Quarles and two hapless women—an attack that had gained him nothing, unless he had intended it as a warning?

The fact that the assailants had been wearing tunics that were easily recognized meant that they were not members of Tse-Jin Woo's bodyguard at all, but hired thugs who had donned the uniforms to throw their pursuers off the scent. And that would mean that no one would ever be able to trace them, Ethan decided grimly, and felt a surge of uncontrolled fury at the thought.

"I believe it's time you returned to the party, Miss Warrick. You are the guest of honor, after all, and I imagine they'll be wondering what's happened to you."

"I don't think," China said frostily, "that you have any right to dismiss me without telling me what you're going to do."

"Oh, but I can and I will," Ethan told her unpleasantly. "The identity of those men in Singapore needn't concern you—at least no more so than what your mother is going to think when it's discovered you've been engaged in an intimate conversation with a man of my caliber alone on the terrace."

"Perhaps you are accustomed to being pursued by assassins, Captain," China said frigidly, "but I most certainly am not. And seeing as I have become an unwitting target in a conflict between yourself and some unmentionable person you've offended in the past, I believe I have every right to be concerned, even though you claim I do not. As for finding the prospect of being involved with murderers no more disturbing than being caught entertaining you alone on the terrace—" She fixed him with a withering glance. "You rate yourself too highly, sir. Good night."

Turning her back on him, China crossed the terrace with an angry swish of silk, and Ethan was left staring with compressed lips at the swaying curtains through which she vanished. After a long moment he clattered down the garden steps, never noticing—indeed, having forgotten all about—the pair of children who stood in the shadows of a nearby tree.

"Oh, Brandon, what do you think he means to do?" Philippa whispered once they were alone. Though she hadn't understood a great deal of the exchange between the tall sea captain and her lovely sister, she had been thoroughly frightened by the look on the captain's face.

Brandon, who had understood enough to draw the conclusion that China had been attacked in Singapore because of something Ethan Bloodwell had done, jammed his hands

into his trouser pockets. "I don't know," he said helplessly,
and wished vehemently that his father were still alive.
Father would have known instantly what to do!

"Do you think he'll hurt China? I heard Damon say he
was a bad man!"

Brandon considered the question before shaking his
head. "I don't think so. He couldn't mean to hurt her if he
kissed her, could he? It's somebody else. That Wang Toh
person, I think. Come on."

"Where are we going?" Philippa demanded breathlessly
as she hobbled beside him down the raked path leading
not to the far end of the house where their bedrooms lay
but to the covered archway of the eastern portico—and
Damon's private study. "What are we going to do?"

"I don't know yet," Brandon replied, his jaw set at a
stubborn angle that anyone who had known his father and
grandfather would have had no trouble recognizing. "I
don't know yet, but I'll think of something!"

_____ *Chapter Fourteen* _____

Rajiid Ali, his hawkish features obscured by a flowing kafiya, emerged from the doorway of a waterfront brothel to find Nappy Quarles awaiting him in the shade of a nearby fig tree. Without speaking the two men fell into step and turned south along the waterfront, oblivious to the roustabouts, rickshaws, and pedestrians that jostled and fought one another for room on the crowded streets.

The morning had dawned clear, yet afternoon had brought more clouds from the west; leaden thunderheads that rumbled ominously and promised heavy rain. Lightning danced across the distant mountains of Malaysia and a sudden gust of wind set the blocks and lines of the anchored ships tapping and clanking restlessly. Another puff ruffled the glassy water and lifted the long ends of Rajiid's robes as the two men turned down the wide, palm-edged street leading to the sprawling coral house.

"I was unable to learn a thing," Rajiid said darkly. "By Allah, they were naught but ignorant dogs."

Nappy's nut brown face hardened. "The cap'n won't like us coming in empty-'anded. Not again."

"I offered princely bribes. If they truly know nothing then they cannot be expected to speak—even for a price."

"I was 'opin' you'd found something," Nappy confessed unhappily. "Leastaways enough to set Cap'n Ethan on the right trail after them buggers wot 'urt Miss China."

"Inshallah." Rajiid shrugged. "It is in the hands of God to decide if they will be caught."

Nappy snorted. "From the way 'e's actin' you'd think it were in the 'ands of Ethan Bloodwell 'isself! Rum curious cove, 'e's become," he added, slapping irritably at the mosquitoes that swarmed in a whining cloud above his head. "'E weren't this anxious ter catch 'em when it first 'appened!"

"Curious indeed," Rajiid agreed, for never had he known his captain to pursue a hopeless cause quite so doggedly. The youths who had attacked Nappy Quarles and the two Englishwomen had doubtless melted into the teeming streets of Canton days ago and would never be found. And the bodyguards of Tse-Jin Woo would be of no help either, first because he, Rajiid, was an Arab and they would tell him nothing when he questioned them, and secondly because neither he nor the captain had been in Singapore long enough to recruit the spies one needed to infiltrate their ranks—at least not those who could be trusted.

Rajiid wished there was some way he could convince the captain of the futility of his pursuit. But the captain had been afflicted with a curious madness since his return from the Warrick island two days earlier and would not listen to reason. Allah forgive him! He was intractable to the point of foolishness and in this particular instance there was no hope of changing his mind.

"Why, Mr. Quarles, Rajiid, what a pleasant surprise!"

At first neither Nappy nor the frowning Rajiid recognized the Englishwoman in the daffodil yellow walking dress who descended upon them, her features obscured beneath an outrageous hat with a floppy brim liberally strewn with artificial flowers. It was only when she tilted her head at a coquettish angle that Nappy was compelled to utter a groan which he quickly and successfully hid behind an energetic fit of coughing.

"Afternoon, Mrs. Clayton. I thort you was sailin' for India on the *Steengraffe?*"

"Not until tomorrow evening," Julia replied cheerfully, and regarded Nappy with considerable interest. "I understand Captain Bloodwell has taken up residence in a house here in Singapore."

"Right, 'e 'as. We calls it the Coral 'Ouse. 'E's—"

Seeing the negative movement of Rajiid's head, Nappy broke off abruptly, then shrugged and decided there was little sense in hiding something from Julia Clayton that she obviously already knew. Besides, she couldn't possibly be so foolish as to entertain the notion of visiting the captain at his home, not after he had made it clear to her that he wasn't interested!

But apparently Julia Clayton had exactly that in mind, for she was, at the very least, the sort of woman who never took the word "no" for an answer. Smiling brightly, she remarked that she would be ever so delighted to bid Captain Bloodwell farewell before she left Singapore, and did Nappy have any objections to showing her the way to his house?

While Rajiid muttered an appropriate Arabic oath, Nappy shook his head and tugged uncomfortably at his eyepatch. "It wouldn't be right, Mrs. Clayton. You oughtn't to be goin' there."

Julia's lips thinned. "Whyever not?"

"Because the Coral 'Ouse were once used for—er—Wot I mean is, there ain't never been no wimmen received there, no proper white wimmen, anyways, if you catch my meanin'."

Julia dismissed his fears with an airy laugh. "Oh, I'm sure there's nothing to worry about! I'm leaving Singapore for good tomorrow and don't care one bit what people will choose to think about me. Since I shall never see them again, what could it possibly matter?"

Nappy did not know how to answer her. The root of the problem lay not so much in what anyone would think seeing Julia Clayton enter Ethan Bloodwell's house, but in the manner in which the captain, preoccupied with other problems, would receive her. In view of the mood in which he had found himself of late, Nappy heartily suspected that the encounter would not be pleasant.

"I have my maid with me," Julia resumed, gesturing to a stout Malaysian woman who followed at a respectful distance, "so you needn't worry that I won't be properly escorted."

Rajiid made a sound of disapproval low in his throat and turned rudely away while Nappy sighed deeply. One couldn't exactly disoblige a lady, not if she happened to be the kind who would create an unpleasant scene if her wishes were not granted.

"All right, then, I'll take you," he growled, and hoped fervently that the captain's disapproval would end up descending on a more deserving head—Mrs. Clayton's, for instance—than his own.

Julia's answering smile was tinged with triumph as she fell into step beside him. Five days of stifling heat and unbearable boredom had convinced her that she had made a dreadful mistake in leaving England to see the world, for nothing had turned out even remotely as she had envisioned it. Singapore was hot, filthy, and dull beyond compare, and she still chafed at the fact that Ethan had changed his mind about taking her away from it. Being stranded in a foreign country without the likelihood of finding a man willing to improve her circumstances was a deplorable situation, and when Julia had awakened this morning with the relentless rain clattering once again on the roof of the cramped quarters she had rented, she had flown into a rage.

She would not, absolutely would not, sail for India aboard the *Steengraffe*. Why on earth would she want to leave one hatefully humid country in order to take up residence in another? Nor was Julia about to return to England and revive the vicious gossip surrounding her disastrous affair with Charles Pinkerton. She had been mistress to many men, a kept woman whose beauty and charm had enabled her to rise far above her humble origins and maintain the lavish lifestyle she craved. Why couldn't she use those same skills here in Singapore, most notably on Ethan Bloodwell, instead of starting all over again in Calcutta, where her prospects would doubtless be far less favorable?

"'Ere you go, Mrs. Clayton. The Coral 'Ouse."

Opening the wrought-iron gate, Nappy stood aside to allow her to enter while Rajiid vanished wordlessly around the rear of the house. "The cap'n mayn't be 'ome," he warned, lifting the weathered brass knocker.

"I don't mind waiting."

"I were afraid o' that," Nappy muttered beneath his breath, and prayed that Lal Sri would have a clever enough excuse to prevent her coming inside. Unfortunately it was not Lal Sri who opened the door, but Captain Bloodwell himself, a gurgling Gem Warrick tucked beneath his arm.

"What is it, Piaget?" Ethan inquired, thinking that the physician, who had left the house not five minutes earlier after pronouncing the infant recovered, had forgotten something. A frown drew his brows together when he saw Julia on the steps, and Nappy was hard-pressed not to laugh as her startled eyes fell on the Chinese baby who tugged energetically at the sun-bleached hair curling below the captain's collar.

"Why, Ethan," she said, recovering herself admirably and sweeping inside to take Gem from him, "what a darling child! Is it yours?"

"My dear Julia, what a preposterous notion!" The suggestion of a drawl in Ethan's voice deepened as he sent a narrowed glance at his steward that spoke volumes of displeasure.

"Mrs. Clayton were comin' to say cheerio," Nappy explained quickly. "She's leaving wiv tomorrow's tide. We met 'er on the street and she asked to come along. Rajiid waren't able to find out a thing, by the way."

Julia saw the anger that flared briefly in Ethan's lean face and wondered with interest what it was that Rajiid had been after. She lowered her head quickly and cooed at the baby, hoping to hide her curiosity from Ethan's probing eyes.

"What about you, Nappy?"

"It didn't go so well neither, Cap'n. There ain't many in this town wot's got much of a mem'ry. Not even the kind an 'andsome bribe'd jog."

"I see."

There was something unnerving about the manner in

which those two simple words had been uttered and Julia groped about for some way to break the tension that had settled almost palpably over the elegant entrance hall.

"If the child isn't yours," she said after a moment, "where did she come from?"

"From Badajan."

Julia lifted startled eyes to Ethan's and saw that he was regarding her with a measure of grim amusement, as though it pleased him to toy with her and thereby dispel some of his own restless anger.

"From—from Badajan? I'm afraid I don't understand."

"'Er name be Gem Warrick," Nappy said helpfully, thrusting a gnarled finger in the infant's direction.

"Warrick?" Julia's eyes widened. "How can she possibly be a Warrick? She's Chinese!"

"She be Miss China's 'arf-sister," Nappy explained, realizing the captain could not be relied upon to provide Julia with a civil answer. "We been lookin' arfter 'er. She's gettin' o'er bein' ill."

"Yes, I can see that. She's awfully thin, but what is she doing here? Why isn't she at King's Wheal with her family?"

She listened with a frown as Nappy explained, then glanced sharply into Ethan Bloodwell's face. How had China Warrick managed to convince him to take the child into his home?

"My dear Julia, it was either that or turn the child out into the streets." Apparently Ethan had understood quite clearly the thoughts racing through her brain, and the twitching of his lips gave evidence of his amusement at the nature of her musings. "I may be an unscrupulous adventurer, but I'm not about to have the death of an infant on my conscience. Provided, of course, that I even have one."

"What's going to happen to her if China's mother refuses to allow her to stay at King's Wheal?" Julia asked. "What a terrible thing to do to such a darling little creature! But then I imagine it's a point of pride, isn't it?"

"Miss China ain't decided what's to be done wiv 'er yet," Nappy said unhappily. "It won't do to keep 'er 'ere, and it ain't likely she'll take the little nipper back to the village where she came from."

"Whatever she chooses to do with her had better be done quickly," Ethan pronounced curtly. "I have no wish to turn my house into a foundling asylum."

"Why don't you let her stay with me?" Julia asked impulsively.

Both men regarded her with astonishment.

"Well, why not?" Julia demanded in annoyance. "I have my own rooms on Geylang Road. She can stay there until China finds a suitable home for her."

"I thought you were sailing for India?" Ethan reminded her with a knowing grin.

Julia tossed her head. "I've decided not to go. From what I've heard it's no more civilized than Singapore and even hotter this time of year. So, will you let me take her or not?" She was surprised to discover that it had suddenly become terribly important to her that she be entrusted with the child, though she couldn't exactly explain why. Perhaps it was because it gave her a reason to remain in Singapore, yet had she examined her feelings more closely Julia would have been profoundly startled to realize that it was not mere selfish interest that had prompted her to make the offer. Julia Clayton, the ambitious beauty who had ruthlessly clawed her way from the poverty of her Sheffield roots to the glittering drawing rooms of London, had inexplicably found herself undone by a pair of smiling green eyes.

"I suppose there's no harm in it," Ethan said after a thoughtful pause. "Provided Miss Warrick has no objections."

"She couldn't possibly," Julia said coolly.

"God above, another one!" came a startled voice from behind them. "Where in hell do you find 'em, you devil's spawn, eh?"

No one had noticed that the front door had been left ajar and that a grinning face topped with unruly blond hair was peering around it to take in with considerable interest the scene unfolding before him.

"I've yet to figure out what it is about you that brings the ladies flocking, Bloodwell," Tyler Crewe complained as he sauntered inside. "I've turned this city on its beam ends plenty of times and never found anything as charming as this."

"Perhaps you've been going about it the wrong way, Tyler," Ethan said helpfully, but something in his tone gave Captain Crewe pause.

Lord above, now what had put young Bloodwell in such a fine fettle, he wondered? Surely not the lady regarding him with such longing in her eyes? Not quite as pretty as the first one—that Warrick lass, wasn't it?—but clearly of a more willing temperament if he read her looks a'right.

Regrettably Tyler was unable to give her the attention she warranted, for something in the hard lines of Ethan Bloodwell's face warned him that his mood was volatile. And knowing that look far too well, he took it upon himself to take command of the situation, slyly suggesting that it might be wise of Mrs. Clayton to take her leave before the servants took to gossiping about her.

Julia was only too happy to escape with Gem, and Nappy, quick to seize the advantage, ushered her hastily through the front door while Tyler followed Ethan into his study and brusquely demanded an explanation for the disquieting tension that had settled over the household. Knowing full well that it had nothing whatsoever to do with the lovely woman or the Chinese infant, he was expecting any number of explanations, yet he was not at all prepared when Ethan obliged him with a terse account of the assault made on China Warrick and his steward upon their arrival in Singapore.

"So you think this Tse-Jin Woo is responsible?" he asked when Ethan finished speaking.

"No. I'm more inclined to believe his signet was used as a decoy by the real assailants, but unless I can question his bodyguards I can never be sure."

"It's entirely possible that Tse-Jin Woo did order the attack," Tyler said thoughtfully, picking at his teeth with the blade of his *kris*, the curved Malayan dagger he carried with him wherever he went. "Maybe he didn't have any reason to make trouble for you or the Warrick girl, but who can tell how those yellow bastards think? You need to find those attackers, otherwise you'll never know."

"I've sent my crew to scour the city but to no avail.

Rajiid even went up to the kampongs to see if perhaps they
fled there when the incident first occurred."

"And had they?"

Ethan stirred restlessly. "No. They've all but vanished
from the face of the earth, which doesn't surprise me in
the least. Damn it! My hands are tied until I can have a
crack at Tse-Jin Woo."

"Which brings us to the subject of spies," Tyler pointed
out. "I'm at your disposal."

Ethan regarded him for a moment in silence. "Can you do
it, Tyler?"

"Consider it done," the big man said, grinning. "I've a
friend in the Society of the Oxen what owes me a few
favors. They've got ears and eyes in every household in
this city, and if any of Tse-Jin Woo's men were responsible
for that attack they'll find out. By the way, do you have
any whiskey? I'm cursed tired of drinking this brandy of
yours."

Stepping around the desk in the small, book-lined study,
Ethan obligingly poured the requested drink. "What is it
you want in return?" he inquired as he offered the glass,
knowing perfectly well that Tyler Crewe never performed
simple favors. "I must warn you," he added, thinking of
the last time they had struck a bargain together, "that I'm
rather limited on capital."

To his surprise the request was relatively simple.

"I should want," Tyler announced after taking a long
swallow from his glass, "a closer acquaintance with the
brown-haired beauty you so unceremoniously ushered
through the door when I arrived. Or are there others I
should see before making my choice?"

"Others?"

"Yes, others! Twice now I've walked into this house to
find you engaged in a dramatic confrontation with some
fiery beauty I've never seen before!"

"I assure you there are no others."

Tyler grinned. "Just as well. I happen to think the dark-
haired woman is more to my taste, and you know how
much I like the tall ones. Pretty as she is, I can't say I'd
care to sweep China Warrick off her feet. Might break her
spine if I did. Still, if she's anything like her father and

grandfather," he added thoughtfully, "she's probably more resilient than she looks. Bad-tempered lot, those Warricks, and proud as the devil. Honest, too, though you wouldn't expect it with the money they've got, or had, at any rate."

"Had?" Ethan inquired interestedly.

Tyler nodded. "I think they've run into trouble since Race Warrick drowned last year. Doesn't surprise me any, not the way that upstart stepson of his throws his wealth around. Say, this isn't bad stuff. Got another glass? Thanks. Now, where was I?"

"Weighing the virtues of Julia Clayton, the woman you want me to introduce you to," Ethan replied helpfully.

Captain Crewe ruminated for a moment, then said, "I'll take her, I suppose."

"She may prove dangerous," Ethan warned.

"All the better." Tyler's grin was wide and wolfish. "I like a woman what poses a bit of a challenge." Leaning forward he said in a dramatic whisper that filled the air between them with boozy breath, "Let me have her, old friend, and I'll see there's a spy in Changi by eventide tomorrow."

Inasmuch as Captain Crewe was a man of his word, the spy was duly recruited and the men of Tse-Jin Woo's bodyguard carefully interrogated, though with sadly disappointing results. To a man they scoffed at the notion that any member of their rank would be dishonorable enough to accept a bribe, especially one for the laughable purpose of attacking a pair of helpless women and an elderly man with only one eye.

"I'm afraid you're going to have to believe 'em," Tyler Crewe concluded, meeting with Ethan on the downstairs terrace of the Coral House several days later. "It's a matter of honor, you know. The mere thought of accepting a bribe disgusts them. I found out, too, that Tse-Jin Woo's grandfather taught Kingston Warrick to speak Chinese. He was one of the first Europeans to learn it, did you know that? You can't find stronger ties than the Warricks have with Tse-Jin Woo and his family. You could even call it friendship, though it's hard to believe a concept like that can exist between Westerners and those damned suspicious Chinese."

Ethan rose and prowled restlessly to the end of the terrace where he stared into the distance for a time without speaking. "Then I suppose we'll never know who was responsible," he said at last, and his expression grew hard. "Bloody hell! That doesn't leave me with much of a choice!"

Lal Sri, stepping onto the terrace at that moment to inform his master that the evening meal had been laid out, was curtly interrupted and charged with the execution of a series of quite incomprehensible instructions. Tyler Crewe was equally mystified by Ethan's brusqueness, yet when his repeated demands to know what the devil all this nonsense was about were simply ignored, he lost his temper and threatened to resort to physical violence to gain the answers he sought.

"You've tried that before, Tyler, remember?" Ethan inquired blandly.

The burly captain made a face. "Aye, you're right. And it cost me a few cracked ribs."

"Not to mention a broken nose," Ethan recalled without sympathy. "In any case it was richly deserved as you were in the process of rifling my safe for silver ingots."

"You were drunk," Tyler accused, "and fast asleep in the arms of that alluring Persian courtesan— God, what was her name? Big, black eyes and lips like rubies! Had you over the barrels, didn't she? I never dreamed you'd wake up, let alone be in sufficient command of your faculties to fight me."

"Or trounce you thoroughly."

"Aye, that, too," Tyler conceded with a scowl.

The suggestion of a smile curved Ethan's hard, slashing mouth, and after a moment the tension eased from his face and he said obligingly, "I'm going to Badajan, Tyler, just as soon as I write a letter to a friend in Djakarta who happens to owe me a favor."

"Why back to Badajan?"

"To settle a matter that should have been attended long before this," Ethan said darkly.

Tyler threw up his hands and made an undignified sound. "Once again I find you speaking in riddles!"

The pale eyes mustered him calmly. "Am I? It's really quite simple. Someone in my past, and I don't yet know who, has embarked on a ruthless game of vengeance against me. Though normally it wouldn't give me the least cause for concern, he has unwisely chosen to involve an innocent young woman, and the fact that I cannot discover who it is has convinced me that at present I can do nothing to protect her."

"I take it you mean the Warrick girl?"

Ethan's face was suddenly a stranger's face, remote and enigmatic. "Aye, the Warrick girl. Are you returning home tonight, Tyler?"

"I was thinkin' I might."

"Then you'll be so good as to deliver the letter for me?" Without waiting for an answer, he strode back into the house where he penned a quick letter at his desk while Tyler waited impatiently at his elbow. Thrusting it into his hands, Ethan remarked that he had quite a lot to do and would Tyler please excuse him? Without another word he quit the study, calling loudly for Lal Sri.

"Impatient bastard," Tyler remarked to the deserted room, and could only hope that he wasn't planning to do anything ill-advised, like going to Changi to make trouble with Tse-Jin Woo.

But it was Damon Warrick that Ethan Bloodwell intended to see, and upon arriving on Badajan aboard a sampan that Lal Sri had procured for him, he walked quickly up to the house. A robed manservant answered his knock on the door and explained regretfully that the young master was entertaining visitors and could not be disturbed.

"You will come back tomorrow, yes? It is late now and supper is being served. Tomorrow, yes?" He tried to shut the door as he spoke only to find it barred by a muscular arm and an accompanying look that suggested it would be unwise of him to resist.

"Please tell your master that I will keep him no more than a quarter hour," Ethan said, and despite this civilly uttered message the manservant hastened fearfully away, leaving Ethan on the darkened veranda listening to the whirring of the fruit bats in the garden and the rustle of the bougainvillea in the wind.

Moments later Damon Warrick appeared on the light-flooded portal, hostility and suspicion darkening his thin features. "What is it, Bloodwell? What do you want? I've a delegation of merchants from Macao awaiting me in the dining room and you've got some bloody nerve to pop up on my doorstep threatening my servants!"

"I've come for my two hundred pounds," Ethan told him coldly, "and I warn you that I won't leave without them this time."

For the space of a full minute there was stunned silence on the veranda.

"Is that a threat?" Damon demanded at last.

"If you like."

Damon bridled. "What in God's name makes you think I have any intention of—" His words were abruptly broken off as the lawn behind the broad-shouldered captain filled suddenly with shadows; two men, no, three, all of them armed, the most sinister being an Arab in flowing robes who carried a curved dagger with a blade that glinted ominously in the square of light falling from the house door onto the grass.

Captain Bloodwell, too, had drawn a weapon from his breeches, a pistol with a barrel that glinted cold blue steel. "Well?" he inquired softly. "Are you going to pay me or not?"

"Will you shoot me if I don't?" Damon scoffed with forced bravado.

Ethan's lips curved. "I might."

A flicker of fear showed briefly in Damon's eyes and he refrained with difficulty from slamming the door in the captain's grinning face. The man was bluffing—he had to be! No one would dare cut down an unarmed man in his own home, not even Ethan Bloodwell and his cursed vigilantes!

"Damn you, I haven't got that kind of money!" Damon hissed, the sweat beginning to trickle into his eyes. "King's Wheal is nearly bankrupt!"

"I thought as much," Ethan said, lowering the pistol. "I didn't think I'd get the admission out of you any other way. What about China's inheritance? Did you fritter that away, too?"

Damon regarded him blankly. "China's—inheritance?"

"Come, come," Ethan said impatiently, "don't try to make me look the fool. Her father couldn't have left everything to you. He would have made some provisions for her, and for Brandon and Philippa."

Hot color rushed to Damon's face. "And if he did? What are you suggesting?"

"I'm not suggesting anything. But the consensus seems to be that you've run King's Wheal into the ground in the months since your stepfather's death. And to recompense, your mother came up with the brilliant scheme of entertaining clients in time-honored fashion: offering opium, women, eunuchs, anything to tempt them to pay a higher price for their orders. Very clever, I'll admit, and it's obvious to me that China has no idea what the two of you have been up to."

"So what? Will you tell her?" Damon challenged.

Ethan thought of the stricken look on China Warrick's face when she had discovered the truth about her father's relationship to the infant girl Gem. "No."

Emboldened, Damon demanded, "Then what is it you want? I seriously doubt you came here merely to insult my business acumen, and it couldn't be those two hundred pounds, not if you're aware, and I think you must be, that I couldn't pay you even if you threatened to kill me."

"Believe me, if I really intended to kill you, I wouldn't waste my time with idle threats. I came to find out whether Race Warrick left his children an inheritance; in China's case a dowry."

Damon swallowed convulsively, the captain's blunt words having served to quell completely his momentary surge of confidence. All at once he looked his twenty-one years, youthful, inexperienced, and extremely uncertain. "What is it you're after? Are you trying to blackmail me?" The hinges creaked a protest as he gripped the doorlatch with a white-knuckled hand. "What does China's inheritance have to do with any of this?"

"It's quite simple, actually." Tucking the pistol back into his belt though the men behind him continued to brandish theirs, Ethan said lightly, "I'm willing to accept China's dowry—or inheritance, if you wish—in place of those two hundred pounds, provided you haven't spent it yet."

"No, I haven't. At least not all of it. But surely you must realize you'll have to marry her to take possession of her money!"

"I'm quite aware of that," Ethan replied, and suddenly the tone of his voice was neither affable nor mild nor even, in Damon's opinion, remotely human. "You can rest assured that I've thought the matter over quite carefully. I've summoned an acquaintance from Djakarta, a former barrister, to draw up the necessary papers. As soon as he arrives you will sign over the sum of your sister's dowry to me—and I will make China my wife."

_____ *Chapter Fifteen* _____

China Warrick, her face white and strained, turned her
mount down the overgrown jungle trail leading from the
cluster of production sheds to the modest cottage in which
Darwin Stepkyne lived. A stifling hot dawn was breaking
over the slumbering island, covering the mountains with
a layer of haze and silencing the nocturnal creatures scur
rying back to their roosts. The biscuit-colored riding habit
China wore clung damply to her back and shoulders while
the feathers in her veiled hat drooped like wilted flowers.
There were shadows beneath her lovely eyes and the chignon confining her bright red hair was pinned in haphaz-
ard fashion, for she had plaited it in haste.

Darwin was sipping coffee and making notes in his
ledger when the clopping of hooves on the tightly packed
earth brought him outside, barefooted and in shirtsleeves.

"Miss Warrick, what is it? What's happened? There's
nothing wrong at the house, is there?"

China did not know how to begin to explain what had
brought her here in such a hurry. Shortly after midnight
she had been awakened by the sounds of an argument,

and upon realizing that the voices were coming from Damon's study, she had thrown a wrapper on and gone down to investigate. She had found the study door ajar and her mother and brother engaged in the act of hurling cold, angry accusations at one another. Unwilling to eavesdrop, she had slipped away without speaking, but the utterance of a certain name had halted her in her tracks and she had tiptoed back and heard the words that had stiffened her with shock and caused her lips to move in soundless denial.

"I will not marry Ethan Bloodwell," she had told herself in a choked whisper once she fled back to her room, lying with wide, unseeing eyes in the darkness. "I will not, I will not!"

But it was obvious to her that her mother had already decided as much and that Damon was prepared to sign, though with apparent reluctance, the papers that would make it binding.

It occurred to China that she had been sold exactly like a slave or some other possession of equally little value, sold for the sum of two hundred pounds to a man who was neither respectable nor kind and who most assuredly did not care in the least about her. It was appalling to envision life as Ethan Bloodwell's wife, forced to share a house with his undoubtedly numerous mistresses while he sailed around the globe in pursuit of adventure, amusing himself by breaking every law he encountered merely because it pleased him to do so.

"I'll have to run away," China decided, yet the thought filled her with flaring anger, and she knew at once that she would not. No one, not even Ethan Bloodwell, was going to drive her away from Badajan again!

She knew he had made the offer only because Damon had refused to pay him his two hundred pounds, and being thoroughly unscrupulous, had doubtless asked questions among her father's acquaintances and discovered that China Warrick's dowry entailed at least that amount.

How clever of him to have come up with such a rewarding alternative, China thought, quivering with outrage and wishing they were standing face-to-face this very moment so that she could have the pleasure of telling him exactly what she thought of him. But he would only laugh, as he always laughed at everything she said, and treat her with the callous disregard of an adult toward a spoiled, unmanageable child. She had never been anything more to him than an exasperating burden and he had infuriated and hurt her cruelly at times with his refusal to take her seriously.

Against her better judgment, China found herself remembering how he had kissed her that night on the terrace and thinking of the slow delight that had followed on the heels of her initial shock, the breathless emotions that had dragged at her heart and filled her with wonder and not a little fear. In his arms she had found herself confronted with feelings she had never dreamed existed and which had disturbed her with their compelling intensity. And later, and perhaps somewhat shamelessly, she had been able to recapture them merely by brushing her lips with the tips of her fingers and remembering the feel of his mouth against hers.

It infuriated her that she should be thinking of something as meaningless as a kiss when by rights she should be plotting Captain Ethan Bloodwell's timely demise. Propping her elbows against the sill, she stared across the moonlit courtyard, the hot breeze lifting the crimson hair that spilled unbound over her shoulders. Only the tinkling of the fountain and the scratching and scurrying of some foraging animal, perhaps the children's beloved mongoose Ibn Bibi, broke the onerous silence.

She would not leave Badajan and she would not marry Ethan Bloodwell, of that she was certain, yet how to insure that neither came true? Oh, if only she were already married or at the very least betrothed to another man so that Ethan Bloodwell could have no claims upon her whatsoever!

Suddenly China grew still and her mouth opened in a breathless gasp. Why not? Why not marry another man? While Ethan Bloodwell might arrogantly consider himself far superior to his fellow men, he was certainly not God and couldn't possibly possess the power to put sacred vows asunder! A smile curved China's lips and, dismissing him with a toss of her head, she began to lay her plans.

"Are you certain you're well, Miss China?"

Darwin's anxious words brought her back to the present. She uttered a short laugh and two spots of color burned in her cheeks. "I'm quite well, Darwin," she assured him. "I've come to ask a favor of you."

Had Darwin been more observant he might have noticed that her nervous laughter held a trace of hysteria, but he saw nothing save the dusky green glow of her eyes and felt the fierce love that cramped his heart as he boldly took her hand in his.

"A favor? Certainly, Miss Warrick! Anything you wish!"

"I should like," China said clearly and without hesitation, "for you to marry me."

"I—I beg your pardon?"

China was tempted to laugh at the absurd look that crossed Darwin's face, but she did not. There was little time to waste, and she must convince Darwin of the urgency of her proposal before someone at King's Wheal awakened to find her gone.

"Let's go inside where we can talk." Taking his lax hand in hers, she pulled him into the house.

"Oh, it will never work," Darwin said after she had given him a thorough account of the situation.

"Yes it will," China insisted. "My mother won't be able to do a thing to stop us. Once she learns of it, it will be far too late." Regarding him, China sighed tiredly, for every doubt Darwin uttered served to seriously shake her own resolve. Yet she had only to think of Captain Bloodwell and how pleased with himself he probably felt at this very moment, and her jaw tightened in a manner that was startlingly reminiscent of her great-grandfather in one of his rare tempers.

Looking at her, Darwin had no choice but to give in, simply because he could no longer bear to see the hopeless look on her face and because his love for her overshadowed reason until nothing mattered except sparing her from the filthy hands of Ethan Bloodwell—and damn the consequences!

"Very well, I'll do it!" he said, and this time it was he who spoke at length. They would, he told her decisively, leave at once for Singapore in search of the Reverend Hubert Challoner who was, in Darwin's opinion, the only member of the city's small collection of clergymen who could be called upon to marry them without Malvina Warrick's consent.

"He's lived in Asia for the past forty years, perhaps longer," he explained. "Though it's probably unkind of me to say this, he's getting on in years and tends to be rather confused about things at times. It shouldn't be too hard to fabricate a tale that will satisfy him as to why we must marry in haste."

"I suppose we'll have to give him false names," China added. "Though I wonder if it will be legal?"

"Of course it will," Darwin assured her. "And it's probably wise we do. That way the ceremony won't give rise to any gossip since Reverend Challoner would doubtless recognize your name. It's better your mother hears it from us and not from some chattering group of natives arriving here on the next packet."

It was all so simple, he was thinking to himself, too simple, in fact, and as he accompanied China to the docks he was assailed by a host of new doubts. Though he would never admit as much to anyone, least of all China, Darwin was terrified of Malvina Warrick. He had spent the better part of ten years—nearly half his life—doing his best to avoid her sharp tongue and quick temper, and knew perhaps better than anyone that she cared for nothing and no one save Damon, her first-born son.

From his own father Darwin had heard the tale of John Gilkenny, a New South Wales rancher, who had been twenty-year-old Malvina Shepherd's first and only love. Whatever girlish sweetness she might have possessed seemed to have died within her the day he had been trampled to death by a vicious stallion. She had left Australia shortly thereafter, vowing never to return, and taking nothing with her but the life which, unbeknownst to her, grew within her womb. That, and the opals her father had presented her on her wedding day—rare green opals that he had mined himself nearly forty years ago and given first to his beloved wife, Lady Delia Linville.

Beautiful and clever, Malvina Gilkenny had soon managed to catch the eye of the very young and impressionable grandson of the legendary Kingston Warrick. And when it became obvious to her that she was to bear John Gilkenny's child, she had coolly seduced him and managed by that score to convince him the child was his. Impulsively and against the adamant wishes of his ailing father, Race Warrick had offered to marry her.

The marriage was a great mistake. Even Race, in love with the graceful, patrician beauty, quickly came to realize as much. The moment he saw the squalling, black-haired infant, he knew that it could not be his, and the enormity of Malvina's betrayal destroyed completely the love he had heretofore fancied to feel for her.

There remained only the child, and Race was prepared to raise it as his own, for he did not believe that an infant should be blamed for the sins of its parents. But Damon grew up to be his mother's child, rejecting entirely the attentions of the man who would have willingly called him son, and clinging to the glorified and greatly exaggerated memories of John Gilkenny that Malvina laid inexhaustibly before him.

He was a spoiled and lazy boy without the proud, restless ambition that drove all Warrick men, and Race did his best to breach the impossible gap between them—until China was born. Red-headed, green-eyed China, as lusty, gay, and full of life as her charming, irreverent great-grandfather, had worshipped her father and been adored by him in turn, and it became obvious at an early age that she had inherited all the stubborn tenacity and driving ambition of the Warrick men who had gone before her.

It was China who filled the empty place in Race's heart, China who labored diligently and solemnly as only an adoring child could to learn the trade her father practiced, and China to whom he intended to turn over King's Wheal's reins once age forced him to step aside—until Malvina Warrick awoke to the fact that her beloved son stood in danger of being disinherited, and saw to it that the child was sent away to the gloomy English estate of her uncle.

All this and more Darwin had learned while growing up on Badajan and doing his best to master the art of plantation management from his ill-tempered but hard-

working father. All this and more, and none of it had
mattered to him during the years he had studied in England or when he returned East to step into his dying
father's shoes—until China Warrick had returned to the
island, beautiful beyond compare and oblivious to the injustice her mother had done her by sending her away.

Looking at her now, as she stood beside him waiting
anxiously for the *Tempus* to be made ready for sailing,
Darwin felt an overwhelming surge of love for her. She
could not know the treachery of which her own mother
was capable, could not know that Malvina would strike
like a cobra if anything dared to threaten her beloved
Damon's existence. And marrying Darwin Stepkyne would
threaten it indeed, for Ethan Bloodwell would doubtless
have taken her far away from Badajan while Darwin intended to see that she remained. Perhaps one day he would
find the courage to tell her what he had never dared tell
anyone else: that Race Warrick would still have left King's
Wheal to her if death hadn't robbed him of the opportunity,
and that the inheritance he had planned for Brandon and
Philippa had already been spent, and that the once ov-
erflowing coffers were bare.

Oh, yes, Darwin knew exactly how badly the Warrick
finances stood, how Damon's total lack of business sense
had forced them to auction off their holdings on Sumatra
and in Singapore, and that the teak plantation south of
Kuala Lumpur had already been sold, secretly, to Sir
Joshua Boles. Nothing remained of the vast empire
Kingston Warrick had built save the island itself and the
lustrous gold silk that was coveted by half the world,
and which Damon was rashly and desperately selling to
anyone who would offer a good price for it, even if it
meant accepting their credit. But China knew none of
these things and Darwin was ashamed that he did not
have the courage to tell her.

The sun, climbing beyond the mountain peaks, had
burned off the early-morning haze and hung suspended
above the breathless sea, mirroring itself on water that
seemed as hot and glassy as molten metal. Both Darwin
and China relaxed visibly once the *Tempus* cast her lines
and gained momentum across the wind-ruffled water, her

squares of white canvas bellying taut. Though Darwin could have handled the helm himself, he had insisted on taking Lam Tan with them so that Malvina would be unable to question him once the *Tempus*'s disappearance was discovered.

China sat silent in the bow of the yacht, the heel of her riding boot tapping restlessly on the polished teak deck. She knew that she must hide every outward indication of her fears from Darwin lest his courage fail him and he insist on turning back. She was glad he had agreed to help her and yet she had never felt so wretched and miserably alone in her entire life.

The traffic between the Singapore wharves and the ships anchored in the roads was brisk, and the *Tempus* was forced to trim sail and jib as she maneuvered her way through the profusion of tongkangs, sampans, and fishing boats scurrying to and fro amid the lumbering East Indiamen and salt-blistered frigates. Making her fast against a wooden piling that rose from the length of the worn watersteps, Lam Tan leaped nimbly over the side and handed Darwin ashore.

"Will watch missy very careful," he promised cheerfully, and Darwin, his expression filled with misgivings, vanished down a narrow, twisting alley leading to the inner city.

It had been agreed, since Darwin did not know exactly where the minister lived, that China would wait aboard the *Tempus* rather than risk being recognized on the crowded streets. Darwin had promised to fetch her as soon as he had located the Reverend Challoner, and they would then proceed to his residence along less frequented roads, which to China's way of thinking was a wise precaution.

Staring restlessly about her, China stiffened as two men wearing the flowing white robes of native Arabs emerged suddenly from one of the shuttered houses facing the pier where the *Tempus* lay moored, and began strolling in the direction of the bustling warehouses. China recognized one of them as Rajiid Ali, but not the other, for his face was turned away from her, yet her heartbeat quickened in

alarm. If Rajiid was here on the waterfront, then it was
entirely possible that his captain was somewhere nearby.

She watched anxiously as the tall Arab turned to say
something to his companion, and when both of them threw
back their heads and laughed she could not help but experience a small shock. Though she still could not see the
other man's face, she had had no trouble recognizing that
deep, familiar laugh.

Sending her chair clattering across the deck, she disappeared down the hatch and waved the startled Lam Tan
into silence. Endless moments passed and she breathed a
sigh of relief as the two men continued on their way without turning their heads in her direction.

Despite the fact that it was unbearably hot in the tiny
cabin, China dared not leave it for fear they might return.
Fortunately Darwin came back sooner than she had anticipated, and she hurried up on deck to meet him. The
moment she saw his face, however, she knew that something had gone wrong, and her heart sank.

"What is it? Couldn't you find him?"

"I found him all right," Darwin said grimly, "but I'm
afraid he's dead."

"Dead!"

"His housekeeper told me he died two nights ago and
that they buried him yesterday. Can you imagine? Yesterday! It's utterly absurd, isn't it? Whatever are we going
to do now?"

"Surely there must be someone else who can marry us?"

"I don't know," Darwin said with a sigh. "It's doubtful
anyone else will agree to it without your mother's consent.
You're not of legal age, after all."

"But they have to!" China's eyes were wide, and her
desperation tore at his heart. "If no one agrees to help us,
I'll have to marry *him* and I'd—I'd rather die!"

"A most charmingly uttered sentiment," said a calm
voice. "I take it, Miss Warrick, that you are referring to
me?"

China's head came around, and her expression went
rigid as her gaze fell on the billowing length of a white
jubbah, and traveled higher: to the dark, hostile face of
the man who wore it. Her heart seemed to check and her

breath caught in her throat and for a long, dragging moment there was utter silence on the wharf.

The frothing wake of a passing dhow gurgled against the *Tempus*'s hull and in the stillness the din of the crowded pier seemed to drown out even the sound of her own erratic breathing. Men shouted and cursed as wooden crates and casks, roped bundles and baskets were carried and dragged and scraped across the planks. Birds screeched and monkeys chattered and the murmur of the wakening city filled the humid sky.

Far in the distance a church bell rang the Angelus to the mournful accompaniment of a howling pack of pariah dogs, and Ethan turned abruptly to Rajiid and made a swift, barely discernible movement with his head. Leaping down onto the deck, the tall Arab cornered the startled Darwin and Lam Tan against the hatchway, drawing a knife from his robes and affecting a menacing stance while Ethan strolled casually down the watersteps and came to stand before China with a thoughtful frown on his face.

"It would seem," he said in a tone that was exceedingly affable and therefore all the more unnerving, "that you are ever full of surprises, Miss Warrick. I gather your brother knows nothing of your plans, for surely he would have mentioned them last night. Were you planning to elope with Mr. Stepkyne?"

"I—" China found she could not speak at all. Clearing her throat, she tried again, but Captain Bloodwell seemed altogether uninterested in what she had to say.

"It's fortunate I recognized your sails and that red hair of yours," he resumed, "or I never would have known you were here." He shook his head in mock resignation. "I cannot tell you how disappointed I am to discover that you find the notion of marrying me so intolerable that you would contemplate something as absurd as this to escape it."

"Now, listen here, Bloodwell—" Darwin began angrily, but was checked by a curt movement from Rajiid and an accompanying expression on the captain's face that convinced him of the prudence of remaining silent.

"I can see that it was wrong of me to trust you," Ethan

continued, his eyes returning to China and speaking suddenly in a tone that no one had ever used with her before. "You're equally as perfidious and cunning as the rest of your sex, and it's time I stopped playing the obliging gentleman and simply took from you what I want."

"You—you wouldn't dare!"

"I wouldn't? Apparently you don't know me very well at all. A pity for you, Miss Warrick, but then that's all you can expect from a filthy renegade like me, isn't it?"

As he spoke he reached down and scooped her without warning into his arms. Though China gasped and struggled, he merely laughed and lifted her onto the worn planks of the pier.

"Darwin!" she screamed although it did her no good, for Ethan clamped his hand roughly over her mouth and dragged her away. Rajiid, waiting behind long enough to assure himself that neither Darwin nor Lam Tan would make a move to help her, bowed insultingly before hurrying after them.

China was shaking with shock and outrage by the time Ethan released her in the shade of the Coral House's blossom-scented garden. No sooner was she free of his arms than she darted wildly for a nearby gate. She felt something catch at the skirts of her habit and then she was spun around to land hard against his chest. Tears welled in her eyes and she heard him say coldly, "Try that again and I'll give you something to really cry about. I've never hit a woman before, Miss Warrick, but I'm sorely tempted to try."

Looking up into Ethan's face, China saw that he meant it, and it seemed as if her heart had forgotten how to beat in steady rhythm but was stopping and jerking and making her pulse pound dizzily in her temples. She found that she didn't even have the strength to demand what he intended to do with her. His quiet threat had served to undermine her as surely as his rough handling had done, and suddenly it was as if the oppressive heat surrounding her flared up in whirling, dancing bands before her eyes, and she wavered.

"Serves you right for wearing those goddamned heavy petticoats and stays," she heard him say from a great, yawning distance, and felt herself being lifted once again into his arms. She struggled feebly, but the darkness was already reaching out for her, and the last thing she remembered before it engulfed her entirely was the sound of the strong, steady beating of his heart against her cheek.

Chapter Sixteen

"Oh, come, Darwin, what's the worry? What harm can Bloodwell possibly do her? He's going to marry her, after all."

"What harm?" Darwin Stepkyne echoed, red-faced and incredulous, "He's taken her prisoner in that house of his, for God's sake, and had the nerve to threaten me with a pistol! Does that sound like a man who intends to treat her kindly?"

"Darwin! Whatever is the meaning of this?" came an arctic voice from the open door of the study. "Is it necessary to raise your voice so that all the servants may hear?"

"I'm sorry, Mrs. Warrick," Darwin said without the least sign of contrition, "but your daughter has been abducted by a madman and your son seems to find it no cause for concern."

"Abducted!"

"She wasn't abducted, Mother," Damon interjected with a dour glance in Darwin's direction. "It's Bloodwell. Apparently he's decided not to wait until the marriage papers have been signed. He's taken China to that house of his in Singapore."

"What on earth can he mean to do with her?" Malvina demanded. "And what was she doing in Singapore to begin with?"

"She said she had a pressing errand to run and asked Darwin to accompany her." Damon's eyes went to the flushed face of his plantation manager, not believing for a moment that the stammered explanation Darwin had given him was the truth. "Apparently Bloodwell was on the wharf when the *Tempus* docked and simply spirited China away."

"That hook-nosed Arab henchman of his went so far as to threaten me with a knife," Darwin put in. "And when I tried to get into the house I was shot at!"

"Dear me," Malvina murmured.

"I've been trying to explain to Darwin that there's bloody little we can do about it," Damon said crossly. "If I were to appeal to the Commissioner or ask the Far East Fleet to spare marines for a rescue, it would only draw unwanted attention to the situation."

"Is that all that matters to you?" Darwin demanded, losing his patience for perhaps the first time in his life. "Avoiding unpleasant scenes? You know bloody well that fornicating scum hasn't got honorable objectives in mind! More likely than not he'll ruin her and send her back with a polite note to the effect that she isn't exactly what he had in mind for a wife!"

"Please be quiet, Darwin," Malvina said crisply. "There's no need to overdramatize. Captain Bloodwell may be a cad but he's not a fool. If he has truly led my daughter astray, then he'll have no choice but to marry her, and King's Wheal will have lost nothing in the bargain."

"And if he doesn't marry her?" Damon inquired.

"Oh, he will," Malvina said confidently. Her eyes gleamed and she clasped her hands to her breast in the manner of a woman contemplating something infinitely pleasing. "In fact, I'm beginning to believe that this has worked out for the best."

"You can't be serious!"

Malvina gazed curiously into Darwin's wild face. Now,

why on earth was the boy being so difficult about this? Surely he wasn't fond of the girl himself? Dear me, perhaps he was!

"Oh, but I'm afraid I am," she assured him tartly. "Very much so, my dear boy. And Damon's perfectly right. We can't risk making a spectacle over something like this. Captain Bloodwell may have acted impulsively, but I don't believe his behavior was governed by irrational thinking. He strikes me as the sort who never acts without considering the consequences most carefully."

Furthermore her daughter was not the sort of woman capable of driving a man to lose his head, she was thinking though she did not say as much aloud. Beautiful, yes, but lamentably prim and prudish and not at all the sort, Malvina firmly believed, to prompt a man like Ethan Bloodwell to toss two hundred pounds into the gutter for the sake of a simple romp.

"There's something else I think you should know," Darwin said hesitantly.

"Yes? What is it?"

Darwin knew that Malvina would be furious once she learned that he and China had been on their way to Singapore to elope. But how else could he make it clear to her that Ethan Bloodwell had abducted her daughter in a fit of rage and that in his present frame of mind he was capable of doing anything to her, anything at all?

"I'm afraid I wasn't being exactly truthful when I told Damon that China asked me to accompany her to Singapore in order to run errands. Actually we—"

"Mistress! Mistress!"

The breathless arrival of a disheveled serving woman who burst into the room waving a piece of paper and babbling in an incoherent mixture of English and Malay put an end to Darwin's stammered confession. For the space of a full minute the three of them did their best to decipher her frantic explanations, all without success, until Malvina ordered her into silence and took the paper from her.

"Where did you get this?" she demanded sharply, reading it.

The serving woman's voice was thick with unshed tears. "I find in Master Brandon's bed. I wonder why they not come down for lessons. Mr. Lim waiting in schoolroom. Him very angry, so I look in rooms. No Master Brandon. No Missy Philippa. Beds no slept in. I find note on pillow. I come to you as fast as can." She moaned and wrung her thin hands.

"Be quiet, Jumai," Damon said crossly. "What does it say, Mother?"

"It's from Brandon. It seems he and Philippa have run away from home."

"What!"

"If this note is to be believed, they stowed away aboard the *Malhão* last night," Malvina said.

"Luis Queidós's ship?" Damon burst out. "Whatever for?"

"Because for some inexplicable reason Brandon wants to go to Canton. That's where Captain Queidós planned to deliver the silk he purchased last night, isn't it?"

Damon frowned. "I believe so. But why Canton, for Christ's sake? And why run away at all?"

"Brandon didn't say."

"They couldn't have! All the way to Canton? I won't believe it!"

"I'm afraid you must," his mother said tartly. "Brandon isn't the sort to play jokes like this."

"Those ignorant little fools!" Damon's fist crashed furiously onto the desktop. "Canton is over two thousand miles away! Whatever could they be thinking?"

"I've no idea," Malvina replied. "Brandon merely says that China needn't worry because he intends to see that she comes to no harm." Tossing the crumpled piece of paper into the wastebasket she regarded her son with baffled eyes. "What on earth do you suppose he meant?"

"Good God, I wish I knew! They must have taken leave of their senses! Brandon's old enough to understand the dangers of stowing away aboard a merchant ship, and as for taking Philippa with him—" Damon broke off and tugged energetically at the bell pull. "We'll have to go after them, of course, before the *Malhão* gets much farther."

"How? Aboard the *Tempus?*" his mother inquired scornfully. "You'd be lucky to get five knots out of her even in a brisk wind."

"What about the *Aurora?*" Darwin suggested. "She's due in today, isn't she?"

"We can't count on that," Damon said curtly. "Even a few hours' delay would mean taking the chance of missing them entirely." He began to pace angrily. "By God, I could throttle Brandon for this! I'm sorry, Mother, but I haven't the faintest idea how we're to fetch them back."

"Or how to rescue China, either," Darwin added bleakly.

Damon turned to regard him blankly, for in view of Jumai's shocking disclosure that the children were missing he had forgotten entirely about her.

"Darwin," Malvina said quickly, "do you know whether Captain Bloodwell's brigantine is still anchored in Singapore Harbor?"

"I would imagine it is," Darwin allowed cautiously, "though I didn't actually see it."

"You're not thinking of asking him for help?" Damon inquired with appalled comprehension.

Malvina regarded him with arched brows. "Why not? Do you have a better idea?"

"Good God, Mother, the man's a veritable pirate! What makes you think he'll agree to lend assistance to charitable causes?"

Malvina's lips tightened. "Charitable? My dear boy, with two hundred pounds at stake you can hardly call this a charitable request! The way I see it he doesn't have a choice. Either he agrees to help us bring the children back or there won't be a wedding or a dowry, either!"

She strode from the study, calling loudly for Al-Haj, and both Damon and Darwin were left to wrestle with their own misgivings. It was perfectly obvious to Darwin that Ethan Bloodwell would never offer his assistance selflessly, even if the welfare of two innocent children hung in the balance. And Damon, in thinking the matter over, came to a similar conclusion.

"Good God," he said again, and to no one in particular, "I hope it's not too late. For the children or for China."

Darwin's eyes met his across the cluttered desk and then each looked quickly away, neither willing to reveal to the other the depths of his concerns, yet it was obvious that the two of them were in utter agreement.

* * *

When China returned to her senses it was to find herself lying on an Eastern-style bed in a room with a high, domed ceiling and countless arching windows. The furniture that filled it was of delicate Oriental design, inlaid with mother-of-pearl, its veneer protected from the damp climate by daily rubbings of scented oil. A pleasant breeze stirred the silken wall hangings that served in place of doors and filled the air with the fragrance of flowers.

"It must be raining again," China thought in confusion, hearing the warm murmur of water, but when she turned her head she saw that the sound came from a tile fountain standing in the center of the room. She lay for a moment watching the setting sun dance on the waterspout and reflect shivering patterns of light across the walls, and gradually her senses cleared and she became aware of the fact that someone had removed her heavy gown and petticoats and that she was lying beneath a single sheet with nothing but a loose silk garment wrapped about her.

She remembered then the dreams she had had, and realized that they must have been real, for how else could she explain how she came to be here? Dimly she recalled being carried up a flight of spiral stairs and delivered into the competent hands of two women who had undressed and bathed her with cool, scented water. Their soothing chatter had served to gentle her into an exhausted sleep.

China's eyes flew open in alarm as she recalled vividly the madness of Ethan Bloodwell's behavior. Tossing the cover aside, she came swiftly to her feet and was promptly overcome by a wave of dizziness that made her grope for the bedrail for support.

"That was foolish of you, my dear child. The floor happens to be made of stone, and had you fallen you would have given yourself a splendid concussion on top of that heat stroke."

China looked up and, in the golden light of the sunset that ignited the walls and furnishings, saw Ethan standing amid the drawn curtains separating her room from a plant-filled balcony. He was still wearing his Arab robes, and the impenetrable look that had been on his face earlier remained.

"Would it have mattered to you if I had hurt myself?" China inquired, but not in the tone she would have liked to use, for she was suddenly afraid, and the tremulous whisper with which she spoke betrayed her more clearly than anything else might have done.

"I would not have wanted to see you injured after Seeta and Janri worked so hard to bring your body temperature down."

"Seeta and Janri?"

Ethan grinned and sauntered inside. "Two of the servants Prince Shaweh graciously provided with the house. This chamber is part of the women's quarters, by the way, and as Seeta and Janri have resided here for the past seven years I didn't have the heart to turn them out. Besides, comely servants are always an asset."

"Concubines, you mean!" China said, for she was not at all ignorant of the trade the denizens of the house had originally practiced.

Ethan shrugged. "If you prefer to call them that: concubines, then. But you needn't fear that I intend to make you one of them."

"How generous of you," China said stiffly. "Now if you would be kind enough to return my clothes to me, Captain, I will trouble you with my presence no longer."

"Oh, I'm sure of that, but I'm not prepared at the moment to let you go." He grinned as he saw her eyes widen and then dart past his shoulder. "There's no sense in trying to flee, either. The women's quarters are on the third story of the house and it's quite a drop from the balcony. Furthermore, the windows have been barred and the doors barricaded since early this morning to discourage any—er—unwanted intruders."

"Has someone been looking for me then?"

He laughed unpleasantly. "Why should they? In view of the fact that we are shortly to be married your brother has obviously seen no reason to think it odd that you were brought here. And poor Darwin, who I will allow did make a heroic effort to rescue you, was easily thwarted with a pistol."

China went white. "You shot him?"

"Dear me, no. Rajiid merely discharged a few shots into

the air, but it was enough to make him turn tail and run. I imagine he ran straight to the British High Commissioner or some other glorified figurehead of Her Britannic Majesty's imperial forces in order to plead for help, but as this house happens to belong to an Indonesian prince and therefore enjoys diplomatic immunity—"

But China was no longer listening. Having caught sight of herself in the floor-length mirror that hung on the far wall, she realized with a gasp of horror what had not been clear to her before: that she was wearing little more than a robe of embroidered vermilion silk, loosely sashed at the waist and ending at midthigh. She blushed scarlet with shame, and Ethan, seeing her expression, turned his head to follow her gaze to her reflection, and a slow, knowing smile curved the corners of his mouth.

Their eyes locked in the glass, causing the color to burn deeper in China's cheeks. She turned her face away and a taut stillness settled over the room. It was at that moment that the sun slid unnoticed behind the horizon, painting the sea and the garden and the house in a glorious wash of colors. It streamed through the windows, igniting China's hair first red, then gold, then red again and warming the ivory perfection of her skin. There were suddenly golden flecks in her dark green eyes that Ethan had never noticed before, and the alternating shadows gave a rosy cast to her full lower lip that drew his gaze to her mouth—and abruptly changed the expression on his face.

Paralyzed with fear China watched him, sensing instinctively that in his present frame of mind he was far more dangerous than she had ever imagined. It was obvious to her now that he had been drinking, perhaps not enough to make him lose command of his faculties, but enough to give him the same heavy-lidded eyes and indolent air she had noticed the first time they had met in his quarters aboard the *Kowloon Star*.

He must, she thought in panic, be thoroughly enraged by the fact that she had tried to cheat him of his money by attempting to marry Darwin Stepkyne. And if it was true, as he claimed, that her brother had raised no protest at her abduction, then she alone must deal with him.

Ethan's smile deepened and became an ugly thing, dark

and full of menace, and his words uncannily echoed her
innermost thoughts. "Do you think I mean to punish you
for what you tried to do?"

"I don't know," China whispered.

"I was indeed prepared to throttle you at first," he said
unkindly. "Surely you have more sense than to wed that
mewling, milk-bearded cub! He's not the man for you, my
treacherous little firebrand, but you're not quite woman
enough yet to understand that."

"And I expect you're going to change that?" China
snapped, and realized at once that she had said the very
worst thing possible. Looking up into his quiet, watchful
face, she realized with a sense of cold, mounting panic that
this was precisely what he had had in mind all along.

"No!" she whispered, her eyes wide and incredulous.
"Oh, no! You can't—you wouldn't—"

She did not even finish the sentence, but ducked beneath his arm and tried to run toward the door. Perhaps
she might have reached it had her hair not been left unbound by the serving women who had lovingly untangled
and brushed it, and as it streamed unbound behind her
like a fiery banner, Ethan was just barely able to lunge
out and grab it.

Jerking hard, he sent her spinning around to land
against his chest, her breath coming in gasps and tears of
pain trembling on her lashes. The sash of her scarlet robe
fell to the floor and Ethan deliberately slid his hands inside, taking her by the hips and bringing her closer, her
naked breasts brushing against his chest. She tried to
struggle free but he merely held her tighter, her body
arching against the length of his, the intimacy of the embrace shaming her and flushing her with heat.

"Don't fight me, China," he whispered, and before she
could reply he lowered his head and kissed her.

China gasped, for it was not at all like the kiss on the
terrace at King's Wheal but urgent and demanding, the
kiss of a man who has waited too long to claim what he
desires. And Ethan desired her with an urgency that was
torment in itself, and the oil she had unwittingly poured
on the fire by daring to run away with Darwin Stepkyne

had driven him to take leave of his senses and kidnap her, and to make her his regardless of the cost.

Nappy had pleaded frantically and the disapproving Rajiid had quoted a sura from the Koran on the virtues of forgiveness and restraint, yet the fire had been burning so hotly within him that even their protests and several potent drinks had done little to quench it. And whatever promises he had made to himself on the unsteady ascent to the rooms in which she lay had been forgotten the moment she had faced him with the sun setting gloriously behind her, igniting her hair and her skin and convincing him that she was not a flesh-and-blood woman but a pagan goddess—until he had touched her and knew that it was not so. She was a woman, unbearably lovely and achingly desirable, and Ethan could no longer deny that he had wanted her, and her alone, from the very first.

The scarlet robe rustled softly as it fell to the floor, and his lean, dark hands molded her to him so that she could feel the hard, alien heat of his desire through the folds of his jubbah. Though China gasped and shivered, she made no move to struggle free, for a languorous delight was filling her blood at the touch of his mouth on hers. She was no longer afraid but alive and willing, and eager to learn what mysteries awaited her at his hands.

The moment he kissed her she realized that it could not have been otherwise between them, and perhaps she, too, had fallen victim to the beguiling spell woven by the sunset, for she offered no resistance as Ethan lifted her into his arms and laid her gently on the bed. His robe fell away and he was bending over her, lean and brown and disconcertingly masculine, and China's eyes traveled wonderingly across the ridged expanse of his muscled chest to his flat, tapering belly, and lower still: to the evidence of his desire that had risen and hardened at the very first touch of their lips.

Ethan saw the color flare to her cheeks and the gold-dusted lashes flutter over her eyes, hiding her expression from him. Leaning forward, he cupped his palm beneath her chin and tilted it, and his heart twisted oddly when he saw not the expected fear and revulsion in her gaze, but a dawning sense of wonder and shy, answering need.

With a groan he bent over her, his lips capturing hers, and heard her gasp as he slid his heated body down the length of hers until his manhood came to rest between her thighs. It was in his mind to tell her not to be frightened, that he could not possibly hurt her when he loved her so, yet even as the words were framed on his tongue she reached out to touch him with a small, seeking hand. He sucked in his breath at the intimacy of that hesitant gesture, and for the first time in his life knew a heart-stopping pleasure that was almost pain, because she was here beside him and because she so obviously seemed to want him.

"China," he whispered into her ear, and his breath stirred the silken tendrils curling at her temple. "China, I'm afraid it's going to hurt you, and I can't do anything to prevent it."

"It doesn't matter," she whispered in turn, lifting starry eyes to his. Slipping her arms about his neck she brought his head down and her lips traced a shy path from his cheek to the corner of his mouth. Ethan kissed her fiercely and with all the longing for her that he could no longer deny. Her thighs opened beneath him and he entered her, feeling the quiver that fled through her slender body at the savage ending of her girlhood. When she raised her eyes to his he saw the pain that clouded their emerald depths, yet even as his heart turned over and seemed to stop its beating she smiled at him tenderly and moved shamelessly against him.

Ethan groaned and thrust deeper, filling her slowly before drawing back and then entering her again in a rhythm that was as ancient as time itself. She clung to him, her arms about his neck, moving with him as though they had performed the ritual of the mating dance a hundred times, a thousand times over. And who was to say that perhaps they had not, in some other time, in some other, long-forgotten life? For this was Ethan, the one man China suddenly knew she had been born for, and she uttered his name in a whispered caress that he could not possibly have heard and yet somehow did, and he caught her to him and claimed her with a wild, savage thrust that swept both of them to the brink of oblivion.

China felt the explosion deep within her, spreading

through her and drowning her in a wrenching moment of piercing ecstacy. Her heart seemed to cease its frenzied beating and she gasped and teetered as the rapturous spasms bore her aloft, then gentled her slowly back to awareness: of Ethan still a part of her, his warm, hard body upon hers, of his lips caressing her, and finally, of a drowsy, wonderful peace that crept over her like a velvet sigh and eased her into a deep and dreamless sleep.

_____ *Chapter Seventeen* _____

China awoke alone to the murmur of the surf and the fluttering of a moth that batted itself relentlessly against the fluted glass of a nearby lamp. The sky beyond the darkened windows was awash with stars, and pushing aside the mosquito netting surrounding her bed, she stood staring up at them with her arms propped against the sill. It was a beautiful night, more beautiful than any she could remember in her life. A cool wind had dispelled the clouds and the humidity, and the stars shone down from the heavens with a brilliance that fingered the frothing surf with pearlescent light.

It could not be so very late, for the subdued sounds of the city, the throbbing hum that was the heart of Singapore, came to her softly amid the rustling of the palm fronds and the tinkle of the fountain in the room behind her. China closed her eyes and allowed the wind to play with her hair, which fell in an unbound crimson curtain to her hips.

She had never been aware before this night how delightful it could be to feel the breeze caress one's naked skin, and for the first time in her life she took pleasure in the perfection of her smooth young body. Had this sensuality been a part of her before, perhaps buried beneath the confining stays and corsets she had been forced by convention to wear? Or was it Ethan and the slow, languorous pleasure with which he had loved every inch of her that had awakened her to the awareness of her own woman's body?

When had it happened? The first time he had loved her? Or when she had been brought abruptly from sleep by the touch of his hard, demanding mouth and he had taken her again... and yet again?

"I cannot seem to get enough of you," he had murmured, and there had been wonder as well as amusement in the pale eyes that had looked at her. She had shivered in response, though this time not with fear, and he had taken her into his arms and kissed her so that everything in creation had been swept away but the slow, burning pleasure of his seeking lips.

She blushed at the shameless longing kindled by the memory, and would have turned away from the window but for a sudden movement in the garden below that froze her in her tracks. A shadow showed itself briefly against the whiteness of the flowerbeds, the shadow of a man who moved deliberately up and down the shell walks and paused now and again to test the latches of the gates.

China stood very still watching him, and presently it occurred to her that he must be a watchman, and she remembered then what Ethan had said about barricading the house against intruders. Making a thorough search for her clothes, she could find neither her riding habit nor the lavish undergarments that had accompanied them. A brief inspection of the inlaid chest of drawers by the bed revealed nothing more than a strip of scented muslin and a sarong of the sort Malaysian women commonly wore. China left it untouched in the drawer, for she had no desire to wander about the house clad in the tight-fitting, ankle-length article that would, she knew, bare her shoulders and the tops of her breasts for everyone to see. Nor was she about to leave the women's quarter wrapped in little more than a bedsheet.

"Why, I believe this will do quite nicely," she said aloud, her gaze falling on a sandalwood trunk whose brass-hinged lid, upon being opened, revealed a variety of women's shirts and silken pantaloons. Selecting a rather simple gold tunic and lavender trousers embroidered with matching thread, China slipped them on and, surveying herself in the floor-length looking glass, burst into laughter. Despite her un-Eastern red hair she could easily have passed for a member of the Coral House's harem, for the outfit was not only unorthodox in its cut but utterly and outrageously garish in color, a necessary prerequisite, in China's mind, for ladies of dubious morals.

And yet—and yet what had been different about what she herself had done? Ethan had used her until his passions were well sated, and not once had he said he loved her or murmured some endearment that might have made everything seem less sordid and improper to her now. And where had he gone once she fell asleep beside him? To yet another dark, scented room where a different woman lay waiting to receive him?

The colorful costume that had made her laugh only a moment ago was suddenly nothing more than the glaring evidence of her own unbearable vulgarity. China was ashamed of herself and of what Ethan had done to her, and with a choked cry she stumbled for the door and would have fled the room had someone not appeared on the threshold: a tall, dark shadow who caught her by the arms and demanded to know what on earth was the matter.

"Can't you see for yourself?" China gasped. "I look like a palace concubine and it's all your fault!"

Ethan's brows rose. "My fault?"

China struggled free of his grasp and stared accusingly into his amused blue eyes. "My habit should never have been taken away from me! It's your fault that I—that we—"

"That I made love to you and thereby necessitated the removal of your clothes?" he inquired bluntly.

Hot color burned in China's cheeks. "Yes," she said hoarsely, and was shocked when he burst into laughter.

"And how else would you have had me do it? By re-

maining fully clothed? I'll confess it's a novel idea, my love,
though hardly satisfying."

The blush on China's cheekbones deepened and she
wished that he would not refer to what had happened in
such a shockingly direct manner, and as for actually laughing about it—!

"China," he said softly, and when she raised her eyes
to his she saw that he was no longer smiling but was
regarding her intently. "You must never be ashamed of
what happened between us. And as for looking or feeling
like a concubine, you do yourself a grave injustice."

China found she could not answer him, for she seemed
to have lost the ability to speak. Mesmerized by the compelling look in those pale, smoldering eyes and the dark
and very strong hands that rested intimately about the
curve of her hips, she could only stare up at him without
speaking, her lips parted and trembling slightly as her
quickening breath escaped them.

Finding himself similarly undone by a pair of wide green
eyes fringed with gold-dusted lashes, Ethan uttered a groan
and, lowering his lips to hers, kissed her deeply. China
slipped her arms about his neck, glorying in his kiss and
the awakening passion their touching bodies kindled.

"My red-haired enchantress," Ethan whispered against
her lips. "What spell have you woven that leaves me unable to resist you? One kiss, one look into your eyes and
I can think of nothing but wanting you, taking you now,
this moment and for always. Come here, little firebrand."

"Bloodwell Captain? Master?" The sound of Lal Sri's
querying voice and the furtive rapping on the outer bedroom door caused Ethan to release her with a curse. Opening the door a crack he spoke through it curtly, then listened
with ill-concealed impatience before issuing a series of
orders in a voice far too low for China to hear. Closing the
door behind him he turned and regarded her thoughtfully
and she knew at once that something had happened to
change his mood. She was shaken by the galling disappointment of the discovery.

"Is anything wrong?" she inquired.

"No. But I must go out for a time. Lal Sri has been

instructed to fetch Janri in the event you require anything.
You need only ring the bell there."

"Ethan, wait!" she called out as he reached for the door.
"What about me? When can I go home?"

He stood regarding her with something that was very
like impatience. "My dear girl, you can go home any time
you wish. You're not a prisoner here." And once again he
was the hateful, mocking stranger.

"I see."

"It's barely midnight," Ethan went on, consulting his
watch. "If you like I could ask Nappy or Rajiid to escort
you back to Badajan now. Unless you think it would be
better if I made my excuses to your mother and brother
personally? In which case it might be wise to wait until
morning."

"I suppose that would be better," China agreed slowly
and wondered why the thought of going home should make
her feel so wretched. She found she couldn't bring herself
to look at him, much less ask the question that trembled
on her tongue concerning their marriage and whether he
still wanted her in view of what had happened. Reminding
herself bleakly that it was her money he desired and certainly nothing else, China gazed at him steadily, wishing
she had the courage to frame that hateful question and
yet dreading its answer. For a long moment there was
silence in the softly lit room, broken only by the tinkling
of the fountain and the distant crooning of the surf. Then
Ethan gave her a mocking bow and wordlessly shut the
door behind him.

China stood for a moment listening to the sound of his
footsteps receding on the landing, then whirled and, on
her knees, began rummaging wildly through the teak
trunk. She was determined not to remain in Ethan's house
another minute, nor was she about to permit him to escort
her home as though he were gamely returning some object
he had merely borrowed for the night. It would be far more
tolerable for her if she were to face Damon and her mother
on her own terms, for that way she could also explain to
them that she had no intention of marrying Ethan Bloodwell now or ever! Considering, of course, that he still wanted

her after he had crudely sampled the fare he would be acquiring!

"I'll pay him the money myself," China vowed, "if I have to steal or cheat or—or kill someone to get it!"

When she appeared downstairs several minutes later she was wearing a pair of thin gold slippers with absurd curling toes that she had found in the bottom of the teak chest, and a heavy veil that thankfully served to obscure her features. Though it seemed unlikely that she would meet anyone she knew, China was not about to take the chance of being recognized and thereby humiliating herself even further. The outlandish costume was bad enough, and apparently Lal Sri, encountering her in the hall where she struggled with the heavy bolts on the front door, seemed to be of the same opinion, for upon discovering that she intended to leave the house thusly clad, begged her to reconsider.

"Is not safe for missy outside. Is dark and streets full of bad men. Will wait until Bloodwell Captain returns, yes?"

"No," China said firmly. Having made up her mind to go home, she was not about to let anyone stop her. Yet realizing that Lal Sri was right in claiming her costume would invariably draw the attention of Singapore's unsavory populace, she asked if he would be kind enough to provide her with adequate protection, whereupon he vehemently shook his head.

"I am not permitted to leave house with Bloodwell Master gone," he informed her regretfully. "Sayyid Rajiid Ali is not here either and Mr. Nappy is sleeping. No can wake. He angry when Bloodwell Captain bring missy here. Drink too much, I think. Now no one can wake."

" A clever solution for avoiding the unpleasant," China observed tartly. "Did Captain Bloodwell say how long he would be gone?"

"He say not very. He go visit a friend in Geylang Road."

"At this hour?" China queried in surprise.

"Oh, yes, missy! He go away much at night. It is the Jule friend he has gone to see this time."

China's breath caught in her throat. "The Jule friend? You can't mean Julia Clayton?"

Lal Sri beamed. "Yes, yes, the Jule Clayton. She send message for him to come."

And Ethan had gone, without explanation, without hesitation, and the implication of what it meant caused the breath to pass in an audible gasp from China's lips and a hot, hard lump to rise in her throat.

"He couldn't have!" she whispered, knowing perfectly well that he was capable of doing exactly that, and knowing, too, that denying the truth to herself would in no way make it any less real or tolerable.

"Yes, he go," Lal Sri assured her, anxious to convince her of the fact. "He tell me so himself. It is not first time, missy."

With a gasping sob China wrenched open the door and stumbled out into the night, ignoring Lal Sri's startled cry and the puzzled greeting from the watchman by the gate, who thankfully made no attempt to stop her. If the darkened streets were haunted by unsavory men, if the doorways of the dimly lit saloons were filled with menacing shadows, China did not notice. She ran blindly, her mind in a turmoil.

Her eyes filled with stinging tears as she reached the wharf and she found herself confronted by a myriad of darkened ships that rose and fell with the quiet breathing of the tide. China looked about her and her heart seemed to leap into her throat, for there, incredibly, moored against enormous pilings whitened by the ravages of time and the droppings of innumerable gulls, lay the *Aurora D.*, King's Wheal's privately owned schooner.

China broke into a run and soon several faces appeared at the rail, drawn by the sound of her cries. A voice she thought she recognized cried out in a mixture of shock and disbelief, "My God, it's China!"

Sobbing with exhaustion and relief, she stumbled up the gangplank to fall gratefully into Darwin Stepkyne's waiting arms. He held her awkwardly, patting her shoulder and murmuring endearments and telling her things that at the moment made very little sense: how they would have come sooner but for the *Tempus* having snapped her mast in a sudden squall that had swooped down on them in the Strait, how Damon's wrist had been broken by a falling spar and necessitated their return to Badajan where Darwin had waited in a fever of impatience until the *Aurora D.* made port three hours later, and how he had been just about to leave the ship in search of her when she had appeared through the darkness. All this and numerous other details passed in and out of China's whirling consciousness like so much spindrift in the wind.

It was only when Darwin inquired hoarsely if that "filthy blackguard" had hurt her that China seemed to become aware of the fact that she was being addressed.

"I'm sorry, Darwin," she said distantly. "What did you say?"

"I asked if he hurt you," Darwin repeated urgently, though scanning her tear-stained face he could see no signs that, to his mind, indicated that she might have been ravished. Unless one took into consideration her costume, which was certainly outlandish enough to warrant grave misgivings, and the more he looked at it the more it began to remind him of harems and zenanas and of the mysterious Eastern ladies who spent their lives practicing unmentionable and immoral acts.

"What's happened to your clothes?" he demanded, thrusting away the dreadful thought and beginning to quiver with righteous indignation. "Did he—did that swine—"

He got no further, for Captain Horatio Creel, informed by a breathless mate that Miss China Warrick had just come on board, had hurried down from the weather deck, his burly fighter's physique wrapped in a gold-braided frock coat, a welcoming grin on his whiskered face.

"God's blood!" he bellowed, checking in astonishment at the sight of her, the smile fading into disbelief. "What ye be wearin', lass? Go below an' be takin' those off!"

"I'm afraid I haven't anything else to wear," China said softly.

Captain Creel regarded her for a moment in thoughtful silence, her pale, exhausted face not going unnoticed, and then said gruffly, "I suppose they baint so bad. Keep 'em if you like, lass."

"But surely you can't expect her to—" Darwin began.

"There be time later for arguin', lad," the captain interrupted. "Tide be turnin' godrotting fast. If we don't sail now, we don't be catchin' the little 'uns. Runkle!" His voice rose. "Loose them headsails, blast you! Up anchor! We beed wastin' enough time!"

"Aye, aye, sir!" came a muted cry forward.

"Godrotting lubbers," Captain Creel muttered beneath his breath and touched his cap deferentially in China's direction. "We'll find 'em. Don't you be a'fearin'."

He hurried away and China turned to Darwin and asked urgently, "What little ones? Who is it we've got to find? What was he talking about?"

Darwin had no choice but to tell her. "Damon suggested we say nothing to Captain Creel about your abduction," he finished at last. "Given Horatio's love of the dramatic, we were afraid he might insist on storming Bloodwell's house in order to get you out. And Damon felt that would only exacerbate the situation."

"Then what did you tell him?"

"I made up some garbled story about your having gone to Singapore to enlist help in finding the children. I imagine Captain Creel had enough on his mind plotting a course after the *Malhāo*, because he didn't think to question it."

"How could you be so certain that Captain Bloodwell was prepared to let me go?"

Darwin's face reddened and he said uncomfortably, "I couldn't be certain at all. But by the time the *Aurora* arrived you'd been in his clutches for over eight hours and naturally I thought—that is, we all assumed—" He coughed and looked away. "We assumed that Bloodwell had had enough time by then to do whatever it was he—"

Darwin broke off, for China had turned toward him as he spoke and there was something in the calm, steady gaze looking back into his that made him flush hotly and rob him of the willpower to finish the damning thought.

The *Aurora D.* had cleared the harbor by now and as her sails filled with wind she heeled slowly to larboard and began to gather speed. Water slapped and gurgled against her hull, and the lines and beams creaked and whispered in response to the coaxing of the breeze, and China stood at the rail with her eyes dark and remote.

Miserable and helpless, Darwin stood beside her, and the silence stretched like a yawning gulf between them.

At Captain Creel's orders the schooner's crew crammed on more canvas, scurrying aloft to shore and trim the humming lines in order to extract every ounce of speed from her straining sails. A wake began to froth beneath the *Aurora*'s weathered stern, trailing away into the darkness behind her, and with the wind blowing full in her face and tugging gently at the ends of her veil, China could feel the terrible numbness within her give way gradually to a measure of hope. Surely they would catch the *Malhão* before it was too late?

Captain Creel, pausing beside her long enough to take note of her exhausted face, dourly ordered her below, and it was a measure of her weariness and despair that China obeyed without argument. Lying in the hot darkness of the tiny cabin graciously lent her by the first mate, she tried not to think of anything, not of Brandon and Philippa or Damon's broken wrist or of the fact that she could never marry Darwin in view of what had happened to her. Nor did she allow herself to dwell for a moment on the thought of Ethan Bloodwell and the rented rooms he kept for Julia Clayton somewhere on Geylang Road.

____ *Chapter Eighteen* ____

Luis Morales de los Queidós, captain of the Portuguese-registered schooner *Malhão*, stood in the greenish twilight on the aft deck and flicked the glowing end of a thinly rolled African cheroot over the rail. The wind took it instantly, whirling the ashes out of sight, and he cast his eyes to the heavens where the first evening stars flared and glittered in the descending darkness, and thanked the Blessed Virgin for his fortune. His holds contained over a hundred bolts of Badajan silk, valued at thirty-five thousand pounds sterling on the British market—the equivalent of well over a lac in Chinese currency. And every single golden yard of it had been purchased on credit.

"Thirty-five thousand pounds sterling," Captain Queidós murmured to himself, liking the sound of it. "And not a single escudo did you have to spend!"

Chuckling softly, he propped his arms against the rail and began to whistle through his teeth. He was a spare man of little more than medium height, his face scarred and his eyes dark and insolent. Like the complement of men who made up the *Malhão*'s crew, he was half Spanish and half Portuguese, but his loyalty belonged to neither country. His ship might be registered in Lisbon and his flag locker might contain the green and orange arms of his native land, but Luis de los Queidós served no one but himself, and least of all the fat, foul-mouthed mandarin Wang Toh Chen-Arn, for whom the silk was intended.

"Intended, yes, but received? Never!"

His lips parted in a satisfied grin. In less than three hours the *Malhão* would rendezvous with another ship, a fast, low-slung Chinese lorcha of the sort that smuggled opium up and down the China coast. And though its masthead would flutter the telltale purple dragon crest, it would not belong to Wang Toh's fleet nor be crewed by Wang Toh's barbaric henchmen, but commanded by Captain Queidós's half-brother Pedro. And as had been arranged in advance, the *Malhão*'s cargo would be transferred smoothly and surreptitiously aboard the lorcha while the schooner's crew slept oblivious in their bunks. As soon as the transfer was completed the lorcha and its fabulous wealth of Badajan silk would vanish along with the *Malhão*'s captain into the darkness.

"Wang Toh may look far and low, but he will never find me," Captain Queidós said to himself with a chuckle, for the lorcha would make instantly for Rangoon where a buyer for the silk already awaited him. And once the goods changed hands, he, Luis Morales de los Queidós, would be a man of great wealth and would buy himself a fabulous house in Rome and a dozen beautiful mistresses to occupy it.

And what of the schooner and her crew? The captain shrugged, for their fate did not concern him. Undoubtedly the vengeful Wang Toh would have her blown out of the water and the men taken hostage, yet since the *Malhão* was owned by a private Portuguese trading firm and not Captain Queidós himself, the loss did not trouble him in the least.

A sneer replaced the lingering smile on his thin, tobacco-stained lips. It was the deplorable practice of the powerful merchant firms, who paid less than one percent of their profits to the men who risked high seas, pirates, and swift-striking typhoons to transport their goods from one continent to another, that had driven him to accept the princely bribe offered by Wang Toh in the first place. Luis de los Queidós was not a fool and he had come to realize years ago that a vassal would always remain so— and that the power to rise above his humble means lay in his own hands; his, and Wang Toh's.

Captain Queidós had never met Wang Toh face-to-face. Few Europeans had. But Queidós knew quite a bit about him, for he had made it a point to learn everything he could about the man he intended to betray. A high-ranking civil official, Wang Toh had grown far too wealthy and powerful from the proceeds of the notorious Opium War for the peace of mind of the Emperor, and had, after the Treaty of Nanking, been assigned to Kansu province far in the north—a position amounting to little better than exile.

But public officials, by Chinese law, could serve only three years in any one province, and he was next sent to Shansi, where, by the end of his term, he had managed to bribe, steal, and buy sufficient votes so that last year he had been returned to Kwangtung. His hatred for the Ching dynasty was legendary although the face he showed the Emperor was loyal and benign. Few people knew or even suspected that he was covertly organizing secret societies that schemed to overthrow the Manchus, and de los Queidós was of the opinion that he was scheming to make himself emperor as well.

If not emperor, then at least the richest man in all the Middle Kingdom, for how else could one justify his mad decision to buy every scrap of Badajan silk produced this year and last? Surely he was scheming to bankrupt the Warricks and then pounce like a tiger to devour their leavings. He had bought huge amounts of the coveted silk, and when Damon Warrick refused to sell him more, had directed other merchants to buy it for him—always on credit.

Apparently Damon, or perhaps his more worldly mother, had begun to feel the money squeeze at last, because Captain Queidós had had a devil of a time procuring so many bolts—the last that were to be produced that season—without payment up front. But he had wheedled and pleaded and finally agreed to purchase an extra two hundred yards while feigning great reluctance, and laid down without argument the twenty-five percent Damon had demanded as advance against the account Queidós assured him would be settled by the end of the month.

Of course, that would never happen, nor would Wang Toh, whose advance money it had been, receive those priceless bolts of shimmering gold.

"No, my fat yellow friend," Captain Queidós murmured complacently. "You will have to find someone else to settle your unscrupulous affairs for you. Luis de los Queidós will be too busy fornicating with his concubines in his palace in Rome!"

He threw back his head and laughed, and the sound swirled away in the teeth of the wind. Behind him on the main deck the brass bell clanged the change of watch and Captain Queidós could feel a shaft of nervous excitement stab through his belly. It wouldn't be long now.

"Captain!"

He whirled, his thin face dark with impatience. "What the devil is it, Francisco? I thought I gave orders not to be disturbed?"

"Yes, I know, but Sanchez has found something in the hold. He thought you should take a look."

"Did he? And what was that half-wit doing in the hold against my orders? Surely not helping himself to a length of silk, eh?"

"Oh, no, Captain! He heard a noise and went to investigate."

Captain Queidós's eyes narrowed. "A noise? What was it?"

Francisco hesitated, aware that his captain was more than a little drunk and in an extremely agitated frame of mind. *Deos!* That could only mean more floggings before morning, and he shivered, for he had endured more than his own share of them on this particular voyage. What had made the captain so anxious? Surely he was not worried about the safety of the cargo in their holds?

"Well, Francisco? I don't like to think that you are deliberately hiding something from me."

The young man swallowed, recognizing the sadistic gleam in the captain's eyes. "Sanchez claims he has found

a pair of stowaways who—" He broke off without warning
and stared incredulously beyond the rail. *"Deos!* What is
that?"

Captain Queidós turned and peered into the darkness,
and his heart seemed to check and the saliva in his mouth
ran dry. It was a lorcha, bearing down on them with incredible speed, her silk sails blackened with dye to hide
her approach from the vigilant eyes of the *Malhão*'s lookout. Lanterns had been hung on her ancient prow, and it
was these that Francisco had seen, for they were being
ignited one after the other now that she had sped into
range. As light flooded the foredeck Captain Queidós could
clearly see Wang Toh's grinning purple dragon fluttering
demonically on the masthead.

"Mother of God!" he whispered, because the flickering
yellow light had also illuminated something else, something that could not be real and yet had to be, for Francisco
had seen them, too, and was nearly weeping with terror
recalling his earlier fear of pirates. In the bow of the lorcha,
kneeling in a menacing line with their oiled breastplates
gleaming in the light, were half a dozen armed Mongol
archers.

Luis de los Queidós's eyes bulged, but it was not the
fear of death that brought the scream to his lips, for he
never saw the deadly arrows that were launched from the
tautly strung bows to imbed themselves in his chest. It
was something else that tore the sound from his lungs and
sent it echoing into the vast silence of the grave: the sight
of his brother Pedro's head, blood-soaked and grinning
hideously, impaled on a pike and displayed like the spoils
of battle on the lorcha's weathered bow.

Graying dawn, creeping through the slits of the reed
matting covering the porthole, awakened China from a
fitful sleep. Quickly dressing in her silk shirt and lavender
trousers, she ascended the ladder and hurried through the
mist to the aft deck where Captain Creel stood engaged
in earnest conversation with the *Aurora D.*'s youthful
coxswain. Both men fell silent at the sight of her, for without the benefit of a brush or comb China had been forced

to plait her hair into a single braid that dangled well below her hips and added to the raffishness of her appearance.

In response to her anxious question, Captain Creel assured her that the schooner was making excellent time and that a rendezvous with the *Malhāo* could safely be predicted by six bells that evening.

"Deck, there! Sails abaft!"

Captain Creel's head came up and China's heartbeat checked for a frozen moment, but of course it could not be the *Malhāo,* she argued with herself, for how could the Portuguese schooner have ended up behind them?

"It's a clipper, sir!" the lookout shouted. "She's flyin' the Stars and Stripes!"

"Thot be *Orion,*" Captain Creel remarked, taking the offered telescope from his coxswain. "She's bound for Hainan, I'll wager."

China felt the tension ease from her, relieved that it was nothing more than an American clipper traveling a trade route across the China Sea. A cabin boy appeared on deck, and Captain Creel inquired if she cared for breakfast.

She was ravenously hungry, and taking a biscuit and a mug of hot tea she seated herself on a nearby bench. She had eaten nothing since the night before last—the very same night that Brandon and Philippa had left their beds and crept aboard Luis Queidós's schooner, bound for Canton and God alone knew what sort of danger.

China shivered and thrust away the panic that had been gnawing at her heart and mind like a creeping black specter ever since Darwin had told her the children were gone. She mustn't allow herself to think of the horrifying things Ethan had said about Wang Toh's greed and cunning, for it would only serve to drive her mad with fear, and she knew that she must remain calm and perfectly in control if she was to be of any help to the children.

"It won't be long until she passes us, will it?" she observed.

"Who?" Captain Creel inquired, bent over his charts.

"The *Orion.*"

"Yus, she be fast a'right. Give her another half hour or so. Tyler Crewe, thot be her cap'n, be a right impatient

bastard—beggin' your pardon, miss," he added hastily
when the sound of breaking glass alerted him to the fact
that he had been guilty of a thoroughly improper slip of
the tongue.

Turning his head, he saw that China had sprung to her
feet, smashing her cup on the deck and splattering her
trousers with hot liquid. Yet she seemed not in the least
dismayed by the accident; was not, in fact, even aware of
what had occurred, for she was staring in horror across
the wind-rippled water at the white stains of the *Orion's*
topsails.

"Tyler Crewe? You can't possibly mean he's the captain
of that ship!"

"Why not? Beed sailin' these waters near as long as I
have. Baint the most trustworthy cove you'll ever come
across, but I've met worse'uns." Captain Creel cocked his
head to one side. "Be you acquainted?"

"Yes, no, I mean— Oh, I should have known Ethan
wouldn't let me go so easily!" China's brow furrowed and
she fell silent. Presently she lifted her eyes to his and said
in a tone that was oddly breathless, "Captain Creel, do
you have the authority to marry people on board your
ship?"

He scratched his nose with a dirty thumbnail. "Eh...
I suppose I do."

"Could you do it right now? At this very moment?"

"Well, seein' as I've the Good Book in m' locker—" He
regarded her with drawn brows and inquired suspiciously,
"What be you askin' for, Miss China?"

"Because," China said urgently, "I should like to marry
Darwin Stepkyne. Immediately, before the *Orion* catches
us."

To say that Horatio Creel was taken aback by China's
request was to do grave injustice to the truth, for he was
so astonished by her words that for the space of a full
minute he could do nothing but gape at her and wonder
if she had taken leave of her senses. It took a considerable
amount of argument on her part and that of the hastily
summoned Darwin to convince him that their desires were
mutual and genuine and that the need to act with haste
was imperative; and still precious minutes were lost as he

did his best to point out to them the folly of their intentions. It was only when Darwin heatedly informed him that the *Orion* was in all likelihood carrying a passenger who intended to marry China for unscrupulous reasons and wholly against her wishes that he relented and agreed to perform the ceremony.

"Not without doubts," he growled, shaking his head and surveying with considerable misgivings the pair of anxious young faces before him. Godrot the joss that had taken Race Warrick's life and left his innocent daughter with no one but that fool stepson of his to look after her! Race would never have allowed his beloved daughter to marry someone as clearly unsuitable as Darwin Stepkyne, and the wedding he had doubtless envisioned for her would not have included the bride being called upon to appear in a crumpled harem costume with her hair dangling in an outlandish braid down her back.

"Deck, there! We've a ship in't channel! Starboard bow!"

"What be she?" Horatio bellowed back, cupping his hands.

"Schooner from the look of 'er, sir!"

There was a scuffle of running feet to the rail.

"It couldn't be the *Malhão!*" Coxswain Runkle protested as his captain snatched up the telescope. "She'd have made better time than this!"

"What is it, Captain Creel?" China inquired breathlessly, for she could see nothing on the gold-washed horizon save the shadows of scudding clouds and the toppling flight of feeding cormorants.

Horatio was slow to answer, for he could not himself explain what he was seeing in the circular field of his telescope. It was a schooner as the lookout had claimed, but one he couldn't identify and whose appearance brought to mind the eerie images of a ghost ship. Her canvas was down and her ratlines trailed behind her, and he could detect no movement at all on her numerous decks.

"Let's have a look, Mr. Runkle," he said, and the coxswain hurried away, shouting orders as he went.

As the *Aurora D.* drew closer it became obvious even without the aid of a spyglass that no one stood watch at the schooner's helm. She was drifting with the current, her masts rising bare into the paling sky.

"God above, her canvas be cut clean away!" Arthur Runkle exclaimed.

"It's almost as if there's no one left aboard," Darwin added uneasily.

As he spoke, a cloud of black birds rose from the schooner's deck, swooping and dipping over the oily water before settling with flapping wings into the empty rigging to watch the *Aurora*'s approach. The name *Malhão* was by now clearly visible on her motionless stern, and the wind, shifting slightly, suddenly brought with it the unmistakable stench of death.

Captain Creel lowered his telescope and grimaced. "Runkle, see if you can raise 'em."

But hailing the drifting schooner with the speaking trumpet proved thoroughly ineffective. Nothing greeted them save the restless fluttering of the carrion eaters watching balefully from the yards, and Captain Creel briskly ordered the *Aurora*'s launch readied and an armed boarding party assembled.

"I'm going with you," China said immediately.

Horatio shook his head. "There be dead men on't ship. No tellin' wot killed 'em."

"Please remember that my brother and sister happen to be aboard her as well," China said imperatively, quite undaunted by the likelihood. "You cannot stop me going with you."

"Oh, yes he can," Darwin said angrily. "Don't be stupid, China! Suppose it's cholera that killed them?"

"Cholera!"

The frozen look on her face made him instantly regret his hasty words and it was with a feeling of profound relief that he heard Captain Creel say crisply, "Baint no disease aboard her, lad. Cholera wouldn't strip her rigging or cut them lines. Men beed doin' thot. Men wot beed long gone."

China paled. "You're not suggesting they were attacked by pirates?"

"I baint suggesting nothing," Captain Creel said harshly though he was helpless to keep those exact suspicions from showing on his anxious face.

"Then I'm going with you," China said urgently, and there was suddenly something in her expression so strongly reminiscent of Race Warrick in one of his intractable tempers that Horatio Creel felt a superstitious prickle flee down his spine. His mouth pulled down at the corners and he was silent for a long moment. Then he sighed deeply.

"Get in't launch, child. But you'll not be settin' foot on *Malhão*'s deck. Be thot clear?"

"You must be mad!" Darwin's face was red with fury. "China isn't going over there with you!"

"Yes I am," China said clearly, and though Darwin pleaded and entreated and finally lost his temper, she could not be persuaded to listen to reason.

"You don't have to come with us if you don't want to," she pointed out in a tone that was as rigid as her stubborn face, and the unintentional though galling intimation of cowardice in her words effectively persuaded Darwin to abandon the argument.

A tense silence hung over the crowded launch in which the dip and swish of the oars and the creaking of the oarlocks seemed unnaturally loud, and as the small boat drew closer to the drifting schooner the stink of corruption became stronger and more horrible. The muscular tars numbered among the boarding party turned their heads away and fingered their weapons, and China sat in the stern between Captain Creel and Darwin and stared deliberately at nothing. Her face was little more than a white oval against the surging blue of the water, and only her hands betrayed her, for they were white-knuckled and trembled convulsively as they lay in her lap.

In the shadows of the schooner's salt-blistered hull the air was noticeably cooler and the smell of death not as strong, yet the ominous silence seemed to grow more menacing, whispering about them and taunting them to ascend the dangling ladder and see for themselves what horror had been wrought on the deck above.

Able-bodied Seaman Timmons McNee was the first man over the side, and when he saw what lay scattered on the sun-baked boards about him he tottered to the rail and vomited helplessly. The *Malhão*'s crew had been hacked to pieces. Everywhere was stacked the grisly evidence of car-

nage: dismembered limbs and bloated corpses, severed
heads with black, gaping mouths and eyesockets that had
been picked clean by the carrion eaters or were writhing
with the burrowing industry of clouds of blowflies. The
heat and the baking sun had served to dry the blood that
had soaked the planks and run into the scuppers, and
Seaman McNee, clutching the rail and gasping for breath,
could feel it crackle beneath the soles of his shoes.

"They be dead, Cap'n. All of 'em." His voice was little
better than a hoarse croak, and those waiting in the launch
below could feel the hair prickle on their scalps at the
sight of his face, for surely they were looking at a man
who had peered into the very depths of Hell.

"No!"

It was an incoherent cry from China that startled Horatio Creel from the paralysis that had gripped him. Turning his head he saw her scramble for the ladder, and he
lunged to intercept her.

"Wait, child!" His hand closed about her sleeve but the
fragile fabric tore in his grasp and before anyone could
stop her she had hauled herself over the side.

"Brandon! Philippa!"

Her desperate scream was answered by an explosion of
wings as the scavenging birds took flight, circling with
raucous cries though China took no notice of them or of
the inhuman things that littered the deck and filled her
nostrils with the terrible stench of putrefaction.

"Brandon! Philippa! Where are you?"

There was a corpse sprawled across the companionway,
an arrow imbedded in its throat, its wide, unseeing eye-
balls shriveled by the blistering sun. Gasping, China stumbled over it and scrambled down the ladder into the blazing
inferno below decks where the scurrying of rats and her
own tearful voice did little to disrupt the onerous silence.

A glimmer of light showed beneath a door at the end
of a long and stifling passageway, and China opened it to
find herself in a crude midships galley where the last smoldering embers of a coal fire burned in the stove and thick,
choking smoke hung in the air. The cook, if this was indeed
what the pitiable thing stretched on the floor had once
been, had obviously been preparing the evening meal when

the attackers had leaped upon him, for he still held an iron skillet in one bloodied hand. China, seeing that half of his fingers were missing and that cockroaches scuttled and scratched amid the offal, backed away, her throat tight with rising nausea, and stumbled over another corpse that lay propped behind the door.

She screamed and staggered to her feet, slipping in the oil and blood and refuse, and fled down the companionway only to crash headlong into someone who had leaped down the ladder at the sound of her cry. She screamed out in terror and struck at him with her fists only to feel herself being taken into a tight embrace.

"Hush, China. Don't be frightened," a familiar voice whispered in her ear.

"Ethan!" China breathed in a sob of relief.

He held her hard against him and the shock and fear were suddenly more bearable. After a moment she began to shiver violently and she lifted her head from his shoulder and turned her tear-stained face to his.

"Brandon and Philippa—"

"Yes, I know. Captain Creel told me."

"I can't find them anywhere," China went on in a frightened whisper. "Everyone's dead! Oh, Ethan, did you see what they did to them?"

Ethan nodded grimly, his lips compressed and his eyes narrowed with anger, seeing what the shock and the terrible anxiety of the past few days had done to her. Feeling the trembling of her small form against him, he lifted her into his arms and carried her into the spacious stern quarters that had once belonged to the captain of the *Malhão* and which had been swept wonderfully clean of the heat and the stench by a crisp breeze that blew through the opened shutters.

Settling China into a padded chair, he poured a drink from an engraved silver flask and she lifted it dutifully to her lips and coughed as the fiery liquid burned her throat. After a moment, however, a pleasant warmth began to steal through her and presently her shivering subsided and she looked up at Ethan with eyes that were no longer clouded with panic. A shock fled through her as she saw how haggard he appeared, but there was no time to analyze the emotion that cramped her heart in response, for Ethan had propped his hands on the desktop before her. Leaning down so that his face was very nearly touching hers, he demanded in an ominous voice, "What in God's name did you mean by running away like that? Didn't it even occur to you that the Singapore streets are no place for a woman dressed the way you are?"

China could only blink at him wordlessly as he delivered a lecture that appalled and cowed her with its violence and which might have gone on and on as his fury was further exacerbated by the meekness with which she endured it had the cabin door not burst open to reveal an incredulous Darwin and Horatio Creel.

"You've no right to speak to Miss Warrick that way!" Darwin protested with certainly justifiable indignation. "If there's anyone to be blamed for what's happened it's you and your contemptible, selfish reasons for snatching her from the Singapore pier!"

"Be quiet, lad," Captain Creel said curtly, not caring particularly for the sudden stillness that settled over the lean frame as Ethan straightened and turned to regard them. "You were right, Bloodwell," he added heavily and as though Ethan had spoken aloud. "The little 'uns baint aboard."

Ethan's eyes narrowed and his face seemed to age. China found herself thinking unexpectedly that this was probably how he would look in another twenty years, and she bit her lip and averted her face and wondered why the image of Ethan as a tired old man should make her heart ache so.

"Where do you suppose he be takin' 'em?" Captain Creel wondered aloud.

"Taking who?" Darwin demanded. It annoyed him that the burly schooner captain seemed to have developed an instant, if not liking, then trust in Ethan Bloodwell. And it further annoyed him that China did not seem to find his presence here the least bit odd, treating it as a matter of course despite the fact that she couldn't possibly have seen the *Orion* arrive nor Captain Bloodwell and his muscular tars come aboard.

"Who is it we're after?" he demanded of Captain Creel.

"Do you mean to say someone removed the children from the ship? Is it that Chinaman everyone's been talking about?"

Horatio did his best to explain patiently that his men had, at Captain Bloodwell's behest, made a careful search of the holds only to find neither the silk that had been purchased on Badajan two nights previously nor a trace of Brandon and Philippa Warrick. And on the further evidence of the arrows found imbedded in the bodies of the *Malhão*'s captain and crew, and identified by the Arab Rajiid Ali as Mongolian in origin, it could be safely assumed that the attack had taken place under the orders of the notorious Chinese mandarin Wang Toh Chen-Arn.

"How can you be sure?" Darwin persisted.

This time it was Ethan who answered. "Because Wang Toh, to the best of my knowledge, is the only Chinese who employs Mongolian archers as bodyguards. It's said the Emperor distrusts them and has forbidden them on the threat of death from entering Canton, though Wang Toh apparently takes them with him wherever else he goes."

"And be usin' 'em to do his godrotting filthy pirating," Horatio added in disgust. "Twenty-two years I beed sailin' China seas and never seen nothing like this. Godrotting savages!"

"Can you be certain they took the children with them?" China asked, swallowing hard. "How do you know they weren't killed and thrown overboard?"

Though it was Captain Creel she addressed, her eyes had gone to Ethan's face, and the sight of her ravaged expression filled him with a flaring rage. He found that he had to turn away without answering, and it was Horatio who assured China that Brandon and Philippa were valuable hostages and would not be so thoughtlessly discarded.

"And we'll be catchin' 'em afore they make Hong Kong," he promised. "Captain Bloodwell be goin' after 'em with *Orion*. She be a sight faster than my *Aurora*."

"Where is Captain Crewe?" China asked in bewilderment, for it had suddenly occurred to her to wonder how Ethan had come to be here. "Is he waiting for you on board his ship?"

Ethan shook his head. "I imagine he's still in Singapore."

"In Singapore?" She regarded him with wide, baffled eyes. "I don't understand. How did you manage to convince the *Orion*'s crew to bring you here?"

Ethan grinned. "I didn't have to. I simply borrowed her."

"You borrowed her?"

"Why not? The *Kowloon Star* was being refitted with new canvas and wouldn't have been ready to sail until tomorrow at least. And as the *Orion* was conveniently moored in the Singapore River and her captain safely ensconced in the arms of a most obliging lady elsewhere in the city—"

"Just a moment, there," Darwin interrupted furiously. "Don't you think enough time's been wasted as it is? Shouldn't you collect your crew and set off after the children?"

"Certainly," Ethan said. "China, are you coming with me?"

She took his offered hand without hesitation and the color immediately rushed to Darwin's face.

"China! You're not really thinking of going with him?"

"Whyever not?" she inquired.

"You know perfectly well what will happen the moment you do!"

"No, I'm afraid I don't," China said clearly.

"If you're concerned about Miss Warrick's virtue, Mr. Stepkyne," Ethan put in blandly, "you can always come with us to protect her."

"Best be goin'," Captain Creel urged into the tense silence that settled over the cabin and made the air seem unbearably hot and close. "It be little 'uns I'm thinkin' of." His troubled gaze fell on China. "It baint for me to keep you here," he added heavily, "though I'd rather you didn't go. I suppose Cap'n Bloodwell be lookin' after you proper, and seein' you be travelin' with your fiancé—"

"Fiancé?" Ethan interrupted sharply.

"Aye, young Darwin here. They be plannin' to wed. Or didn't you know?"

"No." Ethan's eyes narrowed as they fell on China's stricken face. "It will be a singular honor to welcome you and your betrothed aboard the *Orion*, Miss Warrick," he gibed, and made a thoroughly insulting obeisance in her direction. "I do hope, however, that you won't consider it ill-mannered of me to suggest that we dispense with further amenities and take our leave immediately?"

China's lips tightened in response to his mocking tone and she lifted her chin and nodded. Nothing in her bearing or her expression revealed to him the depths to which he had hurt her. "Are you coming, Darwin?"

"I suppose so," Darwin said glumly.

Stepping into the harsh sunlight China scarcely noticed that the bodies littering the *Malhão*'s deck had been tossed overboard on Captain Bloodwell's orders. Ignoring the interested scrutiny of the *Orion*'s assembled crew, she nodded stiffly to the bowing Rajiid and stepped into the waiting launch where she seated herself with her back turned deliberately away from Ethan, and during the voyage back to the *Orion* did not speak at all.

Chapter Nineteen

"I believe the first thing we should do is get you out of those clothes," Ethan observed coldly once he had ushered China below decks and the _Orion,_ under command of the hatchet-faced Rajiid Ali, had hoisted anchor and laid a course due north for Hong Kong. "Though I'd trust my own crew to behave themselves where you're concerned, I cannot say the same for Tyler's. They're a surly bunch and agreed to sail with me only on promise of ample payment."

"It would seem no one of your acquaintance knows the least thing about loyalty," China pointed out critically. "I find it hard to believe that they would agree to abandon their own captain purely for the sake of profit. How is it," she added tartly, "that they trusted you sufficiently to permit you to abscond with their ship?"

"They know me well enough," Ethan replied briefly and entirely to her dissatisfaction. He stood regarding her for a moment in thoughtful silence, thinking to himself that she looked far too beautiful and tempting what with the morning sun pouring through the unshuttered stern windows of the cabin and igniting the golden highlights in her crimson hair. She seemed so small and slender in the silk trousers with their gripped ankles, and so impossibly fragile, that it was all he could do to keep from taking her into his arms and smoothing the lines of exhaustion from her face.

But he knew that he mustn't touch her; not only because he could not in all honesty assure her that her brother and sister would be returned to her unharmed, but because she had made no effort to deny the shocking disclosure that she and Darwin were to be married—even after everything that had happened between the two of them in the dark, scented bedchamber of the Coral House.

"You needn't worry about me, Captain," China was saying stiffly, finding it equally difficult to think of anything else now that Ethan was standing before her. In his salt-stained clothing and with his disheveled hair and wild, unshaven face, he looked disconcertingly like a pirate, but there was something in his haggard features that brought a curious ache to her throat. She found it impossible to keep her gaze from falling to his lean, dark hands and remembering how they had roved her body, touching her in intimate places and awakening feelings she had never dreamed a man ever could.

"You needn't worry," she repeated with considerably more hostility than the situation warranted. "I have no intention of leaving my cabin until Wang Toh's ship has been sighted."

"Suit yourself," Ethan replied brusquely and turned away without seeing how she flinched in response. Perhaps if he had, things might have turned out differently between them, for the almost imperceptible gesture would have made clear to him that he still possessed the power to wound her, and made him realize further that he could not possibly have done so had China's feelings for him been wholly impervious ones. And such was China's own pain and despair that any sign of softening on Ethan's rigid face would surely have done away entirely with the walls she had erected between them, and she would have forgiven him anything and everything—even his clandestine liaison with Julia Clayton.

But because Ethan's back was turned to her and because

he could think of nothing but the blinding rage that the vision of China married to Darwin Stepkyne aroused within him, the moment and the opportunity vanished, and left in its stead a rift that yawned empty and uncrossable between them. Wordlessly and with a chilling finality, he shut the cabin door behind him.

Throughout that long and trying day China remained below, and though the heat and the unbearable worrying eventually took their toll, she could not bring herself to make an appearance on deck. Darwin, concerned by her listlessness and the remote, colorless voice with which she addressed his anxious questions, finally took his fears to Ethan, thinking that however much he might dislike and distrust the older man, he could at least be called upon to offer his worldly advice in the matter of offering comfort to a clearly apprehensive female.

But Captain Bloodwell merely observed uncharitably that seeing as Miss Warrick was Darwin's future wife and not his own, it was up to Darwin to find a way to assuage her fears in the matter of her abducted brother and sister.

"But suppose we never find them?" Darwin persisted, voicing the concern that lay too uncomfortably heavy on Ethan's own conscience. "What on earth shall I do then?"

"My dear fellow," Ethan remarked curtly, "if you plan to saddle yourself with an emotional and quite unpredictable wife, you'd better learn how to manage her. I will warn you that spending your life with someone as stubborn and opinionated as Miss Warrick isn't bound to be easy."

Darwin said through clenched teeth, "I cannot honestly believe you could be so unfair and judgmental toward her when you know perfectly well what China has suffered since returning home from England, part of which or perhaps even all of which has been because of you! And that, incidentally, is precisely why she wishes to marry me and not you!"

"And that is precisely why I'm letting her go," Ethan interjected with an unsettling gleam in his eyes, "and why I've decided not to break every bloody bone in your body. Though I will confess, Mr. Stepkyne, that I am sorely tempted to try. Now, if you'll excuse me, I've a ship to sail."

With a brief and thoroughly insulting nod he turned

away. Darwin opened his mouth and shut it again while the color receded slowly from his face. He couldn't be sure whether those quietly uttered words had been seriously meant, but in view of Ethan Bloodwell's unsavory nature it might be wise to take them at face value and abandon any further effort to communicate civilly with him. China was fortunate indeed to have escaped marriage to him. The very idea of a match between them was such a highly offensive notion, in fact, that Darwin resolved to hold to his convictions no matter how much the captain might threaten him with physical abuse.

Twilight fell swiftly that night and still the darkening sea and the vast, star-hung horizon remained empty. It had been a discouraging day for everyone, even the members of the clipper's crew, for every man jack among them had been uncommonly moved by the quiet suffering on China Warrick's face when she had made a brief appearance on deck earlier that afternoon after sails had been sighted on the northern horizon. It had turned out to be nothing more than a British frigate beating before the wind in the direction of Singapore, and as soon as her white ensign had been unquestionably identified, China had slipped wordlessly below, but not before her sad face had aroused the better instincts of every man who saw her.

Evening fell and China hesitantly accepted an invitation to dine with Captain Bloodwell and the *Orion*'s officers, not because she was particularly hungry, but because the waiting had become intolerable and she was quite prepared to exchange the loneliness of her hot, stuffy cabin for any form of companionship—even Ethan's. Stepping into Tyler Crewe's quarters, she was rather startled to find the paneled walls hung with colorful Persian tapestries and the wire-fronted bookcases cluttered with a surprising number of expensive *objets d'art*. Ethan Bloodwell, dressed in his work clothes, seemed entirely out of place as he rose from his chair to greet her. The *Orion*'s officers, on the other hand, had made a touching effort to appear presentable, and the scent of freshly applied pommade mingled strongly with the victuals steaming on the nearby table.

Darwin was quick to guide China to a chair next to his,

deliberately steering her away from the one that had been placed at Ethan's right. Though Ethan could not possibly have failed to see it, he merely signaled the hovering steward to serve the meal, his expression unreadable.

"Would you like wine, Miss Warrick?" the *Orion*'s first mate inquired with a kindly smile.

"Thank you," China said politely, "but I don't think I'd care for any."

"Under the circumstances," Ethan said with the faintest suggestion of a drawl, "it might be wise to fortify yourself, Miss Warrick. The night promises to be a long one."

"How long do you think it will be before we find them?" China asked anxiously.

"There's no reason to believe we'll sight Wang Toh's ship before morning," Ethan replied brusquely. "Not unless something's happened to delay him, though it doesn't seem likely."

There was a sudden scramble of feet on the deck above and Darwin demanded sharply, "What is that?"

"Cap'n Bloodwell!"

It was only a faint cry, like a whisper on the wind, but Ethan started at once for the companionway, shouldering the bewildered Darwin aside. The *Orion*'s acting first mate met him on deck, handing him a telescope and gesturing without speaking to starboard. It was difficult to pierce the dim, starlit darkness with the circular glass and Ethan cursed the fact that he had left his own spyglass locked away in his sea chest aboard the *Kowloon Star*.

"'S a clipper, ain't it?" the first mate inquired. "Her mainsails're down and she's dropped anchor, but I don't think it's us she's waiting for." He backed away involuntarily as Ethan lowered the telescope, startled by the expression on the captain's face. He had seen men look like that when they were plunged into the grip of a cold, uncontrollable urge to kill.

"Helm alee, Mr. Fine," Ethan said harshly, "and be quick about it. See that her head's kept into the wind. You've got thirty seconds or you're over the side, is that understood?"

Without waiting for a reply he strode to the weather

deck where he exchanged a few words with Rajiid before vanishing below.

"Where's he gone? What the devil's he up to?" Darwin demanded, coming up on deck with China behind him.

"Lord help me if I know," the first mate growled, and hurried off to carry out his orders.

"Why don't you ask Rajiid?" China suggested.

"What? Speak to that surly heathen?" Darwin burst out. "You must be mad! He won't—Where are you going, China? China!"

Rajiid, hearing her soft footfalls on the deck behind him, turned and made a deep bow. It was true that he cared little for women in general, and English ones in particular, but he had come to respect China Warrick in his own way and suspected that the captain's feelings for her were not as indifferent as he might have everyone believe.

"What is it, Rajiid?" China inquired worriedly. "Has Wang Toh's ship been sighted?"

"It is the Imperial One's ship," Rajiid acknowledged enigmatically, "yet it is the captain's ship as well."

China regarded him blankly for a moment, her upturned face illuminated in the flickering light of a cabin lantern, and Rajiid found himself thinking with a start of surprise that she was really quite beautiful despite the fact that hers was not the sort of beauty he could readily understand or appreciate. He wondered why he had never noticed it before.

China's face cleared suddenly and she exclaimed, "Oh! Do you mean the *Lotus Star*? But I thought—Wasn't she destroyed?"

"It is what we had been led to believe. The Imperial One must have salvaged her, and now he is one of very few Chinese to possess such a ship."

And with it the awesome speed of which only a clipper was capable, China thought. "What does Captain Bloodwell intend to do?" she asked.

"Allah forgive him, he is a fool," Rajiid said shortly. "He would deliberately seek an audience with the Imperial One. It is madness, great madness to enter a jackal pit alone and unarmed and believe one will not be turned upon."

China's face turned white. "Why would he do such a thing? Surely Wang Toh won't set my brother and sister free simply because Captain Bloodwell requests it!"

Rajiid angrily shook his head. "He has been beset by demons now that he has seen his ship. I am afraid he will not listen to reason or accept the fact that there is nothing he can do."

China was silent a moment, considering the truth of Rajiid's observations. Presently she asked in a whisper, her throat so tight that she could barely speak, "Will they kill him?"

Rajiid shrugged his shoulders and spoke with an equanimity he was far from feeling. "Inshallah. It is in the hands of God."

"I know. What is written is written," China quoted bitterly. She wished she had at least a measure of the Arab's faith so that she, too, could accept the notion that a man's death was predetermined from his hour of birth, and since there was nothing one could do to alter it and certainly no reason to rail against it, there really was no need to be afraid.

But she was afraid, more afraid than she had ever been in her life. When she saw Ethan come up on deck she found herself gripped with a paralyzing terror that had nothing whatsoever to do with her own safety or that of Brandon and Philippa.

Turning his head, Ethan saw her standing white and drawn by the aft deck railing. He frowned and approached her with a purposeful stride. "There's something I want you to do for me before I go," he stated coolly.

China regarded him warily. "What is it?"

His tone was curt. "I want to see you safely married to Darwin Stepkyne before I leave. As acting captain of the ship I'm the only one who can perform the ceremony and I—What's the matter? It's what you've wanted all along, isn't it?"

"No—yes, I mean I never—"

"For God's sake, China," Ethan said impatiently, "I haven't time to argue with you! At the risk of sounding tediously melodramatic, it's entirely possible that I won't be returning once I set foot aboard the *Lotus Star*, and I want to make certain you'll be adequately cared for in the event you are carrying my child."

A wave of color flared upward from China's throat to her hairline. She could only stare at him blankly and wonder with an odd twist of breathless hope if perhaps it might be true....

Seeing the look on her face Ethan could not help but laugh, though it was faintly bitter. "The possibility never occurred to you, did it? Surely you must realize that sometimes when a man and a woman—"

"Don't," China said in an almost inaudible whisper. "Don't, please." She paused. "Do you really want me to marry him?"

"My dear young woman, you've already taken great pains to prove to me how reprehensible you find the notion of marrying a former China trader like myself, and Darwin seems to be your choice of preference."

Taking a deep breath, China decided in that moment to lie, calmly and deliberately, for the first time in her life. Not only because she knew there was no other way to sway him from his purpose but simply because she suddenly found the idea of marrying Darwin Stepkyne a thoroughly unappealing one.

"Oh, Ethan, Darwin and I can't get married," she said quickly. "You see, Mother told me that Darwin and I are related. My father didn't only keep Oriental mistresses. He—"

"I understand," Ethan interrupted curtly, and though China's garbled and highly improbable account would normally have aroused his suspicions, he was too distracted by his driving fear for her and by the fact that he could very well make a fatal error once he found himself confronting his hated enemy aboard the *Lotus Star*. But what else could he possibly do? He was one of the few Europeans who had ever met Wang Toh face-to-face, who understood the workings of his devious mind, who knew the proper tactics to use in the subtle warfare that would accompany his appeal to free the Warrick children.

"If there is a child and you want it to have a name," China said slowly, "shouldn't it at least be yours? I mean, seeing as you would be the father?"

The blue eyes were suddenly far too close and there was
something oddly urgent in the deep voice that China had
never heard before. "What is it you're trying to say, China?"

She never had the chance to speak, for a cry of alarm
from the forward lookout suddenly rent the air. China
turned her head and saw an ominous shadow swoop down
on them from out of the darkness. It was a lorcha, the
fearsome eyes painted on its prow seeming to stare in a
diabolical manner that made her breath catch in her throat.

"Ethan—"

Before she could utter another word, Ethan seized her
by the arm and dragged her below. Thrusting her into the
stern cabin he forced a pistol into her hands.

"Do you know how to use this?"

She nodded.

"Then lock the door behind me. Shoot anyone who tries
to force his way in. And under no circumstances are you
to leave the cabin until I return. Is that clear?"

"What is it? Has Wang Toh—"

The sound of musket fire drowned out her words, and
the muffled cries and running feet that accompanied it
could mean only one thing: the *Orion* was being boarded.

Ethan's heart cramped at the sight of China's terror,
but he could do nothing for her here. Hurrying topside he
saw that the *Orion*'s crew had been set upon by a horde
of Chinese pirates wielding cutlasses and knives, and without hesitation he discharged his pistol into the face of a
man who lunged at him.

Bringing the butt of the empty weapon crashing against
the jaw of another, he heard the bones splinter with the
force of the blow. Scooping up the dead man's cutlass he
hacked and slashed his way back to the gangway, positioning himself in front of the steps and trying to block
out the chilling image of China trying to defend herself
with only one bullet. He wheeled as another man lunged
for him, sidestepped neatly, whirled and killed him, and
knew with cold certainty that he would allow no man to
gain entrance to the decks below.

A Chinese who had scrambled onto the companionway
housing dropped down on him from above, and Ethan
grabbed him by the throat. Flipping him onto the deck,

he heard the man's neck snap as he fell. Crewmen were swarming over the main deck, their muskets flaring in the darkness. Through the burning haze of powder smoke Ethan saw Darwin Stepkyne take aim and fire into the melee and then jerk about, his face contorting, as a knife caught him in the side. Without moving away from the steps he guarded, Ethan drew out the knife concealed amid his clothing and, hurling it with brutal accuracy, saw it imbed itself in the throat of the man who leaned over Darwin's inert form.

Clawing and gasping, the Chinese toppled. Ethan whirled and hacked at another who came out of the darkness to avenge the killing. A cutlass caught him a glancing blow on the side of the head, but before the deadly blade could do more than cut his temple, the weapon was hurled away and the man who wielded it uttered a grunt and fell. It was Rajiid who stood behind him, calmly wrenching the hilt of his knife from the Chinaman's back and salaaming gravely before vanishing into the smoke-filled blackness.

Wiping the blood and sweat out of his eyes, Ethan looked about him and realized with numb despair that his men were losing. Though a great number of dead Chinese littered the deck, more and more were coming aboard to replace them, swarming like rats over the *Orion*'s sides and attacking in waves that were increasingly difficult to repulse.

With uncharacteristic indecision, Ethan wondered if he should call a surrender. Should he give in now before all of his men were killed? How best to keep China safe? By fighting to the bitter end or by giving in and hoping that the killing would stop and she would not be harmed?

His vision blurred and his wound throbbed and he knew that he could no longer trust himself to make a decision with any reasonable judgment. But even as he continued to jab and slash at those Chinese who came too near, the sounds of battle were beginning to die away and as he looked around he saw that a fierce contingent of warriors was disarming the last of his men and herding them against the great cabin wall.

A heavy silence suddenly weighed down upon the ship, broken only by the sound of the wind sighing through the rigging and the terrible moans of the wounded and dying. Ethan lowered his cutlass and slumped wearily against the cabin wall.

"I wish to speak to your master," he said in Cantonese to a knife-wielding warrior walking nearby.

The Chinese turned away obligingly and Ethan found he had to close his eyes against the dizzying pounding in his head. In the next moment, however, he had forgotten everything: the dead and dying, the pain of his wound, the fact that his ship had been assaulted by Wang Toh's bloodthirsty men. For a movement at the top of the companionway had brought his head around, and he found himself staring incredulously into China Warrick's white face.

China had been listening with helpless panic to the sounds of the battle being waged above her head. The screams of the wounded and the thuds and grunts and the deadly clang of swords had echoed horrifyingly into the silence of the deserted cabin and she had been hard-pressed to keep from putting her hands over her ears to shut out the sound of it. Though she had locked the door as Ethan had commanded, she had opened it several times, indecision quickening her breathing and leaving her trembling on the threshold, not knowing whether to stay below or hurry topside in the event she might be able to help.

When the sounds of ferocious battle had given way at last to an utterly chilling silence, she had fled instantly up the stairs. Stepping out into the hot night, the heavy dueling pistol held in one hand, she had spotted Ethan immediately and her heart had jerked to a stop at the sight of the blood running down his face.

For a frozen moment in time they stood staring at one another, China paying no attention at all to the Chinese about them, seeing only the pain and weariness etched into Ethan's haggard features. And Ethan was thinking absurdly to himself how impossibly lovely she appeared to him amid the carnage littering the Orion's decks. Abruptly his mind cleared and a savage rage swept over him.

Bearing down on her, his eyes a dark, luminous blue with the force of the anger that shook him he said hoarsely, "Damn you to hell! Didn't I tell you to stay below?"

China, gazing up into the lean, sun-browned face that was barely recognizable because of the blood and the bruises that were beginning to swell and darken it, felt her heart cramp within her and knew in a moment of appalled comprehension that she loved him.

"Oh, Ethan, your face!" she whispered, her shocked words cutting through his blistering denunciations to effectively silence him. "Does it hurt very badly?"

Ethan was distracted from replying by the sound of a rope slapping against wood. He turned quickly to see two of the *Orion's* seamen lowering the boarding net under the watchful eyes of an armed Chinese guard. A moment later a dinghy that had been launched from the lorcha appeared through the darkness and a gaunt Chinese in an embroidered silk robe swung himself with difficulty over the side.

One of the guards gestured toward Ethan, and the elderly Chinese approached him without haste and bowed gravely. With a wave of his blue-veined hand he indicated the bodies of the dead men being laid out in rows on the deck below him.

"Wang Toh hopes lesson learned, savvy?" he said in the clipped pidgin with which most Chinese addressed English-speaking Europeans. "We can send many times more other warriors, never mind."

"Lesson plenty learned," Ethan responded in kind, and a flicker of surprise showed briefly on the ancient face before the Chinese's features became composed and unreadable once more.

"You come see Wang Toh quick, savvy?"

"Savvy," Ethan said and felt hot hatred wrenching his guts. There had been no need for Wang Toh to prove his advantage over them by launching an attack on the *Orion*. Not only did the *Lotus Star* in all likelihood possess ten times the number of men, but Brandon and Philippa Warrick were aboard her, and surely Wang Toh must have known that Ethan would obey any summons willingly enough in order not to endanger their lives. The deaths of the *Orion's* crewmen had been entirely avoidable; purely the result of the mandarin's love of warfare and killing.

"Wang Toh want others, can," the elderly Chinese added imperiously.

Ethan, not having expected this, could feel the cold
sweat break out on his brow. What others? Wang Toh could
not possibly know that China was aboard the *Orion* and,
for that matter, could only have surmised that Ethan himself commanded the clipper in Tyler Crewe's place.

Presuming to behave as though the question was not
in the least unexpected Ethan inquired coolly, "What others, heya?"

The ancient Chinese's rheumy eyes swept slowly over
the officers and crewmen who were assembled before him.
"Cow chillo can," he said abruptly, his gaze falling on China,
who stood very white and still at Rajiid's side.

"Cow chillo noa can," Ethan said immediately, knowing
that the "girl child" in question had been recognized despite the emissary's almost casual request. "Cow chillo
stay here."

The Chinese made a stiff and regretful bow. "I goa then.
Quick-quick. Werry sorry, never mind!"

Ethan, realizing that none of them stood a chance if the
emissary were to return to Wang Toh's ship without them,
felt the cold sweat chill him and knew that he must gamble
heavily if he hoped to buy sufficient time to save their
lives.

"Others can," he said without haste. "Wang Toh want
others can?"

"Cow chillo can." It was a polite but unarguable request.

Ethan closed his eyes and for a moment the pain of his
wound lashed at him. It was no use. The old man had
obviously been given his orders and it seemed that China
was not about to escape Wang Toh's devious grasp. Unless—

Opening his eyes Ethan spoke curtly in Arabic to Rajiid,
and everyone, including the frowning emissary, was taken
aback when the Arab whipped a curved knife from the
folds of his robes and thrust the blade directly beneath
China's chin.

"Cow chillo noa can," Ethan said coldly. "Frien' kill cow
chillo plenty quick, never mind. Wang Toh see noa, savvy?"

It was, of course, a bluff, but Ethan was grimly pleased
to note the expressions of incredulous horror that crept to
the faces of the crew. Studying them intently, the ancient

Chinese could not help but believe that Ethan meant what he said. At any rate the orders he had been given did not include forcing the opposition into a reprisal that would result in the death of a most coveted hostage.

After pondering the situation for a moment he inclined his head and said resignedly, "Cow chillo noa can. You can, savvy?"

Ethan, striving hard to hide his enormous relief, said calmly, "Can."

Signaling Rajiid to release China, Ethan found himself instantly surrounded by an angry mob demanding explanations. They had to be forced into submission by cuffs and blows from the Chinese guards, and in the brief interim provided by the confusion, Ethan was able to shoulder his way to China's side.

"Rajiid wasn't really going to harm you."

"I know," she said calmly, and with eyes that were overly bright she glanced at his temple. "You're still bleeding. Surely that man there will allow you to have it bandaged?"

Ethan grinned humorlessly. "I'm afraid the state of my health matters very little to them."

"You're going with him, aren't you?" China asked numbly. "Rajiid says that's the *Lotus Star* out there and that Wang Toh owns her now."

"Not for long," Ethan told her lightly, and seeing the sudden paling of her face, his mouth tightened and he added with a curt laugh, "My dear young woman, I'm not nearly as addle-brained as you seem to believe. I've no intention of sacrificing the lives of your brother and sister by instigating some foolish plan to recapture my ship."

"But you just said—"

"My God, China, do you really have so little faith in me?" he was compelled to ask. "After all this time am I still nothing more to you than a black-hearted knave without a compassionate bone in his body?"

China ached to tell him that she couldn't remember when she had last thought of him that way, and that what terrified her was not so much the fact that he intended to risk Brandon and Philippa's freedom in some wild scheme to win back his ship, but simply the thought of losing him. She knew that Wang Toh would never give up one thing without taking another, and she couldn't bear the notion that Brandon and Philippa were going to be set free if it meant that Ethan had to die.

Seeing the stricken look on her face and misinterpreting it as guilt because she did, in fact, still think of him as nothing more than a conscienceless cad, Ethan laughed bitterly and bowed in her direction. "Thank you for the sincerity of your sentiments, Miss Warrick."

Without waiting for her reply he remarked politely to the Chinese emissary who had pushed his way between them that he was quite prepared to meet with Wang Toh and shouldn't they make haste before the Imperial One grew impatient?

And with an armed trio of Chinese guards accompanying him he strolled casually to the launch, whistling a tuneless melody softly between his teeth.

Chapter Twenty

Wang Toh Chen-Arn, imperial mandarin of Kwangtung and proud owner of the magnificent clipper *Lotus Star,* sat on a raised dais lavishly padded with silk cushions in the spacious aft quarters that had once belonged to Ethan Bloodwell. A teak screen handpainted with fearsome purple dragons divided the sleeping area from the rest of the lavishly furnished cabin and a nightingale preened itself in a gilded cage near the brocade-hung windows. Armed guards flanked the door of the cabin both inside and out, and a half-dozen robed retainers waited anxiously in an adjoining room to be summoned by their master.

Wang Toh, dining on fried prawns and delicate dim sum from a crimson-lacquered tray, was feeling immensely pleased with himself. Not only had his lorcha recovered the silk that the Portuguese swine devil had planned to steal from him, but its captain—Wang Toh's eldest son by his second and favorite wife—had also taken possession of an unexpected and highly valuable prize: the first-born son and youngest daughter of the English barbarian Race Warrick.

Though it was doubtful that the crippled girl child would be of any use, Wang Toh had refrained from ordering her flung overboard, for he could not yet be certain that she might not prove so in the end. Barbarians, Wang Toh had learned long ago, placed a ridiculous value on the lives of their female offspring, though even the most ignorant Chinese knew how utterly worthless they really were.

Laying his carved ivory chopsticks aside, Wang Toh crossed his hands over his enormous, silk-covered belly and studied the jeweled sheaths that protected his four-inch-long fingernails. It had not surprised him that Ethan Bloodwell, the barbarian captain of the *Lotus Star*, had come in pursuit of the Warrick children, for Wang Toh's spies had informed him days ago that Ethan Bloodwell coveted King's Wheal Plantation, and in order to take possession of it had planned to make the eldest Warrick daughter his wife. But of course there could be no wedding until the children were safe.

It was a great pleasure to have all of them in his grasp, Wang Toh decided gleefully: the barbarian Bloodwell, the Warrick children, and the eldest daughter with the insulting name of China, which was the name the first barbarians to sail up the majestic Pearl River had given his beloved land. Joss had been good to Wang Toh Chen-Arn, very good indeed. Without joss Race Warrick would never have died before his affairs were settled, leaving Badajan in the hands of his weak and ineffectual stepson. And joss had provided Wang Toh with greedy Asians and European traders who had descended like locusts on the island following Warrick's death, each one of them engaged in rapacious schemes and frantic takeover bids that had accomplished nothing more than to mask Wang Toh's own covert activities as he secretly bought up every scrap of silk cloth on credit and pushed the Warricks ever further toward bankruptcy.

He had intended to make his final squeeze once the *Malhão*'s cargo was safely in the *Lotus Star*'s holds, but now joss had dealt him a different set of cards and he was delighted to play his hand accordingly. Delighted!

"What is it, you worthless piece of dung?" he inquired contemptuously of a quaking servant who had crept into his presence, knocking his head repeatedly on the floor. It pleased him that his slaves were terrified of him, and he knew that they would fear him even more now that he had ordered thumb screws placed on his elderly sixth uncle Jin Chen H'ung. Ayee yah, but had the fool not deserved it? Even the lowliest peasant would have seen through Ethan Bloodwell's bluff and known instantly that he would never have China Warrick killed merely to prevent her being brought aboard the *Lotus Star*.

A pity that his son Ho Kuang Chen had been slightly injured during the attack on the *Orion* and had been absent from the final confrontation, for he would never have fallen for such a transparent trick. Still, Ho Kuang's decision to attack the American clipper after recovering the *Malhāo*'s cargo of silk had been both fortuitous and profitable, for the unexpected capture of Ethan Bloodwell had given Wang Toh Chen-Arn the final advantage. Ayee yah! His joss was great indeed.

"Speak!" he commanded, his hooded eyes falling on the kowtowing servant. He was able to make out just enough of the creature's frightened gibberish to understand that the barbarian captain's wound had been cleaned and bound and that he was ready to be brought into the mighty lord's presence.

Wang Toh's eyes narrowed with fiendish enjoyment. "Send him to me."

In the sweltering darkness amidships, Ethan was doing his best to keep his boiling temper in check. The fact that Wang Toh had ordered him held in the smallest cabin aboard the ship—an airless cubbyhole formerly used for surplus ship's stores—was a deliberate slight that had not gone unnoticed. And Ethan, whose rage had begun to simmer the moment he had seen the number of Chinese seamen who occupied the berths and hammocks that had once housed the men of his own loyal crew, knew that Wang Toh was playing the game of cat and mouse purely for his own enjoyment.

He felt a certain measure of gratitude to the obese mandarin, however. The *Lotus Star* had suffered considerable damage when she had been captured, and he had been impressed despite himself with the skill that had gone into repairing her torn hull and superstructure and in the mending and maintenance of her canvas. From what little he could see in the smoky light of the swaying lantern hanging on an overhead beam, the cabin in which he found himself was scrupulously clean, the deck swept free of cobwebs, and the brasswork neatly oiled and polished. The physician who had tended Ethan's wound had washed his hands carefully in an enameled bowl of hot water before treating it, and the bandage he had used to bind it had been made of freshly laundered gauze. Ethan's bloodied and sweat-stained clothing had been taken away, and the pongee robe provided in its stead was clean and refreshingly cool.

Yet it was the fate of his ship and of the Warricks that occupied his troubled and increasingly angry thoughts now. He knew he had to act soon, before he was summoned into Wang Toh's presence. His sweltering cell had once been used for storing surplus sacks of grain and barrels of flour, and in order to protect them from the gnawing ferocity of the large and ever-present shipboard rats, the walls had been lined with thin strips of tin plating. Ethan worked at them with a splintered piece of wood pried from the underside of the berth and soon was able to remove them without difficulty.

He tapped along the length of the exposed wooden wall and discovered that a window that had once separated the tiny anteroom from the adjoining one still remained. To his bitter disappointment it was barred from the other side, and no amount of pushing and straining on his part could open it. With an exclamation of disgust he dropped onto the sagging mattress, his head in his hands. Even if he could manage to prize it open, there was little enough he could do in the way of escaping until he had located the missing children. And even then he had to consider the fact that the Orion had been seized by Wang Toh's men and that there was no way Rajiid could help them.

Ethan lifted his head abruptly at the sound of a furtive scraping and scratching that came to him through the breathless heat radiating from the lantern, and for a moment he was mystified as to its origin. In the next he had sprung to his feet and thrown himself hard against the window, laughing aloud as he felt it give. He pushed again, harder, and the shutter swung open with a muted crash, bringing a string of invectives to Ethan's lips. Yet it appeared that the guard outside had heard nothing untoward, for all remained silent in the corridor. When Ethan at last turned his head he was shocked to find himself gazing at none other than Brandon Warrick, whose small, incredulous face was staring back at him from the far side of the frame.

"It—it *is* you, Captain Bloodwell!" the boy whispered. "I heard someone banging on the wall and I opened the window to see who it was. What's happened to your face?"

"An accident," Ethan said briefly. "Where's your sister?"

"She's locked in the next room, but I can talk to her through the wall." Brandon's expression brightened considerably. "Have you come to take us home?"

It would have been an unconscionable breach of honesty to offer the child false assurances, and Ethan found he could not bring himself to lie with those solemn green eyes pinned hopefully upon him. "I'm going to try," was all he could promise. "You're not hurt, are you? Either one of you?"

Brandon shook his head and dropped his voice to a hoarse whisper. "It isn't us Wang Toh wants to hurt. It's China."

Ethan stiffened. "What do you mean?"

"I heard them talking. The guards that brought us here, I mean. Wang Toh speaks Mandarin and I don't, but the guards that took us away talked Cantonese and I do know a little of that. China taught me some and my father did, too. He said it was important to speak it because we have so many Chinese clients."

"What did they say?" Ethan inquired, and Brandon's brow puckered as he strove to remember.

"I'm not really sure. I think Wang Toh had your house in Singapore watched. That's how he found out you wanted King's Wheal for yourself and that you were going to marry China to get it. Philippa thinks it's because you're in love with her, but I overheard them saying something about

Father having left King's Wheal to China and not to Damon and that the only way it could be yours was if you married her. Why? And why would that make him want to hurt her?"

"Who?" Ethan prompted, his mind reeling.

"Wang Toh. They said Wang Toh hired some men to kill China when she came back from England because King's Wheal was hers and not Damon's. They laughed about it and one of them said he could have killed her a lot easier and for a lot less money than Wang Toh paid those—those—"

Brandon's words trailed away and his mouth drooped and suddenly there were tears in his eyes. "I can't remember what he called them." He stretched his hand through the window and his fingers clutched desperately at Ethan's sleeve. "I wanted to help her. That's why I ran away with Philippa. We heard what you said to her on the terrace and I thought—I thought—" The drooping lips began to quiver and Ethan quickly laid his hand over Brandon's small one.

"You did the right thing, lad," he said reassuringly.

"I did?"

"Well, almost. It wasn't wise of you to run off without telling anyone, but as for helping China, here's what we can do..."

The tousled head bent closer and Ethan outlined his plan in a manner that even a frightened little boy could understand, and which brought an excited gleam to the wide green eyes long before he had finished speaking. Seeing it, Ethan could not help but experience an odd twisting of his heart, recalling how often China, too, had faced the near impossible with a similar show of courage.

Yet this time things would be exceedingly dangerous, and as Ethan watched the shutter swing into place over Brandon's freckled face he found himself in the grip of considerable uncertainty—and was extremely disconcerted by it. So many depended on him: Brandon and Philippa, Rajiid and the captured men of Tyler's *Orion*. Yet all of them paled in significance when compared to China's anxious and impossibly beautiful little face and the realization of how much she meant to him.

Strange how intolerable the thought of never seeing her again could seem, and strange to think that he might very well die without ever knowing if the passion they had shared together would bear fruit in a child. Or, even, for that matter, whether or not China had ever loved him. . . .

Ethan came cursing to his feet, furious at the madness of his thoughts, but they were mercifully destined not to torment him long. The sound of a key turning in the lock reminded him at once of the task at hand. Affecting a deliberately casual pose, he disposed himself on the bunk with his hands propped behind his head, and only the coiled tension of his long body gave evidence to the fact that his ease was an illusion.

He was greatly relieved to see that only two guards had come for him. When he made no move to rise, the older one nudged him impatiently with the barrel of an ancient blunderbuss. Ethan uncrossed his arms and rose obligingly, moving in the manner of a tightly wound spring that is slowly and carefully uncoiled, and prayed that Brandon's timing would be right.

It was.

"Hey, you! Wat for you no see me, heya?"

The unmistakably cheeky pidgin and the curly head that grinned at them from behind the window before slamming the shutter back into place was nicely calculated—and successful—in bringing the pair of Chinese heads around. It then was an astonishingly simple matter for Ethan to seize the matchlock and slam it hard into the back of the first guard's neck and ram it into the stomach of the second who collapsed to his knees where another blow effectively subdued him.

Tossing the clumsy weapon aside, Ethan rapped sharply on the shutter and instantly Brandon's face appeared, his eyes widening at the sight of the immobilized guards.

"You did it!" he said admiringly.

"Get your things together," Ethan ordered, searching the bodies of the unconscious Chinese for the keys. Though he knew that it would be wiser to kill them, he found he had no taste for it, and quickly gagged them and tied them securely to the bunk, using the strips of leather that had been intended for his own hands.

Philippa, rescued from her dark and miserably cramped cabin, was unable to walk as her crutches had been left behind on the *Malhão*, and Ethan was obliged to carry her. Brandon followed close behind, his belongings tied firmly about his waist in a knotted scrap of silk cloth.

Their escape was negotiated for the most part in utter darkness, but there was no hesitancy as Ethan had designed the layout of the clipper's lower decks and it was a simple matter to wind his way through the familiar maze of bulkheads and passageways that crisscrossed the *Lotus Star*'s daunting holds. In the dark bowels below the waterline, where foraging rats scratched and fought amid forgotten crates and casks and the smell of bilge was overpowering, he set Philippa down and, stooping, ran his hand along the length of an exposed beam.

Ah! There it was, apparently untouched and undetected by Wang Toh's industrious carpenters. The latch sprang open easily, and as he thrust the panel aside the sweet scent of cool night air blew into their faces.

"It's a trap door, isn't it?" Brandon exclaimed eagerly, crouching to look. "Did you hide treasure in here?"

Ethan grinned. "No, I didn't, I'm sorry to say." Of course Brandon was not to know that he had on occasion smuggled human cargo as well as the usual consignments of opium and silver bullion. Human cargo of a dangerous nature, in fact, for there had invariably been a price on the heads of the terrified men who had been brought secretly and in the dead of night aboard the ship: political activists, exiled Chartists, persecuted or wrongly convicted and desperate men, and though the *Lotus Star* had been stopped and searched by numerous naval squadrons, she had never failed to deliver up to safety every single man she had protected.

Ethan cautioned the two children not to light any tapers in the event the smoke would draw attention, and provided them with a dust-covered bottle of claret in place of water to drink. With the stern admonition not to reveal their presence to anyone but himself, he slid the panel back into place behind them and left.

There was little time to lose as the absence of the guards who had been sent to fetch him would soon be noticed. It was fortunate that he, better than anyone, was privy to the many secrets the clipper carried with her—among them the installation of several cleverly concealed peepholes the former owner of the *Lotus Star*, a notoriously cunning Englishman who had smuggled opium for the British East India Company, had used to great advantage. Ethan was pleased to discover that they still existed, and by concealing himself in a narrow recess of the corridor well out of sight of the guards posted before Wang Toh's door, he was able to slide back a panel of wood and study the cabin behind it.

Little remained of the spare but functional furnishings that had served him well for a number of years, replaced now by the lavish cushions, the lacquered screens, and the immodest opulence with which Wang Toh had surrounded himself. The mandarin, as Ethan well knew, abhorred sea travel, and had apparently attempted to make his quarters as comfortable as possible in the event it was necessary to leave Canton. And nothing could have prompted him to undertake this lengthy journey save the recovery of the silk that had left Badajan in the holds of the Portuguese schooner *Malhão*.

Wang Toh, older, grayer, and far more overweight than Ethan remembered, sat cleaning his teeth with an ivory pick on a raised dais covered with the same emerald and vermilion silk that draped his own immense frame. His beard was ragged and nearly white and his oiled queue was shot with gray. His eyes, cunning and evil as ever, were half hidden amid folds of fat. Deciding that he had seen enough, Ethan slid the peephole shut and picked up the knife he had taken from one of his felled Chinese guards.

The sight of Wang Toh majestically enthroned in the cabin that had once been his own had fueled his temper, doing away with any qualms he might have suffered on the question of whether or not to kill him. Regrettably, there was no time to plan a proper attack, and he knew that he would have to act quickly.

It was a simple enough matter to dispose of the guards flanking Wang Toh's door, for the companionway leading to the stern quarters was dimly lit and he was able to steal up behind the first without being seen. And because the second one did not turn his head until he heard the sound of their panting struggle, Ethan was able to grab him by the throat and kill him instantly.

With reckless disregard for his own safety, he burst through the cabin door, knocking aside a terrified servant and overturning a low lacquered table upon which a wafer-thin tea service had been laid. Hacking at the guard in green silk trousers who lunged at him, he leaped upon the dais, his sea boots clattering, and seized the startled mandarin by the throat.

"Were you so certain of your victory that you sent your archers back to the lorcha?" he inquired, his breathing harsh, the blade of his knife pricking the vulnerable flesh beneath Wang Toh's numerous chins. "That was foolish of you, my friend."

"Perhaps," the mandarin responded after a long moment. His Chinese enemies had long mocked and despised him for his mastery of the barbarian tongue, but Wang Toh had decided from the very first that it would prove far easier to manipulate the Western savages by speaking their own language, and that pidgin was a crass and thoroughly useless tool for the subtleties of the negotiations he practiced. Therefore, once he had managed to recover from the shock of this unexpected attack, he was able to observe blandly and in nearly flawless English, "Time has changed you little, Ethan Bloodwell."

"And you," Ethan responded through clenched teeth.

"You will kill me now, perhaps?" the mandarin inquired curiously.

Ethan inclined his head. "I would remind you of the fable of an old Chinese scholar you spoke of many years ago."

The stout shoulders shook with silent mirth. "Ah! This of course is one a barbarian as you would not forget. It is a fable that tells us: do not show mercy to a dangerous animal."

Wordlessly, Ethan nodded.

"But perhaps you would wish to hear my say?"

"I know everything I need to," Ethan answered shortly. "It doesn't matter how you discovered that it was China

Warrick who inherited King's Wheal, but the fact that you tried to have her killed does matter; a great deal, in fact."

"Are you certain it is everything you know, Ethan Bloodwell?" Wang Toh inquired softly.

The knife blade did not waver. "I can guess the rest. Now that Brandon and Philippa Warrick are in your grasp you will demand the drafting of a deed, signed by China herself, granting you undisputed ownership of King's Wheal Plantation in exchange for their freedom. Given that you own most of the silk produced this year and that Damon Warrick was forced to borrow heavily, and from creditors who, unbeknownst to him, were financed by you yourself, no one should find the eventual transfer at all suspicious."

Wang Toh nodded contentedly.

"Of course you'll have to put China and her brother and sister to death afterward," Ethan continued, "and perhaps scuttle the *Orion* and her crew, for you dislike complications and witnesses to your crimes, but China is not to know that. How, I wonder, did you intend to make your excuses if the British government happened to protest the murder of three of its innocent subjects? Or America, for that matter? They're a rash and hot-tempered lot who don't take kindly to having their ships boarded and captured, much less sunk with all hands lost."

Wang Toh waved a hand that, with its jeweled sheaths and talon-like nails, strongly resembled the claws of a predatory animal's. "There are ways to make killings seem accident. Even you know that, Ethan Bloodwell. And if there is protest I have only to seek help from friend, your British plenipotentiary, who is ever willing to accept a bribe, never mind! How do you think your *Lotus Star* became mine and my men were taught to sail her, heya?"

He uttered a wheezing chuckle, seeming to have forgotten the blade that was pressed uncomfortably against the fleshy folds of his throat, and his bright and cunning eyes met Ethan's cold stare. "You do not know everything, friend. There is more to show. The best for last—is that not barbarian custom? I will summon slave, heya?"

Ethan's hand tightened about the hilt of his knife and he considered the possibility that he could well be inviting disaster. There was something in those calm and deceptively affable eyes that told him the mandarin was not afraid or even mildly concerned by the likelihood that death awaited him at the hands of a determined madman. Then again, he could be bluffing, but Ethan realized he couldn't risk the possibility and that there was little to be gained by killing Wang Toh now, if something of import indeed remained overlooked.

He said curtly, "Summon him, but no tricks. I can kill you faster than you think."

Wang Toh's lips curved. "No tricks. No cheat."

The servant who had been huddling unmoving on the floor crept away at a clipped command from his master, and for a long moment there was silence in the elegant quarters as both men waited. Ethan made no move to relinquish his hold about the mandarin's throat, not having dismissed entirely the possibility that he was about to fall victim to an ambush.

Swift and deadly as Wang Toh's archers might be, he would still have enough time to drive the knife blade home before he died, and were that to happen he had no other choice than to hold to the belief that Wang Toh's death would give Rajiid the advantage he needed to rescue Brandon and Philippa Warrick and set the *Orion* free.

But when the servant returned, prostrating himself at Wang Toh's feet, Ethan's heart turned over and his mouth went dry at the sight of the scrap of silk cloth the man held in his hands. He recognized it at once as the veil China had pulled over her face when she had fled the Coral House and which he had last seen her wearing on board the *Orion*. It instantly made clear to him something that should have dawned on him before: that Wang Toh had ordered China taken captive the moment he had learned of her presence on board the other clipper.

Of course there was no need to question the obvious or doubt the evidence of his own eyes, and while Ethan had been quite willing to slit the mandarin's throat on the chance that China would go free, he was not about to behave so recklessly when her life would be forfeit the moment he acted. This way, perhaps, there might still be hope, and though he was forced to grapple with the killing rage that closed his throat and nearly blinded him, he managed to subdue it at last and let the knife clatter to the deck.

"You make wise choice, Captain Bloodwell," Wang Toh pronounced supremely, and signaled his servant to remove the weapon.

You bastard, Ethan thought to himself. You'll die for this, I swear it!

But his face revealed none of his thoughts and it was with a remarkably level voice that he asked to see her and was rather astonished when his request was granted.

Moments later China was led into the room by two heavily armed Mongol guards. Her frightened eyes went instantly to Ethan's and he saw the shock and the weariness within them give way to enormous relief. She started toward him but was prevented by the restraining hand of one of the guards. Ethan tensed as he saw her wince but could do nothing more than force himself not to move and demand curtly, "Have they hurt you?"

She shook her head. "Oh, Ethan, where are Brandon and Philippa? Have you seen them?"

"You needn't worry about them," he said quickly, hoping to reassure and convince her without revealing that they were, for the time being, quite safe, and that one of Wang Toh's prime bargaining chips had, in point of fact, already changed hands.

"You needn't worry about me, either, Ethan," she said with quiet dignity. "I've no intention of giving him what he wants, not King's Wheal or Badajan, and certainly not when he is holding my brother and sister hostage. He had his uncle tortured because he failed to bring me here, and if he thinks that he can do the same with me, he is quite mad!"

A nearly imperceptible movement of the mandarin's jeweled hand brought the guards before her, affecting a menacing stance that could not be misconstrued. China fell silent although there was a look of triumph on her lovely face as she lifted her chin to stare scornfully at the obese warlord.

Whatever else might happen, she was content in the knowledge that her words had caused the white, strained lines about Ethan's mouth to disappear. She knew that she had managed to still his concern for her and with it the frustration and helplessness she knew would cripple his judgment and prevent him from turning his energies toward rescuing Brandon and Philippa—and saving himself.

Ignoring her guards with deliberate calm, she lifted her proud eyes to his. "It's Brandon and Philippa I'm thinking of, Ethan. It's entirely possible Father left King's Wheal to me, but I'm quite certain he made provisions for me to keep it only as long as it takes Brandon to come of age. That means I'm really quite useless to Wang Toh though he refuses to acknowledge as much. It's the Warrick males who have always laid claim to King's Wheal."

"It's all right, China. There's no need to go on. I understand," Ethan said.

Quite suddenly China's slim hands twisted together and betrayed the fear she had been trying so hard to hide from him. In a breathless whisper that filled him with a fierce and futile ache she asked, "You'll help them, Ethan, won't you? No matter what may happen?"

Knowing perfectly well that she was asking him to forget about her own safety and think instead of Brandon and Philippa's, a rush of helpless anger hit him full in the face. Damn her! Surely she must know that he could never make such a promise because in doing so he would be sealing her fate as assuredly as Wang Toh was attempting to do! He began to shake his head, but the movement was checked by the answering look on her face, which was suddenly no longer calm, but ravaged and intolerably afraid.

"Please, Ethan! I can't bear to think that something might happen to them."

"In God's name, China," he said, "I'll do what I can for them. I swear it!"

He saw the tension drain from her, leaving her looking unbearably young and vulnerable. He would let her believe what she wanted, for it was clear to him that the promise he made had at least served to restore her courage.

There was no need for them to say anything more; each had understood the other perfectly. But as Wang Toh indicated to the guards to lead her away, China shook herself free and said clearly, "Oh, Ethan, I almost forgot. Rajiid asked me to tell you that the fire started on the forecastle during the attack was put out without damage. He expects the *Orion* to be ready to sail at dawn."

Ethan's hard gaze came to rest challengingly on Wang Toh. "Provided you'll let her go."

"It is possible," the mandarin allowed grandly, but his eyes were cold and hooded and it was clear that his thoughts were elsewhere.

But where? Ethan, led away to another cell by a different set of guards, could only hope that it was China's plea to spare the lives of her brother and sister rather than her own self that had captured the warlord's attention. Not, he prayed, the seemingly innocuous message she had delivered on behalf of Rajiid Ali. That, as Ethan well knew, contained a meaning of far greater significance than Wang Toh Chen-Arn could ever imagine.

The fire on the forecastle referred to a signal fire, and if he could somehow manage to raise one, Rajiid Ali, who had presumably devised a plan to get free of his Chinese captors, was prepared to attack the *Lotus Star* at dawn. But how was he, Ethan, to escape from his cell in order to do so? His hands were now bound; a necessary precaution, Wang Toh had explained with an apologetic smile, as he had proved himself a criminal unworthy of trust. The cell to which he had been taken was a former munitions locker constructed during the days of the Opium War when the clipper had been a runner for John Company and had, of necessity, been armed. The locker was windowless, reinforced with thick and impenetrable wood, and as an added precaution the Chinese guards outside the door had been doubled and issued extra weapons.

It would be futile, Ethan knew, to test his strength against the iron-braced beams and strutted walls, and at any rate his hands were lashed behind him with thongs that cut into the flesh and could not be loosened however much he worked at them. For the first time in his life, and with a whispering edge of panic that thoroughly disconcerted him, he realized that he had reached the end of a road from which there was no turning back, and that this time, and partly through his own selfishness, he had helped bring about the capture and perhaps the ultimate deaths of three innocent people.

Of course he could not be blamed for the manner in which Brandon and Philippa Warrick had fallen into Wang Toh's clutches, but Ethan did not have to remind himself that it was his own unkind words to China on the terrace at King's Wheal the night of her party that had prompted the children to run away in the first place. And if he hadn't been so preoccupied with his own affairs, he would have realized straightaway that it was Wang Toh Chen-Arn, not Damon Warrick, who was responsible for the family's financial troubles, and would have taken immediate steps to put an end to the mandarin's ruthless squeeze.

Instead he had behaved in an unforgivably stupid manner, blundering about as though he were both addled and blind, and committing the sort of gross errors of judgment one would expect from a scrubbed and beardless weanling fresh out of the classroom.

Despite his great self-loathing and the burning urgency that flailed at him at the thought of China being held captive and perhaps tortured at Wang Toh's hands, he could do nothing but pace through the hot, sweating darkness and admit to himself that there was no way to escape or send a signal to Rajiid before it was too late. The thought was an intolerable one.

The rasp of the enormous metal bolt on the far side of the door brought Ethan's head around, and he blinked as a bright shaft of light stabbed his eyes after nearly an hour of total, impenetrable darkness. All but blinded he was dragged outside and brought face-to-face with a lean Chinese youth dressed in the leather and chain-mail garb of a warrior, his left wrist encased in a leather guard, a quiver of arrows strapped to his back. A puckered scar ran from the corner of his right eye well into his hairline, and it was the ferocity and cunning in those eyes that cautioned Ethan to play carefully.

The heart of the matter was, of course, the missing children. When Ethan blandly disclaimed any knowledge of their whereabouts, the Chinese with the eyes of a wolf calmly removed a knife from his belt and slit open the skin between the base of Ethan's right thumb and forefinger. The wound was not deep, but the pain was shattering, for Ethan's hands were still tied behind his back and the nerves were raw and tingling.

"My father grows old," the archer pronounced in guttural Cantonese, "and is inclined to show mercy to his enemies. I am not like him."

Ethan's eyebrows rose. "And if I cannot tell you what you wish to know?"

Wang Toh's son bared his teeth in a smile and the knife moved again, slicing through the bonds so that Ethan's hands were suddenly free. "Bind him," he ordered tersely to one of the guards. "I would not have him bleed to death until I have finished with him." Indicating the blood that ran freely from the wound, he said to Ethan, "I would want you to feel this pain and remember it, Captain. It will help you appreciate the suffering of the Warrick woman when her fingers are cut off, one after the other, until your memory is restored."

Ethan felt as if the air had been driven from his lungs in a single, savage thrust. His hands came up instinctively to deal a blow, a gesture of utter insanity given the odds, and yet he was no longer capable of rational thinking. Grinning, Ho Kuang Chen raised his knife and waited.

It was difficult to say who was more surprised, Ethan or his captor, when a compact little body appeared seemingly out of nowhere and hurled itself against Ho Kuang's legs and toppled him to his knees. Ethan recovered first, striking the Chinese swiftly in the face with the heel of his boot and rolling him into a position so that as he slammed the magazine door behind him, he could hear an agonized scream and the sickening crunch of breaking bones as the man's fingers caught in the hinges.

The startled guards moved swiftly to Ho Kuang's defense, and Ethan grunted in pain as the shaft of a weapon caught him full in the belly. Another blow landed on his head, reopening the cut on his temple, and all at once it seemed as if he had been leaped upon by a half-dozen frenzied creatures when in truth it was only three. He felt himself going down amid a profusion of arms and legs and wondered dully why none of them had as yet dealt the killing blow. Could it be that they had been given orders not to kill?

"Captain Ethan! Here!"

He felt the hilt of a knife smack into his open palm, and though it was slippery with blood he gripped it tightly and drove it upward with all his might, feeling it slice through muscle and imbed itself at last in hard bone.

Someone above him was screaming and abruptly the weight upon him was gone. Ethan leaped to his feet, wrenching the knife free. Then he was fighting like a demon possessed, for one thought only penetrated the killing fog that surrounded him: what they would do to China if he were to lose.

Driving the blade of his knife through the throat of a Chinese who was already bleeding badly from an earlier thrust, Ethan stood back to watch him fall, then whirled and tensed himself for the next attack—and was left blinking in astonishment when he found the corridor before him empty and the deck beneath his feet littered with bodies.

Abruptly his strength ebbed away and he became aware of the fact that his head and wounded hand were throbbing. The stink of blood and sweat filled his nostrils, and for a moment he leaned against the wall, panting and swallowing convulsively.

"Captain Ethan? Shouldn't we hide them before somebody comes?"

Ethan's head came up and in the flickering light of one of the lanterns that burned on an overhead beam he saw Brandon Warrick's face, white and very anxious, regarding him from the far side of a bulkhead behind which he crouched.

A tired smile lit his lean features. "Aye, lad, I suppose we'd better."

The task was done quickly and in silence. Ethan found Ho Kuang Chen unconscious behind the narrow, iron-braced door and waited until Brandon had slipped out into the corridor before bending to slit his throat. It was not a task he relished, yet it had to be done, and his expression was grim as he stepped out into the corridor and locked the munitions door upon the grisly remains. Looking down, he became aware of the sickly cast to Brandon's face and it occurred to him that the boy had just witnessed his first killing.

"I'm afraid I was hopelessly ill the first time," Ethan said with an understanding smile.

"You—you were?"

Ethan nodded and began unwrapping the blood-soaked gauze about his head. Cutting away a clean strip with which to bind his hand, he rewound it tightly. He couldn't afford to be weakened by the loss of blood, not now, when he would need every ounce of strength he possessed.

"I was fourteen years old and newly shipped out on a London merchantman named the *Wayang Pandjii*. We were carrying a shipment of plate home from Arabia when we were boarded by pirates off the coast of Algiers."

Brandon's eyes widened. "Did you have to kill them?"

Ethan nodded grimly. "Yes, indeed, since they were doing their bloody best to kill us. We were lucky to be able to drive them off without losing more men than we did." Even now he could recall, quite vividly and with a lingering sense of shame, the fear that had sickened him even more than the stench of the blood and the sight of the dead men who had littered the freighter's decks.

"And they were real pirates?" Brandon inquired with awe.

"Real pirates," Ethan said dryly, "but I daresay no more bloodthirsty than these devils." A frown pulled at the corners of his mouth. "Now what in God's name are you doing here? I thought I told you to stay below."

"I know, but Philippa and I were afraid you weren't coming back, so I decided to try and find you. I've been looking everywhere for you. At first I didn't know how to help you get away from those men, but then I remembered how we had surprised the other ones. I just wanted to help you and China," Brandon confessed in a tremulous whisper.

Ethan clamped him firmly on the shoulder. "You probably saved our lives, lad. I've no idea how else I might have gotten away. Is Philippa all right?"

"Yes. She promised she wouldn't get scared and try to follow me."

"Did anyone see you?"

"No," the boy said decisively. "It was dark and I made certain to hide whenever I heard anybody coming."

Ethan regarded him for a moment in silence, not knowing quite what to make of him and wondering, as he had on numerous occasions in the past few months, what sort of man Race Warrick must have been to sire such astonishing offspring.

"Come on, then," he said softly and with a measure of gruff fondness. "We might as well try to find China."

Pausing only long enough to pick up some scattered arrows and Ho Kuang's bow, Ethan motioned Brandon into silence. With their shadows falling small in the lamplit corridor before them, they set off in search of China.

Chapter Twenty-one

In the end it was Brandon who was responsible for finding her: Brandon, who had braved the darkness and the fear of discovery to search for hours in the sweltering holds and amid decks overrun with Chinese, forcing himself to keep a tight rein on his panic and telling himself over and over that Captain Bloodwell would not be angry with him for breaking his promise and leaving his sister and the relative safety of their hiding place behind. He himself did not know what had driven him to disobey the order, unless it was the despair that filled him at the thought of what his own foolishness had led them to, and the fact that he could no longer sit by and do nothing while Captain Bloodwell risked his life to rescue them.

It was fortunate that the boarding and capture of the clipper *Orion* had served to fully occupy the *Lotus Star's* Chinese crew, for Brandon would not have escaped detection quite so easily had the situation been different or the crewmen below decks more vigilant. And it was fortunate that he had grown up in the company of Malaysian children who had taught him to shimmy up coconut palms and swing effortlessly from the stilts of the kampong huts that stood high above the tidal mud flats, for without that skill he could not have climbed out of the hold or hidden himself by scrambling amid the overhead beams whenever anyone came near.

And if the Cantonese he had learned from the Chinese boys in the villages of Badajan had not been perfected under the tutelage of his older sister and, later, his father, he might not have understood the words that Ho Kuang Chen, the mandarin's son and captain of the pirate lorcha, had said as he ordered the munitions locker opened and the barbarian prisoner removed, unaware that a small figure crouched in the shadows behind him, listening with wide, staring eyes and a pounding heart to all that was said.

"They found out we were gone, you know," he told Ethan in a somber whisper further muffled by the oppressive darkness of the corridor leading to the midships galley down which they hurried. "Wang Toh was mad because China wouldn't sign some kind of paper and he wanted her to see us. To help make her sign, I think. I didn't even know China was here! They weren't really going to cut off her fingers, were they?"

"I've no doubt they would have," Ethan said grimly, seeing no reason to lie to the boy. There seemed little reason to add that unless they found her quickly, China could be expected to suffer a fate far worse than the loss of her fingers once Wang Toh discovered that Ethan, too, was gone and that his eldest son lay brutally murdered on the deck below him. He thrust the thought away as soon as it occurred to him, but apparently his fear must have prompted him to speak out loud, without being aware that he had done so, for suddenly Brandon exclaimed, "But I *do* know where to find her!"

"What?"

"China! I think I know where she is."

Ethan whirled and gripped the small shoulders hard. "Where?"

"I'm not really sure. I heard that man with the arrows say she was...He called it—" His voice trailed away and only with difficulty did Ethan suppress the urge to shake him.

"Think hard, Brandon. What did he say?"

The boy's brow furrowed and abruptly his eyes filled with tears. "I'm sorry, Captain, I can't remember. I thought I could but I can't. He said something about the *fan quai* and I—"

"The *fan quai*? Do you mean Chinese demons?"

"Yes. He said she was being kept in the place where the barbarians worshipped their demons and it— What is it? Why are you laughing? Did he mean a church?"

Anything but! Ethan thought wryly, for he had never professed himself to be of a particularly religious bent, not, at any rate, the sort that would drive a man to express his devotion by erecting a chapel aboard his ship. But the mention of barbarian demons could mean only one thing, or so he hoped: a reference to the stained-glass window depicting the three Magi bringing gifts to the infant Jesus, which Nappy Quarles had won after a night of drunken gambling from a disreputable Arab chieftain, a certain well-known trader of antiques, precious stones, and narcotics, who had plied his wares in the ancient port cities of the Persian Gulf and went by the name of Sheik Abdul Al-Hassid.

It was probable that the sheik, who was really no more than a thief and a pirate, had come by the window by disreputable means, but as it was large and cumbersome and, to him, of very little value, he had presented it gladly to the one-eyed steward, who had taken a most absurd fancy to it. And Nappy, turning a deaf ear to the gibing of the rest of the crew, had proudly installed it above his cot, a truly grand embellishment to the cramped and otherwise spare quarters he was content to call home.

It was possible, but not entirely certain, that the *Lotus Star*'s Chinese crew, being by nature superstitious and mistaking the glass for an object of religious worship, had feared to remove it and thereby anger the Christian fan quai housed within it, which would assuredly have reaped untold misfortune upon their heads. And as Nappy's cabin was located at the top of the companionway, within calling distance of Ethan's own, it was entirely possible that Wang

Toh had ordered China held there until such a time as she would agree to sign King's Wheal over to him.

"By God, it's a chance worth taking," Ethan murmured to himself, for he had no idea where else to begin the search.

With Brandon watching wide-eyed and uncomprehending, he entered the midships galley where he spent the next few minutes removing the lids of the heavy wooden barrels stacked behind the door, smelling and tasting the contents until he found the one he was looking for.

"Soybean oil," he told Brandon. "Let me have your shirt. Better yet, have you got a handkerchief?"

Brandon did, slightly grimy but otherwise usable, and Ethan dipped it into the oily liquid, folded it carefully and wrapped it securely about the head of one of the arrows. As a precaution he repeated the procedure with another, this time using a strip of gauze cut from the bandage about his hand.

The idea that had occurred to him when he had first seen the bow and quiver that Ho Kuang Chen carried seemed almost laughably simple, and he was plagued with doubts over its possible success. Yet inasmuch as it seemed unlikely that a second and more suitable solution would occur to him, he was forced to content himself with this and not with considering the appalling number of things that could go wrong—and what would happen to China and the children if they did.

He could scarcely believe that no alarm had as yet been raised, but if the unbelievable were true and their absence had still gone unnoticed, he could only assume that the situation would change at any moment and that they must proceed with utmost haste.

Though Brandon was visibly tired he kept pace without complaint, clutching Ethan's hand whenever an abrupt turn in direction plunged them into the utter darkness of a deserted companionway, and moving with utmost caution when they were forced to pass by doors standing partly ajar and from which issued the low snores of sleeping crewmen.

Ethan found himself growing convinced that Wang Toh's encroaching age, his laziness, and above all, his smug conviction of his own infallibility, had lulled him into a critical and dangerous sense of security, for how else could one account for the lack of guards and the inattention of those at action stations throughout the ship? The only other explanation that occurred to him was one he dared not contemplate; the possibility that Wang Toh had sent most of his men to the *Orion* because of some unforeseen development there was something too frightening to consider.

One step at a time, Ethan cautioned himself. Thinking ahead and worrying about things he could not foresee was not only counterproductive but deliberate madness. As for the luck that had sustained him until now, he would simply have to hold to the belief that it would not fail him, not when they had finally succeeded in ascending the rung ladder to the upper deck and were crouching in the shadows near the wall, peering down the dimly lit passageway leading aft to Nappy's cabin.

The smell of lantern oil and garlic-fried fish was strong here, and Ethan could only assume that Wang Toh was passing the time in which the barbarian prisoners were ostensibly being tortured by dining in a leisurely fashion. He was grimly pleased to note that the guards standing before the closed door had lapsed into slouching stances of inattention, and he hoped their negligence would serve in his favor. Though the passageway was dimly lit and filled with the grimy haze of lantern smoke, Ethan wasn't entirely convinced that it would be a simple matter to enter Nappy's cabin without being seen.

He felt Brandon lean against him and whisper worriedly in his ear, "How are you going to get in?"

It was a question Ethan had already asked himself at length and which he had been despairing of answering, yet quite unexpectedly he found himself saying as though he had known all along, "Through the privy. There's a small door leading into the back of it. That's how the waste buckets used to be emptied without anyone having to enter the cabin. I doubt our Chinese friends are aware of it."

"It must be very small," Brandon said and added curiously, "Shouldn't I go instead of you? I'm smaller, after all, and I could probably squeeze through without making any noise."

After some deliberation Ethan decided that this might be the wisest solution, especially as it would free him to keep watch on the guards and cover Brandon in the event they were seen. "Go on, lad," he urged, "but for God's sake be quiet!"

He watched the boy slip into the narrow opening behind the privy door and took up his knife, positioning himself to the best advantage in the shadows of a nearby beam. Endless minutes ticked by and Brandon did not return and still the guards remained motionless before Wang Toh's door.

Sweat chilled him as Ethan's imagination presented him with a plethora of agonizing possibilities: that the privy door was locked from the cabin side or, worse, that it had been boarded shut long ago by the *Lotus Star*'s Chinese captain. Or perhaps Brandon had managed to gain entrance into Nappy's cabin only to find China not there, or worse and most unthinkable, that she was lying on the bunk wounded or beaten or that Ho Kuang Chen had lied to him and her fingers had already...

Ethan ground his teeth in helpless frustration. Too long, his mind whispered; Brandon was taking far too long. Yet even as he fought a battle with himself on the score of intervening, he heard at last the creaking of a hinge in the darkness behind him.

There was a whispered movement in the distant shadows and Ethan's heart seemed to turn over and stop, knowing at once that it was China. Reaching out his hand, he pulled her quickly down beside him. She was breathing heavily and her face was pale beneath the veil she had wrapped about her, but Ethan knew without having to ask that she was unharmed. An absurd light-headedness seized him and he took her into his arms. One of his hands came up to caress the back of her neck and China sighed, turning her face wordlessly against him.

Neither of them spoke, and when Brandon appeared behind them Ethan slowly released her. "What took you so long?" he whispered.

Breathing heavily, Brandon thrust a bottle into his

hands. "I found this in Nappy's cabin. I think it's brandy. Do you suppose it will help your hand stop hurting?"

Ethan laughed softly and took the bottle from him. Helping China to her feet, he motioned Brandon into silence and led them quickly away.

It happened just before they reached the upper deck and were about to step into the cool night air, and though Ethan had been expecting as much long before this, it was still a crippling blow. There was a sudden trample of feet on the deck above and unintelligible voices raised in alarm, and suddenly the gangways and the corridors were swarming with seamen shouting in Chinese that the Imperial One's son had been slain and that the barbarians were somewhere loose on the ship.

It was too late to turn back or find a place to hide; too late, in fact, to do anything but push China and Brandon toward the ladder and cover them from the rear, praying that China had understood his harshly whispered orders and would keep to the shadows as she and Brandon made their way aft. He waited only long enough to make certain that no one had spotted them, then leaped up to the ladder himself and, turning in the opposite direction, ran across the deck to conceal himself between a rack of belaying pins and the canvas coaming that rimmed the closed entry port.

He worked quickly, taking no notice of the stampeding feet about him. His senses were acutely alive, every nerve end raw with the tingling anticipation of battle. Had it not been for his fear for China and the children, he would actually have been whistling softly through his teeth at the thought of slaking at last his long-plaguing thirst for revenge.

A ripple of wind fingered his cheek and, lifting his head, Ethan scanned the pennants fluttering on the masthead. A sense of urgency, of time running out, sobered him, for the wind had backed two points and it would soon be dawn. Though the sky was still blazing with untold stars and he could see nothing but darkness beyond the rail, he knew the night would be giving way quickly to a relentless, graying light and take with it their only means of escaping detection.

He finished quickly, then crept back across the deck, and touched the tip of one of the arrows to the flame of a lantern burning on the cabin wall. The oil-soaked rag ignited instantly. A shout went up on the deck behind him and Ethan, his heart hammering, strung the bow and fired.

Archery had not been numbered among the subjects taught at the Cork Asylum for Orphans and Foundlings, nor was it one of the skills Ethan had acquired over the course of a lifetime as a trader and disreputable adventurer. Nonetheless the arrow went over the rail and into the water where it was extinguished with an audible hiss.

With the second arrow, Ethan drew the bowstring back as far as the limits of his strength would allow. The arrow came away clean, drawing a finger of fire across the dark sky before plunging into the sea. Ethan did not wait to see if it had traveled in an arc high enough to be seen by the *Orion*'s watch, for the planking was shuddering with the onrush of approaching seamen and he managed to dive headfirst down a yawning gangway just as an arrow, this one launched by an expert marksman, whistled past his head and into the cabin wall. The yelling lot started to chase him, and Ethan tossed the bow aside and ran, hoping that by diverting the pack he would manage to clear the way for Brandon and China to reach the poop unchallenged.

He could not know that both of them had been prevented from doing so because of the number of seamen drawn to the weather side of the main deck by the launching of his arrow. Instead they were crouching against the cabin wall with only the scanty protection of a wooden bench to conceal them. Listening with a pounding heart to the hoarse shouts of the Cantonese crewmen, China shivered and found herself praying a soundless request: "Please, God, let him elude them."

Brandon pressed close. "Don't be scared, China. He knows the ship better than any of them. It won't take long for him to get Philippa and—"

Without warning China's hand clamped down on his mouth. She had seen a pair of legs encased in cloth leggings and soft-soled shoes coming to a halt directly in front of their hiding place. In the utter stillness that descended she could hear Brandon's quick, frightened breathing and she tightened her hold on him and willed herself not to move. Long minutes dragged by and still the man did not stir. China felt the hair at the nape of her neck prickle and lift like that of a cornered animal. Unable to stand the suspense any longer, she turned her head and found herself staring directly into the dark, startled face of the Chinese who had stooped to peer behind the bench at the exact same moment.

His eyes were only inches from her own. China saw the recognition dawn within them and his jaw drop as he gave vent to a cry of alarm. Acting purely on instinct and in order to stop at all costs the cry from leaving his lungs, she groped behind her for the brandy bottle Ethan had given her. Lifting it, she hit him full in the face and saw his features dissolve in blood.

Screeching in pain, he reached for her and China hit him again. This time, and quite by accident, the bottle shattered and a fragment of glass pierced his throat, severing his jugular vein. Feeling the warm spurt of blood on her hand, China dropped the bottle and shrank away, covering her ears in a vain attempt to shut out the terrible, bubbling wheeze of his dying moans.

"We'll have to hide him," she said with a gasp, breathless with nausea as the dreadful twitching of his body finally stilled. "Quickly—before someone comes!"

They dragged him beneath the bench, China pulling on one leg and Brandon the other. Then, taking Brandon firmly by the arm, she hurried him across the open expanse of deck and thrust him behind a collection of barrels beneath the poop where Ethan had said he would meet them. Slipping down beside him, she buried her head in the crook of her arm and fought for breath.

"It won't be long now, will it?" Brandon asked, and China's heart contracted painfully at the uncertainty she heard in his weary voice.

"No," she said firmly, and prayed that she was speaking the truth. "I've a feeling we won't have to wait very long at all."

In the end they found themselves waiting considerably longer than either of them had expected, and China, shivering uncontrollably although the night was far from cool, could not rid herself of the nagging certainty that Ethan was dead. If this was love—and she knew that it was—it had brought with it such unendurable pain that China wasn't entirely certain she cared for the emotion at all.

An untoward stillness settled over the ship as though it, too, were breathlessly awaiting the paling of the sky, and perhaps Brandon sensed something of the hushed expectancy, for he stirred uneasily. "Do you think she's out there?"

China turned to peer into the darkness where the unseen ocean murmured beyond the clipper's stern. "Who?"

"The *Orion*. I wish we could see her from here. Ethan said if she wasn't there anymore we'd never—"

"Don't, Brandon," China implored with a shudder.

"But if we can't—"

"Hush!" China whispered. "Someone's coming!"

She felt the tremor that ran through his small body and held him tightly to her, her heart knocking painfully against her ribs.

"China? Brandon? Are you there?"

China's heart leaped into her throat and for a dreadful moment it seemed as if she could no longer draw breath, but then she heard Brandon give a gasp of relief and wiggle out of her arms.

"Oh, China, it's Ethan!"

China came slowly to her feet, moving as though she were in the grip of utter exhaustion. Philippa lay fast asleep in Ethan's arms and she reached out wordlessly to take the child from him. She did not trust herself to speak, or even to look at him, for she knew that both the tone of her voice and the expression in her eyes would instantly betray her love for him, but it seemed as if every fiber of her being was aware of him and exulting in the fact that he had returned unharmed.

"Was it very awful?" Brandon was asking. "Did you have to kill a lot of bad men?"

Lifting her head and seeing Ethan's expression, China was profoundly grateful that Philippa had fallen into an exhausted sleep, for the look on his face told her that her sister had thankfully escaped bearing witness to something that he could not—or would not—put into words.

"We've got to get back to the *Orion*," was all he said. "They're still looking for us below, but I don't think we can count on being safe here much longer."

"How?" China asked hopelessly. "They'd see us the moment we tried to lower one of the boats."

"We'll have to wait until Rajiid makes his intentions clear," Ethan said roughly. It was all he could do to keep from pulling her into his arms and burying his face in the sweet-smelling softness of her hair, and he found himself thinking suddenly and with pained longing of the rapturous delight they had shared in the cool of the Coral House.

Already he regretted the harshness with which he had spoken and he stretched out his hand to her, but China had moved out of reach and was bending quietly over Philippa's sleeping shadow. Watching her small hand smooth the unruly curls that fell across the little girl's brow, it occurred to Ethan that she scarcely looked much older than a child herself in her oversized tunic and wide-legged pants. A feeling of such fierce, protective love overcame him that he was forced to turn away, afraid that his face would betray him should she happen to look up and find him watching her.

Watching her? God's fury, had exhaustion and pain so weakened him that he had failed to notice the fact that China's face was of a sudden clearly visible in the lifting darkness? Could he really have failed to notice that the dawn lay like a sullen slash of gunmetal gray against the black horizon? Time was clearly running out, and Wang Toh would assuredly have been informed by now that the barbarian prisoners were nowhere below decks, and he would order the search continued aloft where there was no place left for them to hide.

As if to justify his fears, he heard the groaning of a gangway hatch in the darkness behind him and the hollow echo of footsteps on damp planking. Men, a great number of them, were coming this way.

"China," he whispered imperatively, but she was already beside him, pointing at the sudden movement of a dark, hulking shape across the oiled blackness of the water.

Ethan's heart skipped a beat and he was hard-pressed to still the exultant shout that rose to his lips as he saw the *Orion* hurling toward them, her mainshrouds looming through the clinging tentacles of early morning mist.

"She's coming for us, isn't she?" Brandon cried in an excited whisper. "Oh, China, aren't you glad?"

"I don't know," she replied, staring anxiously at Ethan, frightened by the sudden stillness that had settled over him. "What is it, Ethan? What's wrong?"

"Get down!" he ordered sharply, and jerked them behind the crates. It was suddenly clear to him why Rajiid had made reference to the forecastle of a ship in the coded message China had delivered for him. Yet knowing what it meant did not entirely convince him to accept the evidence of his own eyes at seeing the row of neat, black squares visible along the *Orion*'s port hull. Guns, his disbelieving mind told him. Tyler's ship was armed with guns; a half-dozen nine-pounders from the look of them. But how in God's name had Rajiid found out about them and managed to free the gun crew in order to fire them?

Without warning a yellow flame leaped from each of the opened ports and a hollow explosion rumbled on their heels. The deck jerked and yawed beneath their feet as cannonballs smashed into the defenseless *Lotus Star*'s hull, but the shots were well forward and presented no danger to the little group huddled astern. Ethan, aware that Rajiid had deliberately waited until the *Orion* had drawn ahead of the *Lotus Star*'s jib before firing so that the forecastle and not the stern would be hit, found himself laughing aloud.

"Well done, my friend," he whispered. "Well done!"

Brandon gave a crow of excitement as the squeal and rumble of the gun trucks came to them clearly across the stillness of the water and the cannons, newly loaded, were fired once more.

"Bloody sessions to you, Rajiid!" Ethan shouted, and his exultant laughter rang out once again.

This time the *Lotus Star* took the shots full broadside, lurching drunkenly in response to the deafening cannonade. Pandemonium broke loose on her decks, the deck watch working feverishly to put out a fire that suddenly flared

to life and raged across the bow while others hurled themselves up the ratlines and scrambled onto the yards in a
vain attempt to loosen the mainsails and take the ship out
of range.

Footsteps slapped across the planking and Ethan put a
finger to his lips. "They'll be turning the wheel over," he
warned. The bowsprit swung around and the enormous
rudder creaked and groaned as the *Lotus Star* fell away.
It was far too late, though. The damage had already been
done and the fire, aided by a freshening wind, was burning
out of control. Smoke was billowing aft; thick, choking
clouds of it that brought tears to China's eyes and made
the children cough helplessly.

The *Orion*'s guns rumbled a third and last time, and
China could hear the screams of the men in the rigging
as they were shaken loose from the yards like so many
pieces of overripened fruit from a tree. A writhing body
smashed through a crate behind them in a twisted tangle
of arms and legs, and Philippa screamed and buried her
face in China's neck.

"China!"

She felt her arm being taken in a painful grip and
looked up to find Ethan towering above her, the light of
the flames flicking harshly over his face. "There's a boat
waiting below," he told her in a voice made hard with
urgency. "Are you willing to try to reach it?"

Her breath caught on a gasp. "A boat? Yes, of course!
But how are we going to get to it? Someone is bound to
see us if we use the boarding nets."

Ethan had already considered the question the moment
he had seen, incredibly enough, the prow of the tiny boat
break free of the darkness and the upturned face of a
seaman in the bow searching the aft rail for a sign of them.
"I may be able to lower you down with a rope. If we tie
the knots securely, there shouldn't be any danger of falling.
And if we stay hidden behind the bulwark, I don't believe
anyone will see us."

"The children must go first, Ethan," China said firmly.

"I'll take Philippa down myself," he promised.

It was far easier than he would have supposed, for the
fire had by now reached the main deck and was licking

greedily along the netting and the masts, and frantic efforts were being made to prevent the flames from crawling into the rigging and igniting the sails. Those men who had not been killed or wounded in the cannonball blasts were scrambling to put it out, and no one spared so much as a single thought for the escaping prisoners. The wind itself had died abruptly and the smoke lay thick and choking on the decks. Though it seared their lungs and blinded their eyes, neither China nor Ethan would have wished away the protective cover it afforded them.

The rope, hastily removed from a nearby rack, was tied securely about Philippa's waist. She clutched Ethan tightly as he went with her over the side.

"Don't be afraid," he soothed, feeling her shiver as she looked down and saw the black water looming far below the hull and the tiny, bobbing boat that had drawn alongside and was being steadied with the aid of a gaff.

"I'm not afraid," she assured him with a child's solemn honesty. "Not with you. China said you can do anything and China wouldn't lie."

Ethan made no reply, for there was nothing he could say in response to that, and at any rate he was forced to conserve his strength. His injured hand was bleeding again, making the rope precariously slippery. Though China had obeyed his instructions and had knotted the rope tightly at four-foot intervals, he felt as though it might slip from his grasp at any moment, and the added weight of the small body securely lashed to his own seemed to be dragging him inexorably downward.

But Ethan had grown into manhood on board a fighting merchant ship, and shimmying down ropes and ratlines was a skill he had perfected when boys his own age were still wearing short pants and studying in the schoolroom. But there was also the fact to consider that he hadn't slept for well over thirty-six hours and that his left hand was by now completely useless.

Taking into account his exhaustion and the length of the descent, it was a miracle that he made it at all, and Ethan found himself muttering a prayer of thanks as Philippa was lowered into the waiting hands of their rescuers. There were two oarsmen in the boat, able seamen Ethan didn't know, but the third, a dark-headed fellow with a face disfigured by smallpox scars, went by the name of Franklin Cheney and Ethan had dealt with him enough in the past to know that he could be trusted.

Rajiid's wisdom in selecting Cheney was quickly made apparent when he asked no questions but merely handed Philippa aft and ordered her wrapped securely in a blanket. "You'll be needin' this'n, Cap'n," he added in a coarse undertone and thrust a loaded pistol into Ethan's hands. "We'll be coverin' you best we can from 'ere."

Tucking the pistol into the folds of his robe and the ends of the robe into the tops of his sea boots, Ethan issued a curt order on what was to be done in the event someone chanced to see him, and taking the rope between his stiff and bloodied fingers, he began his ascent.

The fact that he could even attempt such a thing in the condition he was in was due more to sheer determination than any strength that was left him. His arms and shoulders were soon badly cramped, and twice he lost his footing when his boot slipped on the mist-soaked hull, slamming him against the rough wood and scraping the side of his face.

The moment his head appeared at the rail, China and Brandon hauled him over the side.

"Come on, lad," he said briskly to Brandon. "I'm not at all willing to roast alive." He tied the guy lines while China watched, her knuckles pressed to her mouth. With a cheerful wave, Brandon's curly head disappeared beneath the rail.

"Now it's your turn," Ethan said lightly when a tug on the rope signaled the boy's safe descent into the waiting boat. He did not need to add that China must make haste, for the fire was raging out of control and every breath they took was searing torment. They had been incredibly fortunate so far in that only one Chinese had seen them—and that quite by accident when he stumbled aft in the vain hope of finding cooler air to breathe—and Ethan had killed him without remorse.

But there would be others soon, for some of the casks stacked beneath the poop contained drinking water which the crew would need in order to combat the fire once the forward supply was exhausted. The heat was growing intolerable and Ethan's robes were soaked with perspiration. Lifting China onto the rail, he moved to slip the knot over her head, but his hands halted abruptly in midair.

"I'm sorry, China. It isn't any use."

Her eyes widened. "What do you mean?"

"I simply cannot let you go until you've given me your word you'll marry that Stepkyne fellow."

"Darwin?" she asked blankly.

"Damn it, we've been over this before," Ethan said impatiently.

"Oh, Ethan, I don't intend to argue with you," she said bleakly. "Darwin is dead." Seeing the shock that crept to his face she added, "There wasn't time to tell you before they took you away. And afterward I forgot all about it because I was so afraid for the children and for—for you."

Her voice had dropped to a whisper and the last word was all but inaudible, but Ethan heard it nonetheless and suddenly he was gripping her shoulders so hard that she winced.

"You were afraid for *me?*" he asked incredulously.

She nodded without looking at him.

"Then will you marry me instead, China?" he inquired savagely, and was aware that it was fear alone that roughened his voice, fear that she would refuse him or, worse, betray her aversion to him with a simple flicker of her beautiful eyes.

But China's eyes did not turn away from his, and there was no sign of scorn or derision in them; only a measure of something that had been there before, perhaps from the very beginning, and which betrayed itself in the slight tremor of her voice as she said softly and without hesitation, "Yes."

"Oh, my love, my dearest love—"

Taking her into his arms, Ethan captured her lips in a kiss that was tender and loving and so unhurried that they might have been lying in the sandalwood-scented room of the Coral House with nothing before them but the enchanted hours of their wedding night.

"You'll have to go now," he told her, releasing her at last, and his voice was unsteady.

"You sound as if you mean to stay here," China observed, startled.

"I'm afraid so. I can't go back with you until I'm certain Wang Toh is dead."

"That's ridiculous!" China gasped, her eyes bright with sudden anger. "What difference does it make if he's dead?"

"I cannot spend the rest of my life afraid to let you out of my sight for fear of what he'll do to you," Ethan said harshly. "Because he's treacherous and evil and because I killed his favorite son, he'll hunt us down without remorse. And I will not permit my wife to become a fugitive or hide her away in exile for fear he'll catch wind of our whereabouts. Could you, China? Would you wish that sort of life for us?"

"*Any* sort of life with you is better than losing you altogether! I'm sorry, Ethan, but if you insist on staying, then so will I."

"For God's sake, China, don't be stupid! You'll only be in the way!"

"How?" she challenged. "Surely you can't expect to outwit all those men alone?" She jerked her head in the direction of the burning deck. "Besides, it's too late for you to do anything about Wang Toh. The fire's seen to that. Come away while you can, please!"

"I'm sorry, China, I can't."

Her lips thinned. "Then I won't, either."

"Damn you!" he said. "This is no time for misguided heroics!"

"Misguided?" she cried, tears welling in her eyes. "Is it wrong of me not to want to lose you? I won't let Wang Toh take you away from me! I won't!"

For a moment they regarded one another as antagonists, China's level eyes filled with a stubborn calm and Ethan's with frustrated anger. Then suddenly he lifted her into his arms and before she could guess his intent the rope tightened about her waist and she was being lowered over the rail.

"Ethan! Please!"

"I'm sorry, my love," she heard him say above her, "my life—" The rest of his words were drowned out as a shout went up behind him. Straining to see through the smoke,

China had a brief glimpse of Ethan's face and a confusion of others, all of them Chinese, struggling wildly above her before the rope abruptly went slack.

She struggled and cried out as she went down. Then, suddenly, the rope lurched and her head struck the gunwhale of the waiting boat. Pain exploded in a myriad of colored lights and everything around her went black.

Chapter Twenty-two

There was something wet and very cold pressing on her forehead, soothing the throbbing pain, and when China opened her eyes it was to see a vaguely familiar face swim above her in a circle of hazy lantern light. A face that was disconcertingly young and very anxious and which relaxed visibly when she made a feeble effort to rise.

"Oh, it's glad I am you're awake, Miss Warrick! We were so afraid your injury was serious!"

China's lips moved soundlessly and she wet them with a parched tongue and tried again. "Bran—Brandon and Philippa? My brother and sister?"

"They're below with the quartermaster, miss. He's put them to bed. Has six little ones of his own back home, Mr. Cooper does. No need to worry about them."

"You're—you're David—"

"David Bourne, miss. And you're safe back aboard the _Orion_, I'm happy to say." He took the compress away and dipped it in a bowl of water. China saw that the light that had been shining over his shoulder was not a lantern, but the sun, dancing and shivering in warm white bars through the slats of a porthole shutter.

She lifted her head to look about her and instantly regretted doing so, for the pain seemed to flow in hot, pulsing bands from her neck and shoulders to her temples and she groaned aloud.

"Oh, miss, please lie still! You've a fracture and you'll only make it worse if you move!" David said anxiously.

Struggling feebly against the rising nausea, China clutched at his arm. "How long have I been here, Mr. Bourne?"

"About two hours, miss. Mr. Cheney brought you here to the saloon because we were afraid to move you any further. Mr. Fine, the first mate, asked me to look after you."

A wave of color flared across David Bourne's smooth cheeks. Being assigned to nurse an unconscious female alone in the ship's saloon had been embarrassing enough, but now that she was awake David was acutely aware of the unintentional but patent intimacy fostered by the close quarters in which they found themselves. And since the shutters had, of necessity, been barred against the rising heat of the morning, the saloon was filled with shadows that only served to underscore his feeling of isolation.

Perhaps if Miss Warrick had been wearing more conventional attire—tightly laced stays and petticoats, for instance—and long sleeves and a collar that concealed her white skin, David's discomfiture might not have been so acute. At least it was a relief for him to note that she seemed not at all concerned to find herself being ministered to by an improperly chaperoned male while attired in little more than the thin silk garments of a woman of the East.

In truth, China had forgotten entirely that she was wearing them and wouldn't have troubled herself over maidenly modesty even if she hadn't. There were other and far more sobering considerations on her mind, and when David turned back to her with the intention of laying the wet compress across her forehead once more, he was shocked to find her standing unsteadily before him, holding to the back of a nearby chair, her face a pale oval against the shadows.

"Miss Warrick!"

"Please, Mr. Bourne, will you take me outside? I must see for myself what happened to the *Lotus Star*."

He regarded her blankly. "The *Lotus Star*? Is that a person, miss?"

It occurred to China that Wang Toh must have changed the clipper's name, and that she, Ethan, and Rajiid were the only ones who knew its former name. But because she didn't intend to waste time on explanations, she turned a stubborn face to David's pleading and started for the door.

A sun the color of glowing white wine had risen beyond the mizzen-mast yards, casting its hot light on the pitch-stained planking. Narrowing her eyes against the glare, China did not at first see the shroud-wrapped bundles that were laid out neatly on the aft deck below her. It was the murmuring voice of Thomas Fine, the *Orion*'s first mate, that brought her head around and made her breath catch in her throat as she understood the import of the Psalms he was intoning from the book in his hands. The clipper's crew, bareheaded, sweating, and silent, were gathered in a half circle around him, their shadows shimmering through the heat haze on the deck. Of necessity the service was a hasty one, for the dead had to be dumped overboard before the heat and the blowflies could inflict their damage upon them.

Clutching the rail with a trembling hand and shading her eyes because she found she could not tolerate the brightness, China stared down at them without speaking, a small, unnoticed observer in the torn garb of a concubine. Her eyes were enormous in her pointed face, and David Bourne, coming to stand beside her, felt his heart check when he saw the frozen horror of her expression.

"There are so many of them!" she whispered, appalled.

"Most of them are Chinese," he assured her quickly. "Though we did lose a few of ours, too. Mr. Foster, the sailmaker, for one, and the captain's steward, and that Arab friend of Captain Bloodwell's—"

"*Rajiid?*"

"Yes, I suppose that was his name. Fought like a tiger

to the end, he did. It was his idea to blast the Chinese clipper with Captain Crewe's guns, and he led the charge to free the ship with only a tulwar to protect him. I heard the men say they'd never seen that kind of courage."

China began to cry, silently and grievously, her slim shoulders bowed. Tan Ri, the elderly munshi who had lived on Badajan for as long as China could remember, had told her once that it was every Moslem's wish to draw his last breath within sight of the Kaaba "in the arms of the Prophet and of the guardian angels." Yet Rajiid Ali had not lived to make the hajj, the holy pilgrimage to Mecca, and now there was no one to sprinkle his body with zemzem water and recite the prayers that should accompany him on his journey. Nor would he be laid to rest in the land of his birth, but China derived an odd sense of comfort recalling that Tan Ri had also told her that Muhammad himself had once observed, "The best grave is one you can wipe away with your hand."

She watched in silence as the shroud-wrapped body was lifted up on the bier, and was gratified by the respect in the faces of the men who raised their hands in salute.

"*Labbaika allahumma labbaika*—I am here, God, at your command," China whispered softly. It was the only Moslem prayer she knew, yet she felt certain that Rajiid, had he been able to hear the chant, would have understood.

There was a muted splash and the body was gone; China turned away, blinded by tears. It was for Ethan she sorrowed as well as Rajiid. Ethan would never have the chance now to bid farewell to the friend who had—Ethan! Her heart seemed to jerk to a halt.

It seemed entirely impossible, yet in view of the dizzying pain and all the turmoil she had endured, she had forgotten completely about him. Yet the shock of remembrance, when it came, seemed to crash over her with the force of a physical blow. She ran to the rail, her eyes wide and her lips parted, scanning the hot, glassy water and seeing nothing at all.

"Mr. Bourne! The Chinese ship! Where is it?"

"No cause to be frightened, miss. She's scuttled."

"Scuttled!"

"We had six nine-pound cannons riddling her with holes,

miss. And someone must have set off a magazine amidships, because she exploded a short time after Mr. Cheney brought you aboard. At first we thought it must have been the deck fire done her in, but a big ship like that—" He broke off and sucked in his breath as he looked at her, seeing the agony that had suddenly filled her young, unguarded face.

"Mr. Fine took a party across once the fire died down," he continued, feeling quite unsure of himself. "Those of her crew that were left alive threw themselves overboard as soon as our boats drew alongside. I've heard the Chinese rarely allow themselves to be taken prisoner."

"And Captain Bloodwell?" China whispered through bloodless lips.

"The ship was sinking fast, miss," he said reluctantly. "The boarding party searched as much of it as they could. They never did find him. Some of the men think it was Captain Bloodwell who set off the magazine, though why he'd want to try something as suicidal as that just doesn't make sense. It isn't at all like him, and there must have been a safer way to get those heathen to surrender."

China turned without speaking and walked away. David was tempted to go after her, but a call from the lookout stayed him. "Deck, there! Sails on the larboard quarter! It's a brig from the look of it!"

There was a scramble of feet across the planking, and the *Orion*, idling southward with only her fore and topsails set while her crew went about the solemn task of disposing of its dead, shuddered in response to the coaxing of the helmsman as he turned her closer into the barely discernible wind.

"Is she striking colors, Mr. Thatcher?" the first mate called, cupping his hands.

In the wind-stilled heat of the morning the lookout's words were clearly audible. "No, sir! There's no mistaking her, though. It's the *Kowloon Star*, Ethan Bloodwell's ship!"

"Larboard tack, men!" the first mate ordered immediately. "Loose those headsails! We might as well intercept her."

With her canvas tightly hauled and the yards set to make best use of the slight but steady breeze, the big clipper was able to close the shivering silver distance quickly. And a scant half hour later her soaring jib boom had drawn abreast of the brigantine's bow and the *Orion* came hard about, hull and timber shuddering and groaning a protest. Moments later the two ships were gliding in tandem through the brilliant blue of the tropical sea, broached so close that the speaking trumpet Thomas Fine lifted to his lips was little better than a useless affectation.

"God rot you, Fine!" a voice bellowed quite audibly from the *Kowloon Star* before the first mate could speak. All eyes were drawn to the gesticulating form of Captain Tyler Crewe, who was leaning over the brigantine's windward rail. "Are you mad or is there a reason for this godrotting brinkmanship? And where's Bloodwell? I'll tear him limb from limb for absconding with my ship! God rot the lot of you! You're all beached for this, each and every one of you! Now get off your arses, I'm coming aboard!"

Tyler's wrathful words were enough to galvanize his exhausted crew into action. With renewed energy they leaped to the entry ports and lowered the nets. Falling into line with suitably respectful expressions, hats clutched dutifully in hand, they waited nervously to welcome their rightful captain aboard.

Tyler Crewe's anger seemed to have run its course surprisingly swiftly. When he crossed the deck to speak to First Mate Thomas Fine, there was no trace of the irate color that had flushed his face earlier. "What's untoward, Tom?" he inquired almost affably. "I saw the damage from Bloodwell's ship. Run into trouble with them Chinese fellows?"

"You knew about them, sir?"

"Hell, yes! Intercepted the *Aurora* on our way out from Badajan. Her skipper told us what happened. I take it you found the little ones? You'd not be coming back otherwise, eh? Not Bloodwell's way to give up." His bristling blond head swiveled questioningly. "Where is that double-dealing son of a whore? Can't say I'll promise not to break his collarbones for stealin' m'ship, but before I do I'm going to have to shake his hand for—"

He broke off and his countenance darkened as he became aware of the unsmiling faces around him. "Now, what in hell is wrong with you men?" he inquired suspiciously, and propped his hands on his hips. "A little bitty lorcha couldn't have given you that much trouble, could it? Mr. Fine! The *Orion*'s guns've been fired, haven't they? I could smell it when I came aboard!"

"Yes, sir, I'm afraid they were."

"I'd like to know which of you disloyal bastards told Bloodwell about them guns to begin with," Tyler snapped, glowering. "Supposed to be a secret and you know god-rotting well they ain't legal!" He hawked and spat into the scuppers. "Oh, hell! I just hope once you did decide to waste the grape you blew those slant-eyes out of the water!"

"Sir—"

"Where is he, eh?" Tyler's good humor was genuine and so thoroughly impervious to disruption that he had alto-gether failed to pick up the obvious signs of disaster around him. It was a leathery brown hand moving to stay him that made him aware of it, and he glanced about quickly. "What is it, Quarles? You got some idea what your cap-tain's about?"

Nappy, who had scrambled up the nets behind him, did not reply. He had spotted China Warrick standing at the far rail, and she had turned as though knowing he was there so that her eyes met his for a brief and frozen instant. Then she had bowed her head and looked away, and Nap-py's wizened face seemed to age and sag in on itself.

"So that's it," he breathed. Pushing his way past the startled captain, he reached out stiffly to take China's hands in his. She stumbled toward him gratefully and Nappy held her, crooning words of comfort that made no sense, and his seamed face, though infinitely weary, was tender.

A lantern was swaying from an overhead beam, and when China awoke at last from a sleep of total exhaustion she lay quite still watching the dancing fingers of copper light oscillate across the rough-cut walls of the cabin. The creaking of timber and the gentle murmur of the wind and water were familiar sounds, and she welcomed them as one might the soothing chatter of an old and trusted friend. It was, in fact, far easier to close her eyes and listen, and pretend that everything was as it had been before, than to acknowledge what she could not, *would not* accept.

The cabin door creaked imperceptibly on its hinges. China's head came around to see the smiling face of Julia Clayton.

"Oh, China, I can't tell you how glad I am you're awake! I was worried that Tyler had given you too much laudanum. You've been asleep since yesterday morning and here it is evening again! How is your head? Does it hurt very much?"

"Not really."

"Still, you must have cracked it very badly." Bustling inside, Julia set down her tray and reached up to adjust the lantern. Following the movement with her eyes, China became aware of the color that touched Julia's normally pale cheeks as she lifted her face to the light.

"You called him Tyler," she observed. "Do you mean Captain Crewe?"

Julia's color deepened and she busied herself with the folded towels she had carried in with her. "I think he is going to ask me to marry him," she said at last and in a rush that was as shy and charming as a schoolgirl's.

"And will you?" China inquired without surprise.

Julia hesitated for the barest of moments, then nodded. "I know it seems strange. We aren't in the least suited and Tyler is nothing at all like the man I envisioned myself marrying. But each of us seems to—to fill something that's missing in the other, and I suddenly can't imagine myself ever being happy without him. I suppose that sounds rather silly, doesn't it?"

"No," China said softly.

Julia's relieved sigh was clearly audible. "I can't tell you how glad I am that you understand, China. It must be so hard for you, having lost your fiancé so tragically."

"My fiancé?"

"Why, yes! Horatio Creel told us that you and Darwin were going to be married. And we heard from Thomas Fine that he was killed during the raid on Tyler's ship. I'm so sorry for you, China, truly I am."

Though she knew that Julia was expecting some sort of reply, China turned wordlessly to stare up at the slowly swaying lantern. After a moment Julia said, "Here, drink some tea. You're frightfully pale and I'm certain you haven't eaten anything in days."

"No, thank you, Julia. I'm not hungry." China lifted her hand and shakily brushed the hair out of her eyes, looking very white and exhausted as she lay against the pillow, and an awkward silence descended between them. After a moment Julia rose, her muslin petticoats rustling loudly in the stillness. "I'll come back later, dear," she said with forced cheerfulness. "In the meantime why don't you try to rest?"

China made no reply as the cabin door closed softly on Julia's retreating form.

"Well? How's the Warrick girl?" Tyler Crewe inquired as Julia ascended the ladder to join him on the aft deck. He was propped against the binnacle smoking a cigar and staring moodily into the humming rigging. The breeze that had sprung up at sunset had strengthened to a gusty wind and the *Orion* was hauling well, the straining sails cracking like thunder and glowing pewter gray in the starlight. A frothing wake drew an ivory path in the water behind her, and on her larboard stern the ghostly form of the *Kowloon Star* rode docilely at heel.

Julia shook her head and drew a light shawl tightly about her shoulders. "I'm glad you suggested that I come with you, Tyler. I think she really needs another woman with her at the moment. I've never seen her looking so tired and defeated. It isn't like her at all."

"It's only natural for a girl to cry when she loses her man," Tyler soothed. "She's a scrappy little thing. Won't take her long to get over it. I got to admire her, though," he added after a moment. "Young Brandon told me some of the things they'd been through. Bloodwell said she had courage. I suppose he was right." He sighed and flicked the butt of his cigar into the water and for an appreciable length of time neither of them spoke.

"I can't believe he's dead," Julia said at last.

"I can't either," Tyler said promptly, as though she had given voice to his own thoughts. "Always valued his god-rotting hide too much to risk it playing hero."

"I think perhaps China knows what made him do what he did," Julia said slowly, "but I've a feeling she won't tell."

"I think the best we can do for her now is get her home to her mama," Tyler added. "Don't you agree, love?"

"I suppose so," Julia said doubtfully. "I only wonder if that's what China wants?"

China herself had not bothered to ponder the likelihood that the *Orion* was bound for Badajan and home. At the moment she was lying quietly in the bunk where Julia had left her, her eyes on the rafters above, thinking of nothing at all. When she turned it was to see a teapot and a bowl of soup sitting untouched on the tray beside her.

Though she had eaten nothing for well over twenty-four hours she found she had no appetite and turned away with a grimace of distaste. But although she didn't feel like eating, she found that it was equally impossible to continue lying there watching the swaying lantern trail its maddening tattoo across the walls and the shutters and the thin sheet that covered her. China rose at last and crossed the cabin to peer idly into the tiny square of glass that served as a mirror. A shocking black bruise discolored her temple, but she found herself regarding it with more indifference than horror.

It was strange, actually, but nothing seemed to matter to her anymore. She felt curiously like an observer—or an outsider, someone who wasn't herself and who perched on some lofty position high above the cabin floor viewing in a detached manner the comings and goings of a certain peculiar creature by the name of China Warrick.

"China? May I come in?"

She turned slowly, and for the first time, briefly, the rigid whiteness of her face faded beneath a faint tinge of color. "Why, hello, Brandon. Of course you can."

He dashed inside and hurled himself thankfully into her arms. China could feel agonizing pain wash over her, but fought grimly to thrust it away because she could not yet let anyone inside, not even Brandon.

She held him close, and he buried his small face gratefully against her, and wept. China soothed him as best she could, and eventually the stormy tide abated.

"I saw the *Lotus Star* sink, China," he confessed in a choked whisper as they both sat down on the bunk. "They didn't want us to see, but after Mr. Cooper put us to bed I came back on deck and watched. Mr. Fine said she sank really fast because she'd been blown up from inside." He lifted his enormous green eyes to hers and added tremulously, "Did you know—everybody says it was Ethan who blew her up. They said there must have been a mun— muni—a powder room in her holds and that's how he did it."

"I've heard that, too," China said.

"Mr. Fine said they tried to find him but that they didn't have enough time. They had to get off the ship or else they would've drowned, too." His brow puckered. "Why, China? They keep saying Captain Ethan is dead. I don't believe it. He can't be!"

China opened her mouth to speak, then stopped. She had no words with which to comfort him. Instead, she asked gently, "Where's Philippa?"

Brandon pulled a disgusted face, his attention instantly diverted. "Playing with that tom cat Captain Crewe keeps on board. It's a horrible thing, China! Fat and ugly with only one eye and no tail to speak of, but Philippa thinks it's grand. She wanted to ask the captain if she could take it home, but I told her it would only fight with Ibn Bibi and sharpen its claws on Mama's furniture."

"You probably did the right thing," China agreed, amused by his wisdom. She was relieved that Philippa seemed to be suffering no lingering nightmares in view of the horrors she had endured.

"China?"

She smoothed his unruly red curls. "Yes, love?"

"It's my fault that Captain Ethan and Rajiid and Darwin are dead, isn't it?"

China's caressing hand froze and dropped to her side. "Of course not! What makes you say such a thing?"

"Because if I hadn't talked Philippa into running away, none of this would have happened."

Without warning she seized his arms, making no effort

to soften her expression even though he flinched at the sight of her angry face. She was aghast, and trembling with a real, consuming fury. She shook him roughly as she said, "Don't you dare say that, Brandon Warrick, ever again! I'll have none of that, do you hear? Ethan and Rajiid would have gone in pursuit of Wang Toh whether you and Philippa were taken on board his ship or not. They've been bitter enemies for years and years and Ethan knew perfectly well what his hate and vengeance would one day cost him."

"But—"

"But nothing! Wang Toh Chen-Arn is dead, and not one of them—Ethan, Rajiid, or even Darwin—would have done anything different to see that end achieved."

After mulling for a moment or two in silence, Brandon raised his head and said with typical Warrick obstinance, "You know what, China? I still don't believe Captain Ethan is dead. No matter what anybody says!"

"Hush, Brandon," China said with a breathless catch in her voice, but she was thinking to herself that she didn't believe it either.

And she said as much, clearly and imperiously, to Nappy Quarles when the two of them met in the humid sunshine on the main deck the following morning. Regarding him with level eyes in a face that was far too pale for Nappy's liking, she spoke with a calm conviction that left him disturbed and distinctly uneasy. One of Julia Clayton's chip straw hats covered China's bright red curls, the floppy brim hiding the bruise on her brow, and she was dressed in a gown of ivory muslin trimmed with dark green ribbon. Because it, too, was one of Julia's and was therefore far too large for her, she had hemmed the trailing skirts and stitched back the sleeves, to the effect that she looked like a small child, bedraggled and pale and so obviously unhappy that Nappy spoke to her sharply, the words bursting from him before he was even aware of his intent to speak.

"You ain't ought ter be mournin' 'im, miss! Pretty is as pretty does, I allus say. Don't think 'e'd be wastin' 'is time wringin' 'is 'ands if the shoe were on t'other foot!"

A flicker of surprise crept into China's shadowed eyes. "Are you talking about Darwin?"

"Don't makes me out the fool!" Nappy told her severely. "Those lubber-brains can think wot they likes—*I* knows yer too well! Grievin' for t' Stepkyne cove, indeed! Bah!"

He turned away with an angry exclamation because she was looking at him in a way that made him want to shake her, or at the very least ball his fists and rage at God for the injustices He had committed. But instead he merely clumped to the rail where he stood with his small shoulders bowed and his mouth working, feeling his age and the pain weighing down on him unendurably. Time, in its insidious, uncaring way, had finally caught up with Nappy Quarles and he knew what it meant to be old and infinitely tired.

He heard the whispered rustle of fabric and turned to find China standing there beside him, her hands gripping the rail so hard that the knuckles showed white. She did not look at him, but stared out across the flickering heat haze toward the *Kowloon Star,* which idled a mere cable length away awaiting Nappy's return in order that it might tack west into Singapore Harbor.

"I refuse to believe he's dead, Nappy," she said so softly that at first he thought her voice was nothing more than the murmur of the wind and the water. "I'd know if he was. I'd *feel* it."

The lines that age and sun and character had etched into Nappy's leathery face seemed to deepen and his own hands curled angrily about the worn wooden rail. "The *Lotus Star*'s gone, child," he said deliberately, not caring that he was being unkind. "Tom Fine saw 'er sink. There was a few bodies and debris wot floated to the surface. They pulled in each and ev'ry one to 'ave a look. None of 'em was 'im."

China said nothing in response and after a moment he straightened with a weary sigh and remarked that the *Kowloon Star* was waiting and that he had only come aboard to bid her farewell.

"What are you going to do now that you're alone?"

Nappy shrugged and tugged irritably at his eyepatch. "Doan know yet. There's Coral 'Ouse an' t' *Kowloon Star* to be thought of. Somethin'll 'ave ter be done wiv 'em. Cap'n Ethan kept 'is private papers locked away in 'is sea chest, but I can't be certain 'is final wishes and the likes was wrote in 'em." He sighed deeply, and added resignedly, "I suppose I'll 'ave to takes a look. Though I'll tells you 'onest, miss, I don't be wantin' to."

"You'll tell me what you're going to do, won't you?"

"'Ssst! Do yer thinks I'd up an' leave wivout a word to you?"

The ghost of a smile lifted the corners of China's mouth and she shook her head without speaking. Impulsively, she threw her arms about him, and Nappy returned the hug warmly, though with an obvious measure of self-consciousness.

China watched the jolly boat cross back to the waiting ship, the dipping oars flashing in the hot sun, and though Nappy must have known she was there, his grizzled head did not turn. She continued to stand there at the rail as the boat was taken up and the crew scrambled aloft to haul in the brigantine's mainsails. After a moment the *Kowloon Star* began to heel gracefully to the opposite tack as the men at the braces gently guided the yards around and the sails tightened and filled with wind. China saw the white spray break and dash across the brigantine's bow, and then the ship was lengthening the distance between them, her colors snapping stiffly as she eased cleanly into the new course.

It was only a short time later, after the brilliant white sails had grown smaller and eventually disappeared on the horizon, that the *Orion*'s lookout picked out Badajan with its familiar green-humped volcano lying amid the countless mountainous islands that were flung across the surging blue water. China sent Brandon below to collect their belongings, and shook her head as she watched a big orange tom rise from its sunny place on the scuttle and attach himself to Philippa, purring and rubbing his scarred head against the crutches the *Orion*'s carpenter had made for her.

"Looks like they've sent someone out to meet you, Miss Warrick."

China turned in surprise to find Captain Crewe at her elbow. "They have?"

"Here, see for yourself."

She took the offered glass from him and squinted through it. She was able to make out the distant masts of the *Tempus* thrashing through the whiteheads. She caught her breath and for the first time she found herself wondering what she was going to say to Damon when she saw him. She didn't want to talk about Darwin's senseless death, yet she knew that Damon would demand explanations, and he clearly had a right to expect them.

"I wager you'll feel a sight better once you're home," Tyler said awkwardly. "Times like this it's good to have family."

"Yes, I suppose that's true," China said with an odd note of wonder, for she had quite suddenly realized how badly she wanted to be back at King's Wheal and in her mother's arms.

"China? Could you wait a moment before you go? There's something we simply have to discuss. Do you mind?"

China turned with a small twinge of dismay to find that Julia Clayton had joined them at the railing. After a moment she took a deep breath and inquired warily, "What is it?"

Julia's eyes went to the man beside her. "Tyler, would you be a dear?"

Captain Crewe turned up his palms in supplication, bowed wordlessly, and, with obvious relief, left them.

"It concerns Gem," Julia said the moment the two women were alone.

China's eyes widened, for she had been expecting any number of admissions from the unpredictable and quixotic Julia, but nothing at all like this. "Gem? You want to talk to me about Gem?"

"Yes, of course. I'm the one who's been taking care of her, after all." Julia made a small, surprised movement with her head. "Didn't you know?"

"I might have, and forgot. What about Gem?"

"I wanted to remind you that you'll have to decide soon what's to be done with her. Ethan told me your mother was against Gem living at King's Wheal with you, and it won't do to return her to the Coral House."

"Don't worry, Julia, I'll think of something," China said doggedly.

"She can stay with Tyler and me until you've decided
what to do," Julia offered.

"Thank you, Julia, but I really think I can look after
her myself."

China's chin had lifted almost imperceptibly as she
spoke, and seeing it, Julia experienced a sharp stab of
frustration and wondered how Ethan Bloodwell had ever
managed to retain his patience in the face of this thoroughly exasperating Warrick pride.

"To be honest with you, China," she went on, "I've grown
fond of the child myself. If you don't mind and if you trust
me with her, she's more than welcome to stay with me
until you've had some time to think. I left her with Jules
Piaget, by the way. Such a dear man, and quite good with
children despite the fact he's a middle-aged bachelor. You'd
really have nothing to worry about, China. I swear it. Tyler
has plenty of room and it won't be the least disreputable
because we're to be married as soon as it can be arranged."

"Oh, Julia, that's wonderful!" China said and meant it.
At least someone she knew, China thought with a bitter
twist of her soft lips, was happy.

"I've Gem to thank for bringing Tyler and myself together, you know," Julia confessed on a gay little laugh,
relief giving her tongue imprudent license. "Do you believe
I was wicked enough to send Ethan a note the other night
saying the child was sick and that he should come at once
to see her? It was utter fabrication, of course, and when
he arrived to find Gem playing and smiling and drinking
her milk with her usual voracious appetite he was unbelievably annoyed."

Taking China's sudden silence for attentiveness she resumed with the lightheartedness of someone who is relieved to be shed at last of a small but nagging burden.
"Of course it was wrong of me to deceive him that way,
but I simply had to see him. I imagine it's rather hard for
you to understand, but as I've told you before I am a woman
with certain needs, and Ethan—"

"I understand," China whispered.

Julia uttered a somewhat embarrassed laugh. "He didn't
say a word to me, you know, He just looked at me in that
way he has of making you feel like a thoroughly unmiti-

gated fool and walked out the door. I supposed that was the end of it, and I guess it would have been if he hadn't met up with Tyler outside a waterfront saloon. Tyler had been drinking, and was quite interested to learn I was home alone. When he knocked I let him in, thinking Ethan had come back. I suppose that's when it happened. When we fell in love, I mean."

She stopped unexpectedly and regarded China with anxious eyes. "Is something wrong, dear? Do you have another headache?"

"It's nothing, Julia," China said quickly. "And I promise I'll think about what you said. Now, if you don't mind, I'd better see to my things. Excuse me."

Her step was somewhat unsteady as she crossed the tilting deck, but it was not because the *Orion* was moving under full sail to the coaxing of a whining wind, but because everything around her, the hot planking, the soaring mainmast, the long shadow of the cabin wall, had blurred before her tear-filled eyes. Blindly, she groped her way aft and knew a terrible agony of guilt for having condemned Ethan so unfairly.

Ten minutes later, at the bellowed orders of Captain Crewe, the *Orion* dropped canvas and turned her head into the wind, and the *Tempus* tacked about and hauled in her jib in order to draw alongside. As the skiff drifted to a halt beneath the clipper's hull, Philippa, who had been leaning over the railing to watch, cried excitedly, "Oh, look, China, there's Damon! And—and Mama!" She waved and called out and wiggled so much that she nearly squirmed out of the arms of the seaman who held her aloft.

Malvina, hearing her youngest daughter's faint cry above the howling wind and the thunder of the *Orion's* flapping sails, lifted her arm and waved, and China was shocked to see how white and drawn she looked. It seemed as if her mother had aged immeasurably, and the cause, though not immediately apparent, was nonetheless irrevocably entrenched within her mother's very soul: Malvina, faced with the terrible likelihood of losing three of her four children at the murderous hands of a bloodthirsty madman, had found the maternal feelings she did not believe she possessed suddenly and agonizingly thrown into her face like a brutal dash of ice water.

The torturous nights of waiting had left her thin and disheveled, and there were streaks of gray in her chestnut hair that China had never noticed before. Tears glimmered in her once-cold hazel eyes, as mother and daughter looked long and searchingly at one another when China stepped at last into the waiting skiff. For a moment neither of them dared move or speak until finally, with a small, glad cry from Malvina, the two women embraced, and it was in her mother's arms that China felt the numbing band about her heart finally shatter and the healing tears come at last.

___ *Chapter Twenty-three* ___

Darwin Stepkyne's personal possessions turned out to be pitiably few, and China spent less than an hour in his cluttered cottage sorting through them. They would be sent to Darwin's elderly aunt in Chester, and though it was probable that the old woman would have no use for them, China herself had no idea how else to dispose of them. Since Mrs. Pomphrey was Darwin's last living relation, China had decided that it was only right she receive them.

Working diligently with the help of one of the serving girls from the house, China managed to clean the cottage and sort Darwin's belongings in an orderly fashion. She was hot and very tired by the time they finished, and outside it was raining again, the warm, driving rain of the northeast monsoon that roared through the liana trees and splattered in noisy gusts against the thatched frond roof.

Gazing outside at the rank brown water that washed across the oozing path, China felt immeasurably weary and depressed. She had expected that the task would be

351

an unpleasant one but had been unprepared for the number of memories that had risen to haunt her. She realized, too, how much she would miss Darwin in the years to come.

China thrust the thought away with a barely perceptible jerk of her head. She didn't want to think of the future, or of anything beyond the tasks that awaited her and into which she had thrown herself with a vengeance that had startled and dismayed her family.

"China, you'll make yourself ill!" Malvina had remarked only yesterday morning when China had announced her intent to sail to Djakarta at week's end to pay visits to several of King's Wheal's creditors.

"I'm sorry, Mother," China had responded quietly but firmly, "I've got to go." She had said nothing more, but her drawn and stubborn expression was not an unfamiliar one to Malvina, who knew the futility of argument—and who also happened to be bleakly aware that when the plantation loans came due at the end of the month the Warricks would not be able to pay them.

China had written to Sir Joshua Boles and several other planters and bankers in the area, politely requesting loan extensions of sixty days, but their replies had been dishearteningly similar. While expressing shock and regret at the unfortunate loss off such a large shipment of Badajan silk and the untimely death of King's Wheal's manager, they hoped that Miss Warrick would understand the impossibility of extending further credit. They did, however, wish to assure her that they would readily stand at her disposal in the event they could offer any further assistance, and hoped that their letters would find her in good health and her family the same, et cetera, et cetera.

"I don't need their lectures or their condescending advice," China whispered to herself, dragging her wandering thoughts back to the present and lifting her eyes to the leaden skies as though seeking enlightenment there. "I need money, a great deal of it, and I need it now!"

Without money the Warricks would invariably lose King's Wheal, and it was the realization that Wang Toh Chen-Arn might still succeed—even in death—in destroying all that was theirs that had galvanized China into instant action upon her return home. She could not permit Ethan's death to have been in vain, and after delivering a blistering lecture to her shocked mother and half-brother on the score of their mismanagement, their dilatory business practices, and their immoral and unforgivable methods of entertaining prospective clients, she had assigned herself the monumental task of filling both her father's and Darwin's shoes.

She was in far over her depth, of course, but China welcomed the hours upon mounting hours of paperwork because it kept her busy and in doing so prevented her thinking of anything other than the tasks at hand. She soon found that grief and madness could be kept tolerably at bay if one immersed oneself entirely in work.

But she could not pretend that the situation was anything less than desperate, and as she rode back to the house on Damon's Arabian with Darwin's belongings wrapped in oilskins on the crupper behind her, she schemed and pondered and wondered what Race would have done in a similar situation.

"New credit?" Damon demanded when she approached him in the study half an hour later with the glimmering of an idea. "Not bloody likely! No one in his right mind would agree to pour good money into a lost cause. We couldn't possibly attract new creditors, either, because I can assure you our troubles are common knowledge. In fact, I'd be willing to wager that Badajan's the hottest topic of gossip throughout all of Southeast Asia at the moment."

Seeing how she stiffened at his words he added hastily, "Oh, I'm not referring to your connection with that Bloodwell fellow or the fact that Brandon and Philippa were kidnapped by a Chinese warlord, though it certainly doesn't make for reassuring prattle. No, it's because Mama and I quite undermined any prospects of building trust in the family."

"I know all about that," China said irritably. "We've been over it before." She suddenly felt sorry for Damon, who was certainly looking pale and thin these days and whose broken wrist was mending poorly and causing him considerable pain.

Apparently, though, the prospect of bankruptcy and the terrible events of the past week had left their mark on Damon as they had on his mother. China had not been particularly surprised, only grateful, when they had agreed to allow her to take charge of the business without forcing her to resort to the matter of her father's pillaged will in order to convince them.

Though the Warricks were, for all appearances, once again a united family, prepared to put the past behind them and work together in saving their beloved island, there was still a great deal of unacknowledged pain lurking beneath that hopeful surface, and China knew that one had only to scrape it just a little before it would come after them in howling pursuit. She didn't want that to happen; indeed, she dreaded the possibility that anything might divide them at a time when they must do their desperate best to work together. So now she said patiently and reasonably, "I'm not talking credit, Damon. I'm talking about investors. People who are willing to put up money for a share in future production. We've a hatch ready to start cocooning in less than two weeks. If all goes well, we can anticipate—"

"You mean open the business to the public? Allow others access to our books and a voice in decision making? It's unthinkable, China! Why, Race would never—even Kingston would be turning in his grave if he knew!"

"I don't care too much for the prospect, either," China confessed unhappily, "but it's only to give King's Wheal some operating capital so that we can pay off our most pressing debts. We can make the terms of the agreement for a specified period only, or for a certain percentage of the crop. It doesn't mean we'll be losing the plantation altogether."

"We're in no position to bargain," Damon reminded her bleakly. "We'd have to make unheard-of concessions, and make them gladly, if we're to coax anyone into investing in a nearly bankrupt enterprise."

"That depends on how cleverly one goes about negotiating," China said calmly.

Looking at her Damon felt a stirring of admiration. Standing before him with her pointed little chin imperiously raised and that riotous red hair smoothed back into a dignified chignon, he could see so much of Race Warrick in her that for a moment madness seized him and he could almost believe she could succeed. But then the image faded and she was once again nothing more than his little sister China, innocent and inexperienced and painfully pale and small.

"I'm sorry, China, it simply won't work. We'd be smart to sell out to Boles, take his offer and get away from this sweltering, mosquito-infested island as fast as we can."

"Let me try, Damon, please? We've naught to lose."

His lips curved in a bitter smile and he shrugged because it suddenly didn't matter to him one way or the other. He was tired, tired and defeated and quite willing at last to admit that his mother had been wrong about him, wrong in assuming her beloved son could hold his own against the greed and the power of the men who had coveted Badajan silk from the moment its pale golden beauty had captured the imagination of the civilized world.

Damon was prepared to admit that he was inept, lazy, and an unspeakably poor businessman. And though he had truly believed his mother's vehement claims that he could run King's Wheal as well as any Warrick, the bitter lessons had at last been learned. Furthermore he was, quite simply, weary of trying. It was clear to him that China was fighting a hopeless battle, but he could not bring himself to shout at her or shake her or try any number of other ways to make her see reason.

"Oh, very well, why not? Do whatever you please, but make certain you tell Mama about it."

"Thank you, Damon."

For the first time since her return home a week ago a smile curved her lips. Damon had the uneasy impression that she had been prepared to act on her idea whether she had gained his approval or not. He wasn't sure whether the realization angered or relieved him.

"I do believe," said Malvina reflectively as they sat on the veranda after dinner that evening, "that it might be wise to draw up a list with the names of likely people we could approach on the matter of investing. And we shouldn't confine the prospects entirely to Southeast Asia. Race had numerous connections in India and influential friends in John Company, not to mention stock in several private firms in London. One of them might be interested."

There was silence from her two older children until China said slowly, "Are you saying you approve of my suggestion?"

Malvina smiled ruefully. "Not entirely, but I certainly cannot think of anything better. Can you, Damon?"

"No, I'm sorry to say."

China turned her head to stare thoughtfully into the darkened garden and wondered with no small measure of uncertainty if the course she had chosen was in point of fact the right one. Suddenly she found herself longing desperately for Ethan, wishing she could tell him her doubts and ask his advice. She instantly realized the error of that particular train of thought when a raw ache closed her throat and forced her to blink back scalding tears.

The night air was surprisingly cool and fresh, for the rain had stopped at sunset, and a moon the color of bleached bone was ascending slowly into the heavens. Below the shadow-filled stretch of lawn the sea murmured against the beach and lent its voice to the nightly chorus of rustling palm fronds, clicking beetles, and the sawing of the cicadas in the jungle beyond. It was the night song of Asia, as dear to China as the outline of the mountains around her and the indistinct faces of her mother and brother.

A breeze stirred the flowering creepers climbing up the balustrade and shook a cascade of petals onto the grass. China, aware of the cruel romance of the night, found herself aching with loneliness. She was grateful when her mother broke the spell by rising to her feet and smoothing her skirts.

"I'm going to say good night to the children. Jumai should have them ready for bed by now. Why don't we meet in the study afterward and begin that list?"

She was gone before either of them could reply. China, swallowing the last of the sherry Al-Haj had poured for her, set down the glass with a sigh, and the sound served to bring Damon out of his own reverie.

"Wait a minute before you go, China," he said. "There's

something I've been meaning to give you. Not that it's
worth anything, but I think it only fair that you have the
chance to look at it. Ah, thank you, Al-Haj."

He extended the folded document the servant had
brought him and China took it with an odd pang of reluctance. "What is it?"

Damon gave a faintly derisive laugh. "Believe it or not,
a marriage agreement, signed and witnessed in the usual
manner. You didn't know, did you, that you've been married to Ethan Bloodwell for the past—hmm—two weeks?
A British barrister name of Fenwyck came all the way
from Djakarta to draw it up for your prospective groom.
As you can see, Mother went ahead and signed it."

China had paled at his words, but as she was sitting in
the shadows well out of the moonlight, Damon was unable
to see her face. Having no inkling of her thoughts, he
continued in a conversational manner.

"In view of the fact that he all but kidnapped you, I
suppose we should have had Ethan Bloodwell arrested.
But that was before he arrived on Badajan and found out
the children were gone and was decent enough to volunteer
to go after them. Though he did refuse to go until Mother
signed those papers, of course."

The moonlight sparkled on the facets of the glass Damon raised to his lips. "Brandon told me that Bloodwell
was instrumental in saving your lives," he resumed, "and
while I can't dispute the man's courage, I must tell you
honestly I'm relieved things turned out the way they did.
Just the look on his face when he found out you had gone
with Horatio in pursuit of the children was enough to
convince me—Well, it occurred to me that perhaps the
man was every bit as unprincipled as we suspected. No
telling how miserably he would have treated you once you
became his property."

He cleared his throat and took another sip of wine. "At
any rate the question is moot. Bloodwell's dead and the
contract you have there is meaningless. Mama said we
ought to throw it away, but I thought you might want to
look at it first."

Stretching his arms above his head, he yawned widely

and pushed back his chair. "I imagine she's waiting in the study. Are you coming?"

"In a moment," China said softly.

In fact she remained for quite some time after Damon had gone, sitting with the document untouched in her lap and staring out into the darkness, wanting to cry but finding herself unable to. It was bewildering to think that she had actually been Ethan's wife, and she couldn't understand why he had insisted that she marry Darwin. Why hadn't he simply told her the truth? Had he wanted to give her the freedom to choose? Surely he must have known that it was not Darwin she wanted!

Without warning China bowed her head and scalding tears dripped onto the document in her lap.

"Missy? The family is waiting in the study."

"Thank you, Al-Haj." China swallowed and scrubbed furiously at her eyes. Tucking the document carefully into the bodice of her gown, she paused long enough in the moon-drenched courtyard to wet a scrap of cambric in the fountain and wash her tear-stained face. Smoothing down her skirts she tilted her chin and stiffened her back and swept into the lamplit study to inquire briskly if her mother had any suggestions as to who they should put on their list.

Yet in the end there had been no need for the Warricks to compile one, for morning brought an unexpected and rather surprising solution in the form of two letters delivered to China. One of them was a letter of introduction from Sir Charles Wheatley-Smythe, an elderly London banker who had been a lifelong friend of China's great-uncle Esmund. It was written in an effusive and flowery hand that was reminiscent of a long-forgotten age, and expressed Sir Charles's fervent hope that China had passed a tolerable journey home. He apologized profusely for troubling her so soon after her return to Asia, but as the matter was one that couldn't wait, he begged for her patience and understanding.

"He asks," China said, scanning the flowing lines penned across the near-transparent vellum, "if we would be kind enough to welcome a Mr. Martin Forbes and his traveling companion upon their arrival in Singapore. Mr. Forbes is a writer who has done extensive research both in India and Asia on John Company and those financiers, firms, and houses who are operating independent of it. He wishes to write a book about his findings entitled *Beyond Our Empire: An Analysis of British Business Abroad.*"

"Good God! What a dreadful undertaking!" Malvina exclaimed.

"Sir Charles asks if we would be kind enough to permit Mr. Forbes to interview us and perhaps take a tour of King's Wheal. He assures me that nothing will be written about it without our express approval."

"Just what we need at the moment, what?" Damon interjected with grim humor. "A dry-as-dust writer poking and prying into our private affairs! Hell, he doesn't have to come to Badajan to find out how the Warrick firm is faring. Ask anyone on the street—even the lowliest coolie."

"It isn't Mr. Forbes we need interest ourselves in," China said a trifle sharply. "It's George Stanley, his companion. Sir Charles mentions that Mr. Stanley has come into a considerable inheritance and is looking to turn his interests into an undertaking overseas, something 'with a bit of a challenge.'"

The big leather chair that sat behind Race Warrick's enormous desk groaned a protest as Damon threw his weight forward, and Malvina, who had been writing at her escritoire, turned to regard her daughter in astonishment.

"You can't be serious, dear!"

The ghost of a smile curved China's lips. "Oh, but I am. Apparently it didn't occur to Sir Charles to think of suggesting that we provide Mr. Stanley with connections. He's far too proper and retiring for that, and actually it's Mr. Forbes he's trying to help, but I don't see why we can't take advantage of the opportunity."

"What a devilish stroke of good luck!" Damon cried, and laughed on a note of pure happiness. "And the other letter? What does it say?"

China unfolded it and read quickly. "It's from Mr. Forbes himself, asking if it might be convenient for them to call on us some time this week. They'll be at the Raffles Hotel until Tuesday."

"Then I'll fetch them at once!" Damon exclaimed, forgetting entirely that only a moment ago he had been condemning the unknown author and his traveling companion as unmitigated bores.

"Oh, Damon, dear, I'm not at all certain about this," Malvina said doubtfully.

"Don't worry, Mama," Damon said, grinning. "We'll have the humorless creatures in for lunch. That way you can decide for yourself what you think of them before we dare approach Mr. Stanley."

Malvina's face cleared. "Why, yes, what an excellent idea."

Though admittedly hopeful herself, China was somewhat dismayed by the enthusiasm with which Damon and her mother threw themselves into their plans of welcoming Sir Charles Wheatley-Smythe's acquaintances to Badajan. She did not have a great deal of confidence in the machinations of providence and wasn't entirely certain that a solution to their problems could arrive so neatly at King's Wheal's front door.

Her misgivings were further increased when the gentlemen themselves were delivered to the island the following morning aboard the *Tempus* and she found herself shaking hands with George Stanley, a prattling young toff who reminded her with no little dismay of the irresponsible friends of Freddy Linville. Mr. Martin Forbes made a far better impression upon her, being in his late fifties, tall, soft-spoken, and well educated, and she found herself wishing that their roles could have been reversed and that Mr. Forbes was in point of fact the wealthy investor while his dissolute young companion turned out to be the writer.

She took both men on a lengthy tour of the plantation, and it was Mr. Forbes who displayed considerably more interest in the matter of silk production. Despite her disappointment, China quickly found herself warming to him and the subject at hand so that both of them were soon engaged in a lively conversation that precluded entirely the sullen young man.

"Badajan silkworms," China explained as Mr. Forbes

produced a worn ledger and began taking copious notes, "spend the entire twenty-eight days of their lives engaged in eating. After molting four times they're ready to begin cocooning. Those that have been set aside for egg production emerge two weeks later into moths, mate, and die within three days. The eggs the females lay require a minimum of eight to ten weeks in order to develop."

Mr. Forbes paused in his writing and squinted. "Which gives you close to six generations a year, doesn't it? How very interesting! What about those that aren't selected for egg production? What happens to them?"

China showed him the rows of woven baskets in which the sun-dried cocoons were stored to prevent mildew and rot—an insidious problem on the humid island. It had rained earlier that morning but now a hot sun was shrugging free of the leaden clouds, burning off the mist and spangling the dripping lobes of the trees. Water dripped from the sloping roof of the shed in which they found themselves, and the rugged green peaks of the mountains were lost in the swirling gray sky.

"The cocoons are steamed in order to kill the pupae," she explained. "Afterward they must be allowed to dry thoroughly before we attempt to unwind them. Of course you know it's the cocoon itself that yields the raw silk fiber." She gestured toward the baskets. "We'll be ready to start unraveling these this afternoon."

Mr. Forbes's sallow features lit with interest. Reaching into one of the baskets he allowed a handful of the oblong white tufts to sift through his fingers. "Then these are crop cocoons, not moth cocoons."

China nodded. "They'll be washed in hot water to loosen the thread and then reeled, eight filaments at a time, into yarn. Chinese laborers, most of them young girls, are responsible for the task."

"So you do not use Jacquard machines?" Mr. Forbes inquired, scribbling furiously. "I've seen them in France."

A smile touched China's lips. "No. Badajan silk is loomed by hand. It's a very slow and painstaking process and explains why we produce so very little at a time."

Encouraged by his questions, she explained the reeling process at length, unaware that as she spoke some of the old spirit began to creep back into her voice and her eyes, and that George Stanley, whose wandering attention had been caught by some nuance of her expression, was intrigued by the change in her.

In general George Stanley's tastes were wont to run to tall creatures with dark tresses and bold, promising eyes. He had dismissed China Warrick from the moment of their meeting as being far too small and fragile and young, and, dressed in the unrelieved black of mourning, quite unworthy of note. Yet looking at her now he was inclined to wonder if perhaps he could not be compelled to reconsider.

"May I have a word with you in private, Miss Warrick?" he therefore inquired grandly and with a firmly detaining grip on her arm when she made to lead them into the weaving sheds.

A frown creased China's brow, for she disliked being touched in so forward a manner by a stranger, but seeing that Mr. Forbes had wandered with apparent absorption into the adjoining room and was unaware that he had left them behind, she inclined her head politely. "Certainly, Mr. Stanley. What is it you wish to say to me?"

However glib or cleverly couched, the words he uttered were no more than half finished before a stinging slap landed with astonishing force upon his cheek, halting him in midsentence and bringing the startled Mr. Forbes's head about.

"Why, whatever—"

He stepped back hastily as China Warrick swept past him, her face a pale oval in the gloomy shadows though two spots of color burned high in her cheeks. Her eyes flashed in what was to him a most disconcerting manner, and he wondered what could possibly have happened to rouse this shy young creature to anger.

It was in Malvina Warrick's mind to wonder the same thing when her daughter appeared in the house not ten minutes later, breathless with rage and without the visitors she had graciously offered to guide about the plantation. She was not to be left in ignorance overly long, for China did not hesitate to inform her, calmly and clearly, that she had no further intention of soliciting investors for King's Wheal's sake.

"I'm quite certain George Stanley is not unusual of his kind," she concluded on a note of cold finality, "and if raising money for the plantation means inviting similar advances from equally repulsive individuals, I'd far rather stoop to something as ignoble as stealing!"

Malvina regarded her daughter's angry young face with considerable worry. China seemed so painfully remote and unhappy these days, and she was convinced that it wasn't just this reprehensible attack on her virtue or the pressures of losing Badajan that made her appear so. But as the two of them had never been close she knew the futility of hoping that China would confide in her.

"I'm very much afraid you're right, dear," was all she could think to say. "Now that King's Wheal has garnered such an unfortunate reputation, I cannot see how anyone will take seriously any investment offers we care to make."

China was dismayed to see her mother's handsome features sag without warning into haggard lines. Impulsively she threw her arms about her. "It doesn't matter," she said quickly. "We'll think of something else, I promise."

"Do you think so?" Malvina inquired without much hope.

"I'm certain of it," China said firmly. "I've been thinking of writing some of Great-uncle Esmund's friends in London to see if they might be willing to help us. It will take some time, of course, but surely Sir Joshua will forbear to collect on his loan if he knows the money is on its way."

Malvina brightened. "What a wonderful idea, child! Do you think it will work?"

"It might," China allowed.

Malvina drew a deep breath, her composure restored. "Before you came back from England," she said on a brighter note, "Damon and I were considering the possibility of procuring tussah worms in Kwangtung. You know they produce considerably more silk than ours, and at a faster rate. If we could boost our production just a little, we might still be able to show a profit next quarter."

"No," China said firmly. "Tussah is inferior to mulberry silk, and if we started producing it here on Badajan we'd have no advantage over what's being made in China or Japan. Father would never have considered it, and I don't think we should compromise Badajan silk simply because we cannot find the capital to keep King's Wheal going."

"And if there is no more King's Wheal?"

China bit her lip and made no answer.

"Don't fret, dear," Malvina said, patting her hand. "It will all work out for the best. Wait and see."

"Perhaps you're right," China agreed hopefully, and withdrew to her rooms in order to avoid having to face her visitors again. She was standing at the window when the *Tempus* cast off from the docks a short time later, and she sighed in relief as she watched it vanish into the silvered sun's glare. She could only pray that she had seen the last of the revolting Mr. Stanley.

Turning away, China's attention was caught by her reflection in the pier glass, and she paused for a moment to stare pensively at the small, sad face looking back at her. She couldn't understand how George Stanley could possibly have mistaken her for one of those creatures she had always referred to as "loose women." Surely there was nothing in her guileless young face to suggest that she was no stranger to passion or that a man's hands had once roved the untutored flesh of her body and left his mark upon her.

China drew in a pained breath at the thought and turned quickly away, but the memory did not fade. Indeed, the rustling of her crinolines in the heavy silence reminded her with taunting cruelty of the whisper of silk that had stirred the silence of yet another bedroom, and she could remember quite clearly how Ethan's hands had untied the silk sash about her waist and dropped it impatiently to the floor.

"I can't stand this," China whispered. "I simply cannot stand this!"

Pulling open the door she ran down the length of the inner courtyard, intent on finding Lam Tan so that he might take her away in his boat—anywhere, as long as it was far, far away from Badajan and the unwanted torment of her memories.

It was the sound of a child's broken-hearted weeping

that checked China's flight down the crushed-shell walk to the docks. Turning quickly, she saw Philippa sitting on the terrace steps, her small body wracked with sobs and her auburn curls tumbling untidily down her back.

"What is it?" China asked, quickly gathering the little girl close.

It was Brandon who answered her as he emerged through the row of flowering shrubs planted along the low stone wall. "It's Ibn Bibi, China. He's run away." He turned up his palms in a gesture of defeat. "I'm sorry, Phil. I couldn't find him anywhere."

"He's forgotten us, hasn't he, China?" Philippa quavered. "Because we went away. He probably thought we weren't coming back."

"It's possible," China conceded slowly, though she thought it unlikely that the affectionate little mongoose would have forgotten the pampering of his master and mistress so quickly. More than likely he had returned to the jungle or found a mate among the other mongooses kept in the kampong on the far side of the island.

"Couldn't you try to find him for us, China?" Philippa pleaded.

"I could ask down in the village," she said thoughtfully, "but you'll have to remember that Ibn Bibi was born in the wild. Even though you tamed him he might have decided it was time for him to return to the jungle."

Philippa's brow puckered and she sniffled unhappily. "Does that mean he may not want to come back to us even if you find him?"

"It may. But I'll tell you what I can do," China added quickly, seeing the tears well in the little girl's eyes. "I'll go to Singapore and find you a new pet. Just in case Ibn Bibi doesn't want to come home. Do you know what kind you want?"

Brightening, Philippa did not need to think the matter over. "A kitten," she said promptly, and gave a wiggle of excitement. "An orange one."

"Like Captain Crewe's?" Brandon prompted.

"Yes! Just like that! Oh, China, would you really?"

"I'll try."

"Oh, good!"

Feeling Philippa's arms tighten about her, China could
not help but laugh, and the sound startled her. Idly
smoothing the child's unruly curls, she turned her head
and gazed out across the glittering blue expanse of the
ocean, and it seemed to her as if the pain and the agony
of her love for Ethan could not be contained in so small a
vessel as the sea—and certainly not in the meager confines of her broken heart. Nor could it be dispersed into
the blinding sunshine or the humid skies of Badajan, or
be buried away in all the vast lands of Asia. And knowing
it, she wondered how she would ever find the strength to
carry the weight of all that the Warricks stood for when
she wasn't even certain that she could bear to face another
day without him.

Some time later that night China was awakened by a
nightmare, and though she could remember nothing but
the shivering, sweat-drenching terror with which she came
awake, she found herself unable to shake its paralyzing
hold and drift back to sleep. Throwing aside the sheet that
covered her, she padded barefoot across the warm tiles to
peer out across the bowing, swaying tops of the palm trees
and wondered why the dark mountains and the whispering
jungle suddenly seemed so quietly and insidiously menacing to her.

There was no moon that night, and the stars glittered
and pulsed in a sky that was as dark and black as the
depths of a tomb. China pulled the thin silk fabric of her
night rail closer about her, but it did nothing to stop her
shivering. Far in the distance a night bird called, but the
sound went unanswered for the jungle slept, and the silence was complete and oddly unnerving. Then, faintly
from across the sea, came the distant rumble of thunder
over the hills of Malaysia, and China, hearing it, thought
it odd that a storm could be brewing on such a cool and
cloudless night.

The sound was nonetheless reassuring, for it reminded
her that other lands and other people filled the vast and
lonely world and that Badajan was only one of countless
islands lying in the Indonesian Sea. And there across the
Strait, so close that she had only to fetch her brother's

glass to see the lights glimmering in the shipping lanes of the Outer Road, lay Singapore...and Ethan's coral house.

It had been over a week since China had bid farewell to Nappy Quarles on board the *Orion*. Perhaps it was because he had shared her anguish over Ethan's death or because he was the only one to whom she could admit her unbearable sorrow, but suddenly she yearned to see him and to hear his gruff, familiar voice.

The thought of spending a few hours in his company was such a comforting one that the cold grip of the nightmare seemed to ease somewhat. Making up her mind to go to Singapore tomorrow, China knew that she must take adequate precautions that no one learn of her improper visit to the Coral House.

The reluctance of her mother's friends and acquaintances to call at King's Wheal, and to do little more than send cautiously worded cards of sympathy in the matter of Darwin Stepkyne's death, had been an unexpected blow to her. Gradually it had dawned on her that the Warricks were being cast out from polite society because of their association with Wang Toh Chen-Arn. Damon had told her that the notorious mandarin's death had generated wildly unfounded rumors concerning the Warricks' illicit connections with him. While China knew that time would eventually still the malicious gossip and that the worst of the tales would be conveniently forgotten once the Warricks were again a power to be reckoned with, she was well aware that she should not be risking further damage to her family's name by paying an unsquired visit to Ethan's house.

She would leave at first light, she decided, and travel alone and on foot the short distance along the shoreline from the harbor to the back gate of the Coral House. Few people would be about that time of day, and those that were would invariably be Chinese vendors and Malaysian roustabouts, while the British community wouldn't be going abroad for hours at least.

Feeling satisfied that she could conclude her business with Nappy in the brief space of time before their carriages, victorias, and trishaws would make their first appearances on the boulevards, China promptly dismissed the matter from her thoughts. Rolling onto her side she closed her eyes and fell at once into an untroubled sleep.

Chapter Twenty-four

The moment she was admitted to the Coral House, China knew that it had been a dreadful mistake to come. Not because she had been recognized on the deserted, rain-lashed streets, but because it was not Lal Sri who answered her knock on the door. Instead a slatternly woman in a stained sarong which barely concealed her enormous breasts responded to China's polite Malay with distinctly hostile grunts while holding the door ajar with a bare brown foot. She rudely refused to move aside, and China was forced to press back her crinolines in order to step past her.

Once in the entrance hall the feeling of disquiet grew stronger, for the woman made no move to summon Nappy but continued to stare at her with ill-concealed curiosity. Furthermore and perhaps more painfully, China found herself assaulted by such bitter and conflicting memories that they all but took her breath away.

Here, here in this very spot she had stood and listened to Lal Sri innocently paint Ethan with the damning evidence of infidelity that had caused her to flee his house like some panic-stricken virgin, when in truth he had done no more than hurry out to offer assistance to a sick child. And that winding, carpet-hung stair there at the end of the long hall led to the women's quarters of the house and the sandalwood-scented room where Ethan had ordered her taken when she had succumbed to the heat of the fierce Asian sun. And it was there that Ethan had eventually come to her and...

China turned away with a choked little gasp and, finding the woman watching her with the same dark, insolent eyes, was moved to raise her voice and inquire sharply if any officers of the *Kowloon Star* were in residence. Shrugging her plump shoulders the woman gave her to understand that all of them were gone. China was pondering the wisdom of leaving a message that would doubtless go undelivered when a gruff voice addressed her from behind.

"You oughtn't to 'ave come, miss. They'll talk now you've been 'ere."

"A little more gossip one way or the other won't matter to me," China said ruefully.

"Maybe to you it don't, but I'll not put up wiv it." Nappy was scowling fiercely as he clumped across the hall, but China wasn't fooled for a moment, for she knew that he was trying hard to conceal the fact that he was glad to see her.

As he came out of the shadows she studied him anxiously, seeing what the slow-crawling and anguished week had done to him. It was apparent to her at once that Nappy had been sleeping badly, if at all, for there was a dark, unhealthy smudge beneath his single eye, and he seemed thinner to her and frighteningly shrunken and old.

Growling beneath his breath, Nappy sent the serving woman away to fetch refreshments. "We can talk 'ere, miss," he invited, leading China into a room behind the staircase that she had never seen before.

It was a small room by Eastern standards, but could have comfortably swallowed more than half of Broadhurst's formal Withdrawing Room. A row of tall, arching windows opened onto the overgrown garden and provided a view of Singapore River lying sluggish and brown beneath the humid sky. There were no chairs, only a sprawled profusion of cushions and several low-slung tables of inlaid mahogany and ebony that contrasted sharply with the white-plastered walls and the cool tile floor.

China settled herself as gracefully as her wide skirts would allow. "You said I shouldn't have come," she began, regarding him worriedly. "Why? Has something happened?"

"Only that I've sold t' roof wots o'er your 'ead," Nappy said darkly.

"The Coral House? You've sold it?"

"Yus! No sense in keeping it now the cap'n an' Rajiid are gone. Wot'll I do 'ere alone, eh? Place is too big for a cove the likes o' me! Sold it to some 'Igh an' Mighty from Imperial Fleet. Barstid wot 'as money enough to get 'is 'ands on it quick once I made 'im t' offer."

"And the *Kowloon Star?*"

Nappy looked offended. "Wouldn't part wiv 'er for the world, miss! Too many mem'ries an' the like! I know Cap'n Ethan wouldn't care one way or t'other if 'is 'ouse were gone, but 'is ship be diff'rent. Loved 'er, 'e did, and I don't 'old for sellin' 'er to some fellow 'oo'd mistreat 'er or turn 'er into some pulin' passenger wherry! Too good for thot, ain't she?"

"Yes, I suppose she is. What about you, Nappy? What will you do now?"

"I'm goin' away wiv 'er," he mumbled.

"Where?"

"Back 'ome."

China started visibly. "Back home? You mean to England?"

"Yus. Bain't no sense rovin' the East wivout Cap'n Ethan. Wouldn't be the same, if you knows my meanin', miss. Somethin' missin' now that 'e's dead. The way I sees it I've got nowhere else to go. Might as well live out wot's left to me life in m' own land." He tugged at his eyepatch and looked embarrassed at having made such a disclosure.

"Then I'll be left alone here," China said after a long pause and in a small voice that tore at Nappy's heart.

"You've your fam'ly, miss," he reminded her quickly, "and you won't be losin' your island neither. Cap'n Ethan wouldn't've let it 'appen and I won't neither. Thot's why I'm givin' you the money wot's earned from sellin' t' Coral 'Ouse."

China's head came up and for a brief moment he saw the hope and disbelief that flared across her pale, hollow cheeks before she pursed her lips and said stubbornly, "That's very kind of you, Nappy, but I can't possibly—"

"'Sst! I'll 'aves no coy female words, mind! I told you Cap'n Ethan wouldn't let you lose yer place, and why should I be different, eh? I've no use for money. The lads and me both, we're 'appy wiv the *Kowloon Star,* and we don't need to live like 'eathen princes. I've enow for us, and the rest be yours, miss. Take it."

"Oh, Nappy, I can't."

"Take it! Do you want it all lost? Your island and young Master Brandon and Miss Philippa's future, your 'ome, everything? Is that wot the cap'n died for?"

He saw her blanch as though he had struck her, but he could see that his words had had their desired effect. Color rushed to her cheeks, transforming her instantly into the radiant beauty who had first captured Ethan Bloodwell's attention in faraway Kent. Though Nappy snorted and muttered beneath his breath, he was secretly quite pleased with himself.

The arrival of the fat Malaysian woman precluded further discussion, and it was not until she had set down the tray of refreshments and shuffled out that Nappy was able to turn his attention back to his guest. China was sitting with her face averted, her profile lit from behind, and the pale morning sunlight set her riotous red curls ablaze. Her hands were clasped in the folds of her skirts, and the cumbersome black petticoats billowed on the cushions about her so that she seemed lost amid them, an illusion of fragility that angered Nappy unaccountably and made him wonder if perhaps it was unwise to leave her after all.

But how could he possibly help her further? he wondered helplessly. He was naught but a poorly educated old man who had no claims whatsoever upon China Warrick's life. Yet the fact remained that he could not rid himself of the nagging feeling that he should stay in Singapore to look after her. Why, it almost seemed to him that the ghost of Captain Ethan hovered at his elbow, commanding and exhorting him to care for her.

Because Nappy could not shake the feeling that he was somehow failing his captain, he lapsed into a brooding silence, waiting for China to digest the fact that King's Wheal was safe, and hoping that she wouldn't make too much of a fuss over the money he wished to give her.

"I'll 'aves it no other way," he said unexpectedly, "and Cap'n Ethan wouldn't neither. You'll take the gold, miss, and that's the end of it. I'll not be meetin' the cap'n in some afterlife an' 'im takin' brief wiv me on account I didn't do wot were right by you. And I bain't doin' it because o' some paper 'im an' your brother signed wot says you're 'is legal wife! I've eyes in my 'ead—one wot works, anyway—and any fool could see the cap'n was in love wiv you!"

With a start he saw that China was crying. "There, there, miss," he said awkwardly. "There, there. It ain't so bad."

"I know, Nappy," China whispered, though both of them knew the other was lying.

Though they had at first found comfort in each other's company, they were both suddenly seized with the need to take their leave of each other, and they did so awkwardly and with ill-concealed relief. Hurrying down the walk with her veil pulled across her face, China's steps slowed suddenly as it occurred to her that this might be the last she would ever see of Nappy. Yet perhaps it was better this way. Once Nappy returned to England she would have nothing left but memories, and surely they would fade in time and the pain that ravaged every labored breath she drew from her body would recede to a dull yet tolerable ache.

She bit her lip at the thought because she didn't really want it to end like that. She didn't want Nappy to simply sail out of her life or Ethan to become nothing more than an indistinct face she could no longer envision with any great accuracy. Was that how her love for him was destined to end?

"I can't bear it!" she whispered to herself. "I cannot!"

And she began to run, the tears blinding her, wishing that she had the nerve to forsake everything and everyone here in the East and flee with Nappy back to England. A vision of Broadhurst's verdant parks rose unbidden before her and she could almost smell the crisp autumn air and hear the shrieking of the pheasants across the stubbled fields of harvested rye. She could not credit the longing that swept over her, though she knew it to be utterly ill-considered, for she had not forgotten how Freddy and Cassie had schemed to get rid of her and that in view of what they had done to her she could never return.

"Here, miss, watch your step!"

Without warning someone seized her by the arm and jerked her backward, roughly but effectively preventing her running headlong into the path of a carriage that rumbled across the deeply rutted street. The vehicle passed so close that the off-side wheel grazed her skirts, and the horses tossed their heads, their trappings jangling at the sight of this small apparition in black. China caught her breath on a gasp and lifted her eyes gratefully to her rescuer.

"Oh, thank you, sir! I might have been badly hurt!"

"Why, it's the Warrick girl!" she heard him exclaim, and her heart sank as she recognized the swarthy features of Mr. George Stanley beneath the dripping brim of a tall black hat.

It was regrettable that China's veil should have slipped from her face when he had jerked her out of the path of the oncoming carriage, for it was highly unlikely that he would have recognized her otherwise. And seeing the cunning that rapidly replaced his astonishment, China could clearly imagine what disagreeable thoughts must be playing through his head on the score of finding her wandering the streets of Singapore alone.

Mr. Stanley wasted no time in justifying her suspicions by refusing to relinquish his hold on her arm and inquiring with leering interest if she had perhaps come to seek him out knowing he had rented a room in the Raffles Hotel, whose red tile roof was visible above the swaying crowns of the palm trees behind them.

"No!" China burst out, aghast at the very idea. Then she fell silent, for there was nothing she could say to the contrary that would not look entirely suspicious to him. An explanation about Philippa's kitten seemed ridiculous, and she would not permit Nappy's name and the real purpose of her visit to cross her lips.

Setting her mouth in a stubborn line she said coolly, "Would you please let me go, sir?"

Regrettably George Stanley was of a far too boorish nature to oblige a lady's request. Gazing down into her face, he was determined to make the best use of his unexpected stroke of luck. He'd heard some interesting tales about this fiery little redhead, and perhaps in view of them it would make no difference if she were to be seen in public in a most compromising position. And surely there could be no harm in seeing if his suspicions might not be borne out? She was certainly tempting enough, what with the rain dampening her black muslin mourning and causing it to cling to the sweet lines of her slender body. And that mouth of hers! Yesterday she had fired his blood and left him quite unable to forget her, even after she had gone so far as to deliver that insulting slap to his person.

"My dear Miss Warrick," he said in his most magniloquent manner, "it seems to me that playing at cross-purposes becomes neither of us and wastes a considerable amount of time. Time that could be spent in other, more pleasurable pursuits? I see we understand each other quite well," he added as China uttered a disbelieving gasp. "I'm willing to believe that you, my dear Miss Warrick, are—"

He broke off with a startled expletive as a hand of astonishing strength settled without warning about his wrist. Whirling indignantly, he checked abruptly upon being confronted by an enormous man in a black cloak and tall boots, whose long blond hair clung damply about his bare head.

"If you're wantin' to speak with Miss Warrick, sir, you'll be keepin' your hands to yourself, hmm?"

"Captain Crewe!" China said with obvious relief.

Tyler bowed and said good morning as though nothing

were amiss and as if he were quite accustomed to intervening manfully on her behalf, but there was something
decidedly threatening in his manner that suggested to
George Stanley—who may have been vain and unscrupulous but certainly no fool—that it might be wiser to
continue his pursuit of the Warrick girl at some other, more
provident time. Apologizing profusely for any discomfort
he may have caused her, he tipped his hat and hastened
away into the slanting gray rain.

"Trussed up peacock," Captain Crewe pronounced, looking after him darkly. "You're lucky I happened to be driving past, Miss Warrick. It didn't seem likely you were going
to get away from him without help."

"I know," China said ruefully. "Thank you."

"Now suppose you tell me what in tarnation you're doing
here?" Scanning the length of the rain-soaked street for a
sign of her carriage, or at the very least the presence of a
serving woman, Tyler was not particularly surprised when
he found no evidence of either.

"I came to see Nappy," China admitted. "I suppose I
shouldn't have come alone, but I was afraid to bring one
of the servants. You know how they tend to talk."

Tyler grunted and then regarded her for a moment in
silence. "Come on," he said at last, and handed her up into
a covered carriage standing a short distance up the street.
Issuing terse orders to the Malay driver, he lowered himself into the seat across from her and shook out his dripping
cloak. "I hope nobody sees you bowlin' around town with
me," he said, "but I suppose it's better than having you
fall into the clutches of that crawling python back there.
Where in God's name did you find him?"

China told him, and Tyler had to admire her for the
fact that she hadn't succumbed to an attack of the vapors
as his dramatic Julia would have done. There was a core
of unyielding steel beneath that slim façade, Tyler decided,
and wondered, too, idly but with genuine bemusement,
how a boy the likes of Darwin Stepkyne could ever have
won himself such a rare prize.

"Julia's in Djakarta, by the way," he went on. "Makin'
a big fuss over that little sister of yours." Despite himself
he had to chuckle. "Didn't think she was the type to get

doe-eyed over babies. Ah, here we are," he added as the carriage jolted to a stop against the curb.

Peering through the rain-spattered window China saw that they had halted before the imposing white façade of a tall colonial house set at the far end of a wide green lawn. To the left, other houses of similar opulence occupied lush, flower-filled landscapes, while to the right the new buildings of British government and the hulk of a half-finished hotel could be seen rising above the tops of the swaying palms.

"This," Captain Crewe explained as China regarded him questioningly, "is the home of Sir Adrian Dunsmore, director of the Southeast Asia branch of the London Union Bank. Have you ever met him?"

China shook her head.

"Well, you're going to meet him now. Can't think of a better time with most of the city hidin' out on account of the rain. Besides"—Tyler winked—"I've been tellin' him something about you and he's anxious to get to know you."

"Why would he want to meet me?"

"Because Quarles and I asked him to manage your money, that's why."

China frowned. "My money? But we've always done business with the Charter Overseas Bank!"

"I don't mean the Warrick accounts, provided there's anything left to 'em," Tyler said not unkindly. "I was talking about the money Quarles is going to give you from the sale of Ethan's house."

"You knew about that?"

"I couldn't help knowing what with Quarles laying the whole bundle at my door," Tyler responded. "Said he didn't know the first thing about managing cash, and to tell you the truth, neither do I. That's why you've got to see Dunsmore. He happens to have a pretty high opinion of your father, and he's agreed to help you keep the kites at bay—at least until you can get that next hatch reeled and spun into cloth."

"But I can't possibly accept this," China argued.

"Listen up, m' girl, it's the best Quarles and I can do for you," Tyler said with utter seriousness. "If Nappy were

to give you that money out and out, the law would make
you use every single rupiah to settle your debts. You'd
have nothing left to show for it and no way to keep title
to King's Wheal long enough to get back into production.
This way at least you've got a fighting chance."

"But I can't meet Sir Adrian looking like this!" China
protested. Her head was spinning. The London Union
Bank? They, and every other bank in the city, had already
politely but quite firmly turned down her request for new
loans.

"It's not a bad thing to be dressed in mourning when
you meet with a banker," Tyler said with a reassuring
grin, refraining from adding that this subtle reminder of
tragedy would go a long way in impressing upon Adrian
Dunsmore how imperative it was to save the Warrick plantation from ruin.

"I don't quite know how to thank you, Captain."

"Wait until you get your money," he said gruffly. "You
can thank me then. And Quarles, too."

By God, she really was one hell of a beauty, he was
thinking in surprise as she smiled up at him gratefully.
He knew then why Ethan Bloodwell had been unable to
act in a rational manner around her. And it dawned on
him, too, with no small measure of astonishment, that he
would be doing exactly what he was doing right now to
help keep her from ruin even if he hadn't been impressed
into the task by Nappy's fervent pleadings and a sense of
duty to the memory of his dead friend.

Later that evening, in the heat of a sunset made spectacular by the great banks of crimson clouds that roiled
over the Malaysian hills and sent golden fragments of
sunlight flaring across the darkening sea, China Warrick
strolled through King's Wheal's fragrant garden, and for
the first time since Ethan's death permitted herself to think
of the future. Sir Adrian Dunsmore had assured her that
with luck, hard work, and judicious planning King's Wheal
might very well survive.

To her considerable relief she and the elderly banker
had taken to one another from the start, and he had put
her instantly at ease by spending the first half of what

had turned out to be a lengthy visit reminiscing about her father. China, who had found it difficult to discuss Race Warrick with her own family, had blossomed the moment she was asked about him. Animation had lent delightful character to her face as she spoke of him, prompting Sir Adrian to remark with approval that she had obviously inherited every bit of the fabled Warrick spirit and charm.

Tyler Crewe, sitting forgotten in a nearby armchair but listening with considerable interest, was nearly tempted to conclude traitorously that he had chosen the wrong one of Ethan Bloodwell's spirited pair of women, for he had never known the little Warrick to glow with such warmth as she did when she spoke of her father. He could not know that it was simple relief that brought the words tumbling from China's lips, for she had never been permitted to grieve for Race properly, and the prospect of forgetting for a time everything except that which lay in her happily remembered past was a temptation too great to ignore.

When Sir Adrian turned at last to the subject at hand, he did most of the talking, explaining China's options in a straightforward manner and answering her questions patiently and thoroughly. The confidence he restored within her gave her a measure of hope she had never thought to experience again. When she took her leave of him she was delighted by the fact that he also presented her with a kitten from the litter in his stable, and though there were no orange ones among them, China felt certain Philippa would be contented with the solid gray one she eventually chose.

Promising to bring Sir Adrian the plantation account books, China bid him a grateful farewell and took her leave with the little creature purring in her arms. Now, as she wandered amid the vines of tumbling purple bougainvillea while the sun slid behind the mountains and night sprang into life around her, it occurred to her that she would have to tell her mother and Damon of her association with the elderly banker before she could have access to the ledgers. The prospect did not appeal to her particularly, for she knew that she would also have to explain where the money had come from and why the steward of the *Kowloon Star* had seen fit to give it to her.

But China did not want to talk about Ethan just yet. Not tonight, at any rate, when the beauty of the sunset was little more than a cruel reminder of those hushed, golden evenings she had spent aboard the *Kowloon Star*, haughtily imagining herself to despise the brigantine's captain when in truth he had both fascinated and disturbed her. Strange how his loss had forced her to see herself in a light she had never dreamed of. She had spent the last six years of her life, her entire childhood in fact, yearning to be home, yet it was clear to her now that what she longed for, and the world she had kept alive in her childishly romantic dreams, no longer existed. She was seeing life through the eyes of a woman who had tasted fleetingly of love, but who had found it to be a drugging wine she could no longer live without.

And while she had thrown herself frantically into the task of saving King's Wheal from financial ruin, she knew now that she had done so not for herself, but for Brandon and Philippa. King's Wheal was their future, not hers, and she should have realized as much long before this. The Badajan of China's childhood was gone; the one left in its place was a world she suddenly realized she did not belong to or have any desire to embrace, and the two men she had loved most—Ethan Bloodwell and her father—were dead. There was nothing for her here.

If only things had turned out differently! If only her father hadn't died and Wang Toh had not seen fit to set about destroying what Race had left behind. And if only Brandon and Philippa hadn't been taken aboard Ho Kuang's pirate lorcha, a terrible twist of fate that had precipitated one disaster after another, perhaps Ethan might never have—

China was suddenly quite still, her slim hand frozen about the stalk of a wild and beautiful cymbidium orchid she had been about to pick. Though the night and the jungle were unusually still, it seemed to her as if the very mountains had taken up a great shouting. Her heart, having checked for an interminable moment, suddenly began a frenzied beating that made her breath come in harsh gasps. Of course! Why hadn't she thought of it before? *The lorcha!*

China began to run, slipping on the wet grass and stumbling over the length of her trailing skirts. Lifting them high she raced toward the house and up the steps, calling loudly for Brandon. He emerged from his room at a run and China met him on the landing, grasping his arms with trembling fingers.

"The lorcha?" he repeated in response to her breathless question. His brow puckered. "Of course I remember. Don't you, China? That's how Wang Toh's son brought us from the *Malhão* to the *Lotus Star*. No, I don't know what happened to it after that. It must have been sunk along with the big ship. Wouldn't Captain Crewe have said something about it if it hadn't?"

China's breath caught in her throat. Was it possible? *Could* the lorcha have been sunk? Surely Brandon was right in pointing out that Captain Crewe would have mentioned it to her unless—unless it had managed to slip away unseen just before the sun came up and he had never even known of its existence.

China came slowly to her feet, moving as though she were drunk or suffering the onset of some dizzying illness. It was impossible to still the fierce trembling that had taken possession of her. Dared she entertain the notion that Ethan had managed to escape aboard the lorcha? It was absurd, unlikely, highly improbable, and yet—and yet...

"What on earth is the matter, child?" Malvina demanded, having been drawn from the study by the sound of her daughter's voice. She uttered an involuntary gasp as China turned, for the look on the girl's face was one she had never seen before. It was a face transformed by such breathless, jubilant hope that Malvina found herself groping for the railing.

"China, what is it? What's happened?"

"The lorcha!" China burst out. "That's how Ethan got away! Oh, it must be!" She kissed her mother on the cheek and brushed quickly past her. "I'm sorry, Mother, there isn't time to explain. I've got to find Nappy and

Tyler Crewe. They'll take me to look for him! I know they will!"

She laughed aloud and ran lightly down the steps and a moment later the perplexed Malvina heard the front door slammed behind her.

Chapter Twenty-five

As China flew down the hill toward the deep-water docks, a jagged, tearing flicker of lightning rent the sky and the echo of a thunderclap sounding across the island halted her near the boathouse. She gazed in dismay across the black, tossing water.

A southwesterly wind was driving a line of storm clouds across the Strait, and lightning danced and licked along the distant foothills of Malaysia. Whitecaps built and broke and savaged the wooden pilings of the pier, and the _Tempus_, her newly repaired mast rising black against the sky, reared and plunged against her mooring lines like a maddened horse.

"No can cross till storm blows by," Lam Tan, one of the houseboys who was accompanying her, said regretfully. "Missy will try tomorrow, yes?"

No! China wanted to shout. No, you'll take me now and be damned about the weather! But she knew that the monsoon winds and the fury of a squall were dangerous elements to battle with so small a skiff as the _Tempus_. Her father had once attempted the same at the tiller of the

Bonne Heure and had ended up losing his life—but surely, surely there was *some* way to get word to Nappy?

"Lam Tan! I want to cross as soon as the storm blows over. Can you have the *Tempus* ready? I'll wait in the boathouse."

The youthful Malay bowed, his thin face impassive. He had been captain of the boats when Race Warrick had still been alive, and had been familiar enough with his master's impatient ways to recognize them in his obstinate daughter. Shrugging into his oilskins he jumped down into the bucking boat, well aware that the impetuous Missy Warrick would insist on casting off the instant the wind died so much as a fraction.

In the boathouse the wind sounded a steady, wailing cant, and when the rain began at last it did so in a gusting explosion, battering the tin roof and roaring like the seven furies, all but drowning out the sound of the thunder and the crashing waves. Lightning flared and stabbed beyond the single, square-cut window, illuminating the heaving sea in brief flashes of flaring blue light. China could feel the hair at the nape of her neck prickle and stand on end, and she paced the musty, wooden floor, cursing the weather and the interminable delay.

She would not permit herself to consider the possibility that she might very well be mistaken about Ethan's escape in the lorcha. After all, hadn't she seen with her own eyes how he had been dragged from the rail by a half-dozen Chinese seamen? Yet the moment she began to doubt herself she thrust the thought away with a nervous jerk of her head, and the restless tap of her small, sturdy boots sounded once more across the uneven floor.

Of course Ethan had fled the *Lotus Star* aboard the pirate lorcha! It was inconceivable to imagine that he had not, and China could only assume that for some reason or another he had been forced to detonate the magazine and slip away in the ensuing confusion. Yet an unrelieved voice continued to nag and whisper in the back of her mind: Why hadn't Ethan made straight for the *Orion*? Why had he navigated the lorcha elsewhere? More than a week had elapsed since the *Lotus Star* had been destroyed. Surely he would have had enough time to return?

"No, no, no!" China groaned to herself, and covered her ears as though to drive out the sound of her tormenting thoughts.

She ran to the window and stood on tiptoe to peer outside, but the lightning flared and crackled in blinding bolts and it was impossible to see. She knew that it would be utter madness to attempt a crossing until the storm subsided, and that Lam Tan, loyal as he might be, would staunchly refuse to cast off until it was safe. And as for going alone, China knew that she would not be able to manage the boat herself in such high and fractious seas.

A deafening thunderclap exploded as China turned away from the window, and the tiny boathouse heaved and shuddered. An uncomfortable ringing in her ears drove her to the door. Wrenching the handle she was almost knocked off her feet as it burst open from outside and Lam Tan was hurled in on a blast of wind and pelting rain that knocked the breath from her body.

"Missy—missy!" he called.

"What is it? Lam Tan!"

His face was a queer yellow and the whites of his eyes showed as he leaned against the wall and tried to speak, but his panting Malay was entirely incomprehensible to her.

"Please, you must speak slowly," China begged, but her words were drowned out by another clap of thunder that seemed to shake the boathouse loose from its pilings. The tin roof groaned and rattled and the rain increased in force, pummeling like hailstones so that neither the girl nor the Malay could make themselves heard above the noise.

Hail? China found herself thinking in disbelief. She remembered how hail had fallen during the heavy weather of spring and early autumn in Kent and how the unbelievable roar had filled every room in the big house of Broadhurst as the hard, frozen pellets had bounced relentlessly on the windows and the roof. But surely here in Asia it could not possibly be hailing!

She started for the door only to have Lam Tan restrain her with a clawing grip on her arm. His terrified gibberish alarmed her, and China pulled herself free. She jerked open the door to find herself instantly soaked by the rain

and something else—something that coated her dress and
her lashes and settled in her hair like so much fine powder.
She coughed and tasted its silky raw bitterness on her lips,
and her heart seemed to skip to a stop. It could not be—
it couldn't be—*Ash!*

Unmindful of the rain and the splattering pellets of hot
sand and stone she had mistaken for hail, China raced
onto the dock and turned to look up at the mountains.
Through the darkness she could see a great, heaving cloud
being driven northeast by the wind, and hear the rumble
that came from the depths of Badajan's supposedly inert
and long-slumbering volcano.

Gasping and slipping on the wet planks, she ran back
into the boathouse.

"Lam Tan!" she shouted. "Take the *Tempus* around to
the east end of the island. Keep close to shore. Do you
understand? Close to shore!"

Lam Tan nodded, his face pale and frightened.

"If the volcano erupts, the lava will flow to the west of
the island. Here, across the boathouse and the docks."
China had reverted to English because she did not know
the proper words in Malay, and she prayed that Lam Tan
would understand. "That's what happened in my grandfather's time and it left a path on the lip of the mountain
that will make it easy for the lava to funnel into this time,
too. We must get away."

"I will wait by the mangrove swamp, missy. You will
get family, yes?"

At China's nod he gave her a weak grin. "Lam Tan will
keep boat from running onto roots. Don't worry for Lam
Tan."

She smiled back at him and, taking a deep breath,
stepped out into the maelstrom. Wind and rain clawed at
her skirts and a cloud of gritty ash whirled into her eyes.
China bowed her head and ran, keeping under cover of the
wildly gyrating trees as best she could. The ash was hot,
and she found herself thinking over and over as she pounded
breathlessly up to the house, Thank God it's raining! Without the rain and the wet, humid jungle there would be
horrible fires.

The plantation house was blazing with lights. China

stumbled up the steps and onto the protective embrasure
of the veranda where she was met by her mother and a
babbling confusion of servants. The white clapboards were
blackened with ash and a layer of grime coated the windows. Thunder rumbled and the volcano growled an ominous reply. The veranda boards seemed to sway and
tremble and send the servants into a paroxysm of shrill
screams and sobbing prayers.

"China! Where have you been? I was just sending them
out to look for you!"

Malvina's face was drawn and so white that it seemed
little more than a pale oval against the lightning-torn
darkness. Her hands came out to clutch her daughter, and
their eyes met for a brief and urgent moment.

"Lam Tan is taking the *Tempus* down to the shallows
near the mangrove swamp," China said quickly. "We're to
meet him there."

Malvina's hands trembled as she clasped them to her
bosom. "Oh, I simply don't know if that's wise, child! Perhaps we should—"

A fearsome explosion drowned out her timorous words—
obliterated, in fact, all sound and light and sensation. Suddenly the world of wind and rain and night was ignited
by a soaring plume of fire that roared skyward from the
depths of the mountain amid a showering of fierce orange
sparks. The earth seemed to rock and sway beneath their
feet and the screaming servants scattered like dried leaves
in a whirlwind.

Blinded by the falling ash, China groped her way into
the house only to find that there was scant relief to be
had: The windows had been blown in by the force of the
eruption and through the open doors of the courtyard the
insidious, choking gray clouds writhed and seeped inside.
Carpets, furnishings, priceless glassware, and Asian art
already lay under a steadily thickening cover of powder,
and China, stooping to rip loose a square of her petticoat,
bound it tightly about her mouth and nose, and looked
about her with numb disbelief. This couldn't be happening,
not here, not to King's Wheal!

"China, the children!" Malvina was behind her, gesturing wildly toward the landing. Her voice was muffled

behind the silk veil she had tied in a similar fashion about
the lower part of her face, and China ran across the slippery coating of grime to be met on the stairs by Damon
and Al-Haj. Damon was carrying the sobbing Philippa
tightly in his arms and Brandon, though white-lipped and
trembling, bravely clutched Philippa's tiny, mewling kitten.

"Where's Jumai?" China demanded on a cough.

"Gone! Run away like the rest of them!" Damon shouted
above the roar of the elements.

"I stay to help, missy," Al-Haj said firmly. "We must
hurry, missy. The heat grows fierce."

And with it the danger.

Though the lava, as China had hoped, had begun to
race in a fiery path down the far side of the smoke-envel-
oped mountain, the sparks and the ash continued to fall
so thickly that they were unable to see into the garden as
they came outside to stand in a straggling, shivering line
at the veranda rail.

"We'll have to hold hands and make a run for it," Damon
said grimly. "I'll carry Philippa and you, Al-Haj, go between the mistress and Missy China. Brandon, take hold
of my shirt tail and don't, under any circumstances, let
go. Do you understand? All of you?"

They nodded, their faces showing white and very frightened in the light from the empty house behind them. Damon, murmuring reassuringly to the little girl who hid
her face in his shoulder, started briskly across the lawn.
They followed in single file, each holding on to the person
ahead of them, but even before they had managed twenty
running paces Damon slipped in the oozing mix of ash and
rain on the arching footbridge leading into the garden.

Twisting his body in order to protect Philippa as he fell,
he landed heavily upon his wrist and despite the roaring
of the rain and the thunderous rumbles of the disgorging
mountain, China could hear the sickening snap of the newly
mended bones.

"Damon!"

Shaking her skirts free of Al-Haj's clutching hand, China
went down on her knees beside her brother and saw that
his teeth were clenched and that sweat ran in grimy tracks

down his blackened face. In the next moment another
shower of ash rained down through the trees upon them,
obliterating everything with a fury, and China felt Malvina's hand on her shoulder.

"Give Philippa to me. I'll carry her. You'll have to lead
the way."

"You'll get tired, it's too far!" China protested. "We can
take turns—you and Al-Haj and I."

"Al-Haj is too old. You must lead," Malvina said sharply.
"Don't argue with me, child!"

"There isn't any reason why we can't take turns at the
lead," China said stubbornly, but Malvina would not hear
of it. She did not, she reminded her daughter crisply, know
all the many twists and turns of the footpaths that led
from the manicured gardens down through the choking
jungle to the island's shores.

Born and raised on the flat, dun-colored plains of
Queensland, Malvina had never accustomed herself to the
steaming tropics of Asia, nor had she ever admitted to
anyone how much she feared them. The harshly imposed
laws she had laid down forbidding her children to wander
unsupervised about the island had stemmed from a carefully hidden though nonetheless hysterical certainty that
they would be bitten by a snake or a scorpion or carried
off by a wild and lethal tushed boar.

Malvina had never been blind to the fact that China
and Brandon defied those rules and roamed freely through
the jungle. Nor would she ever have believed that one day
she would be grateful for their intimate knowledge of Badajan's closely grown forests. But she knew that the mangrove swamp where Lam Tan awaited them could be
reached in half the time down one of those same dangerous
paths that her children had explored since infancy. And it
was China, possessing the cool courage and steady nerves
of her father, who must lead them.

The path was overgrown and, in the hot, choking darkness, nearly impossible to negotiate. A burly native wielding a machete might have stood an excellent chance, but
China, at the head of the straggling, tiring line, was hampered by the thick clusters of bamboo and tearing creepers
that pressed in on them. It was impossible to tell if the

volcano's rumbling had ceased, for the steady hail of the stones and grit that hurled through the canopy of leaves above them was far louder than the roar of whitewater and drowned out all else.

The heat was an incredible burning furnace at their backs, and blackbuck, monkeys, and other unseen animals crashed through the underbrush behind them in their panic-stricken flight to the sea. It did not occur to China to take heart at the fact that Badajan's furred and feathered creatures were fleeing along a similar path and that it could only mean that she had been correct in assuming the lava would flow to the western end of the island. She could think of nothing at all, for her mind was numb and her eyes burned with the acrid sting of the ash, and yet she dared not wipe them clear, or look away from the ground beneath her feet that was illuminated by the constant glare of lightning, for fear of losing her way.

But very soon an insidious fear began to seep into her heart, for surely they should have reached the shore by now? Granted they were moving at little better than a snail's pace, and China had been forced to turn back on several occasions after running into an impenetrable wall of creepers, losing valuable time and pricking her fingers mercilessly as she tore her petticoats free. But the length of the path from the garden's end to the muddy, low-lying shore, where Ethan Bloodwell and Nappy Quarles had once landed a jolly boat in the darkness to reconnoiter the island, was no great distance. China couldn't bear to consider the likelihood that they had strayed from the path.

The rotting branch of a liana tree, weakened by its weight of ash and sand, came crashing to the ground directly in China's path, delivering her a glancing blow and painfully scratching the side of her face. She staggered back and those following behind her fell into confusion. Other branches cracked ominously overhead and China could feel the ground move as though something huge and horrible writhed and struggled beneath the very earth.

"China!" Brandon's small hand closed convulsively about her skirts. "What is it? Why is the ground dancing?"

"I'm not sure," she said, panting, and her voice sounded muffled and entirely alien in the unnatural stillness.

"I think the volcano is going to collapse," Damon said breathlessly. "I've heard that it happens when the lava flows out and leaves a hollow beneath the mountain. The whole island may sink. We'll have to run for it. Hurry!"

China groped for Brandon's hand, and as she started forward through the underbrush a bolt of lightning, spiraling hot white through the darkness, flashed before her eyes, and in that brief instance of brightness China saw, impossibly, clearly, the cresting line of surf below her and the gnarled, twisting roots of the mangrove trees that ranked far out into the water.

"Damon!" she called over her shoulder. "The shoreline is directly below us! If we—"

Her words were drowned out as the trees around her began to shake grotesquely, and above the horrible groaning shudders she heard her mother's voice behind her. "We can find it, China! Think for yourself! Take Brandon and run! Run!"

Galvanized by the urgency in Malvina's tone China gathered up her trailing skirts and fled, stumbling and gasping and pulling the sobbing Brandon behind her. Branches snapped in her face and caught at her clothing and hair, and she could feel the stinging trickle of blood on her cheek where the falling branch had slashed it. There was a roaring in her ears that might have been the wind or another eruption or even the blood that pounded hot and frantic through her veins, but China was afraid to look behind her, and nothing slowed her flight until the ground gave way without warning beneath her and she and Brandon tumbled onto the wet, sinking sand.

Scrambling to her feet, China waded out into the water, the waves sucking at her skirts. Cupping her hands, she shouted loudly for Lam Tan. The wind and the crashing surf snatched the words away and she called again and again, until she was hoarse and the futility of what she was doing was inexorably thrust upon her.

Tears of despair welled in her eyes. Lam Tan couldn't have left them, couldn't have met up with some unforeseen accident that prevented his reaching the appointed rendezvous! She refused to believe that they had made it this far only to find the *Tempus* gone and no way to get off the island.

A flume of hot blue fire suddenly exploded without warning from the center of the crater. Though the trees rimming the shore hid the mountains from her view, China could see the fire reflected in the thick black clouds that roiled above the volcano's peak and ignited their underbellies an ugly, slashing red. A furious squall of oily, smoking fallout rained down upon them and China, tearing Brandon along behind her, sought cover beneath the mangrove roots only to be knocked down by the seething water that rushed up from the ocean floor and pulled greedily at her skirts. Floundering frantically through the foreshore waves, she thought she heard Damon's voice behind her.

"—Quake! The island's going to sink! —The water, damn you!"

China caught a glimpse of his face in the glare of the lightning. It was blackened and unrecognizable, and something in it filled her with a queer and primitive horror. Pulling Brandon along behind her, she waded across the sandy shallows toward the trees that grew farthest from shore, hoping to find shelter in their spreading branches in the event Damon was right and the island was sinking.

An unseen wall of churning water knocked her off her feet and swept her with bruising force against a tangle of roots. The ocean closed over her head and China felt the leaden weight of her wet skirts drag her under. Kicking and squirming frantically, she fought her way back to the surface, dashing the stinging salt from her eyes and finding that somehow, impossibly, she had managed to keep a grip on Brandon's collar.

Coughing and gasping, she propelled the boy toward the branches of a nearby mangrove, and Brandon, doing his best to keep afloat, was able to grasp them and haul himself up. Reaching for a handhold beside him, China's fingers were plucked away by a boiling wave that tore her along in its maddened race to shore. She was spun about as though she were a weightless rag doll in the maw of some giant, savaging beast. At long last, and just when it seemed that she could hold her breath no longer, she was shot to the surface like a bobbing cork to discover that the backwash had dragged her far out to sea.

China tread water as best she could, fighting to stay afloat while the unseen currents tugged and dragged at her skirts. Ash and salt water stung her eyes, and she could not see at all in which direction the shore lay. And because there was no rhythmic pull and flow of the tide around her, only a cauldron of seething whitewater, she was totally disoriented.

With the last of her strength she struck out in the most likely direction, guided by the sullen red glow that stained the sky in dizzying, tossing glimpses above her. But her strength was ebbing fast and she could only utter a feeble gasp as a mountain of water closed over her head, filling her nose and mouth and robbing her of her last, precious breath of air. She felt herself being dragged away by the current and then, incredibly, she was being jerked in the opposite direction by something that snagged her firmly under the arms and lifted her into the air as though she weighed no more than a struggling fish on a gaff.

A moment later she was lying on her back with something mercifully solid beneath her, and someone was lifting her head and pouring burning liquid down her throat. She coughed and moved her head and heard someone speak to her in a voice that was oddly unsteady, and China did not need to open her eyes to know that it was Ethan.

"I knew," she said feebly, "I knew you'd come...."

She sighed and turned her face gratefully against him.

_____ *Chapter Twenty-six* _____

A blazing sun, setting over the Sunda Strait, ignited the windows of the three-story house and painted rippling bars of fire on the crests of the waves slapping lazily against the salt-worn docks. A spicy smell of frying *bandeng* mingled with the heady fragrance of flowers in the garden, and beneath the spreading lobes of a breadfruit tree, a wizened storyteller in a brightly dyed batik loincloth entertained a group of children with tales of *kantjil*, the sly little mouse deer.

His singsong voice and the giggles of his audience drifted through the windows that had been opened to permit the cooling breezes into the high-ceilinged rooms, and drew China Warrick's wandering attention. Rising with a rustle of flounces she looked down into the garden, a faint, sad smile curving her mouth.

It was pleasant to slip away for a time from the noisy celebration that filled the rest of the enormous house and find refuge here in this cool and empty room and to listen to the storyteller talk of the crafty little creature and how cleverly he had outwitted his enemies, his voice soothing in the gathering cool of the twilight.

"Then said kantjil to the struggling, snapping jackal, 'Perhaps the next time thou willst think twice before jumping into darkened waters,' and with a chatter that may very well have been laughter, he ran off into the grass."

The children applauded heartily and China clapped, too, and as they caught sight of her leaning over the sill of the window above them they laughed and waved and the storyteller pressed the tips of the fingers of both hands together and bowed.

Stepping into the corridor, China instructed a passing servant to reward the old man. In response to the surprise he displayed at the number of coins she let fall into his palm, she shrugged and said, "Is not the day one of auspicious joy? After all, this is thy master's *shadi.*"

His dark face flashed with a wide grin. "Assuredly, assuredly, miss-sahib," he responded cheerfully and hurried off to carry out her request.

Skirting the doors of the drawing room where the wedding party laughed and chattered amid the clinking of glasses and the musical tinkling of a Javanese gamelang, China wandered onto the terrace where the stones were still hot beneath the thin soles of her slippers, and the dying sun sank in shivering crimson over the cloud-shrouded range of volcanic mountains that stretched along the swampy coastline of Sumatra. The stretch of grass beneath the breadfruit trees was deserted, the storyteller having gone, but she could hear the shrieks and laughter of the native children from somewhere down on the shore, and she thought she recognized Brandon's and Philippa's among them.

China's mood lifted and she found herself heartened by the sound, and wondered how it was that children could forget so quickly? Had it been only yesterday that she and Brandon and Philippa had arrived exhausted and bedraggled at Tyler Crewe's door? It seemed days ago—weeks—even months—and realizing as much, China thought she could understand why her young brother and sister could laugh and play as though nothing at all had happened.

Julia had been there to meet them when Tyler had

carried Philippa inside and China had followed with the staggering Brandon holding tightly to her hand. Julia, who was to be married the very next morning and whose house was already brimming with guests, had gathered them to her bosom like a clucking, worrisome mother hen and had neglected her own wedding preparations until the weary trio had been fed and put to bed.

Despite the noisy celebration, the music, the laughter, and the dancing and singing, China had slept as if dead to the world, slept as she had the night before, when the *Kowloon Star* had carried her across the length of the Java Sea to Djakarta and Tyler's home.

The deep and drugging sleep had been nature's way of healing her battered body and wounded mind and soul, but still she could not understand how she could have slept knowing that Ethan had not accompanied them and after she had been unable to exchange so much as a single word with him before the *Kowloon Star* had laid its course for Java, and his small boat had returned to Badajan to search for more survivors. Yet perhaps that was why she had been able to permit herself the unconscionable luxury of sleep— because she knew that Ethan was alive and unharmed even if he could not be with her. And because, for the first time in so very, very long, she had felt safe and protected and happy.

Wandering idly to the far end of the terrace, China lifted her eyes to the hazy bulk on the darkening horizon that was the island of Bangka. Badajan lay somewhere beyond it, she knew, and it was difficult to imagine on this hot and tranquil evening, with the palm fronds rustling softly and a pair of spindle-legged herons picking placidly through the shimmering sand, that violence of the nature her family had endured could possibly have happened. And yet it had, and though it had brought untold sadness to her life, China could not help feeling that despite everything, incredibly, undeniably she really was happy.

"I shouldn't be," China thought to herself. "It isn't right, it isn't fair."

"Oh, here you are, China! Nahdul told me you'd gone outside. What is it, dear? Are you tired? I hope it wasn't wrong of me to ask you to attend the celebration? Tyler's friends did so want to meet you."

China turned and smiled in response to Julia's worried questions, thinking to herself how radiantly lovely and young and gay Julia looked, and how wrong it was to cause her undue anxiety on her wedding day.

"I thought it might be better if I slipped away for a time," she confessed honestly. "I'm not the best of company and I was afraid someone might notice."

"Oh, my dear, how can you think that?" Julia was both indignant and aghast. "Why, simply everyone has been remarking how brave you are considering your bereavement and everything else!"

"That's very kind of them," China said, and after a moment added truthfully, "Still, I cannot help feeling somewhat out of place. For one thing, this gown you've lent me." She looked down, frowning a little, at the wide ecru muslin skirts with their lavish embroidery of violets and ruffled loops of plum satin that revealed the lavender petticoats underneath, all of which foamed absurdly about her whenever she moved. "It was kind of you to give it to me, but isn't it rather unsuitable for a wedding?"

No sooner had she uttered those words than she lifted her eyes to Julia's and both women burst without warning into spontaneous laughter, for where was the use in considering the impropriety of a particular gown when its wearer was by far the more shocking with the cuts and bruises that disfigured her face?

"Oh, China, it doesn't matter to them!" Julia said at last, wiping the tears of mirth from her eyes. "They know you arrived here with nothing but the clothes on your back—and I assure you that those were torn and blackened and fit for the dustbin! No, no, all of them are most sympathetic, and I hope," she added, suddenly anxious, "that they haven't been—"

"Asking indelicate questions?"

Julia was greatly relieved by the lightness of China's tone. "Yes, I suppose that's what I meant." Her long white train whispered across the terrace as she moved to take China's slim hands in hers. "Why don't you come back inside? Tyler has just opened another crate of champagne."

But China was no longer listening. She was staring fixedly over Julia's shoulder, her eyes frozen with disbelief. Julia caught her breath audibly at the look on that young and suddenly radiant face, and she whirled about quickly to see Ethan Bloodwell standing on the top of the terrace steps above them.

With a choked cry China freed herself from Julia's grasp, and lifting up those trailing, frothing skirts, she ran lightly across the terrace, the sunlight torching her bright red hair and igniting an answering blaze in Ethan's blue eyes.

Meeting her halfway he pulled her off her feet and swept her into his arms, and in full view and unmindful of the guests inside, he kissed her. China's mouth was soft and warm beneath his and he heard her sigh, and her body seemed to melt against him. His hands tightened about the slim line of her back, pressing her hard against him while his lips moved slowly, languidly over hers. And when he released her at last and set her gently down it seemed to China as if there was no ground beneath her feet.

"You look tired," Ethan said, regarding her with a frown. "Haven't you been sleeping at all? I left orders with Nappy to give you laudanum."

China was tempted to laugh and tell him that she had been sleeping far too much, but found that she could make no more than a negative movement of her head because there was suddenly a constriction in her throat that prevented her speaking.

A wry smile curved the corners of Ethan's hard mouth as he noticed the incredulous bride in her magnificent white dress standing rigid on the grass below them.

"Surely you cannot be thinking you're seeing a ghost, Mrs. Crewe?" he said with a grin. "Nappy must have told you I'd returned from the dead."

"Yes, of course he did," Julia stammered. "But I didn't know you and China—I never thought—" Her voice trailed away and her eyes went from China's radiant face to the grinning countenance of the man beside her. Though they stood some distance apart and Ethan had deliberately refrained from touching her again, it almost seemed to Julia that something intangible bound them together as assuredly as though Ethan still held China in his arms.

"I'd heard some odd tale," she added with considerable confusion, "but I never would have guessed." She shook her head and fell silent and then she smiled. "I suppose it doesn't matter, does it? I'm ever so glad you're back, Ethan, and quite obviously unharmed, though I daresay that cut on your forehead will leave quite a scar. A raffish one, of course," she added hastily, not wanting to sound ungracious, and a small yet potent twinge of jealousy gripped her as she looked up into his face and noticed that he was no longer listening to her or even looking at her, but was staring intently at China.

Julia's breath caught in her throat, for she had never seen a man gaze quite that way at a woman, nor had she realized until that moment how carefully Ethan Bloodwell had always guarded his expression whenever his eyes had come to rest on China Warrick. No one could have guessed his thoughts or the depths of his feelings for her.

Ashamed of her jealousy and thinking with sudden longing of Tyler, Julia adjusted her veil and swept gracefully up the steps. "I'm certain you have a great deal to talk about," she said brightly, "so I might as well go back inside. China, be a love and help me with my train."

Now that the sun had set and the humid air was noticeably cooler, many of the guests had ventured outside to stroll through the garden and admire the roses and carefully cultivated orchids. Taking China's hand in his, Ethan led her down an overgrown path that hid them from view. Studying her intently, he could feel a familiar tug at his heart. She looked so young and fresh in her white muslin gown with its absurdly befrilled skirts and lavender petticoats. It occurred to him that he had rarely seen her in anything other than the deep black of mourning. He scowled as he thought of the number of people dear to her she had so recently lost, and hated himself for knowing that he would have to hurt her yet again.

China was gazing beyond the blooming oleanders toward the sea, which had faded from rippling gold to cool, pearlescent silver with the waning of the light. Against the warm, shifting colors of the twilight her profile was sharply defined: the long, smooth line of her throat and her slim little nose, and the sweep of her lovely, gold-dusted lashes. There was gold in her red curls and in the translucent green of her eyes, and Ethan found himself thinking that she was more beautiful than any woman he had ever seen—and so achingly desirable that he wanted her with a need that was almost agony in itself.

By all counts this night should have been their wedding night, and yet he could not force himself upon her while those magnificent eyes remained shadowed and sad and the faint hollows beneath her cheekbones revealed to him the extent of what she had suffered, and that she suffered still. With an effort Ethan tore his gaze from her, loathing himself for wanting her when so much remained left unsaid between them.

"They've been so kind to me, Julia and Tyler both."

China's voice was like the soothing murmur of some cool and distant waterfall, and, hearing it, Ethan relaxed visibly and the hands that had been clenched inside his coat pockets were no longer unsteady.

She told him of her interview with Sir Adrian Dunsmore and the efforts both Nappy and Tyler Crewe had made to spare King's Wheal on her behalf, and Ethan listened without asking questions while the sun vanished beneath the lip of the mountains and night drew across the heavens like a cloth of purple velvet glittering with countless stars.

They had reached the end of the cultivated gardens by the time China finished speaking, and they stood for a moment beneath the spreading branches of an ancient oak, the breeze lifting China's petticoats and brushing them lightly against Ethan's legs. Neither of them wanted to be the first to break the intimate silence, for each of them knew that once those unsaid things were uttered, the peace of the gathering evening would invariably be shattered. And so they merely looked at one another, silently and with longing, until Ethan turned away at last.

"I'm sorry, China," he said harshly. "I expect you know that both of them are dead."

He heard her quick, indrawn breath, yet when she spoke her voice was calm. "Yes, I assumed they were. Nappy told me you'd gone back to look for them. Was it very bad?"

"I found Damon's body floating in the reed grass. There wasn't a mark on him."

"I see," China said. Her face was painfully white against the night. After a small, hurtful pause she asked quietly, "And my mother?"

Ethan frowned. "I'm convinced it must have been a heart attack, because I cannot think what else could have harmed her. She was lying on the sand and there was nothing to suggest an external injury. I don't believe she suffered."

"It must have been because she had to carry Philippa so far," China said slowly and drew a deep breath. "I should have known what was going to happen. It was so still the night before, and I remember thinking how odd it was that there should be thunder without a single raincloud in the sky. Only it wasn't thunder. It must have been the volcano getting ready to erupt." Her voice dropped to a whisper. "And Ibn Bibi knew. That's why he ran away. Why didn't I see it before it was too late?"

"Oh, my love, you mustn't blame yourself!" Ethan's arms were about her, warm and strong and very tight, and China leaned gratefully against him, her face turned into his shoulder, wondering why she should feel so terribly empty and unable to cry. Could it be that the loss of her mother and brother had pierced a heart already too sorely wounded to endure any more? Or could it be the fact that Ethan's safe return had given her back the strength and the desire for life that had been robbed from her before? Unfair as it might seem, under those particular circumstances, how could she possibly weep for what was lost?

Ethan walked slowly with her back through the perfumed darkness and told her the rest of the things that remained on his mind: of Lam Tan, whose body had been found amid the wreckage of the *Tempus*, of Al-Haj, who had been pulled exhausted but otherwise unharmed from the crown of a mangrove tree where he had spent a fearsome night, and of the villagers, Malay and Chinese alike, who had fled the island in their outriggers and flats and had thus escaped the worst of it.

The island had not sunk, as Damon had feared, although a great part of the beaches and low-lying jungle had suffered damage from the towering waves that had been fueled by the shifting of molten rock far below the surface of the earth. Nor did much of the house remain, and from what little Ethan had been able to see from the shoreline below, it having been impossible due to the damage to get any closer, a mudslide or a lava break seemed to have swept most of it down the side of the knoll upon which it had stood for so many years, leaving nothing behind but a twisted foundation.

China listened in silence, saying nothing and asking no questions, and eventually Ethan, too, fell silent, for he had told her all that he could. Not until the brightly lit house appeared amid the dense stands of flowering ornamentals, and the muted strains of music and laughter drifted to them on the warm night air, did he turn to her.

"They'll be celebrating for some time yet and it's growing late. Why don't you come back to the ship with me?"

China could not see his face, for he had turned away from the house as he spoke, and the lights blazing from the windows fell instead on the grass behind him, but his voice was rough and the lean, hard hands that had taken hold of hers were oddly unsteady. Quite vividly she had a recollection of the velvet darkness of another night when those same hands, then deliberate and very sure, had roved her body and awakened in her a need she hadn't dreamed she possessed.

This was Ethan, the man she desperately loved and whom she had thought lost to her forever, and suddenly she wanted nothing more than to feel his hard mouth on hers and those same hands caressing her with the slow delight they had given her once before. Feeling his hold about her tighten, China leaned toward him and raised her face to his, yet even as his hands slid about her waist and he moved to draw her closer, the snapping of twigs in the nearby bushes drove them apart.

"Ethan? Are you there?"

With a groan Ethan released her. "What is it, Tyler?"

"Julia sent me looking for you," Tyler said affably, lumbering into their presence. "She wants to know if you're spending the night so she can have a room readied. Oh," he added, seeing China in the shadows. "The little 'uns have been askin' for you, lass."

China's hand flew to her lips. "Oh, Ethan, the children! I've forgotten all about them!" Reaching down, she gathered up her trailing skirts. "I'd better go in and say good night."

Ethan's hand detained her. "Will you tell them?"

She was silent for a moment, thinking, then shook her head. "Not tonight. It wouldn't be fair. I think Brandon suspects, but he hasn't said anything about it yet."

"And Philippa?"

China's gaze faltered. "She keeps wondering when Mother and Damon are going to return." Without looking at him she added softly, "I'd better go to them. Good night."

Ethan was silent as he watched her vanish around the far side of the house, and it was Tyler who spoke first, lowering himself onto the stone wall behind him with a copious creaking of joints. "Take my advice and marry that girl quick, before she gets any grand ideas in her head."

Ethan's lips twitched and some of the tension seemed to drain from him. "Having second thoughts about marriage already, Tyler?"

"It's just this wedding hullabaloo getting on my nerves," Tyler complained. "Leave it to a woman to want the moon when it comes to her nuptials. Sixty people, Ethan! Sixty! Do you know how many cases of champagne I've had to haul out for them so far?"

"You've probably contributed richly to the number," Ethan said, grinning.

Tyler made a face. "I don't ever drink the stuff, you know that, lad! And that reminds me. I haven't seen you lift a glass since you arrived, and that's no proper way to celebrate your return from the dead." His eyes narrowed. "Want to tell me how you managed that? I know you lead a charmed life, but this is taking things a bit too far. I vow the Devil himself must've had his hand in it!"

"Perhaps he did," Ethan said.

"I don't believe you blew up the *Lotus Star* either," Tyler added thoughtfully, "even to save your own hide. It ain't right, you know, a captain scuttling his own ship."

"Of course I didn't do it," Ethan said darkly. "It was

Wang Toh who ordered the munitions detonated so that he could escape aboard his lorcha."

"Leaving his crew to fend for themselves?"

"Like a bloody rat deserting sinking wreckage," Ethan said curtly. "Not a pretty sight, Tyler, I assure you."

"And you?" Tyler asked curiously. "How did you get away?"

"Much in the same way. Those port guns of yours saved my life, Tyler. The bastards had me collared just after China left the ship, and I was sure that was going to be the end of it when a mast toppled and swept the lot of them overboard."

"So you made for the lorcha," Tyler prompted. "What then?"

Ethan's shoulders lifted. "I found plenty of places in which to hide. And since Wang Toh and his bodyguards never suspected I was aboard, it was a simple matter to dispose of them."

"And you were left to sail the lorcha back alone. That's why it took you so long to return, eh?"

Ethan nodded. "I made straight for Badajan, of course, and happened to run in just as the *Kowloon Star* did. What with the eruption visible all the way to Singapore, Nappy had come over to see if he could help."

Ethan did not need to add, because it was clear from the look on his face, what the sight of the fiery flames engulfing the island had done to him, and without any real measure of surprise Tyler Crewe knew what the Warrick girl meant to him.

"And now, my friend?" he asked. "What happens now?"

Ethan came restlessly to his feet. "God, Tyler, I wish I knew. I suppose I'll have to take up the matter with China in the morning. Though I don't relish the thought of having to remind her that she's orphaned, homeless, and financially ruined."

"You'll stay the night?"

Scowling, Ethan rubbed his jaw. "I think not. I'm back to the ship for a bath and a shave. Cleaned myself up a bit before coming over so as not to frighten her, but I've a feeling there's room for improvement."

"I'm beginning to wonder which of us is the anxious bridegroom," Tyler said with a grin.

"Damn it, Tyler," Ethan responded, "you know bloody well I can't bother her with that now! Not with everything that's happened!" He was seized once again with an entirely futile anger and realized that he dared not face China again that night, quite simply because he did not trust himself to maintain a tight rein on his self-control were he to do so.

Lost in thought he stalked angrily into the house, and as he threw open the library door he froze at the sight of China standing in the shadows by the window. For a long moment they stared at one another without speaking, China's slim hand clutching the book she had fetched down from the shelf, and the sound of talk and laughter drifting from the withdrawing room was unnaturally loud in the stillness.

"Are the children asleep?" Ethan asked at last.

"Yes, thank goodness," she replied. "They were exhausted. I was just going up myself. I couldn't go back in there again." She tilted her head in the direction of the drawing room.

"I understand."

China gazed at him curiously, wondering why he spoke so tersely and why his restless gaze seemed to be deliberately avoiding her. "Ethan," she said slowly, "I'd like to talk to you about the children."

He glanced at her sharply. "Why? Is anything wrong?"

She lifted her shoulders in a helpless shrug. "I've been thinking there's little sense in trying to rebuild King's Wheal in view of what you've told me, and it's Brandon's inheritance I'm worried about."

"For God's sake," Ethan said more harshly than he intended, "this isn't the time to be fretting about that! You're clearly exhausted!"

"But I've already decided what I'm going to do," China told him clearly.

His eyes narrowed. "Oh?"

The slim hand holding the book stirred restlessly. "I'm taking the children back to England."

Ethan's face hardened. "You can't be serious!"

China's lips tightened. "Yes I am. I'm going back to Broadhurst. Surely Freddy and Cassie wouldn't dream of turning us away—not the children, at any rate."

Without warning Ethan bent over her, seizing her arms and jerking her off her feet, his eyes a blaze of anger in his thin brown face. "Are you mad, China? Have you forgotten that they tried to kill you?"

"No, of course I haven't, but—"

"But what? But I haven't anywhere else to go? Is that what you were going to say? By God, I hope not! And I certainly hope you don't think I have any intention of permitting those cousins of yours to raise Brandon and Philippa! If anyone is reponsible for their welfare, I am. I'm going to be their brother-in-law, after all!"

Ethan shook her roughly. "For that matter what makes you think I'll permit you to return to England without me? It may be that we'll decide to go back eventually, but that's something we're going to discuss together. Do you understand me, China?" He frowned and shook her again. "Now, why in bloody hell are you looking at me like that?"

"Oh, Ethan! Are we really going to get married?"

"And why not?" he asked. "I know your mother signed that bloody piece of paper, but I want to make you my wife with a public exchange of vows. Once I believed you wanted the same thing. Has anything happened to change that? Has it, China?"

"That's something you'll have to tell me, Ethan Blood-well!" she said defensively. "All this time I thought you were dead. Dead! And you might as well be because since you've come back you haven't—you've only kissed me once!"

Ethan released her abruptly and, unbelievably, she saw that he was laughing, just as he always laughed whenever she said something that struck him as being utterly preposterous. But this time there was a look on his face that stilled her indignation and caused her breath to catch painfully in her throat.

"Are you telling me," he demanded, his eyes seeming to burn into hers, "that I've been an utter fool for trying my best to be noble and respectful of your grief?"

China lifted her eyes to his. "Surely you must know

that your safe return mattered above all else to me," she whispered.

Ethan did not know which of them moved first, only that China was suddenly in his arms and he was kissing her fiercely.

"Patience, my life," he said softly, setting her aside at last and seeing the disappointment that crept to her dusky green eyes. Lifting her hand he pressed his lips to her silken palm and grinned at her. "Would you have me make love to you here in Tyler's library?"

"Faith, sir"—China laughed suddenly and without a trace of the demurring he had expected—"one place seems as good as another."

Ethan's own laughter held a trace of surprise and he swept her without warning into his arms. "My redheaded witch," he murmured. "Little firebrand..." He laughed again and suddenly his voice broke and his hands stripped away her gown and cumbersome petticoats as though they did not exist. "To think that you were going to return to England without me!"

He pressed her back into the soft cushions of the sofa, his hands roving her body with desperate need.

"Were you, China?" he inquired hoarsely. "Were you really going to leave me?"

"You know I could not," she said softly, and pulled his head down to hers. "Oh, Ethan, I'm so glad you've come back! I want—"

"I know what you want," he said gruffly, and kissed her.

China felt his rising need and gloried in it, responding with a shameless passion to his seeking mouth and roughly tender hands. He shed his clothes, and it seemed to China as if everything faded in that moment but the sight of his hard, bronzed body glowing in the soft light of the lamps. She grew still and a breathless expectancy settled over her.

Ethan's lips covered her delicate-boned face with soft kisses and claimed her mouth at last in a fierce promise of passion. "Sweet, sweet China," he murmured. "To think I very nearly lost you!"

He pressed down on her and China's slim thighs parted.

Her arms wound about his neck and she gasped as he entered her, filling her and becoming part of her. She moved shamelessly against him, burning with need for him, and his ultimate possession of her blotted out all else but her desperate love for him.

Chapter Twenty-seven

Morning had waned before Julia, Tyler, and their wedding guests appeared downstairs to find a lavish meal prepared for them beneath a colorful awning in the center of the rose garden. Ethan and China were already there, China looking fresh and beautiful in a borrowed gown of lemon silk shantung trimmed with ribbon of Paris green.

"Oh, China, it's simply beautiful," Julia said with a sigh, looking about her. "Did you plan this as a surprise?"

"In a way." It was Ethan who answered her, coming up behind China and grinning unabashedly. "We didn't think you'd mind if we usurped a little of your time to celebrate our engagement." He slipped his arm about China's waist. "We're going to be married as soon as we return to Singapore."

"Oh, how wonderful!" Julia cried, embracing both of them. "I'm so happy for you!"

"We are, too." China laughed and her eyes met Ethan's. She blushed at the expression on his face and, knowing he intended to kiss her, raised her lips breathlessly. Without warning she was snatched away by Tyler, who swept her into his arms and kissed her soundly.

Releasing her, he grinned at the glowering Ethan. "It's the best man's prerogative to kiss the bride, ain't it?"

Ethan's brows rose. "Best man?"

"Of course! You didn't think I'd let anyone else stand up with you, eh? For that matter we won't hear of you getting married in Singapore. We'll do it right here, or aboard your ship, if you want. The minister lives a few miles down the road and I know he won't object to coming over twice."

"What a marvelous idea!" Julia cried eagerly. "Oh, China, what do you think?"

"It sounds lovely," China said, considering. "Provided Ethan has no objections."

"Why should I?" Ethan asked, grinning lasciviously. "This way we don't have to wait another night to begin our nuptials."

Calling the guests together, Tyler proposed a toast to the young couple. At Julia's behest China agreed to act as hostess for the hastily convened engagement breakfast, and Ethan retreated reluctantly to the shade of a nearby tree to watch his betrothed pour tea and chat engagingly with those who came forward to congratulate her. Despite his gratitude toward Tyler and Julia, he was reduced to anger as afternoon approached and the general mood grew boisterous and China became the recipient of what were, in Ethan's opinion, far too numerous and indiscreet compliments delivered by Tyler's more raffish friends.

Later, when he thought to have finally won some time with her alone, China was asked to hand round the traditional wedding favors to the children of Tyler's servants, and afterward she took Brandon and Philippa aside for a private conversation. This, of course, Ethan did not begrudge her, and in fact his heart constricted as he watched the three of them remove to a distant bench beneath a rank of cascading bougainvillea where their curly red heads bent close together.

Brandon took the news of his mother's death with quiet courage, and Philippa, though she wept in China's arms, was soon diverted to smiling at the antics of her kitten and a ball of yarn that Julia had found somewhere amid the clutter in Tyler's rambling house.

At three o'clock a formal tea was served in the garden, and the protracted ceremony of toasts and farewell speeches was begun. Afternoon had waned before the last of the guests finally drove off down the tree-lined road leading into Djakarta, or raised sail and swept away in their skiffs across the wind-ruffled water.

"Oh!" Julia exclaimed, collapsing gratefully into a chair on the veranda. "I didn't think we'd ever see the last of them! Brandon, do be a dear and tell Nahdul to fetch something cool to drink. And ask him if Gem is still napping, will you? Though I don't see how she could possibly sleep through all that noise!"

"And you, my love," Ethan said softly in China's ear, "are coming for a walk with me in the garden."

Smiling, China held out her hand to him only to turn on the steps as Brandon came running breathlessly outside. He was waving a scrap of Badajan silk that he had apparently found beneath Gem's cradle when he had tiptoed upstairs to see for himself if she was awake.

"That's the cloth he took with him when we hid away on the *Malhão*," observed Philippa from Tyler's lap as the adults exchanged mystified glances over his excitement. "He kept all his things in it."

"Why, yes, I recognize it now," China said. "Brandon, you had it tied about your waist, didn't you?"

"I don't know how Gem got hold of this," he said, tugging eagerly at the countless knots that bound the cloth together. "I think it was in the pocket of my jacket, and one of the servants must have laid it over the side of her bed. I'd forgotten all about it!"

The knots were impossible for his small fingers to loosen, and Ethan was obliged to help him. A stunned silence broken only by an audible gasp from Julia descended upon them when the cloth fell open at last and its contents spilled into his palm.

"Those—those are Mother's opals!" China whispered.

"They're beautiful!" Julia said.

Indeed, none of them could dispute the fact that Ethan seemed to be holding no less than a king's ransom in his hand. There were more than a dozen opals of every size and shape imaginable: deep, glittering blue and green, and milky white teardrops set in necklaces of white gold trimmed with countless tiny diamonds. The finest of them all was a magnificent black gemstone that sparked and glittered when Ethan held it aloft, the brilliant flashes of color reminding China of the luminescent beauty of a butterfly's wing.

"They're New South Wales opals," she said at last, speaking almost reverently. "My grandfather mined them years and years ago and Mother brought them with her to Badajan as part of her trousseau. Race had several of the stones set, but Mother always complained that she had nowhere to wear them, so the rest of them remained for the most part loose in her jewelry box."

She turned to Brandon with a frown between her eyes. "How on earth did you get them?"

"I didn't steal them, China," the boy said quickly. "I borrowed them."

China's brows rose. "You borrowed them? Whatever for?"

"Because I was going to give them to Wang Toh. But not for keeping. For co-coll—"

"Collateral?" Ethan inquired, startled.

Brandon looked relieved. "Yes, that's it." His solemn gaze went to China's bewildered face. "I heard Mother and Damon talking about it. They were saying they could pay off the money King's Wheal owed if they only had coll—whatever it was, to—to—I think to give them time until the cocoons were ready. Only they didn't say anything about Wang Toh, and I think they didn't even know it was him they owed the money to. It was you who said that about him, don't you remember, Captain Ethan?" he asked, turning to peer up into Ethan's face. "On the terrace the night of China's party."

Ethan nodded, sorting pensively through the glittering stones.

"So you decided to take the opals to Wang Toh yourself? In order to give us more time to pay off our debt to him?" China asked.

Brandon nodded eagerly. "Mama always said she didn't like wearing them and that she might as well not have them at all. I was sure she wouldn't miss them. Wang Toh would only have had them for a little while and then he would have given them back, wouldn't he? Once the money was paid?"

Above the boy's red head China's helpless eyes sought Ethan's. Knotting the cloth and tucking it into his pocket he said briskly, "I think we should talk about that when we have more time, Brandon. If you're going to be a businessman like your father was, you'll need to understand a few things about loans and collateral and security."

Brandon's eager face crumpled. "Did I do something wrong?"

"No," Ethan said gravely. "Not deliberately."

"Just think," Julia added quickly, "if you hadn't taken them with you, they would have been lost in the mudslide."

Brandon's eyes brightened and he tugged earnestly at Ethan's sleeve. "Now we have enough money to fix King's Wheal, don't we, Ethan?"

"I'm afraid there isn't enough for that," Ethan told him honestly. "And the jewels belong to China now. You'll have to ask her what she wants to do with them."

China took a deep breath and said somewhat unsteadily, "We'll talk about that this evening, Brandon. And until we decide what's to be done we'll let Ethan look after them. Do you think that's fair?"

Patently relieved, Brandon nodded, and asked if he and Philippa might have some of the tea cakes left over from the luncheon.

"Come on, lad," Tyler said promptly, rising with Philippa in his arms. "Let's see if we can find them."

Remarking that Gem would be awakening soon, Julia hurried after them so that Ethan and China found themselves alone at last in the cool shade of the veranda. Neither of them spoke right away, and when China went to stand at the railing and gaze out into the heat of the late afternoon, Ethan did not follow, but leaned with his shoulder against the wall and watched her.

"He was only trying to help," he observed at last, and saw her slim hands tighten about the railing in response. "And do what he thought was right."

"I know."

China turned her head a little and he saw the slim line of her profile against the hot green stretch of lawn. "It seems unfair to punish him, doesn't it?" she asked. "I suppose I would have done the same thing at his age."

"I've no doubt of that," Ethan observed dryly.

"But don't you see what it means, Ethan?" China asked, turning to look at him. "We cannot let King's Wheal fall into ruin. It's Brandon's inheritance."

"We won't," Ethan promised, coming to stand beside her. "I've no doubt we'll rebuild it one day. But there are other things to think about at the moment."

"Are there?" She frowned.

His hand came up to caress a curl that had worked its way loose from her chignon, his fingers warm against the nape of her neck. "Our wedding, for one, or have you forgotten?"

"No, I haven't," she said with a sigh and slipped her arms about his waist. "The *Kowloon Star* is still in Djakarta, isn't it?"

Ethan's eyes glinted. "It is. Are you thinking of using Tyler's suggestion that we get married aboard my ship?"

China nodded, tipping her chin and regarding him with promising eyes. "I don't see any reason why we should wait until we get back to Singapore."

"You're an impatient creature," Ethan observed with a laugh. His eyes glinted as her lips curved in response. "What do you have in mind, little firebrand?"

"Why, sir," China said, insinuating herself closer, "isn't it obvious? It might be hours yet before the minister arrives and it seems a pity to waste all that time waiting here until then. Perhaps the two of us should go to Djakarta and make certain everything is in order for the ceremony." She glanced at him archly. "Don't you think it would be wise?"

"Oh, indeed," Ethan agreed, delighted by her boldness. Pulling her to him, he lowered his head and his lips claimed hers in a kiss that was warm with promise.

With a cracking of canvas that was not unlike thunder, the *Kowloon Star* responded almost playfully to her helm. Heeling into the glass blue water with the wind full astern, she swung her bow toward Singapore while the setting sun washed the sky in glorious shades of red and rose above her soaring masts. Ethan had ordered the topgallants set and the foresails shortened, and leaving the grinning coxswain in command, he took his wife's hand in his and led her below.

Nappy Quarles had been in the cabin before them. The stern table had been laid with fresh linen, and a glass bowl filled with orchids and sweetly scented jasmine provided a splash of color against the formal place settings. Nappy had barred the shutters across the windows and lit the tapers, and a bottle of wine stood chilling on the sideboard amid a profusion of delicious-smelling dishes.

"Are you hungry?" Ethan inquired, closing the door behind him and standing for a moment with his hand on the latch, looking down at her.

"How can I possibly think of food after everything we've eaten today?" China asked with a laugh. Collapsing in a sea chair she kicked off her slippers. "It was a beautiful ceremony, wasn't it?" she said, sighing.

Brandon had acted as ring bearer and Philippa had carried a basket of flowers. Julia and Tyler had been matron of honor and best man respectively, and with a beaming Nappy looking on, Ethan and China had exchanged vows on the main deck of the *Kowloon Star* as the brigantine rode quietly at anchor in Djakarta's sun-washed harbor. They were on their way to Singapore now, and China wondered with an unexpected twinge of sadness how long it would be before she saw the Crewes again.

"What is it, love?" Ethan inquired, seeing the shadow that fled across her face.

"I'm wondering if I did the right thing to leave Gem with them," China said slowly. Wandering to the table she idly touched the petals of a glorious pink and yellow cypripedium orchid that hung over the rim of the vase. "I cannot help thinking that we should have taken her with us."

"You think too much, dear," Ethan said gently. "And worry and fret and take too much upon yourself. There are countless Chinese living on Java, and Tyler has promised that Gem will grow up with a clear understanding of

her heritage. When she's old enough she'll have the best
of two worlds to choose from, and no meddlesome relations
to make the decision for her."

"But we will come back to see her, won't we?" China
asked. "I would hate for her to think we've abandoned her
entirely."

"Now you're talking utter nonsense," Ethan said. "The
moment we find ourselves growing tired of English winters
or the stuffy restrictions of British life, we'll simply weigh
anchor and head East for a visit."

He spoke lightly although he knew that it would certainly not be as easy as he made it sound, not if they were
forced to live by the meager means he anticipated for them.
Yet he was adamant about seeing to it that the Warrick
opals would not be pawned in order to put food in their
mouths or clothes on their backs.

"God is a great provider," Rajiid Ali had always been
fond of saying. Rajiid . . . Ethan's heart warmed as he thought
of his friend. He was going to miss him terribly, but seeing
China's small, lovely face before him, he smiled, knowing
he was turning away from an old, familiar way of life and
embracing one that was splendid and new and infinitely
enchanting.

"Are you certain you're not hungry?" he inquired with
a grin, noticing that China had lifted the lid to one of the
chafing dishes and was sniffing appreciatively. "Good," he
continued as she shook her head, "because I don't believe
we'll have much time for eating."

He came up behind her as he spoke and his hands slid
boldly about her waist. China turned willingly and lifted
her face to his, and Ethan laughed softly as he bent to kiss
her.

"Has it ever occurred to you, Mrs. Bloodwell, that there
is nothing in the least modest about you?"

"Indeed, Captain," China murmured, smiling at him
saucily. "Would you like me to show you exactly how immodest I can be?"

Her fingers slid into his hair, drawing his head down
until his mouth covered hers, and her lips were soft and
unbelievably sweet, like nectar to a man starved for their
taste—and Ethan had hungered far too long.

His hand came around to the back of her gown, unfastening the countless pearl buttons before he slid his warm fingers across her shoulders and lowered the rustling material away from her skin. And in the candlelit darkness China's clothes fell one by one to the cabin floor in a whispering dance. On the clean scented linens of the bed she opened herself to the man she loved, pulling the length of his bronzed body down on hers with a lack of shame and an ardor that delighted and enflamed him.

"My love," Ethan whispered hoarsely, just as he had on that long-ago night on board the sinking Chinese ship when he had been filled with the anguish of knowing he would never see her again. "My love and my life—"

His hands worked their magic on her, caressing every rounded curve, every smooth inch of her that the candlelight made golden in the darkness. Her unbound hair spilled across the pillow, a banner of fire that slid in silky waves across his chest.

China was waiting for him, open and loving, her eyes lit with green fire. As Ethan drove deep within her she clung to him and sighed his name, and the timeless rhythm of love swept them away to its passionate end.

Later, much later, when the candles had burned low and they had loved and whispered and laughed, then loved again, they opened the wine and drank, their eyes meeting warm and fulfilled over the rims of their glasses. Watching her, Ethan marveled at the contentment that filled him, for he had never known that a man's hunger could be appeased so completely merely by the presence of the woman he loved. Having China here beside him while the familiar creaking of the beams and the whisper of the tide filled the darkened cabin was like a litany of love; all the elements he would ever need to fulfill him were with him here and now.

He chuckled as he saw her head droop wearily, and his hands were gentle as he took the glass away from her and slipped the silk wrapper from her shoulders. Blowing out the candles one by one he took her in his arms and laid her down in the bed that was touched with slanted bars of silver as the rising moon fingered its way through the shutters. Brushing the heavy curls from China's brow,

Ethan bent his head to kiss her, and though he had intended for it to be nothing more than a tender caress, he found that the innocent gesture inadvertently rekindled his desire.

"I don't believe I shall ever have enough of you, Mrs. Bloodwell," he said huskily, and his arm went beneath her hip, turning her toward him so that their naked bodies fit intimately together.

"If I had known what a selfish, demanding man I had married—"

"Would you have thought twice before accepting him?" Ethan asked, moving languidly, sensuously against her.

"No, I would not," China said, "I would—" But the rest of her words were swept away by his kiss and lost once again in a rising tide of passion.

Some time later that night, in the dark hour just before dawn, Ethan was awakened by the barely perceptible change in the movement of his ship. Coming instantly awake, he made to leave the warmth of the bed but was stopped by a pair of slim arms that wound themselves about his neck.

"What is it?" China inquired groggily. "Where are you going?"

"Topside. Frazier's dropped sail for some reason and I want to know why. It's far too early to be taking on the pilot." He pulled on his breeches and bent to kiss her, but China had sat up at his words, the nightmares of the past few weeks by no means forgotten.

"I'm coming with you," she said decisively, and swung her bare feet to the floor.

"Suit yourself," Ethan responded, and though it was too dark to see his face China was struck with the unlikely suspicion that he was smiling. "Only make certain you put on something decent, hmm? I'll not have my wife traipsing about deck without a stitch of clothing."

He did not wait for her, and it took some considerable time for China to strike a light and struggle unaided into her gown. She was too agitated to bother with her crinolines, and, tucking the trailing skirts over her arm, she hurried down the corridor, taking care not to make any noise as she passed the door behind which Brandon and Philippa slept.

Though it was pleasantly cool on deck, the planking was still warm beneath her bare feet. China could see nothing at first, for the moon had set hours ago, but as her eyes adjusted to the dim starlight she was startled by the unexpected sight of a familiar ship that rose and fell to the coaxing of the tide a scant cable's length away.

The *Aurora D!* What in heaven's name was Horatio Creel doing here in the Java Sea? Searching her memory China thought she recalled that Damon had sent him to Timor in order to register an official report with the Portuguese provincial governor in the matter of the boarding and seizure of the schooner *Malhão*. Of course it was possible that Captain Creel had heard of the destruction of Badajan while in Timor and had been hurrying home when he had intercepted the slower moving brigantine and had hailed her for news.

In that China was only partially correct, for the *Aurora D.* had concluded her business on Portuguese Timor several days earlier and had already paid a call in Singapore before continuing on her way to Badajan. And it was in Singapore, not Timor, that Horatio had learned of the tragic deaths of Damon and Malvina Warrick and the destruction of King's Wheal plantation. Hearing that the survivors had been taken to Djakarta, he had plotted a course immediately for Java and raised sail with the tide, but not before he had agreed to take on board a most unlikely passenger who urgently requested to accompany him.

Hearing his wife's soft footfalls behind him, Ethan dismissed the officer of the watch with whom he had been engaged in earnest conversation, and the young man melted away into the darkness.

"Ethan, what is it?" China inquired with a feeling of dread. "And what is Captain Creel doing? Is he leaving?" For the *Aurora D.* was falling away to starboard as she spoke and taking to the opposite tack, her unfurled sails glinting gray in the starlight.

"I imagine he's putting some distance between us seeing as he won't be disturbing us again until morning."

"Why? What did he have to say to you?"

"Upon learning you and the children were safely on board, Horatio graciously agreed not to trouble us at present. We can expect him at eight bells tomorrow. Oh, and he's bringing a visitor."

"A visitor? Who is it? Ethan, whatever is the matter with you? I vow you are—"

"The most exasperating man you've ever met?" His eyes glinted devilishly as he turned to look down at her.

China was betrayed into smiling. "That's not what I was going to say, but yes, I suppose it's true. Now would you please be so kind as to tell me what's going on?"

Ethan turned from the rail and, unmindful of the deck watch nearby, drew her hard against him. And then he laughed, a sound she had not heard in a great while: free of cares and so unaffected that she could not help but join in.

"It's Roland Biggs, China," Ethan said at last and his tone was serious all at once. "He's waiting on board the *Aurora D.* to see us."

For a moment China had no idea who he was talking about. Then her expression cleared and she said disbelievingly, "Roland Biggs? You don't mean Great-uncle Esmund's solicitor? But why is he here? Is he looking for me?"

She saw Ethan's white teeth flash in the darkness, and then his fingers were tracing the slim line of her cheek in a slow caress. "He is. It would seem, Mrs. Bloodwell, that you're an heiress."

"An heiress?"

"Yes, indeed. According to Horatio you've gained control of Broadhurst estate, and with it the sum of the Linville fortune."

"I don't believe it!"

"I am quite in earnest, my love," Ethan assured her. "It seems that Mr. Biggs has chased across the length and breadth of Asia trying to find you."

"But that can't be!" China protested. "What about Freddy? Surely he didn't simply decide to turn Broadhurst over to me!"

"I'm afraid your cousin is dead, China. Horatio said he'd met with some sort of accident in Battersea."

China's eyes were wide and green in the paling light. "In *Battersea?* What on earth was Freddy doing there? That isn't the sort of area he would normally frequent!"

"I can't imagine," Ethan said with deceptive calm, though he was convinced that Lord Freddy had been robbed and beaten by the sort of men who haunted the Battersea streets, dangerous men who held no high opinion of arrogant gentry. And it was a simple enough matter to take his suspicions one step further and draw the probable conclusion that Freddy had sought them out deliberately, never pausing to consider the foolishness of his actions.

There were seafaring men to be found in the Battersea brothels, Ethan knew, men who shipped out frequently on Orient-bound freighters and who would gladly accept a sack of gold in return for some unscrupulous deed. And Ethan had never forgotten that Freddy Linville had tried once before to rid himself of his innocent young cousin. It wasn't difficult to believe that he was capable of trying it again.

He quelled his rising anger at the thought and reminded himself that the two men who had set out to destroy everything China held dear—Wang Toh Chen-Arn, mandarin of Kwangtung, and Lord Freddy Linville, the ninth Earl Linville—were dead. There remained only Cassie as the last of the ugly weeds that must be pulled in order to put an end to the insidious rot that threatened China's happiness and, with it, his own.

I'll deal with her when the time comes, Ethan thought grimly, and did not know that Cassie Linville had withdrawn to an institution some eighty miles north of London several weeks ago, her brother's violent death having unhinged a mind that had never been quite stable.

Thrusting his unpleasant thoughts from him, Ethan gazed down at his young wife and drew her into his arms. "I hope the fact you're an heiress won't give you cause to rethink the wisdom of marrying a lowly China trader, Mrs. Bloodwell," he said huskily.

"I'm not at all sure," China responded very seriously. "You'll have to wait until we return to Kent and I've had the chance to look over the lordlings residing there. It may be that I find one more to my liking."

"It may be," Ethan agreed gravely, "but I've a feeling your time will be far too monopolized for looking."

His mouth covered hers, moving unhurriedly, languidly, and China's lips parted beneath it, and it seemed to her as if the whole world were being swept slowly away by the tender passion of Ethan's kiss. The wide, dark ocean, the paling sky, the dawn that was beginning to steal across the far horizon, all ceased to exist until there was nothing left but the man who held her in his arms and whose gentle kiss was love itself, wild, impassioned, and never-ending.